Blood Bound

Apparently, as in werewolf fights, battles between vampires have a lot of impressive fireworks before the main show.

In the silence that followed, I heard something, a hoarse mewling noise coming from behind the closed bathroom door — as if whatever made it had already cried out so much it could only make a small noise, but one that held much more terror than a full-throated scream.

I wondered if Stefan knew what was in the bathroom and that was why he'd been afraid when we were in the parking lot — there were things that even a vampire ought to be afraid of. I took a deep breath, but all I could smell was the bitter darkness — and that was getting stronger. I sneezed, trying to clear my nose, but it didn't work. Both vampires stood still until the noise stopped. Then the stanger dusted his hands lightly, a small smile on his face as if there had not been rage just an instant before.

'I am remiss,' he said, but the old fashioned words sounded false coming from him, as if he were pretending to be a vampire the way the old vampires tried to be human. 'You obviously do not know who I am.'

Blood Bound

Patricia Briggs

www.orbitbooks.net

ORBIT

First published in the United States in 2007 by Ace,
Penguin Group (USA) Inc.
First published in Great Britain in 2008 by Orbit
Reprinted 2008, 2009 (three times), 2010

A CIP catalogue record for this book
is available from the British Library.

ISBN 978-1-84149-684-9

Typeset in Garamond 3 by
Palimpsest Book Production Limited, Grangemouth, Stirlingshire
Printed and bound in Great Britain by Clays Ltd, St Ives plc

Papers used by Orbit are natural, renewable and
recyclable products sourced from well-managed forests and certified
in accordance with the rules of the Forest Stewardship Council.

Mixed Sources
Product group from well-managed
forests and other controlled sources
www.fsc.org Cert no. SGS-COC-004081
© 1996 Forest Stewardship Council
FSC

Orbit
An imprint of
Little, Brown Book Group
100 Victoria Embankment
London EC4Y 0DY

An Hachette UK Company
www.hachette.co.uk

www.orbitbooks.net

*This book is lovingly dedicated to
the folks of the Tri-Cities, Washington,
who never knew what was living
in their midst.*

ACKNOWLEDGMENTS

With thanks to Barry Bolstad, who let me pick his brain about police work in the Tri-Cities – and to his wife, Susan, who was patient with us while we talked business at lunch. Thanks also to my sister, Jean Matteucci, who double-checked my German. This book wouldn't be what it is without the contributions over the years of our VWs, VW mechanics, and the folks at opelgt.com. Also a hearty thanks to the usual suspects for service above and beyond the call of duty: Collin and Mike Briggs, Michael and Dee Enzweiler, Ann Peters, Kaye and Kyle Roberson, and John Wilson – and my editor, Anne Sowards. They read it when it was rough, so you don't have to. Special thanks to my terrific agent, Linn Prentis, who takes care of business so I can write. Most of all I'd like to thank my family, who is getting used to 'make your own dinners' and 'go away – I have to finish this three weeks ago last Tuesday.' Without these folks this book would never have been written.

As always, all mistakes are the fault of the author.

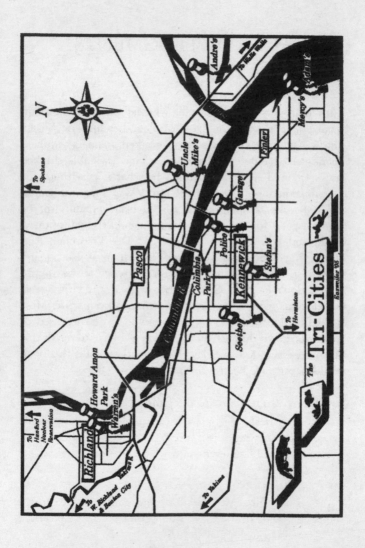

1

Like most people who own their own businesses, I work long hours that start early in the morning. So when someone calls me in the middle of the night, they'd better be dying.

'Hello, Mercy,' said Stefan's amiable voice in my ear. 'I wonder if you could do me a favor.'

Stefan had done his dying a long time ago, so I saw no reason to be nice. 'I answered the phone at' – I peered blearily at the red numbers on my bedside clock – '*three* o'clock in the morning.'

Okay, that's not exactly what I said. I may have added a few of those words a mechanic picks up to use at recalcitrant bolts and alternators that land on her toes.

'I *suppose* you could go for a second favor,' I continued, 'but I'd prefer you hang up and call me back at a more civilized hour.'

He laughed. Maybe he thought I was trying to be funny. 'I have a job to do, and I believe your particular talents would be a great asset in assuring the success of the venture.'

Old creatures, at least in my experience, like to be a little vague when they're asking you to do something. I'm a businesswoman, and I believe in getting to the specifics as quickly as possible.

'At three in the morning you need a mechanic?'

'I'm a vampire, Mercedes,' he said gently. 'Three in the morning is still prime time. But I don't need a mechanic, I need you. You owe me a favor.'

He was right, darn him. He'd helped me when the local

Alpha werewolf's daughter was kidnapped. He had warned me that he'd be collecting in return.

I yawned and sat up, giving up all hope of going back to sleep. 'All right. What am I doing for you?'

'I'm supposed to be delivering a message to a vampire who is here without my mistress's permission,' he said, getting to the point. 'I need a witness he won't notice.'

He hung up without getting an answer, or even telling me when he was coming to pick me up. It would serve him right if I just went back to sleep.

Muttering to myself, I threw on clothing: jeans, yesterday's T-shirt complete with mustard stain, and two socks with only one hole between them. Once I was more or less dressed, I shuffled off to the kitchen and poured myself a glass of cranberry juice.

It was a full moon, and my roommate, the werewolf, was out running with the local pack, so I didn't have to explain to him why I was going out with Stefan. Which was just as well.

Samuel wasn't a bad roommate as such things go, but he had a tendency to get possessive and dictatorial. Not that I let him get away with it, but arguing with werewolves requires a certain subtlety I was lacking at – I checked my wristwatch – 3:15 in the morning.

For all that I was raised by them, I'm not a werewolf, not a were-anything. I'm not a servant of the moon's phases, and in the coyote shape that is my second form. I look like any other *canis latrans*: I have the buckshot scars on my backside to prove it.

Werewolves cannot be mistaken for wolves: weres are much bigger than their non-preternatural counterparts – and a lot scarier.

What I am is a walker, though I'm sure there once was another name for it – an Indian name lost when the Europeans devoured the New World. Maybe my father could have told me what it was if he hadn't died in a car wreck before he knew my mother was pregnant. So all I know is what the werewolves could tell me, which wasn't much.

The 'walker' comes from the Skinwalkers of the Southwest Indian tribes, but I have less in common with a Skinwalker, at least from what I've read, than I do with the werewolves. I don't do magic, I don't need a coyote skin to change shape – and I'm not evil.

I sipped my juice and looked out of the kitchen window. I couldn't see the moon herself, just her silver light that touched the nighttime landscape. Thoughts of evil seemed somehow appropriate while I waited for the vampire to come for me. If nothing else, it would keep me from falling asleep: fear has that effect on me. I'm afraid of evil.

In our modern world, even the word seems . . . old fashioned. When it comes out of hiding briefly in a Charles Manson or a Jeffrey Dahmer, we try to explain it away with drug abuse, an unhappy childhood, or mental illness.

Americans in particular are oddly innocent in their faith that science holds explanations for everything. When the werewolves finally admitted what they were to the public several months ago, the scientists immediately started looking for a virus or bacteria that could cause the Change – magic being something their laboratories and computers can't explain. Last I'd heard Johns Hopkins had a whole team devoted to the issue. Doubtless they'd find something, too, but I'm betting they'll never be able to explain how a 180-pound man turns into a 250-pound werewolf. Science doesn't allow for magic any more than it allows for evil.

The devout belief that the world is explainable is both a terrible vulnerability and a stout shield. Evil prefers it when people don't believe. Vampires, as a not-random example, seldom go out and kill people in the street. When they go hunting, they find someone who won't be missed and bring them home where they are tended and kept comfortable – like a cow in a feedlot.

Under the rule of science, there are no witch burnings allowed, no water trials or public lynchings. In return, the average law-abiding, solid, citizen has little to worry about from the things that go bump in the night. Sometimes I wish I were an average citizen.

Average citizens don't get visited by vampires.

Nor do they worry about a pack of werewolves – at least not quite the same way as I was.

Coming out in public was a bold step for the werewolves; one that could easily backfire. Staring out at the moonlit night, I fretted about what would happen if people began to be afraid again. Werewolves aren't evil, but they aren't exactly the peaceful, law-abiding heroes that they're trying to represent themselves as either.

Someone tapped on my front door.

Vampires *are* evil. I knew that – but Stefan was more than just a vampire. Sometimes I was pretty sure he was my friend. So I wasn't really afraid until I opened the door and saw what waited on my porch.

The vampire's dark hair was slicked back, leaving his skin very pale in the moon's light. Dressed in black from head to heels, he ought to have looked like a refugee from a bad Dracula movie, but somehow the whole outfit, from black leather duster to silk gloves, looked more authentic on Stefan than his usual bright-colored T-shirt and grubby jeans. As if he'd removed a costume, rather than put one on.

He looked like someone who could kill as easily as I could change a tire, with as little thought or remorse.

Then his mobile brows climbed his forehead – and he was suddenly the same vampire who'd painted his old VW bus to look like Scooby's Mystery Machine.

'You don't look happy to see me,' he said with a quick grin that didn't show his fangs. In the dark, his eyes looked more black than brown – but then so did mine.

'Come in.' I backed away from the door so he could; then, because he'd scared me I added snappishly, 'If you want welcoming, try stopping by at a decent hour.'

He hesitated on the threshold, smiled at me, and said, 'By your invitation.' Then he stepped inside my house.

'That threshold thing really works?' I asked.

His smile widened again, this time I saw a glint of white. 'Not after you've invited me in.'

He walked past me and into the living room and then turned like a model on a runway. The folds of his duster spread out with his turn in an effect nearly cape-like.

'So how do you like me *à la Nosferatu?*'

I sighed and admitted it. 'Scared me. I thought you eschewed all things gothic.' I'd seldom seen him in anything other than jeans and T-shirts.

His smile widened even more. 'Usually I do. But the Dracula look does have its place. Oddly enough, used sparingly, it scares other vampires almost as well as it does the odd coyote-girl. Don't worry, I have a bit of costuming for you, too.'

He reached under his coat and pulled out a silver-studded leather harness.

I stared at it a moment. 'Going to an S&M strip club are you? I didn't realize there was anything like that around here.' There wasn't, not to my knowledge. Eastern Washington is more prudish than Seattle or Portland.

He laughed. 'Not tonight, sweetheart. This is for your other self.' He shook the straps out so I could see that it was a dog harness.

I took it from him. It was good leather, soft and flexible with so much silver that it looked like jewelry. If I'd been strictly human, no doubt I'd have been taken aback at wearing such a thing. But when you spend a good part of your time running around as a coyote, collars and the like are pretty useful.

The Marrok, the leader of the North American were-wolves, insists that all of the wolves wear a collar when they run in the cities, with tags that identify them as someone's pet. He also insists the names on the tags be something innocuous like Fred or Spot, no Killers or Fangs. It's safer that way – both for the werewolves and the law-enforcement people who might encounter them. Needless to say, it's as popular with the werewolves as the helmet law was with the motorcyclists when it first went into effect. Not that any of them would dream of disobeying the Marrok.

Not being a werewolf, I'm exempt from the Marrok's rules. On the other hand, I don't like running unnecessary risks either. I had a collar in my kitchen junk drawer – but it wasn't made of nifty black leather.

'So I'm part of your costume?' I asked.

'Let's just say that I think this vampire might need more intimidation than most,' he answered lightly, though something in his eyes made me think there was something more going on.

Medea wandered out from wherever she'd been sleeping. Probably Samuel's bed. Purring furiously, she wound her small self around Stefan's left leg and then rubbed her face against his boot to mark him as hers.

'Cats and ghosts don't like vampires,' Stefan said staring down at her.

'Medea likes anything that might feed or pet her,' I told him. 'She's not picky.'

He bent down and scooped her up. Being picked up isn't Medea's favorite thing, so she yowled at him several times before going back to purring as she sank her claws into his expensive leather sleeve.

'You aren't cashing in your favor just to appear more intimidating,' I said, looking up from the soft leather harness to meet his eyes. Unwise with vampires, he himself had told me so, but all I saw was opaque darkness. 'You said you wanted a witness. A witness to what?'

'No, I don't need you in order to appear intimidating,' Stefan agreed softly after I'd stared at him for a few seconds. 'But *he'll* think intimidation is why I have a coyote on my leash.' He hesitated, and then shrugged. 'This vampire has been through here before, and I think that he managed to deceive one of our young ones. Because of what you are, you are immune to many vampiric powers, especially if the vampire in question doesn't know what you are. Thinking you a coyote, he's probably not going to waste his magic on you at all. It is unlikely, but he might manage to deceive me as well as he did Daniel. I don't think he'll be able to deceive you.'

I'd just learned that little tidbit about being resistant to vampiric magic. It wasn't particularly useful for me since a vampire is strong enough to break my neck with the same effort I'd put into snapping a piece of celery.

'He won't hurt you,' Stefan said when I was silent for too long. 'I give you my word of honor.'

I didn't know how old Stefan was, but he used that phrase like a man who meant it. Sometimes he made it hard to remember that vampires are evil. It didn't really matter, though. I owed him.

'All right,' I said.

Looking down at the harness I thought about getting my own collar instead. I could change shape while wearing a collar – my neck wasn't any bigger around as a human than as a coyote. The harness, suitable for a thirty-pound coyote, would be too tight for me to regain human form while I wore it. The advantage of the harness though, was that I wouldn't be attached to Stefan by my neck.

My collar was bright purple with pink flowers embroidered on it. Not very *Nosferatu*.

I handed the harness to Stefan. 'You'll have to put it on me after I change,' I told him. 'I'll be right back.'

I changed shape in my bedroom because I had to take off my clothes to do it. I'm not really all that modest, a shapeshifter gets over that pretty fast, but I try not to get naked in front of someone who might misread my casual nudity for casualness in other areas.

Although Stefan had at least three cars that I knew of, he had apparently taken a 'faster way,' as he put it, to my house, so we got in my Rabbit to travel to his meeting.

For a few minutes, I wasn't certain he was going to be able to get it started. The old diesel didn't like getting up this early in the morning any more than I did. Stefan muttered a few Italian oaths under his breath, and at last it caught and we were off.

Never ride in a car with a vampire who is in a hurry. I didn't know my Rabbit could peel out like that. We turned onto the highway with the rpms redlined; the car stayed on all four wheels, but only just.

The Rabbit actually seemed to like the drive better than I did; the engine roughness I'd been trying for years to get rid of smoothed out and it purred. I closed my eyes and hoped the wheels stayed on.

When Stefan took us over the river on the cable bridge that dropped us off in the middle of Pasco he was driving forty miles an hour over the speed limit. Not slowing noticeably, he crossed through the heart of the industrial area to a cluster of hotels that sprang up on the far edge of town near the onramp to the highway that headed out toward Spokane and other points north. By some miracle – probably aided by the early hour – we weren't picked up for speeding.

The hotel Stefan took us to was neither the best nor the worst of them. It catered to truckers, though there was only one of the big rigs parked in the lot. Maybe Tuesday nights were slow. Stefan parked the Rabbit next to the only other car in the lot, a black BMW, despite the plethora of empty parking spaces.

I jumped out of the car's open window into the parking lot and was hit with the smell of vampire and blood. My nose is very good, especially when I'm a coyote, but like anyone else, I don't always notice what I'm smelling. Most of the time it's like trying to listen to all of the conversations in a crowded restaurant. But this was impossible to miss.

Maybe it was bad enough to drive off normal humans, and that's why the parking lot was nearly empty.

I looked at Stefan to see if he smelled it, too, but his attention was focused on the car we'd parked beside. As soon as he'd drawn my attention to it, I realized the smell was coming from the BMW. How was it that the car could smell more like a vampire than Stefan the vampire did?

I caught another, more subtle, scent that caused my lips to draw away from my teeth even though I couldn't have said what the bitter-dark odor was. As soon as it touched my nose it wrapped itself around me, clouding all the other scents until it was all I could smell.

Stefan came around the car in a rush, snatched up the leash and tugged it hard to quiet my growl. I jerked back and snapped my teeth at him. I wasn't a damn dog. He could have asked me to be quiet.

'Settle down,' he said, but he wasn't watching me. He

was looking at the hotel. I smelled something else then, a shadow of a scent soon overcome by that other smell. But even that brief whiff was enough to identify the familiar smell of fear, Stefan's fear. What could scare a vampire?

'Come,' he said turning toward the hotel and tugged me forward, out of my confusion.

Once I'd quit resisting his pull, he spoke to me in a rapid and quiet voice. 'I don't want you to do anything, Mercy, no matter what you see or hear. You aren't up to a fight with this one. I just need an impartial witness who won't get herself killed. So play coyote with all your might and if I don't make it out of here, go tell the Mistress what I asked you to do for me – and what you saw.'

How did he expect me to escape something that could kill him? He hadn't been talking like this earlier, nor had he been afraid. Maybe he could smell what I was smelling – and he knew what it was. I couldn't ask him though, because a coyote isn't equipped for human speech.

He led the way to a smoked glass door. It was locked, but there was a key-card box with a small, red-blinking, LED light. He tapped a finger on the box and the light turned green, just as if he'd swiped a magnetic card through it.

The door opened without protest and closed behind us with a final sounding click. There was nothing creepy about the hallway, but it bothered me anyway. Probably Stefan's nerves rubbing off on me. *What would scare a vampire?*

Somewhere, someone slammed a door and I jumped.

Either he knew where the vampire was staying, or his nose wasn't hampered by the scent of that otherness like mine was. He took me briskly through the long hallway and stopped about halfway down. He tapped on the door with his knuckles, though I, and so presumably Stefan, could hear that whoever awaited us inside the room had started for the door as soon as we stopped in front of it.

After all the build up, the vampire who opened the door was almost anticlimatic, like expecting to hear Pavarotti sing Wagner and getting Bugs Bunny and Elmer Fudd instead.

The new vampire was clean shaven and his hair was combed and pulled back into a tidy, short, ponytail. His clothes were neat and clean, though a bit wrinkled as if they'd been in a suitcase – but somehow the overall impression I got was disheveled and filthy. He was significantly shorter than Stefan and much less intimidating. First point to Stefan, which was good since he'd put so much effort into his Prince of Darkness garb.

The stranger's long-sleeved, knit shirt hung on him, as if it rested on skeleton rather than flesh. When he moved, one of his sleeves slid up, revealing an arm so emaciated that the hollow between the bones of his forearm was visible. He stood slightly hunched, as if he didn't quite have the energy to straighten up.

I'd met vampires other than Stefan before: scary vampires with glowing eyes and fangs. This one looked like an addict so far gone there was nothing left of the person he had once been, as if he might fade away at any moment, leaving only his body behind.

Stefan, though, wasn't reassured by the other's apparent frailty – if anything, his tension had increased. Not being able to smell much around that unpleasant, pervasive bitterness was bothering me more than the vampire who didn't look like much of an opponent at all.

'Word of your coming has reached my mistress,' Stefan said, his voice steady, if a little more clipped than usual. 'She is very disappointed that you did not see fit to tell her you would be visiting her territory.'

'Come in, come in,' said the other vampire, stepping back from the door to invite Stefan through. 'No need to stand out in the hallway waking up people who are trying to sleep.'

I couldn't tell if he knew Stefan was afraid or not. I've never been quite sure how well vampires can scent things – though they clearly have better noses than humans do. He didn't seem intimidated by Stefan and his black clothes, though; instead he sounded almost distracted, as if we'd interrupted something important.

The bathroom door was shut as we walked past it. I pricked my ears, but I couldn't hear anything behind the shut door. My nose was useless. Stefan took us all the way to the far side of the room, near the sliding glass doors that were all but hidden by heavy, floor-to-ceiling, curtains. The room was bare and impersonal except for the suitcase, which lay closed on top of the chest of drawers.

Stefan waited until the other vampire had shut the door before he said in a cold voice, 'There is no one trying to sleep tonight in this hotel.'

It seemed an odd remark, but the stranger seemed to know what Stefan meant because he giggled, cupping a hand coyly over his mouth in a manner that seemed more in keeping with a twelve-year-old girl than a man of any age. It was odd enough that it took me a while to assess Stefan's remark.

Surely he hadn't meant it the way it sounded. No sane vampire would have killed everyone in the hotel. Vampires were as ruthless as the werewolves in enforcing their rules about not drawing unwanted attention to themselves – and wholesale slaughter of humans would draw attention. Even if there weren't many guests, there would be employees of the hotel.

The vampire dropped his hand from his face leaving behind a face empty of amusement. It didn't make me feel any better. It was like watching Dr Jekyll and Mr Hyde, the change was so great.

'No one to wake up?' he asked, as if he hadn't reacted in

any other way to Stefan's comment. 'You might be right. It is still poor manners to keep someone waiting at the door, isn't it? Which one of her minions are you?' He held up a hand. 'No, wait, don't tell me. Let me guess.'

While Stefan waited, all of his usual animation completely shut down, the stranger walked all the way around him, pausing just behind us. Unconstrained by anything but the leash, I turned to watch.

When he was directly behind Stefan, the other vampire bent down and scratched me behind my ears.

I usually don't mind being touched, but as soon as his fingers brushed against my fur I knew I didn't want him touching me. Involuntarily, I hunched away from his hand and into Stefan's leg. My fur kept his skin away from mine, but that didn't keep his touch from feeling filthy, unclean.

The scent of him lingered on my fur and I realized the unpleasant odor that had been clogging my nose was coming from him.

'Careful,' Stefan told him without looking around. 'She bites.'

'Animals *love* me.' The remark made my flesh crawl it was so inappropriate coming from this . . . creeping monster. He crouched on his heels and rubbed my ears again. I couldn't tell if Stefan wanted me to bite him or not. I chose not, because I didn't want the taste of him on my tongue. I could always bite him later if I wanted to.

Stefan didn't comment, nor did he look anywhere except straight in front of him. I wondered if he would have lost status points if he'd turned. Werewolves play power games, too, but I know the rules for them. A werewolf would never have allowed a strange wolf to walk behind him.

He left off petting me, stood up, and walked around until he faced Stefan again. 'So you are Stefan, Marsilia's little soldier boy. I *have* heard of you – though your reputation is not what it once was, is it? Running away from Italy like that would soil any man's honor. Somehow, still, I expected more. All those stories . . . I expected to find a monster among monsters, a creature of nightmares who frightens even other vampires — and all I see is a dried-up has-been. I suppose that's what happens when you hide yourself in a little backwater town for a few centuries.'

There was a slight pause after the other vampire's last words.

Then Stefan laughed, and said, 'Whereas *you* have no reputation at all.' His voice was lighter than usual, sounding almost rushed, as if what he was saying was of no moment. I took a step away from him without meaning to, somehow frightened by that light, amused voice. He smiled gently at the other vampire and his tone softened further as he said, 'That's what happens when you are newly made and abandoned.'

It must have been some sort of vampire super-insult because the second vampire erupted, reacting as if Stefan's words had been an electric goad. He didn't go after Stefan, though.

Instead, he bent down and grabbed the bottom of the king-sized box spring and jerk-lifted it and everything above it over his head. He swung it toward the hall door and then around so that the ends of the box spring, mattress, and bedding were balanced for an instant.

He shifted his grip and threw them all the way through the wall and into the empty hotel room next door, landing on the floor in a cloud of Sheetrock dust. Two of the wall studs hung splintered, suspended from somewhere inside the wall, giving the hole in the wall the appearance of a jack-o-lantern's smile. The false headboard, permanently mounted into the wall where the bed had been, looked forlorn and stupid hanging a foot or more above the pedestal of the bed.

The vampire's speed and strength didn't surprise me. I'd seen a few werewolves throw temper tantrums, enough to know that if the vampire had been truly angry, he wouldn't have had the control it took to manage the physics of swinging the two unattached mattresses together through the wall. Apparently, as in werewolf fights, battles between vampires have a lot of impressive fireworks before the main show.

In the silence that followed, I heard something, a hoarse mewling noise coming from behind the closed bathroom door – as if whatever made it had already cried out so much it could only make a small noise, but one that held much more terror than a full-throated scream.

I wondered if Stefan knew what was in the bathroom and that was why he'd been afraid when we were in the parking lot – there were things that even a vampire ought to be afraid of. I took a deep breath, but all I could smell was the bitter darkness – and that was getting stronger. I sneezed, trying to clear my nose, but it didn't work. Both vampires stood still until the noise stopped. Then the stranger dusted his hands lightly, a small smile on his face as if there had not been rage just an instant before.

'I am remiss,' he said, but the old fashioned words sounded false coming from him, as if he were pretending to be a vampire the way the old vampires tried to be human. 'You obviously do not know who I am.'

He gave Stefan a shallow bow. It was obvious, even to me, that this vampire had grown up in a time and place where bowing was something done in Kung Fu Theater movies rather than in everyday life. 'I am Asmodeus,' he said grandly, sounding like a child pretending to be a king.

'I said you have no reputation,' Stefan replied, still in that light, careless voice. 'I didn't say I didn't know your name, Cory Littleton. Asmodeus was destroyed centuries ago.'

'Kurfel, then,' said Cory, nothing childlike in his manner at all.

I knew those names, Asmodeus and Kurfel, both, and as soon as I realized where I'd heard them, I knew what I had been smelling. Once the idea occurred to me, I realized the smell could be nothing else. Suddenly Stefan's fear wasn't surprising or startling at all. Demons were enough to scare anyone.

'Demon' is a catchall phrase, like 'fae,' used to describe beings who are unable to manifest themselves in our world in physical form. Instead, they possess their victims and feed upon them until there is nothing left. Kurfel wouldn't be this one's name, any more than Asmodeus was: knowing a demon's name gave you power over them. I'd never heard of a demon-possessed vampire before. I tried to stretch my mind around the concept.

'You are not Kurfel either,' said Stefan. 'Though something akin to him is allowing you some use of his powers when you amuse him well enough.' He looked toward the bathroom door. 'What *have* you been doing to amuse him, sorcerer?'

Sorcerer.

I thought those were just stories – I mean, who would be dumb enough to invite a demon into themselves? And why would a demon, who could just possess any corrupt soul (and to offer yourself to a demon sort of presupposes a corrupt soul, doesn't it?) make a deal with anyone? I didn't believe in sorcerers; I certainly didn't believe in vampire sorcerers.

I suppose somone raised by werewolves should have been more open-minded – but I had to draw the line somewhere.

'I don't like you,' Littleton said coolly, and the hair on the back of my neck stood up as magic gathered around him. 'I don't like you at all.'

He reached out and touched Stefan in the middle of the

forehead. I waited for Stefan to knock his hand aside, but he did nothing to defend himself, just dropped to his knees, landing with a heavy thud.

'I thought you'd be more interesting, but you're not.' Cory told him, but the diction and tone of his voice was different. 'Not amusing at all. I'll have to fix that.'

He left Stefan kneeling and went to the bathroom door.

I whined at Stefan and stretched up on my hind feet so I could lick his face, but he didn't even look at me. His eyes were vague and unfocused; he wasn't breathing. Vampires didn't need to, of course, but Stefan mostly did.

The sorcerer had bespelled him somehow.

I tugged at the leash, but Stefan's hand was still closed upon it. Vampires are strong, and even when I threw my whole thirty-two pounds into it, his hand didn't move. If I'd had half an hour I could have chewed through the leather, but I didn't want to be caught here when the sorcerer returned.

Panting, I looked across the room at the open bathroom. What new monster was waiting inside? If I got out of this alive, I'd never let anyone put a leash on me again. Werewolves have strength, semiretractable claws, and inch-long fangs – *Samuel* wouldn't have been caught by the stupid leather harness and leash. One bite and it would have been gone. All I had was speed – which the leash effectively limited.

I was prepared for a horrifying sight, something that could destroy Stefan. But what Cory Littleton dragged out of that room left me stunned with an entirely different sort of horror.

The woman wore one of those fifties-style uniforms that hotels give their maids; this one was mint green with a stiff blue apron. Her color scheme matched the drapes and the hallway carpets, but the rope around her wrists, dark with blood, didn't.

Other than her bleeding wrists, she seemed mostly

unharmed, though the sounds she was making made me wonder about that. Her chest was heaving with the effort of her screaming, but even without the bathroom door between us she wasn't making much noise, more of a series of grunts.

I jerked against the harness again and when Stefan still didn't move, I bit him, hard, drawing blood. He didn't even flinch.

I couldn't bear to listen to the woman's terror. She was breathing in hoarse gulping pants and she struggled against Littleton's hold, so focused on him that I don't think she saw Stefan or me at all.

I hit the end of the leash again. When that didn't work I snarled and snapped, twisting around so that I could chew on the leather. My own collar was equipped with a safety fastening that I could have broken, but Stefan's leather harness was fastened with old-fashioned metal buckles.

The sorcerer dropped his victim on the floor in front of me, just out of reach – though I'm not sure what I could have done for her even if I could get within touching distance. She didn't see me; she was too busy trying not to see Littleton. But my struggles had drawn the sorcerer's attention and he squatted down so he was closer to my level.

'I wonder what you'd do if I let you go?' he asked me. 'Are you afraid? Would you run? Would you attack me or does the smell of her blood rouse you as it does a vampire?' He looked up at Stefan then. 'I see your fangs, Soldier. The rich scent of blood and terror: it calls to us, doesn't it? They keep us leashed as tightly as you keep your coyote.' He used the Spanish pronunciation, three syllables rather than two. 'They demand we take only a sip from each when our hearts crave so much more. Blood is not really filling without death is it? You are old enough to remember the Before Times, aren't you, Stefan? When vampires ate as we chose and reveled in the terror and the last throes of our prey. When we fed truly.'

Stefan made a noise and I risked a glance at him. His eyes had changed. I don't know why that was the first thing I noticed about him, when so much else was different. Stefan's eyes were usually the shade of oiled walnut, but now they gleamed like blood-rubies. His lips were drawn back, revealing fangs shorter and more delicate than a werewolf's. His hand, which had tightened on my leash, bore curved claws on the ends of his elongated fingers. After a brief glimpse, I had to turn away, almost as frightened of him as I was of the sorcerer.

'Yes, Stefan,' said Littleton, laughing like the villain in an old black and white movie. 'I see you remember the taste of death. Benjamin Franklin once said that those who give up their freedom for safety deserve neither.' He leaned close. 'Do you feel safe, Stefan? Or do you miss what you once had, what you allowed them to steal from all of us.'

Littleton turned to his victim, then. She made very little noise when he touched her, her cries so hoarse that they would have been inaudible to a human outside of this room. I fought the harness until it cut into my shoulders but it did me no good. My claws tore holes in the carpet, but Stefan was too heavy for me to budge.

Littleton took a very long time to kill her: she quit struggling before I did. In the end the only noise in the room was from the vampires, the one in front of me feeding wetly and the one beside me making helpless, eager noises though he didn't move otherwise.

The woman's body convulsed and her eyes met mine, just for a moment, before they glazed over in death. I felt the rush of magic as she stilled and the rank bitterness, the scent of the demon, retreated from the room, leaving only a faint trace behind.

I could smell again, and almost wished I couldn't. The smells of death aren't much better than the scent of demon.

Panting, shaking, and coughing because I'd half strangled myself, I dropped to the floor. There was nothing I could do to help her now, if there ever had been.

Littleton continued to feed. I snuck a glance over at Stefan, who'd quit making those disturbing noises. He'd resumed his frozen stance. Even knowing that he'd been able to watch that scene with desire rather than horror, Stefan was infinitely preferable to Littleton, and I backed up until my hip bumped his thigh.

I huddled against him as Littleton, the white of his shirt all but extinguished beneath the blood of the woman he'd killed, looked up from his victim to examine Stefan's face. He was giggling a little in nervous pants. I was so scared of him, of the thing that had been riding him, I could barely breathe.

'Oh, you wanted that,' he crooned holding out a hand and brushing it over Stefan's lips. After a moment Stefan licked his lips clean.

'Let me share,' the other vampire said in a soft voice. He leaned into Stefan and kissed him passionately. He closed his eyes, and I realized that he was finally within my reach.

Rage and fear are sometimes only a hairbreadth different. I leapt, mouth open and latched onto Littleton's throat, tasting first the human blood of the woman on his skin, then something else, bitter and awful, that traveled from my mouth through my body like a jolt of lightning. I fought to close my jaw, but I'd missed my hold and my upper fangs hit the bone of his spine and bounced off.

I wasn't a werewolf or bulldog and I couldn't crush bone, only dig deeply into flesh as the vampire gripped my shoulders and tore himself loose, ripping the leash out of Stefan's grip as he struggled.

Blood, his blood this time, spilled over his front, but the wound began closing immediately, the vampire healing himself even faster than a werewolf could have. In despair, I realized I hadn't seriously harmed him. He dropped me to the ground and backed away, his hands covering the wound I'd made. I felt his magic flare and when his hands fell away from his throat, the wound was gone.

He snarled at me, his fangs showing and I snarled back. I don't remember seeing him move, just the momentary feeling of his hands on my sides, a brief moment while I was hurled through the air and then nothing.

2

I awoke on my couch to steady strokes of a tongue-in-the-face wash and Medea's distinctive thrumming. Stefan's voice came as a relief because it meant that he was alive, just like me. But when Samuel replied, though his purring tones bore more than a passing resemblance to the noise my cat was making, there was no comfort to be had from the cold menace under the soft voice.

Adrenaline pumped through me at the sound. I pushed the memory of the night's terrors aside. What was important this minute was that tonight was the full moon and there was an enraged werewolf not two feet from me.

I tried to open my eyes and stand up, but I encountered several problems. First, one eye seemed to be stuck shut. Second, since I seldom sleep in coyote form, I'd tried to sit up like a human. My floundering was made worse because my body, stiff and sore, wasn't reacting very well to movement of any kind. Finally, as soon as I moved my head, I was rewarded with throbbing pain and accompanying nausea. Medea scolded me in cat swear words and jumped off the couch in a huff.

'Shh, Mercy.' All the menace left Samuel's voice as he crooned to me and knelt beside the couch. His gentle, competent hands glided over my sore body.

I opened my good eye and looked at him warily, not trusting the tone of his voice to indicate his mood. His eyes were in the shadow, but his wide mouth was soft under his long, aristocratic nose. I noted absently that he needed a haircut; his ash brown hair covered his eyebrows. There was tension in his wide shoulders, and now that I was fully awake,

I could smell the aggression that had been building in the room. He turned his head to follow his hands as they played delicately over my hind legs and I caught sight of his eyes.

Pale blue, not white, like they would be if the wolf was too close to the surface.

I relaxed enough to be sincerely grateful to be lying, however battered and miserable, on my own couch and not dead – or worse, still in the company of Cory Littleton, vampire and sorcerer.

Samuel's hands touched my head and I whimpered.

As well as being a werewolf, my roommate was a doctor, a very good doctor. Of course, I suppose he ought to be. He'd been one for a very long time and had at least three medical degrees gained in two different centuries. Werewolves can be very long-lived creatures.

'Is she all right?' Stefan asked. There was something in his voice that bothered me.

Samuel's mouth tightened. 'I'm not a vet, I'm a doctor. I can tell you that there are no broken bones, but until she can talk to me, that's all I know.'

I tried to shift so I could help, but all I got was a burning pain across my chest and around my ribs. I let out a panicked little sound.

'What's wrong?' Samuel ran a finger gently along my jaw line.

It hurt, too. I flinched and he pulled his hands away.

'Wait,' said Stefan from the far side of the couch.

His voice sounded wrong. After what the demon-possessed vampire had done to him, I had to make sure Stefan was all right. I twisted, whining with discomfort, until I could peer at the vampire with my good eye.

He'd been sitting on the floor at the foot of the couch, but, as I looked at him, he rose until he was on his knees – just as he'd been when the sorcerer had held him.

I caught Samuel's sudden lunge out of the corner of my eye. But Stefan melted away from Samuel's hand. He moved oddly. At first I thought he was hurt, that Samuel had already hit him, then I realized he was moving like Marsilia, the Mistress of the local seethe – like a puppet, or an old, old vampire who had forgotten how to be human.

'Peace, wolf,' Stefan said, and I realized what had been wrong with his voice. It was dead, empty of any emotion. 'Try taking the harness off of her. I think she was trying to shift, but she can't while she wears the harness.'

I hadn't realized that I was still wearing it. Samuel hissed when he touched the buckles.

'They're silver,' Stefan said without moving closer. 'I can undo them, if you'll let me.'

'You seem to have a lot to say for yourself, now, vampire,' growled Samuel.

Samuel was the calmest, most even-tempered werewolf I knew – though that's not saying much – but I could hear the promise of violence in the undertones of his voice that made my ribcage vibrate.

'You asked me questions I cannot answer,' said Stefan calmly, but his voice had warmed to more human cadences. 'I have every hope that Mercedes will be able to satisfy your curiosity and mine. First, though, someone needs to remove the harness so she can return to her human form.'

Samuel hesitated, then stepped back from me. 'Do it.' His voice was more growl than tone.

Stefan moved slowly, waiting for Samuel to move aside before he touched me. He smelled of my shampoo and his hair was damp. He must have taken a shower – and found clean clothes somewhere. Nothing in that motel room had escaped the murdered woman's blood. My own paws were still covered in it.

I had an immediate, visceral memory of the way the carpet

had squished, supersaturated with dark, viscous fluid. I would have thrown up, but the sudden sharp pain in my head cut through the nausea, a welcome distraction.

It didn't take Stefan long to unbuckle the harness, and as soon as it was off, I changed. Stefan stepped away and let Samuel resume his place at my side.

Anger tightened the sides of Samuel's mouth as he touched my shoulder. I looked down and realized that my skin was bruised and raw where the harness had rubbed, and everywhere were small rust-colored spots of dried blood. I looked like I'd been in a car wreck.

Thinking about cars reminded me about work. I looked out the window, but the sky was still dark.

'What time is it?' I asked. My voice came out in a hoarse croak.

It was the vampire who answered. 'Five forty-five.'

'I need to get dressed,' I said standing up abruptly, which was a mistake. I clutched my head, swore, and sat down before I fell down.

Samuel pried my hands away from my forehead. 'Open your eyes, Mercy.'

I did my best, but my left eye didn't want very badly to open. As soon as I had both of them opened, he blinded me with a penlight.

'Damn it, Sam,' I said, trying to squirm out of his hold.

'Just once more.' He was relentless, this time prying my sore eye open himself. Then he set the light aside and ran his hands over my head. I hissed as his fingers found a sore spot. 'No concussion, Mercy, though you have a sizeable goose egg on the back of your head, a hell of a shiner, and, if I'm not mistaken, the rest of the left side of your face will be purple before daylight. So why does the bloodsucker say you have been unconscious for the past forty-five minutes?'

'Closer to an hour now,' said Stefan. He was sitting down

on the floor again, farther from me than he had been, but he was watching me with predatory intenseness.

'I don't know,' I said, and it came out shakier than I meant it to.

Samuel sat beside me on the couch, pulled off the small throw blanket that hid the damage Medea had done to the back of the couch, and wrapped me in it. He started to reach for me, and I pulled away. A dominant wolf's desire to protect was a strong instinct – and Samuel was *very* dominant. Give him an inch and he'd take over the world, or my life if I let him.

Still, he smelled of the river, desert, and fur – and of the familiar sweet scent that belonged only to him. I quit fighting him and let my aching head rest against his arm. The resilience and warmth of his flesh against my temple helped my headache. Maybe if I didn't move, my head wouldn't fall off. Samuel made a soft, soothing noise and ran his clever fingers through my hair, avoiding the sore spot.

I hadn't forgotten or forgiven him for the flashlight, but I'd get even with him when I felt better. It had been a long time since I'd leaned on anyone, and, even knowing it was stupid to let Samuel see me so weak, I couldn't force myself to move away.

I heard Stefan go to the kitchen, open my refrigerator, and mess around in the cupboards. Then the vampire's scent drifted nearer and he said, 'Get her to drink this. It will help.'

'Help with what?' Samuel's voice was a good deal deeper than usual. If my head had hurt a little less, I would have moved away.

'Dehydration. She's been bitten.'

Stefan was lucky I was leaning against Samuel. The werewolf started to his feet, but stopped halfway up when I whimpered at his sudden movement.

Okay, I was playing dirty, but it kept Samuel from attacking. Stefan wasn't the villain. If he'd fed off of me, I was sure it had been necessary. I wasn't in any shape to step between them, so I chose to play helpless. I only wished I'd had to act a little harder to do it.

Samuel sat back down and moved my hair away from my neck. His fingertips brushed a sore spot on the side that had just blended in with my other aches and pains. Once he touched it, though, it burned and ached all the way down to my collarbone.

'It was not me,' Stefan said, but there was something uncertain in his voice — as if he wasn't entirely sure of it. I unburied my head so I could see him. But whatever had been in his voice hadn't touched the bland expression on his face.

'There is no danger to her beyond anemia,' he told Samuel. 'It takes more than a bite to change a human to a vampire — and I'm not certain Mercy could be turned anyway. If she were human, we'd have to worry that he could call her to him and command her obedience — but walkers are not so vulnerable to our magic. She just needs to rehydrate and rest.'

Samuel gave the vampire a sharp look. 'You're just full of information now, aren't you? If you didn't bite her, what did?'

Stefan smiled faintly, not like he meant it, and handed Samuel the glass of orange juice he'd tried to give him earlier. I knew why he handed it to Samuel and not me. Samuel was getting all territorial — I was impressed that a vampire could read him that well.

'I think Mercy would be a better narrator,' Stefan said. There was a thread of uncharacteristic anxiety in his voice that distracted me from worrying about Samuel's possessiveness.

Why was Stefan so anxious to hear what I had to say? He'd been there, too.

I took the glass Samuel handed me and sat up until I wasn't leaning against him anymore. I hadn't realized how thirsty I'd been until I started drinking. I'm not usually fond of orange juice – Samuel's the one who drank it – but just then it tasted like ambrosia.

It wasn't magic, though. When I finished, my head still hurt, and I wanted nothing more than to crawl into my bed and pull the covers over my head, but I wasn't going to get any rest until Samuel knew everything – and Stefan apparently wasn't going to talk.

'Stefan called me a couple of hours ago,' I began. 'I owed him a favor for helping us when Jesse was kidnaped.'

They both listened raptly, Stefan nodding in places. When I reached the part where we entered the hotel room, Stefan sat on the floor near my feet. He leaned his back against the couch, turned his head away from me and covered his eyes with a hand. He might just have been getting tired – the window shades were starting to lighten with the first hints of dawn as I finished up with my botched attempt at killing Littleton and my subsequent impact with the wall.

'You're sure that's what happened?' asked Stefan without uncovering his eyes.

I frowned at him, sitting up straighter. 'Of course I'm sure.' He'd been there, so why did he sound as if he thought I might be making things up?

He rubbed his eyes and looked at me, and there was relief in his voice. 'No offense meant, Mercy. Your memories of the woman's death are very different from mine.'

I frowned at him. 'Different how?'

'You say that all I did was kneel on the ground while Littleton murdered the hotel maid?'

'That's right.'

'I don't remember that,' he said, his voice a bare whisper. 'I remember the sorcerer brought the woman out, her blood called to me, and I answered it.' He licked his lips and the combination of horror and hunger in his eyes made me glance away from him. He continued in a whisper, almost to himself. 'Bloodlust has not overcome me in a long, long time.'

'Well,' I said, not sure if what I had to tell him would help or hurt, 'you weren't pretty. Your eyes glowed and you showed some fang. But you didn't do anything to her.'

For a moment, a pale reflection of the ruby glow I'd seen in the hotel room gleamed in his irises. 'I remember reveling in the woman's blood, painting it on my hands and face. It was still there when I brought you home and I had to wash it off.' He closed his eyes. 'There is an old ceremony . . . forbidden now for a long time but I *remember* . . .' He shook his head and turned his attention to his hands which he held loosely looped around one knee. '*I can taste her still.*'

Those words hung uncomfortably in the air for a moment before he continued.

'I was lost in the blood' – he said that phrase as if the words belonged together and might mean something more complex than their literal meaning – 'when I came to myself, the other vampire was gone. The woman lay as I remember leaving her, and you were unconscious.'

He swallowed and then stared at the lightening window, his voice dropped an octave, like the wolves' voices can sometimes. 'I couldn't remember what had happened to you.'

He reached out and touched my foot, which was the body part nearest him. When he spoke again, his voice was almost normal. 'A memory lapse is not inconsistent with bloodlust.' His hand moved until it closed carefully around my toes; his skin was cool against mine. 'But bloodlust usually only dulls unimportant things. You are important to me, Mercedes. It occurred to me that you were not important to Cory

Littleton. And that thought gave me hope while I drove us here.'

I was important to Stefan? All I was to him was his mechanic. He'd done a favor for me, and last night I'd returned it in spades. We might possibly be friends – except that I didn't think vampires had friends. I thought about it a moment and realized that Stefan was important to me. If something had happened to him tonight, something permanent, it would have hurt me. Maybe he felt the same way.

'You think he tampered with your memory?' Samuel asked while I was still thinking. He'd scooted closer and slid an arm around my shoulders. It felt good. Too good. I slid forward on the couch, away from Samuel – and Stefan let his hand fall away from my foot as I moved.

Stefan nodded. 'Either my memory or Mercy's is obviously wrong. I don't think he could affect Mercy's, even being a sorcerer. That kind of thing just doesn't work on walkers like her, not unless he made a real effort.'

Samuel made a hmm sound. 'I don't see why he'd want to make Mercy think you were innocent of murder – especially if he thought she was just a coyote.' He looked at Stefan who shrugged.

'Walkers were only a threat for a couple of decades, and that centuries ago. Littleton is very new; I would be surprised if he's even heard of anything like Mercy. The demon might know, one never is quite sure what demons know. But the best evidence that Littleton thinks Mercy was nothing more than a coyote is that she is still alive.'

Goody for me.

'All right.' Samuel rubbed his face. 'I'd better call Adam. He needs to get his clean-up crew to the hotel before someone sees the mess and starts shouting werewolf.' He raised an eyebrow at Stefan. 'Although I suppose we could just tell the police it was a vampire.'

It had been less than six months since the werewolves had followed the fae in coming out into the public view. They hadn't told the human population everything, and only those werewolves who chose to do so came out in the open – most of those were in the military, people already separated from the general population. So far we were all holding our breath waiting to see what would come of it, but, so far, there had been none of the rioting that had marked the fae's exposure a few decades earlier.

Part of the quiet reaction was the Marrok's careful planning. Americans feel safe in our modern world. Bran did his best to protect that illusion, presenting his public wolves as victims who took their affliction and bravely used it to protect others. Werewolves, he wanted the public to believe, at least for a while yet, were just people who turned furry under the full moon. The wolves who had come out first were heroes who put their lives on the line to protect the weaker humans. The Marrok, like the fae before him, chose to keep as much of the werewolves' darker aspects as carefully hidden as he could.

But I think most of the credit for the peaceful acceptance of the revelation belongs to the fae. For more than two decades the fae had managed to present themselves as weak, kindly, and gentle – and anyone who has read their Brothers Grimm or Andrew Lang knows just what a feat that is.

No matter what Samuel threatened, his father, the Marrok, would never agree to expose the vampires. There was no way to soft-pedal the fact that vampires fed on humans. And once people realized there really were monsters, they might just realize that werewolves were monsters, too.

Stefan knew what the Marrok would say as well as Samuel did. He smiled unpleasantly at the werewolf, exposing his fangs. 'The *mess* has been taken care of. I called my mistress before I brought Mercy home. We don't need werewolves to clean up after us.' Stefan was usually more polite than that, but he'd had a bad night, too.

'The other vampire gave you false memories,' I said to distract the men from their antagonism. 'Was that because he was a sorcerer?'

Stefan tilted his head, as if he were embarrassed. 'We can do that with humans,' he said, which was something I didn't want to know. He saw my reaction and explained, 'That means we can leave those we casually feed from alive, Mercedes. Still, humans are one thing, and vampires another. We're not supposed to be able to do it to each other. You don't have to worry, though. No vampire can remake *your* memory — probably not even one who is a sorcerer.'

Relief climbed through me. If I were going to pick things I didn't want a vampire to do to me, messing with my thoughts was very high on the list. I touched my neck.

'That's why you wanted me with you,' I sat up straighter. 'You said he'd done it to another vampire. What did he make the other vampire think he'd done?'

Stefan looked wary . . . and guilty.

'You knew he'd kill someone, didn't you?' I accused him. 'Is that what he did to the other vampire? Make him think he'd killed someone?' The memory of the slow death I hadn't been able to prevent made me clench my fists.

'I didn't know what he would do. But yes, I believed that he had killed before and made my friend think he had done it.' He spoke as if the words left a bitter taste in his mouth. 'But I could not act without proof. So more died who should not have.'

'You're a vampire,' said Samuel. 'Don't try to make us believe you care when innocents die.'

Stefan met Samuel's eyes. 'I have swallowed enough death in years past that more sickens me, but believe as you wish. So many deaths threaten our secrets, werewolf. Even if I cared nothing for any human's death, I would not have wanted so many to die and endanger our secrets.'

So many to die?

His sureness that noise wouldn't disturb anyone in the hotel when Littleton had invited us in became suddenly clear. The thing I'd seen kill the woman would not have hesitated to kill as many people as he could. 'Who else died tonight?'

'Four.' Stefan didn't look away from Samuel. 'The night clerk and three guests. Luckily the hotel was nearly deserted.'

Samuel swore.

I swallowed. 'So the bodies are just going to disappear?'

Stefan sighed. 'We try not to have disappearances of people who will be missed. The bodies will be accounted for in such a way as to cause as little fuss as possible. An attempted robbery, a lover's quarrel that got out of hand.'

I opened my mouth to say something rash, but caught myself. The rules we all had to live by weren't Stefan's fault.

'You put Mercy at risk,' Samuel growled. 'If he had already made another vampire kill involuntarily, he might have been able to make you kill Mercy.'

'No. He couldn't have made me harm Mercy.' Stefan's voice held as much anger as Samuel's, giving a little doubt to the firmness of his answer. He must have heard it, too, because he turned his attention back to me. 'I swore to you, on my honor, that you would take no harm from this night. I underestimated the enemy, and you suffered for it. I am foresworn.'

'"All that is necessary for evil to triumph is for good men to do nothing",' I murmured. I'd had to read Edmund Burke's *Reflections on the Revolution in France* three times in college; some of his points had seemed especially relevant to me, who had been brought up with the understanding of just how much evil there really was in the world.

'What do you mean?' Stefan asked.

'Will my presence in that hotel room help you destroy that monster?' I asked.

'I hope so.'

'Then it was worth what little hurt I took,' I said firmly. 'Quit beating yourself up about it.'

'Honor is not so easily satisfied,' said Samuel meeting Stefan's gaze.

Stefan looked like he agreed, but there was nothing more I could do for him about that.

'How did you know that there was something wrong with Littleton?' I asked.

Stefan broke off his staring contest with Samuel, dropping his eyes to Medea who'd crawled onto his lap and crouched there, purring. If he'd been human, I'd have said he looked tired. If he'd dropped his eyes like that in front of a less civilized werewolf, he might have had problems, but Samuel knew that a vampire dropping his gaze was not admitting submissiveness.

'I have a friend named Daniel,' Stefan said after a moment. 'He is very young, as our kind go – and you might call him a nice boy. A month ago, when a vampire checked into a local hotel, Daniel was sent to see why he had not contacted us for the usual permissions.'

Stefan shrugged. 'It is something that we do a lot; it should not have been dangerous or unusual. It was an appropriate assignment for a new vampire.' Except there was a hint of disapproval in Stefan's voice that told me that he would not have sent Daniel off to confront an unknown vampire.

'Somehow Daniel was sidetracked – he doesn't remember how. Something aroused his bloodlust. He never made it to the hotel. There was a small group of migrant workers who were camping in the cherry orchard, waiting to begin the harvest.' He exchanged a glace with Samuel over my head.

'Like tonight, the mess wasn't pretty, but it was containable. We took their trailers and vehicles and got rid of them. The owner of the orchard just thought they'd gotten tired of waiting and moved on. Daniel was . . . punished. Not too harshly, because he is young and the lust is so very strong. But now, of his own will, he won't eat at all. He is dying from guilt. As I told you, he is a nice boy.'

Stefan inhaled, a deep, cleansing breath. Stefan once told me that most vampires breathed because not breathing attracted human attention. I think, though, that some of them do it because their not breathing is as troubling to them as it is to the rest of us. Of course, if they are going to talk, they have to breathe a little bit anyway.

'In the furor,' Stefan continued, 'no one investigated the visiting vampire who had, after all, spent only one night in town. I didn't even think to question what had happened until I tried to help Daniel a few days ago. He talked to me about what had happened – and something just seemed wrong with his story. I know bloodlust. He could not remember why he'd decided to travel all the way out to Benton City, twenty miles from the hotel where he was supposed to be. Daniel is very obedient, like one of your submissive wolves. He would not have deviated from his orders without provocation. He is not able to travel as I can, he would have had to drive all the way – and driving is not something a vampire in the throes of bloodlust does well.

'I decided to do some investigating of the vampire he was supposed to meet. It wasn't difficult to get his name from the clerk at the hotel where he had stayed. I could find nothing on a vampire named Cory Littleton – but there was a man of that name offering his services in matters magical on the Internet.'

Stefan gave the floor a slight smile. 'It is forbidden us to turn anyone who is not wholly human. Mostly it wouldn't work anyway, but there are stories . . .' He shrugged unhappily. 'I've seen enough to know that this is a good rule. When I went hunting, I expected to find a witch who'd been turned. It never occurred to me he might be a sorcerer – I haven't seen a sorcerer for centuries. Most people today don't have the belief in evil and the knowledge necessary to make a pact with a demon. So I thought Littleton was a witch. A powerful witch, though, to be able to affect the memory of a vampire – even a fledgling like Daniel.'

'Why did you go after him with just Mercy?' asked Samuel. 'Couldn't you have gotten another vampire to go with you?'

'Daniel had been punished, the matter was deemed over.' Stefan tapped his knee, impatient with that judgement. 'The Mistress wanted to hear no more of it.'

I had met Marsilia, the Mistress of Stefan's seethe. She hadn't struck me as the type to be overly concerned about the deaths of a few humans or even a few hundred humans.

'I was considering going over her head, when the vampire returned. I had no proof of my suspicions, you understand. As far as everyone else was concerned, Daniel had fallen victim to his bloodlust. So I volunteered to speak with this stranger myself. I thought I might see if he was someone who could make Daniel remember doing things he had not. I brought Mercy with me as a safety precaution. I really did not expect that he could affect me as he had Daniel.'

'So you don't think Daniel killed the people he thought he did?' I asked.

'A witch who was also a vampire might be able to implant memories, but he couldn't have made Daniel kill. A sorcerer . . .' Stefan spread his hands. 'A sorcerer could do many things. I consider myself lucky that he was so eager to make the kill himself that he did not use the bloodlust he'd summoned in me to make me kill the maid – as I was half-convinced he had. I have become arrogant over the years,

Mercedes. I hadn't really believed he could do anything to me. Daniel, after all, is very new. You were supposed to be a safeguard, but I didn't expect to need you.'

'Littleton was a sorcerer,' I said. 'And some idiot vampire chose to turn him. Who did it? Was it someone from around here? And if not, why is he here?'

Stefan smiled again. 'Those are questions I shall pose to my mistress. The turning might have been a mistake – like our fair Lilly.'

I'd met Lilly. She'd been crazy when she'd been human, and being a vampire hadn't changed that. She was also an incredible pianist. Her maker had been so caught up by her music he hadn't taken the time to notice anything else about her. Like the werewolves, vampires tend to rid themselves of someone who might draw unwanted attention to them. Lilly's extraordinary gift had protected her, though her maker had been killed for being so careless.

'How could it have been a mistake?' I asked. 'I saw your reaction. You smelled the demon before we went into the hotel.'

He shook his head. 'Demons are hardly commonplace these days. The demon-possessed are caged quickly in mental institutions where they are subdued by drugs. Most younger vampires have never run into a sorcerer – you said yourself that you didn't know what you had scented until I told you.'

'Why didn't the demon stop this sorcerer from falling victim to the vampire?' asked Samuel. 'They usually protect their symbionts until they're finished with them.'

'Why would it?' I said, mentally dusting off all I'd ever heard about sorcery, which wasn't much. 'The demons' only desire is to create as much destruction as they can. All vampirism would do is increase Littleton's ability to create mayhem.'

'Do you know something of demons, Samuel Cornick?' asked Stefan.

Samuel shook his head. 'Not enough to be of help. But I'll call my father. If he doesn't, he'll know someone who does.'

'It is vampire business.'

Samuel's eyebrows shot up. 'Not if this sorcerer is leaving bloody messes behind.'

'We'll see to him – *and* to his messes.' Stefan turned to me. 'I have two more favors to ask you – though you owe me nothing more.'

'What do you need?' I hoped it wasn't anything immediate. I was tired and more than ready to clean the blood off my hands, both figuratively and literally, though I was afraid the former was going to be difficult.

'Would you come before my mistress and tell her what you have told me about the happenings of this night? She will not want to believe that a new-made vampire could do what he has done. No more will any of the seethe welcome the news of a sorcerer among us.'

I had no particular desire to meet Marsilia again. He must have seen that on my face, because he continued, 'He needs to be stopped, Mercy.' He took another deep breath, deeper than he needed if all he were using the air for was to talk. 'I will be asked about this night in full court. I will tell them what I have seen and heard – and they will know if what I tell them is true or false. I can tell them the events you say happened, but they cannot know they are true unless you, yourself, will speak for me. Without you there, they will take my memory of the maid's death as fact and your words to me as hearsay.'

'What will they do to you if they don't believe you?' I asked.

'I am not a new vampire, Mercedes. If they decide that I have risked our kind by killing this woman, they will destroy me – just as your pack leader would have to destroy one wolf to protect the rest.'

'All right,' I agreed slowly.

'Only if I can come with her,' Samuel amended.

'An escort of her choice,' Stefan agreed. 'Perhaps Adam Hauptman or one of his wolves. Dr Cornick, please don't take offense, but I don't think you should come. My mistress was taken with you last time, and self-control in such matters is not her strong suit.'

'Tell me when you need me,' I said before Samuel could begin arguing. 'I'll find an escort.'

'Thank you,' Stefan said, then hesitated. 'It is dangerous for you to keep reminding the seethe what you are.'

Walkers are not popular among the vampires. I'd gathered that when the vampires first came to this part of the New World, the walkers here had made themselves enough of a pest that the vampires had killed most of them off. Stefan wouldn't tell me anything more detailed. Some things I'd figured out – like most vampire magic didn't work on me. But I couldn't see how I was any danger to them – unlike, say, a werewolf would be.

Stefan had known what I was for years, but had kept it from his seethe until I'd gone to them for help. He'd gotten into trouble for it.

'They already know what I am,' I told him. 'I'll come. What's the second favor?'

'It's already too light out for me to travel,' he said, waving a vague hand toward my window. 'Do you have somewhere dark I might spend the day?'

The only place for Stefan to sleep was my closet. The closets in Samuel's room and the third bedroom had slatted doors that allowed too much light to go through. All of my windows had blinds, but nothing dark enough to keep a vampire safe.

My bedroom took up one end of the trailer – Samuel's room was on the opposite end. I opened my door to wave Stefan inside, but Samuel came, too. I sighed and didn't fuss. Samuel wouldn't leave me alone with Stefan without a fight I was too battered to enjoy.

My bedroom was littered with clothing, some dirty, some clean. The clean clothes were folded in stacks I hadn't gotten around to putting in my drawers. Scattered among the clothes were books, magazines, and mail I hadn't sorted yet. If I'd known I was going to have a man in my room, I'd have cleaned it.

I pulled open the closet and pulled out a couple of boxes and two pairs of shoes. That left it empty – except for the four dresses hanging on one side. It was a big closet, long enough for Stefan to lie down comfortably in.

'Samuel can get you a spare pillow and blanket,' I said, gathering clothes as I spoke. My need to be clean had been growing since I woke up, and now it was desperate. I needed to get the smell of the woman's death off of my skin because I couldn't get it out of my head.

'Mercedes,' said Stefan in a gentle tone. 'I don't need a blanket. I'm not going to be sleeping, I'm going to be dead.'

I don't know why that was the final straw. Maybe it was the implication that I didn't understand what he was – when I'd just had a graphic example of what vampires could do. I'd been halfway to the bathroom, but I turned back and stared at both men.

'Samuel is going to get you a blanket,' I told him firmly. 'And a pillow. You are going to sleep for the day in my closet. Dead people don't get to stay in my bedroom.'

I shut the bathroom door behind me and dropped the afghan I wore on the floor. I heard Samuel say, 'I'll get some bedding,' before I turned on the shower to let it warm up.

There's a full length mirror on the door of my bathroom. One of those cheap ones with the imitation wood frame. When I turned to put my clothes on top of the sink where they wouldn't get wet, I got a good look at myself.

At first, all I could see was the dried blood. In my hair, on my face, down my shoulder, arm and hip. On my hands and feet.

I threw up in the toilet. Twice. Then I washed my hands and face and rinsed my mouth out with water.

I was not unacquainted with blood. I am sometimes a coyote, after all. I've killed my share of rabbits and mice. Last winter I killed two men — werewolves. But this death was different. Evil. He hadn't killed her for food, revenge, or self-defense. He'd killed her, and four other people, because he liked it. And I hadn't been able to stop him.

I looked back at the mirror.

Bruises bloomed on my ribs and shoulder. Dark purple marks traced the path the harness had run around my chest and ribs. I must have done that while I was struggling against Stefan's hold on my leash. The bruise on the outside edge of my right shoulder was more black than purple. The left side of my face was swollen cheekbone to jaw and red with the promise of a truly spectacular bruise.

I leaned forward and touched my puffy eyelid. I looked like a rape victim — except for the two dark marks on my neck.

They looked sort of like a rattlesnake bite, two dark half-formed scabs surrounded by swollen and reddened skin. I covered them with my hand and wondered how much I trusted Stefan's assessment that I would neither be turned into a vampire nor be subject to Littleton's control.

I took out my hydrogen peroxide and dabbed it over the wounds, hissing at the sting. It didn't make me feel any cleaner. I took the bottle into the shower with me and poured the contents on my neck until the bottle was empty. Then I scrubbed.

The blood was soon gone, though it had turned the water at my feet rusty for a few seconds. But no matter how much soap and shampoo I used, I still felt dirty. The more I scrubbed the more frantic I felt. Littleton hadn't raped me, but he'd violated my body just the same. The thought of his mouth on me made my stomach churn again.

I stood under the hot spray until the water was cold.

3

My bedroom was empty and the door to the closet was shut when I finally emerged from the bathroom. I glanced at the clock. Fifteen minutes to make it to the garage if I was going to open on time.

I was glad no one was there to hear me grunt and groan as I got dressed. No one alive to hear me, anyway.

Every muscle in my body ached, especially my right shoulder, and as soon as I bent down to pull on my socks and shoes, the battered side of my face started to throb. It would hurt me even more, though, if I lost customers because I wasn't open at my usual time.

I opened the bedroom door and Samuel looked up from where he'd been sitting on the couch. He'd been up all night, too; he ought to have gone to bed instead of waiting up to frown at me. He got up and pulled an ice pack out of the freezer.

'Here, put this on your face.'

It felt good and I sagged against the doorway to enjoy the numbness it brought to my throbbing cheek.

'I called Zee and told him what happened,' Samuel told me. 'You can go to bed. Zee's planning on working the shop for you today. He said he could do it tomorrow, too, if you need him.'

Siebold Adelbertsmiter, known to his friends as Zee, was a good mechanic, the best. He'd taught me everything I know, then sold the garage to me. He was also fae – and the first person I'd intended to go to for information on sorcerers.

Even though he sometimes filled in for me when I was

sick, I hadn't even thought about calling him for help with
the garage – proof that it would probably be better if I didn't
try going to work today.

'You're swaying,' said Samuel after a moment. 'Go to bed.
You'll feel better when you wake up.'

'Thank you,' I mumbled before shutting myself back in
my room.

I flopped facedown on my bed, groaned because that hurt
my face again. I rolled until I was more comfortable, covered
my head with my pillow and dozed for a while, maybe for
all of half an hour.

I could smell Stefan.

It wasn't that he smelled bad – he just smelled like
himself, sort of vampire and popcorn. But I couldn't get his
statement about being dead during the day out of my head.
Ugh. There was no way I was going to be able to sleep with
a dead man in my closet.

'Thanks, Stefan,' I told him glumly as I heaved my sore
body out of bed. If I couldn't sleep, I might as well go to
work. I opened the door to the living room, expecting it to
be empty, since Samuel had been up all night, too.

Instead he was sitting at the kitchen table drinking coffee
with Adam, the local Alpha werewolf, who happened to live
on the other side of my back fence.

I hadn't heard Adam come in. Once Samuel started sharing
my house, I'd become careless. I should have realized that
he would come over as soon as Samuel called him, though
– and, of course, Samuel had to call him about the bloodbath at the hotel. Adam was the Alpha, and responsible for
the welfare of all the werewolves in the area.

They both looked at me when I opened my door.

I was tempted to turn around and go back into my
bedroom with the dead man in my closet. Now, I'm not very
vain. If I'd ever been, making my living covered in various

grease and dirt mixtures would have cured me quickly. Still, I wasn't up to facing two sexy men when I had one eye swollen mostly shut and half of my face black and blue.

Stefan, being dead, was unlikely to notice what I looked like – and I'd never dated Stefan. Not that I was dating either Adam or Samuel at the present.

I hadn't dated Samuel since I was sixteen.

I've known Samuel for as long as I can remember. I grew up in the Marrok's pack in northwestern Montana, a were-wolf pack being as close to what I was as my teenage mother could find. It was just chance that her great uncle belonged to the Marrok. Lucky chance, I'd come to believe. A lot of werewolves would just have killed me outright – the way a wolf will kill a coyote who invades his territory.

Bran, the Marrok, in addition to being the ruler of all the North American wolves, was a good man. He placed me with one of his wolves and raised me almost as if I belonged. Almost.

Samuel was the Marrok's son. He'd been there for me as I struggled to live in a world with no place for me. I'd been raised by the pack, but I wasn't one of them. My mother loved me, but I didn't belong in her mundane human world either.

When I was sixteen, I'd believed I'd found my home in Samuel. Only when the Marrok showed me that Samuel wanted children – and not my love, did I finally understand I had to make my own path in life rather than finding someone else's to join.

I'd left Samuel and the pack and hadn't seen either again for more than fifteen years, almost half my life. All that changed last winter. Now, I had the Marrok's cell phone number on my speed dial, and Samuel had decided to move to the Tri-Cities. More specifically, he had decided to move in with me.

I still wasn't quite sure why. Fond of it as I am, my home is a single-wide trailer as old as me.

Samuel, being a doctor, is used to a slightly higher standard of housing. Granted his paperwork nightmare had taken a long time to settle. Only the month before had he at last gotten his license to practice medicine in Washington as well as Montana and Texas. He'd given up his job as a night clerk at an all night convenience store and begun working in the emergency room at the hospital in Kennewick. Despite the increase in his income, he hadn't shown any sign of leaving. His temporary stay in my house had turned into six months and some change.

I'd refused him at first.

'Why not with Adam?' I'd asked. As Alpha of the local werewolf pack, Adam was used to having short-term guests and he had more bedrooms than I did. I didn't ask why Samuel didn't buy his own house – Samuel had already told me that he'd spent too much time alone the past few years. Werewolves don't do well on their own. They need someone, pack or family, or they begin to get odd. Werewolves who get odd tend to end up dead – and sometimes take a lot of other people down with them when they go.

Samuel had raised his eyebrows and said, 'Do you really want us to kill each other? Adam is the Alpha – and I'm a stronger dominant than he is. Now we've both lived long enough to control ourselves up to a point. But, if we're living together, sooner or later, we'd be at each other's throat.'

'Adam's house is only a hundred yards from mine,' I told him dryly. Samuel would have been right about any other wolf, but Samuel made his own rules. If he wanted to live in peace with Adam, he could manage it.

'Please.' His tone was as far from pleading as it was possible to get.

'No,' I told him.

There was another, longer pause.

'So how are you going to explain to your neighbors that there is a strange man sleeping on your front porch?'

He'd have done it, too – so I let him move in.

I told him that the first time he flirted with me, he'd be out on his ear. I told him that I didn't love him anymore, though it might have had more effect if I had been entirely certain of that myself. It helped that I knew that he didn't love me, hadn't loved me when he tried to elope with me when I was sixteen – and he was who-knows-how-old.

It was not really as bad as it sounded. He grew up at a time when women married much younger than sixteen. It's hard on the older werewolves to adjust to modern ways of thinking.

I wish I could hold it against him, though. It would help me keep in mind that he still only wanted me for what I could give him: children who lived.

Werewolves are made, not born. To become a werewolf, you need to survive an attack so vicious that you nearly die – which allows the werewolf's magic to defeat your immune system. Many, many of the werewolf's kin who try to become werewolves themselves die in the attempt. Samuel had outlived all of his wives and children. Those children of his who had attempted to become werewolf had all died.

Female werewolves can't have children; their pregnancies spontaneously abort during the moon's change. Human women can have children with werewolves, but they can only carry to term the babies who have only human DNA.

But I was neither human, nor werewolf.

Samuel was convinced I'd be different. Not being moon called, my changes aren't violent – or even really necessary. I once went three years without shifting to my coyote self. Wolves and coyotes could interbreed in the wild, why not werewolves and walkers?

I don't know what the biological answer to that is, but my answer is that I didn't care to be a broodmare, thank you very much. So, no Samuel for me.

My feelings for Samuel should have been neat and tidily put in the past – except that I hadn't entirely been able to convince myself that all I felt for him was the lingering warmth anyone would feel for an old friend.

Maybe I'd have come to some conclusion about Samuel who had, after all, been living in my home for better than half a year, if it hadn't been for Adam.

Adam had been the bane of my existence for most of the time I'd lived in the Tri-Cities, where he ruled with an iron hand. Like the Marrok, he had a marked tendency to treat me like one of his minions when it suited him, and like a human stray when it didn't. He was high-handed, to say the least. He'd declared me his mate before the pack – and then had the gall to tell me it was for my own protection, so his wolves wouldn't bother me, a coyote living in their territory. Once he said it, it was so – and nothing I could say would change it in the eyes of his pack.

Last winter, though, he had needed me, and it changed things between us.

We went on three dates. During the first one I had a broken arm and he'd been very careful. On the second, he and his teenage daughter, Jesse, took me to the Richland Light Opera Company's presentation of *The Pirates of Penzance*. I'd had a great time. On the third date my arm had been almost healed and there had been no Jesse, no middle school auditorium to cool any passionate impulses we might have had. We went dancing and only his daughter waiting for him at his home, and Samuel waiting for me at mine, had kept our clothes on.

After he'd taken me home, I recovered enough to be scared.

Falling in love with a werewolf is not a safe thing to do —
but falling in love with an Alpha is worse. Especially for
someone like me. I had fought too long to belong to myself,
to allow myself to fall into line with the rest of his pack.

So the next time he called to take me out, I was unexpectedly busy. Avoiding someone who lives next door requires
a lot of effort, but I managed. It helped that when the werewolves became public, Adam's time was suddenly taken up
with trips back and forth between Washington D.C. and the
Tri-Cities.

Though he was one of the hundred or so werewolves who'd
revealed themselves to the public, Adam wasn't one of Bran's
front men — he didn't have the temperament for being a
celebrity. But after working with the government for forty-
odd years, first in the military and later as a security
consultant, he'd developed a network of contacts as well as
an understanding of politics that made him invaluable to
the Marrok — and to the government as they tried to decide
how to deal with yet another group of preternatural creatures.

Between his schedule and my clever avoidance tactics I
hadn't seen him for almost two months.

Even to my monocular gaze, he was beautiful, more beautiful than I remembered him being. I wanted to linger on
his slavic cheekbones and his sensuous mouth, damn it. I
jerked my gaze to Samuel — which was hardly safer. He
wasn't as pretty, but that didn't matter to my stupid
hormones.

Samuel broke the silence first. 'Why aren't you in bed,
Mercy?' he drawled. 'You look worse than the accident victim
I had die on the table last week.'

Adam came to his feet and crossed the living room in
four long strides while I waited like a rabbit in a snare,
knowing I should run, but unable to move. He stopped in

front of me, whistling softly between his teeth as he examined the damage. When he leaned closer and touched my neck, I heard a noise from the kitchen.

Samuel had broken his coffee cup. He didn't look up at me as he set about cleaning the mess.

'Nasty,' Adam said, drawing my attention back to him. 'Can you see out of that eye?'

'Not as well as I see out of the other,' I told him. 'But I see well enough to tell that you aren't on your way to D.C. like you were supposed to be.' He'd had to come back for Moon's Night, but I knew that he'd flown in yesterday afternoon and had been scheduled to fly out an hour ago.

The corner of his mouth kicked up, and I could have bitten off my tongue when I realized I'd just let him know that I was keeping track of his movements. 'My schedule changed. I was supposed to fly out to Los Angeles a few hours ago. D.C. was last week and next week.'

'So why are you still here?'

The amusement left his face and his eyes narrowed as he said curtly, 'My ex-wife decided she is in love again. She and her new boyfriend headed off to Italy for an indefinite period. When I called, Jesse had already been alone for three days.' Jesse was his fifteen-year-old daughter who had been living with her mother in Eugene for the summer. 'I bought her a plane ticket and she should be here in a couple of hours. I told Bran I'm off duty. He'll have to shuffle politicians on his own for a while.'

'Poor Jesse,' I said. Jesse was one of the reasons I'd always respected Adam, even when he frustrated me the most. He'd never let anything, not business, not the pack, come before his daughter.

'So I'll be around for a while.' It wasn't the words, it was the way he looked at me when he said them that forced me back a step. I hate it when that happens.

I decided to change the subject. 'Good. Darryl's a great guy, but he's pretty hard on Warren when you aren't around.'

Darryl was Adam's second and Warren his third. In most packs the two ranks were so close that there was always some tension between the wolves who held them, especially without the Alpha around. Warren's sexual preferences made the tension even worse.

Being different among humans is hard. Being different among wolves is usually deadly. There aren't very many homosexual werewolves who survive for long. Warren was tough, self-reliant and Adam's best friend. The combination was enough to keep him alive but not always comfortable in the pack.

'I know,' Adam said.

'It would help if Darryl weren't so cute,' Samuel said casually as he crossed the living room to stand beside Adam.

Technically, he should have stood behind him, since Adam was the Alpha, and Samuel was a lone wolf, outside the pack hierarchy. But Samuel wasn't just any lone wolf, he was the Marrok's son and more dominant even than Adam if he'd wanted to push matters.

'I dare you to say that to Darryl,' I challenged.

'Don't.' Adam smiled, but his voice was serious. Though he spoke to Samuel, he'd never looked away from me. To me he said, 'Samuel says you're going to need an escort to the vampire seethe sometime in the near future. Call me and I'll find someone to go with you.'

'Thank you, I will.'

He touched my sore cheek with a light finger. 'I'd do it myself, but I don't think it would be wise.'

I agreed with him wholeheartedly. A werewolf escort would serve both as a bodyguard and a statement that I wasn't without friends. The Alpha's escort would turn it into a power play between him and the vampires' leaders with Stefan caught in the middle.

'I know,' I said. 'Thank you.'

I couldn't stay in that room with both men one more minute. Even a human woman could have drowned in the testosterone in the air, it was so strong. If I didn't leave, they were going to start fighting – I hadn't missed the way Samuel's eyes had whitened when Adam touched my cheek.

Then there was the need I had to bury my nose in Adam's neck and inhale the exotic scent of his skin. I looked away from him and found myself gazing into Samuel's white eyes. He was so close to turning that the distinctive black ring around the outside of his pupils was clearly visible. It should have scared me.

Samuel's nostrils flared – I smelled it, too. Arousal.

'I've got to go,' I said, properly panicked.

I gave them a hasty wave as I scuttled out of the house, hastily pulling the door shut behind me. The relief of having a door between me and both men was intense. I was breathing hard, as if I'd run a race, adrenaline pushing the pain of the sorcerer's attack away. I took a deep breath of the morning air, trying to clear my lungs of werewolf, before heading out to my car.

I opened the Rabbit's door and the sudden smell of blood made me step abruptly back. The car had been parked where I always left it: I'd forgotten that Stefan must have used it to bring me back home. There were stains on both front seat covers – both of us must have been pretty bloody. But the most impressive thing was the fist-shaped dent on my dash, just above the radio.

Stefan had been upset.

I pulled into my garage and parked at the far end of the lot next to Zee's old truck. Never trust a mechanic who drives new cars. They're either charging too much money for their work, or they can't keep an old car running – maybe both.

VWs are good cars. They used to be cheap good cars; now they're expensive good cars. But every make has a few lemons. VW had the Thing (which at least *looked* cool), the Fox, and the Rabbit. I figured in another couple of years, my Rabbit would be the only one still running in the greater Tri-Cities.

I let the Rabbit idle for a moment and debated going in. I'd stopped at the nearest auto-parts store and picked up seat covers to replace the ones I'd had to throw away. Judging from the sick looks I'd gotten from the clerk, my battered face wasn't going to be drumming up business for me anytime soon.

But there were four cars parked in the lot, which meant we were busy. If I stayed in the garage, no one would see my face.

I got out of the car, slowly. The dry heat of late morning wrapped around me and I closed my eyes for a moment to enjoy it.

'Good morning, Mercedes,' said a sweet old voice. 'Beautiful day.'

I opened my eyes and smiled. 'Yes, Mrs Hanna, it is.'

The Tri-Cities, unlike Portland and Seattle, doesn't have much of a permanent homeless population. Our temperatures get up well over a hundred in the summers and below zero in the winters, so most of our homeless people are only traveling through.

Mrs Hanna looked homeless, with her battered shopping cart full of plastic bags of cans and other useful items, but someone once told me she lived in a small trailer in the park by the river and had taught piano lessons until her arthritis made it impossible. After that she walked the streets of downtown Kennewick collecting aluminum cans and selling pictures she colored out of coloring books so she could buy food for her cats.

Her white-gray hair was braided and tucked under the

battered old baseball cap that kept the sun out of her face. She wore a woolen A-line skirt with bobby socks and tennis shoes, a size too large. Her T-shirt celebrated some long past Spokane Lilac Festival, and its lavender color was an interesting contrast to the black and red plaid flannel shirt that hung loosely over her shoulders.

Age had bent her over until she was barely as tall as the cart she pushed. Her tanned, big-knuckled hands sported chipped red nail polish that matched her lipstick. She smelled of roses and her cats.

She frowned at me and squinted. 'Boys don't want girls who have more muscles than they do, Mercedes. Boys like girls who can dance and play piano. Mr Hanna, God rest his soul, used to tell me that I floated over a dance floor.'

This was an old argument. She'd grown up in a time when the only proper place for a woman was next to her man.

'It wasn't the karate this time,' I told her, touching my face lightly.

'Put some frozen peas on that, dear,' she said. 'That'll keep the swelling down.'

'Thank you,' I said.

She nodded her head briskly and set off down the road, her cart squeaking. It was too hot for flannel and wool, but then it had been a cool spring evening when she'd died a few months ago.

Most ghosts fade after a while, so probably in a few months we wouldn't be able to converse anymore. I don't know why she came by to talk to me, maybe she was still worried about my unmarried state.

I was still smiling when I walked into the office.

Gabriel, my part-time tool rustler/receptionist was working full time in the summer. He looked up when I walked in and took a startled double take.

'Karate,' I lied, inspired by Mrs Hanna's assumption, and saw him relax.

He was a good kid and as human as it got. He knew that Zee was fae, of course, because Zee had been forced to come out a few years ago by the Gray Lords who rule the fae (like the werewolves, the fae had come out a little at a time to avoid alarming the public).

Gabriel knew about Adam because that was also a matter of public record. I had no intention of opening his eyes further, though — it was too dangerous. So no stories of vampires or sorcerers for him if I could manage it — especially since there were a few customers around.

'Geez,' he said. 'I hope the other guy looks worse.'

I shook my head. 'Stupid white belt.'

There were a couple of men sitting on the battered-but-comfortable chairs in the corner of the office. At my words, one of them leaned forward and said, 'I'd rather fight a dozen black belts at the same time than one white belt.'

He was so well-groomed that he was handsome, despite a nose that was a little too broad and deep set eyes.

I brightened my smile like any good businesswoman, and said, 'Me, too,' with feeling.

'I'm guessing you'd be Mercedes Thompson?' he asked, coming to his feet and walking up to the counter with his hand outstretched.

'That's right,' I took his hand, and he shook mine with a firm grip that would have done credit to a politician.

'Tom Black.' He smiled, showing pearly white teeth. 'I've heard a lot about you. Mercedes the Volkswagen mechanic.'

Like I hadn't heard that one before. Still, he didn't sound obnoxious, just mildly flirtatious.

'Nice to meet you.' I wasn't interested in flirtation so I turned my attention back to Gabriel. 'Any problems this morning?'

He smiled. 'With Zee here? Listen, Mercy, my mother asked me to ask if you want the girls here this weekend to clean again.'

Gabriel had a generous handful of siblings, all girls – the youngest in preschool and the oldest just entering high school – and all supported by their widowed mother who worked as a dispatcher for the Kennewick Police Department, not a high paying career. The two oldest girls had been coming in on a semi-regular basis and cleaning the office. They did a good job, too. I hadn't realized that the film on my front window had been grease – I thought Zee had had some sort of treatment done to it to block out the sun.

'Sounds fine to me,' I told him. 'If I'm not here, they can use your key.'

'I'll tell her.'

'Good. I'm going to head into the garage and stay out of sight today – don't want to scare away customers.'

I gave Tom Black a brisk nod, that was friendly but aloof. Then stopped to say a few words to the other man who was waiting. He was an old customer who liked to chat. Then I slipped into the garage before someone new could come in.

I found Zee lying on his back under a car, so all I could see of him was from the belly down.

Siebold Adelbertsmiter, my former boss, is an old fae, a metalworker, which is unusual for the fae who mostly can't handle cold iron. He calls himself a gremlin, though he is a lot older than the name, coined by flyboys in WWI. I have a degree in history, so I know useless things like that.

He looked like a fiftyish, thinish (with a little potbelly), grumpy man. Only the grumpy part was true. Thanks to glamour, a fae can look like anyone they want to. Glamour is the thing that makes something a fae – as opposed to, say, a witch or werewolf.

'Hey, Zee,' I said when he showed no sign of noticing my presence. 'Thanks for coming out this morning.'

He rolled himself out from under the car and frowned deeply at me. 'You need to stay away from the vampires, Mercedes Athena Thompson.' Like my mother, he only used my full name when he was angry with me. I'd never tell him, but I've always kind of liked the way it sounds when pronounced with a German accent.

He took in my face in a single glance and continued. 'You should be home sleeping. What is the use of having a man in the house, if he cannot take care of you for a while?'

'Mmm,' I said. 'I give up. What's the use of having a man in the house?'

He didn't smile, but I was used to that.

'Anyway,' I continued briskly, though I kept my voice down so the people in the office couldn't hear anything. 'There are two werewolves and a dead vampire in my house and I thought it was full enough to do without me for a while.'

'You killed a vampire?' He gave me a look of respect — which was pretty impressive since he was still lying on his back on the creeper.

'Nope. The sun did. But Stefan should recover in time to face Marsilia tonight.'

At least I was assuming it would be tonight. I didn't know much about the vampires, but the werewolves' trials tend to convene on the spot rather than six months after a crime. They are also over in a matter of hours, sometimes minutes, rather than months. Can't convince your pack Alpha you are less trouble to him alive than dead? Too bad. Pack law, necessarily brutal, was one of those nasty things that Bran was keeping under wraps for a while.

'Samuel told me you are going to be at a trial for the vampire.'

'He called you,' I said, outraged. 'What did he do? Ask you to call him when I got here safely?'

Zee smiled at me for the first time and got out his cell phone. With oil-stained fingers he punched in my number. 'She's here,' he said. 'Made it fine.'

He hung up without waiting for a reply and widened his smile further as he dialed another number. I knew that one, too. But in case I'd missed it, he used names. 'Hello, Adam,' he said. 'She's here.' He listened for a moment; I did too, but he must have had the volume turned down low because all I could hear was the rumble of a male voice. Zee's smile turned into a malevolent grin. He looked at me and said, 'Adam wants to know what took you so long?'

I started to roll my eyes, but it made the sore half of my face hurt worse so I stopped. 'Tell him I had wild, passionate sex with a complete stranger.'

I didn't stick around to hear if Zee passed my message on or not. I snatched my coveralls off their hook, and stalked into the bathroom.

Werewolves are control freaks, I reminded myself as I dressed for work. Being control freaks keeps them in charge of their wolf — which is a good thing. If I didn't like the side effects, I shouldn't hang out with werewolves. Which I wouldn't be doing if I didn't have one living with me and another living on the other side of my back fence.

Alone in the bathroom though, I could admit to myself that even though I was really, really angry . . . I'd have been disappointed if they hadn't checked up on me. How's that for illogical?

When I came out, Zee gave me the next repair job. I may have bought the business from him, but when we worked together, he still gave the orders. Part of it was habit, I suppose, but a larger part of it was that, though I am a good mechanic, Zee is magic. Literally and figuratively.

If it weren't for his tendency to get bored with easy stuff, he'd never have hired me. Then I'd have had to take my liberal arts degree and gotten a job at McDonald's or Burger King like all the rest of the history majors.

We worked companionably in silence for a while until I ran into a job that required four hands rather than two.

While I turned the rachet, Zee, who was holding a part in place for me, said, 'I took a peek under that cover' – he nodded toward the corner of the shop where my latest restoration project lay in wait.

'Pretty, isn't she?' I said. 'Or at least she will be when I get her fixed up.' She was a 1968 Karmann Ghia in almost pristine condition.

'Are you going to restore it or make a street rod?'

'I don't know,' I said. 'Her paint is still the original and there's only a little cracking on the hood. I hate to mess with it unless I have to. If I can get her running well with original parts and Kim can stitch up the seats, I'll leave it at that.'

There are three groups of old car enthusiasts: people who think a car should be left as much original as possible; the ones who restore it better than factory; and the people who gut them and replace the brakes, engine, and suspension with more modern equipment. Zee is firmly in the latter group.

He is not sentimental – if something works better, that's what you should use. I suppose forty or fifty years doesn't mean the same thing to him as it does to the rest of us – one person's antique is another's rusting hulk.

Since a good part of my income comes from restoring rusting hulks, I'm not picky. I have a partnership with an upholstery genius, Kim, and a painter who also likes to drive around and show the cars so we can sell them. After deducting the actual material cost of the restore and the shows, we split the profits according to hours spent on the project.

'Air-cooled takes a lot of upkeep,' Zee said.

'Someone who wants an original condition Ghia won't care about that,' I told him. He grunted, unconvinced, and went back to his job.

Gabriel took my Rabbit out to get sandwiches, then sat in the garage to eat with us. I uncovered the Ghia, and the three of us ate and debated the best thing to do with the car until it was time to go back to work.

'Zee,' I asked as he raised a Passat in the air to take a look at the exhaust.

He grunted as he tapped with his index finger the exhaust pipe where it was badly dented, just in front of the first muffler.

'What do you know about sorcerers?'

He stopped his tapping and sighed. 'Old gremlins go out of their way to stay away from demon-hosts, and it's been a while since humans believed enough in the Devil to sell their souls to him.'

I got a little light-headed. It wasn't that I didn't believe in evil – quite the opposite. I've had ample proof of God, so I accepted that His opponent exists, too. I just didn't particularly want to know that someone who made a deal with Satan was lurking ten miles from my home killing hotel maids.

'I thought it was just a demon,' I said faintly.

'*Ja*,' he said; then he turned and saw my face. 'Devil, demon – English is an imprecise language in these things. There are things that serve the Great Beast of Christian scripture. Greater and lesser spirits, demons or devils, and they all serve evil. The greater servants are bound away from our world, but can be invited in – just as vampires cannot enter a home without an invitation.'

'All right,' I took a deep breath. 'What else do you know?'

Zee reached up and put his hand on the pipe. 'Not much,

Liebchen. The few men I've encountered who claimed to be sorcerers were nothing but demon-bait when I met them.'

'What's the difference?'

'The difference is who's holding the reins.' The exhaust pipe began glowing a bright cherry red under Zee's hand. 'Demons serve only one master well, and those who forget it tend to become enslaved rather quickly. Those who remember might stay in control a while longer.'

I frowned at him. 'So all the demon-possessed start out as sorcerers?'

Zee shook his head. 'There are many kinds of invitations, intentional and not. Sorcerer, demon-possessed, it doesn't matter. Eventually the demon is in control.'

The exhaust pipe made a loud noise and popped back out to its proper shape. Zee met my gaze. 'This creature is playing with the vampires, Mercy. Stay out of its business. The seethe is better equipped to deal with such than you are.'

By five thirty, I was elbow deep in a Vanagon tune-up so I had Gabriel close up the office and tried to send both him and Zee off. My battered face made them more reluctant than usual to leave me working alone, but I persuaded them to go at last.

While Zee had been there, I'd kept the big air conditioner running and the garage doors shut, but, unlike the werewolves, I enjoy the summer heat. So once I was alone, I turned off the cool-air and opened up the bay doors.

'Does that help?'

I looked up and saw that the customer from earlier in the day was standing in the open bay door.

'Tom Black,' he reminded me.

'Does what help?' I asked wiping off my hands and taking a sip of water from the bottle balanced precariously on the car's bumper.

'Humming,' he said. 'I was wondering if it helped.'

There was something about the way he said it that bothered me — as if he was a good friend of mine instead of someone I'd exchanged a few words with. His earlier remark about white belts didn't make him a martial artist, but his body movement as he walked into my garage did.

I kept my expression polite, though the coyote in me wanted to lift my lip. He was invading my territory.

'I hadn't realized I was humming,' I told him. 'This is the last car I'm working on today.' I knew it wasn't his car, because it was one I worked on regularly. 'If Gabriel didn't call you, then we probably won't get to your car until tomorrow.'

'How did a pretty woman like you get to be a mechanic?' he asked.

I tilted my head so I could see him better out of my good eye. Gabriel had told me that if I had kept an ice pack on it longer it wouldn't have swollen up so badly. On good days, my looks were passable, today *hideous* and *awful* were more apt.

If we had been on neutral territory, I'd probably have said something like, 'Gee, I don't know. How'd a handsome man like you get to be such a pushy bastard?' But this was my place of work and he was a customer.

'Same as all the other pretty mechanics, I expect,' I said. 'Listen, I have to get this finished up. Why don't you call tomorrow morning and Gabriel will have an estimate for when you can expect your car to be done.'

I walked forward as I said it. The motion should have pushed him back, but he held still so I had to stop or get too close to him. He smelled of coconut sunscreen and cigarette smoke.

'Actually I picked my car up earlier,' he said. 'I came by tonight to talk to you.'

He was human, but I saw the same predatory look in his eyes that the wolves had when they were off on a hunt. Being in my own garage had made me feel too safe and I'd let myself get too close to him. I had weapons aplenty in the form of wrenches and crowbars, but they were all out of reach.

'Did you?' I said. 'Why?'

'I wanted to ask you how you liked dating a werewolf. Did you know he was a werewolf when you started dating him? Did you have sex with him?' His voice acquired a sudden razor edge.

It was such a shift in topic that I blinked stupidly at him for a moment.

This man didn't smell like a fanatic – hatred has its own scent. When Zee first came out, there was a group of people who'd marched around the shop with placards. Some of them came out one night and spray painted FAIRYLAND in angry red letters across my garage doors.

Tom Black smelled intense – as if the answers to his questions really mattered to him.

Outside, a small-block Chevy 350 pulled into my lot and I recognized its purr. With the last of my trepidation gone, I realized there was only one reason for the questions he'd asked.

I narrowed my eyes at him. 'Hell,' I said in disgust. 'You're a reporter.'

Some of the werewolves coming out deliberately attracted attention on the Marrok's orders: heroes from the military or police and fire departments and a couple of movie stars. Adam was not one of them. I could see why someone would send a reporter out sniffing around him, though. Not only was he an Alpha, but he was a pretty Alpha. I couldn't wait to hear what Adam would say when he found out someone was poking into his love life.

'I can make you rich,' Black told me, encouraged, I think, by my smile. 'When I'm through with you, you'll be as much of a celebrity as he is. You can sell your story to the networks.'

I snorted. 'Go away.'

'Problems, Mercy?' The deep, Texas drawl caused the reporter to spin on his heel. I guess he hadn't heard Warren and his companion walk into the garage.

'No problems,' I told Warren. 'Mr Black was just leaving.'

Warren looked like an ad for 'Real Western Cowboys,' complete with worn boots and battered straw hat. He was entitled: he'd been a real cowboy in the old West when he'd been Changed. He was my favorite of Adam's wolves and beside him was Ben, a recent import from Great Britain – and the leading candidate for my least favorite werewolf. Neither of them had been among the 'outed' wolves, not yet. In Ben's case, probably never. He'd narrowly escaped arrest in his native land and had been quietly shipped off to America to disappear.

The reporter took out his wallet and held out his card. I took it because my mother taught me to be polite.

'I'll be around,' he said. 'Call me if you change your mind.'

'I'll do that,' I told him.

Both werewolves turned to watch him leave. Only after his car was well away did they turn their attention back to me.

'I like what you've done to your face,' Ben said, tapping his eye.

He may have saved my life once and taken a bullet for Adam, but that didn't mean I had to like him. It wasn't just that he'd been sent to Adam's pack to keep him from being questioned in connection with a series of violent rapes in London. I believe in innocent until proven guilty. Rather it was the qualities that had caused the London police to look in his direction in the first place: he was a petty, nasty, and violent man. Everything he said came out like a sneer or a threat, all in this nifty British accent. If he were just a hair nicer, I might have talked to him just to hear his voice, like him or not.

'I wasn't the one who decorated my face, but thanks anyway.' I went back to the van to button it up for the night. I'd lost the momentum that was keeping me working, and all I wanted to do was find someplace to sleep. Someplace without a vampire dead in the closet. Damn it. Where was I going to sleep?

'What are you two doing here?' I asked Warren as I closed the back hatch of the van.

'Adam said we're to stay with you until you hear from the vampires – he thinks it will be sometime soon after dark. He doesn't want you to face them alone.'

'Don't you have to work tonight?' Warren worked grave-yard at an all night gas station/convenience store not too far from my home – he had gotten Samuel a job there when he moved in with me.

'Nah, quit last week. They had another manager changeover and this one wanted to clean house. So I thought I'd quit before I was fired.' He paused then said, 'I've been doing some work for Kyle. It pays better part-time than the convenience store did full-time.'

'With Kyle?' I asked hopefully.

I've known Warren for a long time and had met maybe a dozen of his boyfriends. Most of them hadn't been worth knowing – but I liked Kyle. He was a hotshot lawyer, a terrific dresser, and a lot of fun. They'd been living together for a while when Kyle finally found out Warren was a were-wolf. Kyle moved out. I knew they'd dated a few times since, but nothing more serious.

Warren dropped his eyes. 'Mostly just some surveillance

and, once, guard duty for a woman who was afraid of her soon-to-be ex-husband.'

'Kyle's afraid of us,' said Ben, showing his teeth in a sharp grin.

Warren looked at him and Ben quit smiling.

'You've obviously never met Kyle,' I told Ben. 'Anyone who's been a divorce lawyer as long as Kyle isn't afraid of much.'

'I lied to him,' Warren told me. 'Thing like that will stick in a man's craw.'

It was time to change the subject. Ben might be subdued for the moment, but it wouldn't last.

'I'm going to wash up and change,' I said. 'I'll be right back out.'

'Samuel said you didn't get any sleep last night,' Warren said. 'You have a few hours before the vampires can call on you. Should we stop and pick up some dinner, then head out to your house so you can get a little sleep?'

I shook my head. 'Can't sleep with a dead man in my closet.'

'You killed someone?' asked Ben with interest.

Warren grinned, the expression leaving little crinkles next to his eyes. 'Nope, not this time. Samuel said Stefan had to spend the day in Mercy's closet. I'd forgotten about that. Do you want to catch a little shut-eye at my place? No dead people there.' He glanced at Ben. 'At least not yet.'

I was tired, my face hurt, and I was coming down off the adrenaline rush the reporter had caused. 'I can't think of a thing that sounds better. Thanks, Warren.'

Warren's place was in Richland, half of a two-story duplex that had seen better days. The interior was in better repair than the outside, but it still had that college-student aura defined by lots of books and secondhand furniture.

The spare bedroom Warren put me in smelled of him – he must have been sleeping in there rather than the room he'd shared with Kyle. I found his scent comforting; *he* wasn't lying dead in the closet. I had no trouble falling asleep to the quiet sounds of the two werewolves playing chess downstairs.

I woke in the dark to the smell of peppers and sesame oil. Someone had gone out for Chinese. It had been a long time since lunch.

I rolled out of bed and scrambled down the stairs, hoping that they hadn't eaten everything. When I got to the kitchen, Warren was still dividing Styrofoam-packaged food onto three plates.

'Mmm.' I said, leaning against Warren to get a better look at the food. 'Mongolian beef. I think I'm in love.'

'His heart's occupied elsewhere,' said Ben from behind me. 'And even if it weren't he's not interested in your kind. But, I'm available and ready.'

'You don't have a heart,' I told him. 'Just a gaping hole where it should have been.'

'All the more reason for you to give me yours.'

I pounded my forehead against Warren's back. 'Tell me Ben's not flirting with me.'

'Hey,' said Ben sounding hurt. 'I was talking cannibalism, not romance.'

He was almost funny. If I liked him better, I'd have laughed.

Warren patted me on the top of my head and said, 'It's all right, Mercy. It's just a bad dream. Once you eat your food it will all go away.'

He dumped the last of the rice on one of the plates. 'Adam called a few minutes ago. I told him you were sleeping and he said not to wake you up. He told me Stefan left your house about a half hour ago.'

I glanced out the window and saw that it was already getting dark.

Warren saw my glance and said, 'Some of the old vampires wake up early. I don't think you'll get a call before full dark.'

He passed out the filled plates and handed us silverware and napkins to go with them, then shooed us back out of the kitchen to the dining room.

'So,' said Ben after we'd been eating for a few minutes. 'Why don't you like me, Mercy? I'm handsome, clever, witty . . . Not to mention I saved your life.'

'Let's not mention that again,' I said, shoveling spicy meat in around my words. 'I might get ill.'

'You hate women,' Warren offered.

'I do not.' Ben sounded indignant.

I swallowed, raised an eyebrow, and stared at him until he looked away. As soon as he realized what he'd done he jerked his chin back up so his eyes met mine again. But it was too late, I'd won, and we both knew it. With the wolves, things like that mattered. If I ever met him alone in a dark alley, he might still eat me – but he'd hesitate first.

I gave him a smug smile. 'Anyone who's talked to you for longer than two minutes knows you hate women. I think that I can count on the fingers of one hand the times you've actually said the word "women" and not replaced it with an epithet referring to female genitalia.'

'Hey, he's not that bad,' Warren said. 'Sometimes he calls them cows or whores.'

Ben pointed a finger at Warren – I guess his mother never taught him better manners. 'There speaks someone who doesn't like . . .' He actually had to pause and change the word he was going to use. '. . . er women.'

'I like women just fine,' Warren told him gathering the last of his scattered rice into a pile so he could get it on his fork. 'Better'n I like most men. I just don't want to sleep with them.'

My cell phone rang, and I inhaled, pulling a peppercorn into my windpipe. Coughing, choking, and eyes watering, I found my phone and waved it at Warren so he could answer it while I gulped water.

'Right,' he said. 'We'll have her there. Does she know where it is?' He caught my eye and mouthed 'seethe.'

I nodded my head and felt my stomach clench. I knew where it was.

4

We drove through open wrought-iron gates and into a brightly lit courtyard in front of the huge, hacienda-style, adobe house that served as home for the Tri-Cities' seethe. Warren pulled his battered truck behind a BMW in a circular drive that was already full of cars.

Last time I'd been here, I'd come with Stefan. He'd taken us by the back way into a smaller guest house tucked into the backyard. This time we walked right up to the front door of the main house and Warren rang the doorbell.

Ben sniffed the air nervously. 'They're watching us.' I smelled them, too.

'Yes.' Of the three of us, Warren was visibly the least worried. He wasn't the kind of person to stew about things that hadn't happened yet.

It wasn't being watched that bothered me. What would happen if the vampires didn't believe me? If they believed that Stefan had really lost control, the way he remembered doing, they would execute him. Tonight. The vampires would not tolerate anyone who threatened the safety and secrecy of their seethe.

Not being a vampire, my word wouldn't be worth much here – they might not listen to me at all.

I'd never been certain how Stefan really felt about me. I'd been taught that vampires aren't capable of affection for anyone other than themselves. They might pretend to like you, but there would always be an ulterior motivation for their actions. But even if he wasn't my friend, I was his. If his death were my fault, because I didn't say or do something right . . . I just had to do everything right, had to make them listen to me.

The door opened wide, making a curious groaning noise. There was no one in the entryway.

'And cue the scary music,' I said.

'They do seem to be pulling out all the stops,' agreed Warren. 'I wonder why they're trying so hard to intimidate you.'

Ben had settled down a bit, probably because Warren was so calm. 'Maybe they're scared of us.'

I remembered the vampires I'd seen last time I was here and thought Ben was wrong. They hadn't been afraid of Samuel. I'd seen Stefan lift his VW Bus without a jack, and the seethe was chock-full of vampires. If they wanted to tear me apart they could, and there wouldn't be a damn thing Warren or Ben (if he felt like it) could do to stop it. They weren't afraid of us. Maybe they just liked to frighten people.

Warren must have thought the same thing because he said, 'Nah, they're just playing with us.'

We entered the house cautiously, Warren first, then me, and Ben took up the rear. I'd have been happier with Ben in front of me. He might be willing to take a bullet for Adam, but me, I was pretty sure, he'd have been just as happy to eat.

There was no one in the entryway, or the small sitting room it led into, so we continued down the hall. One side of the hall had three doors with arched tops, all closed, but the other side opened into a very large, airy room with a high ceiling and recessed lights. The walls were covered with brightly colored paintings, some of them spanning floor to ceiling. The walls were painted a soft yellow shade that made it feel bright and cheerful even though there were no windows.

The floor was made of dark clay tiles in a variety of reddish browns. Light, neutral-colored woven rugs were scattered about almost at random. Three couches and five comfy-looking chairs, all a rather startling shade of coral that somehow managed to blend into the rest of the southwestern feel, were set in a loose semicircle around a large wooden chair, that looked as though it ought to have been sitting in a gothic mansion, rather than surrounded by all the sunny colors of the room.

Warren had started down the hallway, but I didn't follow him. There was something about that chair . . .

The wood was dark, but the grain looked like oak to me. It was covered with carvings, from the lion-paw legs to the gargoyle crouched on the top of the tall back. Each of the legs had a ring of brass about a third of the way up. The arms were made entirely of brass wrought with delicate-appearing vines and small flowers and thorns. On the end of each arm, one of the thorns stuck up in a sharp point.

When I was almost close enough to touch the chair, I realized that I'd been sensing the presence of its magic even from the hallway – I just hadn't known what it was. To me, magic usually feels like a tingle, as if I am immersing my skin in sparkling water. This was a dull, bass thrum, as if someone were beating a very large drum while I plugged my ears so I could feel it, but not hear.

'Mercy?' asked Warren from the doorway. 'I don't think that we're supposed to be exploring.'

'Do you smell this?' asked Ben from the level of my knee. I looked down and saw that he was crouched on all fours with his head extended and slightly cocked. He closed his eyes and took in a deep breath. 'There's old blood on that chair,' he said.

I was going to ask him about it, but the first vampire entered. He was one I hadn't seen before. In life he'd been a medium-sized man, Irish, by the red hair. His movements were stiff and graceful at the same time, reminding me of the way a daddy longlegs moves. The vampire brushed past Warren and walked across the room without looking at any of us. He sat down on a small bench I hadn't noticed near the far wall.

The vampire's arrival seemed to answer any doubts Warren had, as he followed the vampire in and took proper body-guard position to my right. Ben rose to his feet and stood just behind and to my left, so I was flanked by the were-wolves.

Over the next few minutes the rest of the seats in the room filled up with vampires. None of them looked at us as they came in. I'd have thought it was an insult, except they didn't look at each other either.

I counted under my breath, fifteen vampires. They made an impressive showing, if only in the expense of their clothing. Silks, satins, brocades in all shades of the rainbow. One or two wore modern business suits, but most of them were in period costume, anything from medieval to the present.

Somehow I expected more dark colors, but I didn't see any black or gray. The werewolves and I were underdressed. Not that I cared.

I recognized the woman who had confiscated Samuel's cross the last time I'd been here when she came into the room. She sat in one of the coral chairs as if it had been a stool, her back upright like a Victorian lady in a tight corset, though she wore an aqua-colored silk dress with rows of beaded fringe from the nineteen twenties that seemed oddly frivolous for her stiff bearing. I looked for Lilly, the pianist, but she didn't appear.

My eyes swung past an old man with wisps of gray hair decorating his head. Unlike werewolves, vampires kept the appearance they had when they died. Even though he appeared ancient, I could be looking at the youngest vampire in the room.

I glanced at his face and realized that unlike the others in the room, he was watching me. He licked his lips and I took a step toward him before I managed to drop my gaze to the floor.

Werewolves might lock eyes for dominance purposes, but they couldn't take over your mind if you held their gaze. Being a walker was supposed to keep that from happening, but I'd certainly felt the pull of his gaze.

A dark haired, young-seeming man with narrow shoulders had entered the room while I'd been playing peekaboo with the old man. Like Stefan, he was more human-seeming than most. It was his clothing more than his face that I remembered. If Andre wasn't wearing the same pirate shirt that he'd been in the night I'd met him, he was wearing its twin. Once he'd taken a seat in one of the plush chairs near the center of the room, he, unlike the other vampires, looked at me directly and smiled in a friendly fashion. I didn't know him well enough to know if he was friend or foe.

Before I could decide how to return his greeting, Marsilia, Mistress of the Mid-Columbia Seethe, came into the room. She wore a brilliant red, Spanish-style riding skirt with a frilly white blouse and a black shawl that suited her blond hair and dark eyes better than I'd have thought it would.

She walked with fluid grace, unlike the last time I'd seen her. Of all the vampires in the room, Marsilia was the only one who was beautiful. She took her time arranging her skirts before she sat down in the chair in the center of the semicircle. Her red skirts clashed badly with the chair's coral fabric. I don't know why that made me feel better.

She stared at us – no, at the werewolves, with an avid, almost hungry gaze. I remembered her with Samuel and wondered if she had a preference for werewolves. It had been because of a werewolf, Stefan had told me, that she'd been exiled from Italy. Vampires didn't have any rules against feeding from a werewolf, but the wolf she'd taken had been the property of a more powerful and higher-ranking vampire.

Ben and Warren, both, had the sense to keep their eyes averted from hers. It would have been instinctive to meet her gaze and try to stare her down, instinctive and disastrous.

Finally Marsilia's voice, deep and lightly accented, broke the silence. 'Go and retrieve Stefan. Tell him his pet made it here and we are tired of waiting.'

I couldn't tell who she was talking to, she was still staring at Warren – on whom she had gradually focused in preference to Ben – but Andre stood up and said, 'He'll want to bring Daniel.'

'Daniel is being punished. He cannot be brought out.' The vampire who spoke sat directly on Marsilia's left. He wore a buff-colored, nineteenth-century businessman's suit, complete with pocket watch and blue-striped silk waistcoat. His moustache was striped like his waistcoat, though in brown and silver. He'd combed his hair back over a small balding spot on the top of his head.

Marsilia's mouth tightened. 'Your aspirations to the contrary, I still rule here, Bernard. Andre, bring Daniel as well.' She glanced around the room. 'Estelle, go with him. Daniel might be difficult.'

The middle-aged woman in her beaded flapper gown stood up abruptly as if someone had pulled on a string above her. As she moved, her beads made a soft chattering sound that reminded me of a rattlesnake. I couldn't remember them making any noise at all when she'd first come into the room.

Andre gave me a small, reassuring smile that no one else could see as he walked by. Estelle ignored us again as she passed. It was deliberate rudeness, I decided, though I preferred it to Marsilia's hungry gaze. I had to resist the urge to take a step forward and block her view of Warren.

If my errand hadn't been for Stefan, I'd have gone out and dragged in a few chairs for us, or maybe just sat on the floor; but I didn't want to antagonize anyone before Stefan was safe. So I just stood where I was and waited for him to arrive.

The minutes crawled by. I'm not very good at waiting, and had to fight not to fidget. I'd have thought that Ben would be worse than I, but neither he nor Warren seemed to have any problem staying still while we waited, not even under Marsilia's steady regard.

The wolves weren't as motionless as the vampires, though. None of the vampires bothered with the small touches that Stefan affected to make humans more at ease, like blinking or breathing.

One by one, as if Andre's leaving was some sort of signal, the vampires turned their gaze on me, their expressions blank. The only exceptions were Marsilia, and the vampire on her right, who appeared to be a boy of about fifteen — so I looked at them.

Marsilia watched Warren, occasionally flexing her long, highly decorated fingernails. The boy just stared off into space, swaying just a little. I wondered if he, like the musical Lilly, was damaged mentally. Then I realized he was swaying in time to the beat of my heart and took a quick step closer to Warren. The boy rocked a little faster.

By the time I heard movement in the hall behind us, he was swaying pretty quickly. Nothing like being prey in a room full of vampires to keep the heart racing merrily along.

I heard Stefan and his entourage coming well before they got to the room.

Estelle brushed past us first, and resumed her seat. Andre took up a position on a couch near the odd, wooden chair.

I didn't have to turn my head to know that Stefan had stopped a few feet behind me – I could smell him. I turned anyway.

He still wore the clothes he'd been in when I last saw him, but he appeared unharmed. He was carrying a young man in his arms who could be no one but his young friend, Daniel, Littleton's first victim.

Jeans and a 'Got Milk?' T-shirt seemed incongruous on someone who looked as though he'd just been liberated from a Nazi death camp. His head had been shaved, and dark stubble turned the pale skin of his scalp blue. It made me wonder if vampires could grow hair.

Daniel's cheeks were so sunken I could almost see his teeth through them. His eyes looked blind, with irises that were startlingly white, and no pupils at all. It was difficult to judge the age at which he'd died accurately, but he couldn't have been older than twenty.

The man in the striped waistcoat, Bernard, stood up – and finally Marsilia quit staring at Warren, and turned her attention to the matters at hand.

Bernard cleared his throat then, in an appropriately businesslike tone, said, 'We are here because early this morning Stefan called us to clean up *his* mess at a motel in Pasco. Five humans are dead, and there was considerable property damage. We were forced to call in Elizaveta Arkadyevna' – I hadn't known Elizaveta worked for the seethe as well as Adam's pack, but I suppose it made sense. The old Russian witch was the most powerful practitioner in the Pacific Northwest – 'because we could see no scenario in which the police would not be called in. The local authorities have accepted the story we manufactured and, according to our contacts, there will be no further inquiry into the case. Other than the monetary cost of employing the witch, no permanent harm has been done to the seethe.' He bit off the last part a little too sharply, as if he wanted to disagree with his statement.

'Stefan,' Marsilia said. 'You put the seethe in danger. How do you answer this?'

Stefan took a step forward, then hesitated, looking at the vampire he held in his arms.

'I can hold him,' Warren offered.

Stefan shook his head. 'Daniel has not fed in too long, he would be a danger to you. Andre?'

Andre frowned, but got up to take the starving vampire into his arms so that Stefan could go stand before the others. I expected Stefan to stand where Bernard had, but he sat in the wooden chair, instead. He slid until he was pressed against the back then grasped each of the brass-studded grace-fully curved arms, closing his hands around the ends as if he hadn't seen the brass thorns sticking up.

Or maybe he had. The thrum of magic I'd been feeling stepped up in tempo and strength, making my ribcage buzz with power. I tried to swallow my gasp, but Marsilia turned to look at me as if I'd done something interesting.

Her regard didn't last more than an instant before she turned her attention to Stefan. 'You choose to offer Truth willingly?'

'I do.'

The chair reacted to his statement somehow. But before I could decide what the flare of energy had meant, the young-looking vampire, the one who was still swaying to my heart-beat, said, 'Truth.'

Most werewolves could tell when someone lied, but it was based on the smell of perspiration and heartbeat – neither of which the vampires had. I knew that there were magical ways of telling if someone lied, too. It was appropriate that the vampire's truth spells would demand blood.

'Speak.' I couldn't tell from Marsilia's voice whether she

hoped he'd be able to excuse himself from the bloodbath at the hotel or not.

Stefan started with his suspicions that there was something odd in Daniel's tale of bloodlust. He explained that when the vampire Daniel had been supposed to contact had returned, he'd seen it as an opportunity to learn more.

'It occurred to me,' he said in an unhurried storytelling kind of voice, 'that if I was correct in my suspicions I was about to confront a vampire capable of enthralling one of our own kind – though Daniel is very young. I thought at the time that the vampire might have been a witch before he was brought over.'

'So dangerous you brought *her* with you rather than another vampire?' Bernard's tone was heavy with contempt.

Stefan shrugged. 'As I said, I thought Littleton was a witch. Nothing I haven't dealt with before. I did not really think I would be facing anything I could not handle. Mercedes was my insurance, but I did not think she would be necessary.'

'Yes,' said Marsilia sharply. 'Let us tell the room why it is that Mercedes Thompson would be someone you would go to for help.' Her eyes were narrowed and her fingers played with the fringe of the black Spanish shawl she wore. I didn't know what she was so angry about, she knew what I was.

'Mercedes is a walker,' Stefan said.

The energy level in the room picked up remarkably, though none of them moved. I would have thought that all of the vampires had been told about me, but apparently not. Maybe she'd been angry because Stefan had forced her to reveal my existence to the rest of them. I *wished* I knew exactly why they were so worried about me – maybe then I wouldn't feel like a chicken in a den of foxes.

The boy next to Marsilia quit rocking. When he looked

at me, I *felt* it, like a flash of ice running over my exposed skin. 'How interesting,' he said.

Stefan spoke hurriedly, as if he were trying to distract the boy from me. 'She agreed to come with me as a coyote, so the vampire would not know that she was anything other than part of my costume. I thought the ruse would protect her, and her partial immunity would help me. I was both right and wrong.'

His recount from that point was very detailed. When he told them that he'd smelled the demon's scent that told him Littleton was a sorcerer as soon as he'd parked my car at the hotel, Bernard broke in.

'There are no such things as sorcerers,' he said.

The boy beside Marsilia shook his head and, in a light tenor voice that would never drop to adult tones said, 'There are. I have met them – as have most of us who are more than a few centuries old. It would be a very bad thing, Mistress, if one of us were a sorcerer.'

There was a heavy pause, a reaction to the boy's comment, but I couldn't tell what it meant.

'Continue, please,' said Marsilia finally.

Stefan obeyed. He'd known that everyone in the hotel was dead when we entered the building. That's how he'd found Littleton so easily: it was the only room where someone was still alive. Stefan had known the woman was in the bathroom before I had. Vampire's senses, it seemed, were better than mine.

I expected Stefan to stop his account of his actions where Littleton had stopped him and changed his memory, but he didn't. He continued on as if the false memory were his true one until the boy next to Marsilia said, 'Wait.'

Stefan stopped.

The boy tilted his head and closed his eyes, humming softly. Finally he said, without opening his eyes, 'This is what you remember, but you don't believe it.'

'Yes,' Stefan agreed.

'What is this?' asked Bernard. I was getting the distinct impression that Bernard wasn't Stefan's friend. 'What is the purpose of volunteering for the chair if you are just going to lie?'

'He's not lying.' The boy leaned forward. 'Go on. Tell it as you remember it.'

'As I remember it,' agreed Stefan and continued. What he remembered of the maid's murder was worse than he'd told us this morning, worse even than what I'd seen, because in his version, he was the killer, bathing in her death as much as her blood. He seemed to be at some pains to remember every moment. I could have done with the short version he'd given me before. Some of the images he called up were going to come back in my nightmares.

When he'd finished, Marsilia stared at him, tapping her fingers on the chair arm, though the rest of her body was very still. 'These are your memories of what happened, though Wulfe believes you no longer trust that they are true. Are we then to suppose that you believe this . . . this *sorcerer* tampered with your memories as well as Daniel's? You, who have never answered to your own maker, *you* believe a new-made vampire – excuse me – *sorcerer* was able to hold *you* in thrall?'

Bernard added, 'And why didn't he give you memories of the other people who died in the hotel? If he wanted to place the fault with you, surely he would have given those deaths to you as well?'

Stefan tilted his head and said thoughtfully, 'I don't know why he didn't give me memories of killing the others. Perhaps I would have had to be present for their deaths. I do have some evidence of his ability to tamper with another vampire's memories. I'd like to have Daniel speak.'

Marsilia's eyes narrowed to slits, but she nodded her head.

Stefan took his hands off the chair carefully. The brass thorns were gleaming black with his blood.

Andre stepped forward and set Daniel's too-thin body on the chair in Stefan's place. Daniel pulled himself into a fetal position, tucking his hands protectively away from the arms of the chair, turning his shoulder when Stefan would have touched him.

'Andre?' Stefan asked.

Andre gave him a dirty look, but turned to Daniel. 'Daniel, you will sit up and take your place in the Questioning Seat.'

The young vampire began crying. With the speed of a crippled old man he straightened in the seat. He tried twice to lift his hands before Andre took them and impaled them on the thorns himself. Daniel began to shake.

'He's too weak for this,' Andre told Stefan.

'You are his maker,' Marsilia's voice was cold. 'Fix it.'

Andre's mouth tightened, but put his wrist in front of Daniel's mouth. 'Feed,' he said.

Daniel turned his head away.

'Daniel, feed.'

I'd never seen a vampire strike. The swift jerk of Daniel's head made me press my hand over the bandages that covered Littleton's fang marks on my neck. Andre grimaced as the other vampire bit down, but he didn't pull away.

It took a long time for Daniel to feed. During the whole while, none of the others moved except for the impatient tapping of Marsilia's bright nails on the cushioned arms of her chair. No one shifted in their seat or moved their toes. I stepped back, closer to Warren, and he put his hand on my shoulder. I looked at Stefan, who normally vibrated like a puppy, but he seemed to be caught up in the same spell as everyone else.

'Stop.' Andre started to pull his arm away, but Daniel's teeth were still embedded in his wrist. Daniel ripped his hands off the chair, tearing a gash in the hand I could see, and curled both hands around Andre's forearm.

'Daniel, stop.'

The vampire whimpered, but he pulled his face away. His hands still held onto Andre. He was shaking as he stared at the blood welling from the fang marks with eyes that glistened like diamonds. Andre twisted his arm away and grabbed Daniel's hands, slamming them back on the chair, impaling him again.

'Stay there,' Andre hissed.

Daniel breathed in great gasps of air, his chest rising and falling unevenly.

'Ask your questions, Stefan,' said Marsilia. 'I tire of this show.'

'Daniel,' Stefan said, 'I want you to remember the night you believe you killed those people.'

Stefan's voice was gentle, but tears welled out of Daniel's eyes again. I'd been taught that vampires can't cry.

'I don't want to,' he said.

'Truth,' said Wulfe.

'I understand,' said Stefan. 'Nonetheless, tell us the very last thing you remember before the bloodlust hit.'

'No,' the boy said.

'Would you rather have Andre question you?'

'Parking at the hotel.' Daniel's voice was hoarse, as if he hadn't used it in a long time.

'The one in Pasco where Cory Littleton, the vampire you were supposed to question, was staying.'

'Yes.'

'Bloodlust begins with a cause. Had you fed that night?'

'Yes,' Daniel nodded. 'Andre gave me one of his sheep when I woke for the night.'

I didn't think he was talking about the kind of sheep with four hooves.

'So what caused you to hunger? Do you remember?'

Daniel closed his eyes. 'There was so much blood.' He sobbed once. 'I knew it was wrong. Stefan, it was a baby. A crying baby . . . it smelled so good.'

I glanced around at the crowd in time to see the elderly vampire lick his lips. I quickly looked back at Daniel. I didn't want to know how many of the vampires were made hungry by Daniel's recount.

'The baby you killed in the orchard?' asked Stefan.

Daniel nodded his head and whispered, 'Yes.'

'Daniel, the orchard is outside of Benton City, a half-hour drive from Pasco. How did you get there?'

Marsilia quit tapping her fingers. I remembered that Stefan had said that a vampire in the grips of bloodlust would never be able to drive a car. Apparently Marsilia agreed with him.

'I must have driven the car. It was there when I . . . when I was myself again.'

'Why did you go to Benton City, Daniel?'

Daniel didn't answer for a moment. Finally he said, 'I don't know. All I remember is blood.'

'How much gas was in your car when you got to the hotel in Pasco?' Stefan asked.

'It was on empty,' Daniel said slowly. 'I remember because I was going to fill it . . . afterwards.'

Stefan turned to his silent audience. 'Bernard. How much gas was in the car Daniel was driving when you found him?'

He didn't want to answer. 'Half full.'

Stefan looked at Marsilia and waited.

Suddenly she smiled, a sweet smile that made her look like an innocent girl. 'All right. I believe that there was someone with Daniel that night. You, I would believe, could drive twenty miles and fill up the car while under the burden of the bloodlust, but a new vampire like Daniel never could.'

Daniel jerked his head toward Stefan. 'That doesn't mean that I didn't kill those people. I *remember* it, Stefan.'

'I know you do,' he agreed. 'You can leave the seat – if Wulfe is satisfied of your truth?' He glanced up.

The teenager next to Marsilia, who'd been cleaning something out from under his nail with his teeth, nodded his head.

'Master?' whispered Daniel.

Andre had been staring at the floor, but at Daniel's words he said, 'You can leave the seat, Daniel.'

'This doesn't prove anything except that there was another with Daniel that night. Someone who drove the car and filled it with gas,' Bernard said.

'That's right,' agreed Stefan mildly.

When Daniel tried to stand up, his legs wouldn't hold him. His hands also seemed to be stuck. Stefan helped him pry his hands free and then picked him up off the chair when it became apparent that despite the feeding, Daniel was still too weak to stand.

Stefan took a step toward Andre, but then he hesitated and brought him back to where the wolves and I were standing.

He set him down on the floor a few feet from Warren. 'Stay there, Daniel,' he said. 'Can you do that?'

The young man nodded his head. 'Yes.' He held onto Stefan's arm though, and Stefan was forced to unwrap the other vampire's fingers before he could return to the chair. He took a handkerchief out of a back pocket and cleaned the arms of the chair until the brass tacks gleamed. No one complained about the time it took.

'Mercy,' Stefan said, putting the handkerchief back in his pocket. 'Would you please come and bear your truth before my mistress?'

He wanted me to go stick my hands on those sharp thorns. Not only did it seem somewhat sacrilegious, thorns and pierced palms, but it was going to hurt. Not that it came as a terrible surprise, not after Stefan and Daniel.

'Come,' he said. 'I've cleaned them so that you will suffer no taint.'

The wood was cool and the seat a little too big, like my foster father's favorite chair had been. After he'd died, I'd spent hours in that chair, smelling his scent, ingrained into the polished wood by years of use. The thought of him steadied me, and I needed all the nerve I could get.

The thorns were longer and sharper than they'd looked when I wasn't about to push them into my flesh. Better to do it quickly than to stew about it. I closed my hands over the ends of the arms and pulled them tight.

It didn't hurt at first. Then hot tendrils of magic snaked in through the break in my skin, streaking up the veins in my arms and closing around my heart like a fiery fist.

'Are you all right, Mercy?' Warren asked, his voice rumbling with the first hint of challenge.

'Wolves have no tongues in our court,' snapped Bernard. 'If you cannot be silent you will leave.'

I was glad that Bernard said something. He bought me time to understand that the magic wasn't hurting me. It was uncomfortable, but not painful. Not worth causing the fight Warren was ready to begin. Adam had sent him to guard me, not to start a war over a little discomfort.

'I'm fine,' I said.

The teenager stirred. 'Not true,' he said.

Truth, huh? Fine. 'My face hurts, my shoulder hurts, my neck hurts where the freaking demon-riding vampire bit me, and the magic of this chair is about as gentle as a lightning strike, but I'm not suffering from anything that will do irreparable harm.'

The boy, Wulfe, resumed his catatonic rocking. 'Yes,' he said. 'Truth.'

'What happened last night?' Stefan asked. 'Please begin with my phone call.'

I found myself telling the story with far more detail than I'd intended to. Certainly they didn't need to know that Stefan's driving had scared me, or the smells of the woman's death. But I was unable to edit, the memories coming out of my mouth as they rushed through my head. It would seem that there was some of the vampire's magic that had no trouble dealing with my walker blood.

That didn't stop Bernard from claiming that it did. 'You cannot have it both ways,' he said when I was through. 'We cannot believe that the seat has power over her and at the same time that she was able to resist a vampire who was able to feed memories into Stefan. Stefan, who of all of us, is able to resist the Mistress's, his *maker's*, commands.'

'The seat isn't dependent upon our power,' Stefan said. 'It functions by blood, but it was a witch who worked the magic. And I don't know if the sorcerer could have done the same to Mercedes as he did to me. He didn't know what she was, so he didn't try.'

Bernard started to say something, but Marsilia held up her hand. 'Enough.'

'Even five hundred years ago, sorcerers were rare,' she told Stefan. 'I have not seen one since we came to this desert. The seat has shown us that you believe that there is a sorcerer, a sorcerer that some vampire turned. But you will have to forgive me for not believing along with you.'

Bernard almost smiled. I wished I knew more of how justice worked in the seethe. I didn't know what I could say that would keep Stefan safe.

'The walker's testimony is compelling, but like Bernard, I have to question how well the seat works on her. I have seen walkers ignore far more dangerous magics.'

'I can feel her truths,' whispered the boy as he rocked.

'Clearer than the others. Sharp and pungent. If you kill Stefan tonight, you'd better kill her, too. Coyotes sing in the daylight as well as the night. These are the truths she carries.'

Marsilia stood up and strode to where I was still held captive in the chair. 'Would you do that? Hunt us while we sleep?'

I opened my mouth to deny it, like any sane person faced with an angry vampire, then closed it again. The seat held me to the truth.

'That would be a stupid thing for me to do,' I said finally, meaning it. 'I don't hunt for trouble.'

'Wulfe?' She glanced at the boy, but he merely rocked.

'It doesn't matter,' she said at last, dismissing me with a wave of her hand as she turned to survey her people. 'Wulfe believes what she says. False or true, we cannot have vampires, any vampires,' she glanced briefly at Stefan to make her point, 'running around killing without permission. We cannot afford the risk.' She stared at the seated vampires for a moment, then turned back to Stefan. 'Very well. I believe that this vampire did the killing – not you. I give you four sennights to find this sorcerer of yours and present him – or his body – to us. If you cannot do it, we will assume it is because he does not exist – and we will hold you responsible for endangering the seethe.'

'Agreed,' Stefan bowed while I was trying to remember what a sennight was. Seven nights, I thought, four weeks.

'You may pick someone to help you.'

Stefan's eyes traveled over the seated vampires without stopping. 'Daniel,' he said at last.

Andre was surprised into protest. 'Daniel's hardly fit to walk.'

'It is done,' Marsilia said. She brushed her hands together, as if to rid herself of the whole matter, and then stood up and walked out of the room.

I started to get off the chair, but I couldn't pull my hands away: they were stuck fast, and wiggling *hurt*. I couldn't make myself pull hard enough to get free. Stefan noticed my problem and gently pried my hands up as he had for Daniel. The sudden warmth as the spell disengaged made me gasp.

As I stood, my glance fell on Wulfe, who was the only vampire still seated in the room. He was staring at me with a hungry look. Bleeding in a room full of vampires wasn't very smart, I thought.

'Thank you for coming,' Stefan said to me, putting a hand under my elbow and turning me away from Wulfe's eyes.

'I don't think I helped much,' I said. Either the chair, or the eye contact with Wulfe had made me dizzy so I leaned a little harder on Stefan than I meant to. 'You still have to hunt down a sorcerer on your own.'

Stefan smiled at me. 'I would have anyway. This way, I'll have help.'

Andre, who'd been standing somewhat to the side, came up to us. 'Not much help. Daniel, even healthy, isn't much better than a human – and starved as he has been, he's weak as a kitten.'

'You could have prevented that.' There was no reproof in Stefan's voice, but something told me that he was angry with Andre over Daniel's condition.

Andre shrugged. 'There was food for him. If he did not take it, I wasn't going to force him. He'd have been driven to feed eventually.'

Stefan handed me over to Warren and then bent to help Daniel to his feet. 'Since you brought him over, it is your job to protect him – even from himself.'

'You've been hanging around the werewolves too long, *amico mio*,' Andre said. 'Vampires are not so fragile. If you had wanted to bring him over, you had plenty of time to do it.'

Stefan's face was turned away from Andre's as he steadied

Daniel on his feet, but I could see the red glow stirring in the chocolate depths. 'He was mine.'

Andre shrugged. 'That is an old argument – and I don't believe I ever disagreed with you. It was an accident. I didn't mean to turn him, but I had no choice other than to let him die. I believe I have apologized enough for it.'

Stefan nodded. 'I'm sorry I brought it up again.' He didn't sound it. 'I will return Daniel to you when I have accomplished the Mistress's will.'

Andre didn't walk out with us. I couldn't tell if he was angry or not. Without normal body scents, the vampires were difficult for me to read.

Warren waited until we were standing by his truck before he spoke. 'Stefan, I'd like to help you. I think that Adam would agree that a demon-riding vampire is not something to be taken lightly.'

'And I,' said Ben, unexpectedly. He saw my look and laughed. 'Been right boring around here lately. Adam's too much in the spotlight for now. He hasn't let us do more than a Moon hunt once a month since the first of the year.'

'Thank you,' said Stefan, sounding as if he meant it.

I opened my mouth, but before I could say anything, Stefan put a cool finger across my lips.

'No,' he said. 'Samuel is right. I almost got you killed last night. If Littleton had had the faintest inkling of what you are, he'd never have let you live. You are too fragile – and I have no desire to start a war with Adam – or worse, the Marrok himself.'

I rolled my eyes – as if I was important enough to the Marrok for him to take on the seethe while he was trying so hard to keep the werewolves looking good. Bran was too pragmatic for that. But Stefan was right; besides, there was nothing I could do that a pair of vampires and werewolves couldn't do better.

'Get him for her,' I told him. 'For that maid and for the others who should be with their loved ones tonight and not buried in the cold ground.'

Stefan took my hand and bowed low over it, touching his lips to the back. His elegant gesture made me conscious of how rough my skin was – mechanic work is not easy on hands.

'As my lady desires,' he said, sounding utterly serious.

5

'Hello?' Adam's voice was brisk.

'It's been nearly a week,' I said. 'Littleton's not coming after me – he's busy playing games with Warren and Stefan.' Warren had kept me more or less updated on the hunt for the vampire-sorcerer, such as it was. Somehow Littleton was always a step ahead of them. 'Call off the bodyguards.'

There was a little silence on the other end of the phone line, then Adam said, 'No. We're not discussing this over the phone. If you want to talk to me, you come over and talk to me. Wear something to spar in, I'll be working out in the garage.' Then he hung up.

'How about some different bodyguards?' I asked the phone plaintively. 'Someone I actually get along with shouldn't be too much to ask.'

I set the phone down and glared at it. 'Fine. I'll just deal with her.'

When I got home from work the next day, I grimly put on my gi and called him again. 'You win,' I said.

'I'll meet you in my garage.' To his credit, he didn't sound smug – proof that Adam is a man of tremendous self-control.

As I trudged across my back field, I told myself it was stupid to be so worried about talking to him. He was hardly likely to jump my bones without permission. All I had to do is keep this on a business setting.

I found Adam practicing high kicks on a sandbag in the dojo he'd made out of half of his garage, complete with a wall of mirrors, padded floor, and air-conditioning. His kicks

were picture perfect – mine would be too if I'd been practicing them for thirty or forty years. Maybe.

He finished his reps, then came up to me and touched
the side of my face. His scent, stronger for his exercise,
enveloped me; I had to fight not to press my head against
his hand.

'How's the head?' he asked. The bruises had faded a bit,
enough that customers didn't look embarrassed when they
saw me.

'Fine.' This morning was the first time I'd woken up
without a splitting headache.

'All right.' He walked away from me, out to the middle
of the padded floor. 'Spar with me a bit.'

I'd been taking karate at the dojo just over the railroad
tracks from my shop for a few years, but even so, I was
doubtful. I am nowhere near as strong as a werewolf. But,
as it turned out, he was the perfect sparring partner.

My teacher, Sensei Johanson, doesn't teach the 'pretty'
karate most Americans learn for exhibition and tournament.
Shisei kai kan is an oddball form of karate Sensei likes to call
'reach out and break someone.' It was originally designed
for soldiers who were facing more than one opponent. The
idea is to get your attackers out of the fight as soon as possible
and make sure they don't come back. I was the only woman
in my class.

The biggest problem I've had is slowing down enough
not to raise questions, but not so much as to allow myself
to get hurt. That wasn't a problem when sparring with Adam.
For the first time ever, I got to fight at full speed and I
loved it.

'You're using aikido?' I asked, backing away after a brisk
exchange.

Aikido is a kinder, gentler method of fighting. It can be
used to break people, too, but most of the moves have a

milder version. So you can lock the elbow and immobilize your opponent, or put a little more force behind it and break the joint instead.

'Running a security business with a bunch of ex-soldiers, I've found it necessary to do a little sparring once in a while. Clears the air,' he said. 'Aikido lets me take them down without hurting them or – before this year – advertising that I'm not exactly human anymore.'

He closed with me again, grinning as he caught my strike and guided it past his shoulder. I dropped down and swept his leg, forcing him to roll away from me before he could do anything nasty. When he regained his feet, I noticed he was panting, too. I took it for the compliment it was.

Though we fought at full speed, we were both still careful about how much force we used. Werewolves heal fast, but their bones still break and a punch still hurts. If Adam hit me full force, I suspected I wouldn't get up soon, if ever.

'You wanted me to pull the guards I set on you?' Adam asked in the middle of a quick exchange of soft-blocked punches.

'Yes.'

'No.'

'The sorcerer thinks I am a coyote,' I explained impatiently. 'He's not going to come looking for me.'

'No.'

I landed a blow that forced him off balance, but didn't fall into the trap of getting too close to him. Grappling with a werewolf is really stupid – particularly one trained in aikido.

'Look, I didn't mind Warren or Mary Jo. Mary Jo even knows one end of a wrench from another and helped out. But Honey . . . doesn't her mate desperately need her to sit and be pretty for his customers?'

Honey's mate-and-husband was a plumbing contractor, Peter Jorgenson. He was a wiry, homely, quiet man who did more work in an hour than most people did in their entire lives. Despite being a bimbo with no appreciation for anything except what she could see in a mirror, Honey loved her husband. Though when she said so, she *always* prefaced it with how she didn't care that – unlike herself – he wasn't a dominant wolf. Not that she ever talked to me: she didn't like me any more than I liked her.

'Peter follows my orders,' Adam told me.

Adam was Alpha, so Peter followed his orders. Honey was Peter's wife, so Peter gave her orders – which she followed. Male werewolves treat their mates like beloved slaves. The thought set my back up.

It wasn't Adam's or Peter's fault that werewolves had yet to come out of the Stone Age. Really. It was just a good thing I wasn't a werewolf or there would be a slave rebellion.

I aimed a kick at Adam's knee that he caught and used to drag me forward and off balance. Then he did something complicated and I ended up face down on the mat twisted like a pretzel while he held me there with one hand and a knee.

He smelled like the forest at night.

I slapped the mat quickly and he let me up.

'Adam. Close your eyes and envision Honey in my shop. She wore three-inch heels today.' The thought of her was like a dash of cold water in my face – which I needed.

He laughed. 'Out of place, was she?'

'She spent the whole day standing up because she didn't want to risk staining her skirt on any of my chairs. Gabriel has a crush on her.' I frowned at him when he laughed again. 'Gabriel is a sixteen-and-a-half-year-old male. If his mother finds out he's flirting with a werewolf, she'll quit letting him work at the shop.'

'She won't find out Honey is a werewolf. Honey isn't out

yet. And Honey's used to male attention, she won't take Gabriel seriously,' Adam said, as if that was the point.

'*I* know that, *Gabriel* knows that – his mother won't care. And she will find out. That's just the way my luck runs. If Gabriel leaves, I'll have to do my *own* paperwork.' I hadn't meant to whine, but I hated paperwork and it hated me back.

Sylvia, Gabriel's mother, had just found out that Zee was fae. She'd been okay with that, because she already knew and liked Zee when she found out. But I doubted she'd be so accommodating about werewolves, especially pretty female werewolves who might be after her boy.

'I don't want to lose Gabriel just because you're paranoid. No more guards, Adam. It's not like Honey would be much of a defense anyway.'

He sighed unhappily. 'Stefan is hunting out this sorcerer full-time. With Warren, Ben, and a few other wolves helping him, it shouldn't be too much longer before they take care of him and you're free. As far as Honey's suitability as a guard goes – she fights mean. She's taken Darryl down a time or two in training.' Most packs don't have 'training.' Sometimes Adam's background as a soldier really shows. 'If Honey weren't a woman she'd be someone's second or third.'

I wasn't surprised that Honey fought mean. I was a little surprised she fought well enough to take down Darryl, even a time or two. As second, he'd have had plenty of experience in real fights, not just training.

I knew why Adam was only sending female guards – for the same reason he sent Warren and Ben to accompany me to the seethe. Warren wouldn't make sexual overtures toward me because he wasn't interested – and Adam knew how much I disliked Ben.

Werewolves are very territorial. Since, supposedly for my protection, Adam had claimed me as his mate before the pack, I was his territory. As far as the pack was concerned, Adam's word was law. Just because I hadn't agreed, didn't change what the pack took as truth. Adam had managed to come to some agreement about it with Samuel. I didn't really want to know what it was because it would only tick me off.

So I got Honey because Mary Jo was working twenty-four hour shifts at the fire department and Darryl's mate Auriele, the only other female in Adam's pack, was in Ellensburg taking a class to keep up her teaching certification. Complaining about Honey wasn't going to get me a different guard – there wasn't anyone else Adam could send.

'Littleton is a *vampire*,' I said, trying to infuse a little logic into the situation. 'He's not going to attack during the daytime. I could make sure to be home before dark until he's caught. He can't get into my home unless I invite him. Not that he would, since he has no reason to think I was anything but a prop for Stefan's costume.'

'I had a talk with the Marrok about sorcerers,' said Adam gently. 'He's the one who told me to put a guard on you, day and night. No one knows what kind of monster a demon-ridden vampire is going to be, he said.'

'I know *that*,' I snapped – if Bran had ordered me guarded, I was doomed. Adam knew it, too.

'Elizaveta told me you called her and asked about sorcerers,' he said.

'Yeah, well, you should be happy. All she told me was that you had given her orders not to tell me anything.' Which wasn't exactly true.

What the witch had said was, '*Adamya says you are to leave it alone. He is a smart man, that one. Let the wolves hunt this sorcerer, Mercedes Thompson. A coyote is no match for a demon.*'

'Warren and Stefan will take care of Littleton,' Adam said. There was sympathy in his voice. He could afford to be sympathetic because he knew he'd robbed me of any chance of argument.

'Stefan and Warren are both out hunting tigers with sling-shots,' I told him. 'Maybe they'll get a lucky hit, and maybe the tiger will turn and kill them both – while Honey wears white slacks and watches me tune up cars.'

I walked over to one of the hanging sandbags and began practicing punches. I hadn't intended to say that, hadn't real-ized how worried I was. Adam could be confident, but he hadn't been in the same room with that *thing*.

'Mercy,' Adam said after watching me a while.

I switched to sidekicks.

'A screwdriver is a very useful tool, but you don't use it when what you need is a blowtorch,' he said. 'I know you are frustrated. I know you want to be in on the kill after what you saw Littleton do. But if you went out with them, someone would get killed trying to protect you.'

'Don't you think I know that?' I snapped. It was scary that he knew me well enough to understand it was waiting while others went after Littleton that bothered me the most. I stopped kicking and stared at the swinging black bag, fighting the urge to kick Adam instead.

I could change into a coyote. I was faster than a human. I was partially immune to some of the vampire's magics, but I wasn't even sure which ones. That was the extent of my preternatural abilities. It wasn't enough to go after Littleton.

If I'd been able to break the harness that night, the sorcerer would have killed me. I knew that, but it didn't diminish the guilt I felt for watching the maid struggle alone. *I* wanted to go after the sorcerer myself.

I wanted to feel his neck under my fangs and taste his blood. I took a deep shuddering breath. What I really wanted, what I hungered for, was to kill that smiling, cadaverous son of a bitch.

'Elizaveta won't go after him,' Adam said. 'Demons apparently have an odd effect on witchcraft. You're not the only one sitting on the sidelines.'

'You know, today one of the TV stations interviewed the sister of the man the vampires framed for the murders.' I kicked the sandbag twice. 'She cried. She admitted that her brother had been having marital problems, but she'd never imagined he would do something like this.' I kicked again, grunting with the effort. 'You know why she'd never imagined it? Because the poor bastard didn't do anything except be in the wrong place at the wrong damn time.'

'None of us can afford for the vampires to come out now,' Adam said.

I could tell the lies bothered him, too. Adam was a straightforward person – but he understood necessity. So did I. That didn't mean I had to like it.

'I *know* the vampires have to hide their presence,' I told the sandbag. 'I know people aren't ready to find out about all the things that hide in the darkness. I understand keeping them hidden saves us all from mass hysteria that would lead to a lot more people dying. But . . . that trucker – you remember, the one who was set up as the murderer – he had kids. They'll have to grow up with the idea that their father killed their mother.' I'd written down their names. Someday, when it was safe, I'd see they knew the truth.

Their pain, the murders, and every time I woke up with the memory of the smell of the poor woman's death, and the sound of Littleton's taunting laugh, all of those things were on the sorcerer's account. I wanted to be on the collection committee.

'He played with her.' I sent the bag swinging with a roundhouse, my best kick, hoping if I spoke the worst of that night, it would stay out of my dreams. 'I bet she knew that he'd already killed those other people. I bet she knew he was going to kill her. He tortured her, cutting her a little at a time so that it would take her longer to die.'

'Mercy,' Adam's voice was a purr, ready to offer comfort, but I wasn't going to fall down that hole. Everything meant too much to werewolves, and too little. If I let Adam comfort me, he could, and probably would, take it as an admission that I acknowledged him as my leader – maybe as my mate. It wasn't his fault, werewolf instincts are very strong. Samuel was safer, though he was a powerful dominant, because he wasn't Alpha of a pack.

Being Alpha was more than dominant. There is magic in the bindings of a pack that gives power to their leader, he can draw on their strength and give some of it back to them. I'd seen Adam's pack heal him and give him the power to force his dominion on another group of werewolves.

Being Alpha also gives a wolf the need to protect – and control – everyone they believe falls under their command. I didn't. But Adam had declared me his mate so he disagreed with me. I couldn't afford to soften my position at all.

I backed up the length of the garage, then ran hard toward the bag. A jumping, spinning back-kick is one of those moves that my sensei said had one purpose – to intimidate. Sure, if it hit, the kick was devastating, but any martial artist who was any good wouldn't allow one to hit because flashy kicks are too slow. Usually.

I launched as hard as I could, spinning fast enough to leave me dizzy. The heel of my foot caught the bag just below the top edge, as it was supposed to. If the sandbag had been a person I'd have broken his neck. I might even have landed on my feet.

The chain that suspended the bag kept it from falling back the way a person would have, and I hadn't expected the force I generated: I landed bruisingly hard on my butt.

I lay back quickly, flat on the floor, but Adam caught the

bag before it could swing back and hit me. He whistled softly as sand started sifting down from a small tear in the seam of the bag. 'Nice kick.'

'Adam,' I said staring up at the ceiling, 'he saved her for dessert.'

'What? Saved whom?'

'The maid. Littleton saved her like a kid hoarding his chocolate Easter bunny. He put the maid in the bathroom, out of sight, because he didn't want to kill her too soon. He was waiting for Stefan.' There were other reasons he could have stashed her in the bathroom – like he'd fed already on the other people he'd killed – but there had been something in his face when he'd brought her out that had said, 'at last.'

'Was he waiting for Stefan in particular? Or for whoever Marsilia sent?' asked Adam, seeing the important part of it before I did.

I thought of how much Littleton seemed to know about Stefan, intimate things, though Stefan had never met him. But it was more than what he'd said that made me certain, it was the way he'd seemed so pleased – as if everything was happening as expected.

'For Stefan,' I said, then continued to the obvious question. 'I wonder who told him Stefan was coming?'

'I'll call Warren and tell him you think someone told Littleton Stefan was coming for him,' Adam said. 'Stefan will have a better idea how Littleton might have found out, and if it means he has a traitor in his camp.'

I stayed where I was while Adam got the phone off the wall and began punching buttons.

We'd spent years as adversaries, two predators sharing territory and a certain, unwelcome attraction. Somehow, during all those years I spent outwardly acquiescing to his demands while making sure I held my own, I'd won his respect. I'd had werewolves love me and hate me, but I'd never had one respect me before. Not even Samuel.

Adam respected me enough to act on my suspicions. It meant a lot.

I closed my eyes and let the flow of his voice surround me and drive away the frustration. Adam was right. I wasn't suited for going after a vampire, any vampire, and certainly not one aided by a demon. I'd just have to be satisfied when Warren or Stefan did it. If Ben killed Littleton, though . . . I didn't know if that would satisfy me. I hated to owe Ben any more than I already did.

Adam hung up the phone. I heard the quiet sound of his feet walking toward me on the padded floor, and the hiss as the mat gave way when he sat beside me. After a moment he untied the top of my gi and pulled it off, leaving me in my T-shirt and white gi pants. I let him do it.

'Passive isn't like you,' he said.

I growled at him, though I didn't open my eyes. 'Shut up. I'm wallowing in misery, here. Have a little respect.'

He laughed and rolled me over until my face was pressed into the sweat-scented mat. His hands were warm and strong as they dug into the tense muscles of my lower back. When he dug into my shoulders, I went boneless.

At first he was all business, finding the knots left by sleepless nights and days of physically demanding work. Then his hands softened and the brisk rubs became light caresses.

'You smell like burnt oil and WD-40,' he said, a smile in his voice.

'So plug your nose,' I retorted. To my dismay, it came out with more sugar than vinegar.

I was so easy. One back rub and I was his. My susceptibility to him was the reason I'd been avoiding him. Somehow, lying on my face with his hands on my back, it didn't seem like a good enough reason.

He didn't smell of burnt oil, but of forest, wolf, and that exotic wild scent that belonged only to him. His hands slipped under my tee and spread wide over my lower back then feathered over my bra strap. I could have told him that sports bras don't have clasps, but then I'd have to take an active part in my own seduction. I wanted him to be the aggressor — a small part of me, the very small part of me that wasn't turning to jelly under his hands, wondered why.

I didn't want to delegate responsibility, I decided lazily. I was more than willing to accept responsibility for my own actions — and allowing him to slide his warm, calloused hands into my hair was certainly an action on my part. I loved a man's hands in my hair, I decided. I loved Adam's hands.

He bit the nape of my neck and I moaned.

The door between the garage and the house popped open suddenly. 'Hey Dad, hey Mercy.'

Ice water couldn't have been more effective.

The hands on my butt stilled as Adam's daughter's quick steps paused. I opened my eyes and met her gaze. She'd changed her hairstyle since last time I'd seen her, going from startling to even more startling. It was no more than a half-inch long and yellow — not blond yellow, but daffodil yellow. The effect was charming, but a little bizarre. Not what a rescuer ought to look like.

Her face went blank as she realized what she'd inter-rupted. 'I'll, uh, go upstairs and watch a show,' she said, not sounding like herself at all.

I scooted out from under Adam. 'And Jesse saves the day,' I said lightly. 'Thank you, that was getting out of hand.'

She paused, looking — surprised.

I wondered uncharitably how many times she'd walked in on her mother in similar situations and what her mother's response had been. I never had liked Jesse's mother and was happy to believe all sorts of evil about her. I let anger at the games her mother might have played surround me. When you've lived with werewolves, you learn tricks to hide what you're feeling from them – anger, for instance, covers up panic pretty well – and, out from under Adam's sensuous hands, I was panicking plenty.

Adam snorted. 'That's one way to put it.' To my relief he'd stayed where we'd been, sinking face down into the mat.

'Even with my willpower, his lure was too great,' I said melodramatically, complete with wrist to forehead. If I made a joke of it, he'd never realize how truthful I was being.

A slow smile spread across her face and she quit looking like she was ready to bolt back into the house. 'Dad's kind of a stud, all right.'

'Jesse,' warned Adam, his voice muffled only a little by the mat. She giggled.

'I have to agree,' I said in overly serious tones. 'Maybe as high as a seven or eight, even.'

'Mercedes,' Adam thundered, surging to his feet.

I winked at Jesse, held my gi top over my left shoulder with one finger, and strolled casually out the back door of the garage. I didn't mean to, but when I turned to shut the door, I looked back and saw Adam's face. His expression gave me cold chills.

He wasn't angry or hurt. He looked thoughtful, as if someone had just given him the answer to a question that had been bothering him. He *knew*.

I was still shaking as I gingerly climbed over the barbed wire fence between Adam's land and mine.

All my life I'd blended in with those around me. It is the gift of the coyote. It's what helps us survive.

I learned early how to imitate the wolves. I played by

their rules as long as they did. If they pushed it beyond reasonable limits because they thought I was less than they, being coyote rather than wolf, or because they were jealous that I did not have to heed the moon's call, then all bets were off. I played my strengths to their weaknesses. I lied with my body and eyes, licking their boots – then tormenting them in whatever way I could come up with.

Wolf etiquette had become a game to me, a game with rules I understood. I thought I was immune to the stupid dominance/submission thing, immune to the Alpha's power. I'd just had a very visceral lesson that I was not. I didn't like it. Not at all.

If Jesse hadn't come in, I would have surrendered myself to Adam, like some heroine from a 1970s series romance, the kind my foster mother used to read all the time. Ick.

I walked across my back field until I stood beside the decrepit Rabbit that served as my parts car, as well as my means of getting back at Adam when he got too dictatorial. If he looked out his back window, it sat right in the center of his field of view.

I'd pushed it out of the garage several years ago when Adam had complained about my mobile home spoiling his view. Then, every time he bothered me, I made it uglier. Right now it was missing three wheels and the rear bumper, all stored safely in my garage. Big red letters across the hood said FOR A GOOD TIME CALL followed by Adam's phone number. The graffiti had been Jesse's suggestion.

I dropped down in the dirt beside the Rabbit and leaned my head against the fender, trying to figure out why I'd suddenly been overwhelmed with the desire to submit to Adam. Why hadn't I felt like this before – or had that been why I'd run so hard? I tried to think back, but all I remembered was worrying about getting so involved with another werewolf.

Could he have made me submit to him on purpose? Was it physiological or parapsychological, science or magic? If I knew it was going to happen, could I resist it?

Who could I ask?

I looked at the car parked in the driveway. Samuel was home from his shift at the ER.

Samuel would know, if anyone did. I'd just have to figure out how to ask him. It was a testimony to how shaken up I was that I got to my feet and headed home with the intention of asking one werewolf, who had made it plain that he was only waiting to make his move on me, about the way another werewolf had made me desire him. I'm not usually that dumb.

I was already beginning to have doubts about the wisdom of my plans by the time I reached the front porch. I opened the door and was met by a frigid blast of air.

My old wall unit had been able to keep my bedroom about ten degrees cooler than the outside, which was all right with me. I like hot weather, but most of the wolves had trouble with it, which is why Samuel had installed the new heat pump and paid for it. A considerate roommate, he usually left the temperature where I set it.

I took a look at the thermostat and saw that Samuel had punched it down as far as it would go. It wasn't forty-two degrees inside, but it was trying. Pretty decent effort considering it was over a hundred degrees outside and my trailer had been built in 1978 before the days of manufactured homes with good insulation. I turned it to a more reasonable temperature.

'Samuel? Why'd you turn the temperature down so low?' I called, dropping my gi top on the couch.

There was no reply, though he had to have heard me. I walked through the kitchen area and into the hallway. Samuel's door was mostly shut, but he hadn't closed it all the way.

'Samuel?' I touched the door and it opened a foot or so, just enough that I could see Samuel stretched out on his bed, still in his hospital scrubs and smelling of cleanser and blood.

He had his arm over his eyes.

'Samuel?' I paused in the doorway to give my nose a chance to tell me what he was feeling. But I couldn't smell the usual suspects. He wasn't angry, or frightened. There was something . . . he smelled of pain.

'Samuel, are you all right?'

'You smell like Adam.' He took his arm down and looked at me with wolf eyes, pale as snow and ringed in ebony.

Samuel isn't here today, I thought, trying not to panic or do any other stupid thing. I had played with Samuel's wolf as a child, along with all the other children in Aspen Springs. I hadn't realized how dangerous that would have been with any other wolf until I was much older. I would have felt better now, if those wolf eyes had been in the wolf body. Wolf eyes on a human face meant the wolf was in charge.

I'd seen new wolves lose control. If they did it very often, they were eliminated for the sake of the pack and everyone who came in contact with them. I'd only seen Samuel lose control once before – and that was after a vampire attack.

I sank down on the floor, making certain my head was lower than his. It was always an interesting feeling, making myself helpless in front of someone who might tear my throat out. Come to think of it, the last time I'd done this it had been with Samuel, too. At least I was acting out of self-preservation, not some buried compulsion to submit to a dominant wolf – I was faking it, not submitting because of some damn buried instinct.

After I told myself that, I realized it was true. I had no desire to cower before Samuel. Under other, less worrisome circumstances, I'd have been cheered up.

'Sorry,' Samuel whispered, putting his arm back over his eyes. 'Bad day. There was an accident on 240 near where the old Y interchange was. Couple of kids in one car, eighteen and nineteen years old. Mother with an infant in the other. All of them still in critical condition. Maybe they'll make it.'

He'd been a doctor for a very long time. I didn't know what had set him off with this accident in particular. I made an encouraging sound.

'There was a lot of blood,' he said at last. 'The baby got pretty cut up from the glass, took thirty stitches to plug the leaks. One of the ER nurses is new, just graduated from the community college. She had to leave in the middle – afterward she asked me how I learned to manage so well when the victims were babies.' His voice darkened with bitterness that I'd seldom heard from him before as he continued, 'I almost told her that I'd seen worse – and eaten them, too. The baby would have only been a snack.'

I could have left, then. Samuel had enough control left not to come after me – probably. But I couldn't leave him like that.

I crawled cautiously across the floor, watching him for a twitch of muscle that would tell me he was ready to pounce. Slowly I raised my hand up until it touched his. He didn't react at all.

If he'd been a new wolf, I'd have known what to say. But helping new wolves through this kind of situation had been one of Samuel's jobs in the pack I'd grown up in. There was nothing I could say that he didn't already know.

'The wolf is a practical beast,' I told him, finally, thinking it might have been the thought of eating the baby that bothered him so much. 'You're more careful what you eat. You aren't likely to pounce on the operating table and eat someone if you aren't hungry.' It was almost word for word the speech I'd heard him use with the new wolves.

'I'm so tired,' he said, raising the hair on the back of my neck. 'Too tired. I think it is time to rest.' He wasn't talking about physically.

Werewolves aren't immortal, just immune to age. But time is their enemy anyway. After just so long, one wolf told me, nothing matters anymore and death looks better than living another day. Samuel was very old.

The Marrok, Samuel's father, had taken to calling me once a month to 'check on things,' he said. For the first time it occurred to me that he hadn't been checking on me, but on his son.

'How long have you felt this way?' I asked, inching my way up onto his bed, slowly so I didn't startle him. 'Did you leave Montana because you couldn't hide this from Bran?'

'No. I want you,' he said starkly moving his arm so I could see that his eyes had changed back to human grey-blue.

'Do you?' I asked, knowing that it wasn't completely true. 'Your wolf might still want me, but I don't think you do. Why *did* you leave the Marrok to come here?'

He rolled away, giving his back to me. I didn't move, careful not to crowd him. I didn't back away either, just waited for his answer.

Eventually it came. 'It was bad. After Texas. But when you came back to us, it went away. I was fine. Until the baby.'

'Did you talk to Bran about it?' *Whatever* it *was*. I put my face against the small of his back, warming him with my breath. Samuel would see suicide as cowardice, I tried to reassure myself, and Samuel hated cowards. I might not want to love Samuel – not after the way we'd once hurt each other – but I didn't want to lose him either.

'The Marrok knows,' he whispered. 'He always does. Everyone else believed I was the same, just like always. My father knew something was wrong, that I wasn't right. I was going to leave – but then you came.'

If Bran couldn't fix him, what was I supposed to do?

'You left the pack for a long time,' I said, feeling my way. He'd left the pack shortly after I had, over fifteen years ago. He'd stayed away for most of those fifteen years. 'Bran told me you went lone-wolf in Texas.' Wolves need their pack, or else they start to get a little strange. Lone wolves were, in general, an odd bunch, dangerous to themselves and others.

'Yes.' Every muscle in his body tensed, waiting for the blow to fall. I decided that meant I was on the right track.

'It's not easy being alone, not for years.' I scooted up a little until I could wrap myself around him, tucking my legs behind his. I slipped the arm I wasn't lying on around his side and pressed my hand over his stomach, showing him that he wasn't alone, not while he lived at my house.

He started to shake, vibrating the whole bed. I tightened my arm, but I didn't say anything. I'd gone as far as I was willing to go. Some wounds need to be pricked so they can drain, others just need to be left alone – I wasn't qualified to know the difference.

He wrapped both of his arms over the top of mine. 'I hid myself from the wolves. I hid among the humans.' He paused. 'Hid from myself. What I did to you was wrong, Mercedes. I told myself I couldn't wait, I couldn't take the chance that another would take you from me. I had to make you mine so my children would live, but I knew I was taking advantage of you. You weren't old enough to defend yourself from me.'

I rubbed my nose against his back in reassurance, but I didn't speak. He was right, and I respected him too much to lie.

'I violated your trust, and my father's, too. I couldn't live with it: I had to leave. I traveled to the far corner of the country and became someone else: Samuel Cornick, college freshman, fresh off the farm with a newly minted high school diploma. Only on the night of the full moon did I allow myself to remember what I was.'

The muscles under my hands convulsed twice. 'In med school, I met a girl. She reminded me of you: quiet with a sneaky sense of humor. She looked a little like you, too. It felt like a second chance to me – a chance to do it right. Or maybe I just forgot. We were friends at first, in the same program at school. Then it became something more. We moved in together.'

I knew what was coming, because it was the worst thing I could think of that could have happened to Samuel. I could smell his tears, though his voice was carefully even.

'We took precautions, but we weren't careful enough. She got pregnant.' His voice was stark. 'We were doing our internships. We were so busy we hardly had time to say "hello" to each other. She didn't notice until she was nearly three months pregnant because she assumed that the symptoms were from stress. I was so happy.'

Samuel loved children. Somewhere I had a picture of him wearing a baseball cap with Elise Smithers, age five, riding him as if he had been a pony. He'd thrown away everything he believed in because he thought I, unlike a human or werewolf, could give him children who would live.

I tried not to let him know I was crying, too.

'We were doing internships.' He was speaking quietly now. 'It's time consuming and stressful. Long irregular hours. I was working with an orthopedic surgeon, nearly a two hour drive from our apartment. I came home one night and found a note.'

I hugged him harder, as if I could have stopped what happened.

'A baby would have interfered with her schooling,' he

said. 'We could try again, later. After . . . after she was established. After there was money. After . . .' He kept talking
but he'd dropped into a foreign tongue, its liquid tone
conveying his anguish better than the English words had.

The curse of a long life is that everyone around you dies.
You have to be strong to survive, and stronger to want to
do so. Bran had told me once that Samuel had seen too many
of his children die.

'That infant tonight . . .'

'He'll live,' I said. 'Because of you. He'll grow up strong
and healthy.

'I lived like a student should, Mercy,' he told me.
'Pretending to be poor like all the other students. I wonder
if she knew that I had money, would she still have killed
my baby? I would have quit school to take care of the child.
Was it my fault?'

Samuel curled his whole body around my arm as if someone
had punched him in the stomach. I just held him.

There was nothing I could say to make it better. He knew
better than I what the chances of his baby being born healthy
had been. It didn't matter, his child had never gotten any
chance at all.

I held Samuel while the sun set, comforting him as best
I could.

6

I left Samuel sleeping and made tuna fish sandwiches for dinner, something I could put in the fridge for him in case he awoke hungry, but he stayed in his room until past my bedtime.

I set my alarm clock for a couple of hours later than my usual wake-up. Tomorrow was Saturday when I was officially closed. I had work to do, but nothing urgent, and Gabriel wasn't scheduled to come in until ten.

When I knelt for prayer before bedtime, I asked God to help Warren and Stefan catch the demon, as had become my usual plea. This time I added a prayer for Samuel as well. After a moment's thought I prayed for Adam, too. I didn't *really* think it was his fault that he turned me into a submissive ninny.

Even though I was all set to wake up late (for me), I got up just before dawn because someone was tapping on my window. I pulled my pillow over my head.

'Mercy.' My window's assailant kept his voice down, but I knew it anyway. Stefan.

I rubbed my eyes. 'Are you asking for quarter? I'm not in a particularly *merciful* mood.' I can make fun of my name, but no one else can. Unless I'm in a really good mood. Or if I start it first.

I heard him laugh. 'For quarters, perhaps. But I have no need to yield, if you are not assaulting me.'

One of the nice things about Stefan was that he usually got my jokes, no matter how lame. Even better, he'd play along.

'You need money?' I asked in mock surprise. 'I can write you a check, but I only have a couple of dollars in cash.'

'I need a place to sleep the day, love. Would you shelter me?'

'All right,' I threw back my covers and started for the front door. There went my plans to sleep in.

The sky was striped with the beginnings of sunrise when I opened the door.

'Left it a little late, Stefan,' I said adding his name so that Samuel – who would have heard me open the door – wasn't alarmed.

Stefan didn't appear to hurry, but neither did he waste much time standing on my doorstep.

I hadn't seen him since the night of his trial. He looked tired. His shoulders were slumped and he didn't move with his usual effervescent energy. 'I sent Daniel home, but I had a tip I had to check out. I thought I'd have time, but my powers lessen as dawn approaches and I found myself on your doorstep' – he grinned – 'begging for *mercy*.'

I escorted him to my bedroom door. 'I thought Warren and Ben were working with you. Why didn't you have them check it out?'

'I sent them home earlier. They have jobs to do today, and even werewolves need sleep.'

'They're working on a Saturday?'

'Warren has a job for his lawyer friend, and Ben had things to do that he couldn't get done when everyone else was working.'

Ben was a computer geek working at the Pacific Northwest Nation Laboratory which was affiliated in some arcane manner with the Hanford Nuclear Site. Darryl, Adam's second, had gotten him the job – and from all accounts Ben was a pretty decent nerd. I think it surprised Darryl, who wasn't accustomed to being surprised.

I pulled open the closet door – Stefan's pillow and blanket were still there from the last time he'd spent the day. 'Are you sure the sorcerer is still here? He could have moved on.'

Stefan looked grim. 'Watch the news this morning,' was all he said before stepping into my closet and closing the door.

The car wreck that had so upset Samuel made the early news. So did the violent deaths of three young men who had gotten in an argument. We were two weeks into a heat wave that showed no signs of letting up anytime soon. There was another Arts festival in Howard Amon Park this weekend.

I assumed Littleton wouldn't have anything to do with the Arts festival or the weather (at least I hoped that a sorcerer wasn't powerful enough to affect the weather), so I paid close attention to the report on the dead men.

'Drugs are a growing problem,' the newscaster said, as EMTs carried black sheathed bodies out on stretchers behind him. 'Especially meth. In the last six months the police have shut down three meth labs in the Tri-City area. According to witnesses, last night's violence apparently broke out in a meth lab when one man made a comment about another's girlfriend. All of the men were high, and the argument quickly escalated into violence that left three men dead. Two other men are in police custody in connection with the deaths.'

On the brighter side, all of Samuel's patients were apparently still alive, though the baby was in critical condition.

I turned off the TV, poured a bowl of cereal, then sat down at my computer desk in the spare bedroom while I ate breakfast and searched the Internet.

The online story had even fewer details than the morning news. On a whim I looked up Littleton's name and found his website offering online tarot readings for a mere $19.95, all major credit cards accepted. No checks. Not a trusting soul, our sorcerer.

On impulse, since Elizaveta wouldn't tell me anything, I Googled for demons and sorcerers and I found myself buried under a morass of contradictory garbage.

'Any idiot can put up a website,' I growled, shutting down the computer. Medea meowed in sympathy as she licked the last of the milk out of my cereal bowl and then cleaned her face with a paw.

Dirty bowl in hand, I checked in on Samuel, but his room was empty. When he hadn't gotten up at Stefan's arrival, I should have realized he was gone. He didn't have to work today.

It worried me, but I wasn't his mother. He didn't have to tell me where he was going anymore than I usually told him my plans. So I couldn't pry, no matter how worried I was. With that thought in mind I wrote him a note.

> S sleeping in my closet.
> I'm at work until?
> Stop by if you need anything.
> Me

I left it on his bed then rinsed out my bowl and left it in the dishwasher. I started for the door, but the sight of the phone on the end table by the door stopped me.

Samuel had been in a bad way last night; I knew his father would want to know about it. I stared at the phone. I wasn't a snitch. If Samuel wanted the Marrok to know about his problems, he would have stayed in Aspen Creek. Samuel had his own cell phone – he could call Bran if he needed help. Which would be when Hell froze over. Samuel had taught me a lot about independence, which was actually an unusual trait for a werewolf.

Bran might be able to help. But it wouldn't be right for me to call him behind Samuel's back. I hesitated, then remembered that Samuel had called Zee to check up on me.

I picked up the phone and made the long-distance call to Montana.

'Yes?'

Unless he wanted it to, Bran's voice didn't sound like it belonged to the most powerful, werewolf in North America. It sounded like it belonged to a nice young man. Bran was deceptive that way, all nice and polite. The act fooled a lot of wolves into stupidity. Me, I knew what the act hid.

'It's me,' I said. 'About Samuel.'

He waited.

I started to say something and then guilt stopped my tongue. I knew darned well that what Samuel told me had been in confidence.

'Mercedes.' This time Bran didn't sound like a nice young man.

'He had a little trouble last night,' I said finally. 'Do you know what happened to him in Texas?'

'He won't talk about Texas.'

I drummed my fingers against my kitchen counter and then stopped when it reminded me of the vampire's mistress.

'You need to ask him about Texas,' I said. Bran didn't ask people about the past as a rule. It had something to do with being very old, but more to do with being wolf. Wolves are very centered in the here and now.

'Is he all right?'

'I don't know.'

'Are there any bodies?' he said dryly.

'No. Nothing like that. I shouldn't have called.'

'Samuel is my son,' Bran said softly. 'You did right to call. Mercy, living in a town with a sorcerer isn't going to make him the safest roommate if something is upsetting him. You might consider moving in with Adam until they find the demon-rider.'

'Demon-rider?' I asked, though I was thinking about what he'd said.

'Sorcerer, as opposed to demon-ridden, as the possessed are. Though there's not much to choose between them, except that the demon-ridden are easier to spot. They're in the middle of the carnage instead of on the sidelines.'

'You mean sorcerers attract violence?' I asked. I should have called Bran for information about the sorcerer earlier.

'Does sugar water attract hornets? Violence, blood and evil of all kinds. Do you think I had Adam send his wolves out to help the vampires with this hunt because I like vampires?' Actually, I had thought Warren and Ben volunteered. 'If there's a sorcerer about, all the wolves will have to hold tight to their control. So don't go around pushing buttons, honey. Especially with the younger wolves. You'll get hurt – or killed.'

He'd been warning me about 'pushing buttons' for as long as I could remember. I don't know why. I'm not stupid. I'm always careful when I torment werewolves . . . then I remembered Samuel's eyes last night.

'I won't,' I promised, meaning it.

But then he said, 'Good girl,' and hung up.

As if he'd never doubted I'd do as he told me. Bran seldom had to worry about people not following his orders – except for me. I guess he'd forgotten about that.

It was a good thing there weren't any werewolves around to annoy. I'd like to think I was grown-up enough not to pick a fight just because Bran told me not to, but, still . . . I wouldn't have poked at Samuel, not in his current state, but it was probably a good thing Ben wasn't around.

*   *   *

Although it was not yet eight in the morning, there was a car waiting for me in the parking lot, a sky blue Miata convertible. Even after our talk last night, Adam had sent Honey out to babysit me again.

Sometimes you wonder what gets into parents when they name their children. I knew a girl named Helga who grew up to be five feet tall and weighed 95 pounds. Sometimes, though, sometimes, parents get it right.

Honey had waves of shimmering golden brown hair that fell over her shoulders to her hips. Her face was all soft curves and pouty lips, the kind of face you'd expect to see in a professional cheerleading outfit, though I've never seen Honey wear anything that wasn't classy.

'I've been waiting here for an hour and a half,' she said, sounding miffed as she got out of her car. Today she was wearing creamy linen shorts that would show every smudge of dirt – if she irritated me too much today, I could always get her with my grease gun.

'It's Saturday,' I told her amiably, cheered by my thoughts. 'I work whatever hours I want to on Saturday. However, I believe in being fair. Since you had to wait for me, why don't you count that as a good effort and go on home?'

She raised an eyebrow. 'Because Adam sent me here to watch you and make sure the boogeyman doesn't come and eat you. And as much as I'd like to see that happen, I don't disobey the Alpha.'

There were a lot of reasons I didn't like Honey.

The car I was working on needed a new starter. That's how it all began. Three hours later I was still sorting through unlabeled dusty boxes in the storage shed that predated Gabriel's reign of order on my parts supply.

'Somewhere in here there should be three starters that fit a 1987 Fox,' I told Gabriel, wiping my forehead off on my sleeve. I may not mind the heat usually, but the thermometer on the outside of the shed read 107 degrees.

'If you told me that somewhere in here you had Excalibur and the Holy Grail, I'd believe you.' He grinned at me. He'd only come out after he'd finished the parts supply order so he still had energy to be happy. 'Are you sure you don't want me to run down to the parts store and pick one up?'

'Fine,' I said dropping a box of miscellaneous bolts on the floor of the shed. I shut the door and locked it, though if I'd left it open, maybe some nice thieves would come and clean it out for me. 'Why don't you pick up some lunch for us while you're out? There's a good taco wagon by the car wash over on First.'

'Honey, too?'

I glanced over at her car where she was sitting in air-conditioned comfort as she had been since I came out here. I hoped she'd had her oil changed recently – idling for hours could be hard on an engine.

She saw me looking at her and smiled unpleasantly, still not a hair out of place. I'd been sweating in a dusty and greasy shed all morning and the bruises Littleton left on my face were a lovely shade of yellow today.

'Yeah,' I said reluctantly. 'Take the lunch money out of petty cash. Use the business credit card for the starter.'

Gabriel bounced back into the office and was on his way out by the time I made it to the door. The air-conditioning felt heavenly and I drank two glasses of water before going back to work. The garage wasn't as cool as the office, but it was a lot better than outside.

Honey followed me through the office to the shop and managed to ignore me at the same time. I noticed, with some satisfaction, that soon after she left the office, she broke out in a sweat.

I'd just had time to get a good start on a brake job when she spoke. 'There's someone in the office.'

I hadn't heard anyone, but I hadn't been listening. I wiped my hands hastily and headed back into the office. I wasn't officially opened, but a lot of my regular customers know I'm here on Saturdays more often than not.

As it happened the face was familiar.

'Mr Black,' I said. 'More car problems?'

He started to look at me, but his eyes ran into trouble as they hit Honey and refused to move off of her. It was not an uncommon reaction. One more reason to hate Honey – not that I needed another one.

'Honey, this is Tom Black, a reporter who wants the skinny on what it's like to date Adam Hauptman, prince of the werewolves.' I said it to get a rise out of her, but Honey disappointed me.

'Mr Black,' she said, coolly extending her hand.

He shook her hand, still staring at her, and then seemed to recover. He cleared his throat. 'Prince of the Werewolves? Is he?'

'She can't talk to you, Mr Black,' Honey told him, though she glanced at me to make it clear that the words were directed at me. If she weren't more careful, she'd find herself outed as a werewolf. If she weren't dumber than a stump she'd have known I don't take orders. Not from Bran, not from Adam or Samuel – certainly not from Honey.

'No one ever told me not to talk to reporters,' I said truthfully. Everyone just assumed I'd be smart enough not to. I was so busy tormenting Honey that I ignored what the implicit promise in my statement would do to the reporter.

'I will make it worth your while,' Black said in a classic assumption close worthy of a used car salesman. He reached into his suit jacket and pulled out a roll of bills in a gold clip and set them on the counter. If I hadn't been so ticked off with Honey – and Adam for sticking me with her – I'd have laughed. But Honey was there, so I licked my lips and looked interested.

'Well . . .' I began.

Honey turned to me, vibrating with rage. 'I hope that Adam lets me be the one to break your scrawny neck.'

Yep. It wouldn't be long before everyone knew Honey was a werewolf. She was just too easy. I ought to have felt guilty for baiting her.

Instead, I rolled my eyes at her. *'Please.'*

Black ignored Honey. 'I want to know what you think about him personally. What is dating a werewolf like?' He gave me a charming smile, though his eyes were still watchful. 'The public wants to know.'

That last statement was too comic-book reporter for me to ignore. It pulled my attention from Honey. I considered Black thoughtfully for a moment. He smelled anxious – and angry. Not the emotions of a reporter about to get the story he wanted.

I pushed the money roll back at him. 'Put that away. I'm pretty upset with Adam right now, so I'd really like to give you an earful.' Especially with Honey watching. 'You may not quote me, but the truth is that, for a domineering control freak, he's pretty damn nice. He's honest, hard working, and generous. He's a good father. He's loyal to his people and he takes care of them. It doesn't make a very good story, but that's your problem, not mine. If you are looking for dirt on Adam Hauptman, let me save you a lot of fruitless effort. There is no dirt.'

I don't know what kind of a reaction I expected, but it wasn't the one I got. He ignored the bills on the counter and leaned down over it, invading my space.

'He's a good father?' he asked intently. The fake smile

vanished from his face. I could smell his anxiety winning over anger.

I didn't answer. I wasn't going to take responsibility for directing the eyes of the press toward Jesse, when Adam had been so careful to keep her out of the way. Besides, the reporter's strange reactions made me think there was something else going on.

Black closed his eyes briefly. 'Please,' he said. 'It's important.'

I took a deep breath and could smell the truth of his words. The first complete truth he'd uttered in my presence. This was very important to him.

I shuffled through possibilities and then asked, 'Who do you know that is a werewolf?'

'Are you a werewolf?' he asked.

'No.' Not that he could have known if I lied, because he was decidedly human.

The same thought must have occurred to him. He waved away his last question impatiently. 'It doesn't matter. If you'll tell me why you say he's a good father . . . I'll tell you about the werewolves I know.'

Fear. Not the kind of fear you feel when unexpectedly confronted by a monster in the dark, but the slower, stronger fear of something terrible that was going to happen. Fear and pain of an old wound, the kind that Samuel had smelled of last night. I hadn't been able to help Samuel, not enough.

I considered Mr Black who might or might not be a reporter.

'Your word you won't use this for a story,' I said, ignoring Honey's raised eyebrows.

'You have it.'

'Are you a reporter?' I asked.

He nodded his head, a quick up and down followed by a get-on-with-it glare.

I thought a moment. 'Let me give you an example. Adam is supposed to be speaking to government officials about legislation dealing with werewolves. He's up to his neck in touchy negotiations. When his daughter needed him, he dropped everything and came back here – though he has a number of trusted people he could have called upon to take care of her.'

'She's human, though, right? His daughter. I read that they can't have werewolf children.'

I frowned at him, trying to see the point of his question. 'Does it matter?'

He rubbed his face tiredly. 'I don't know. Does it? Would he treat her differently if she was a werewolf?'

'No,' said Honey. Black was being so interesting, I'd forgotten about Honey. 'No. Adam takes care of his own. Wolf, human or whatever.' She looked at me pointedly. 'Even when they don't want him to.'

It felt weird to exchange a smile with Honey, so I stopped as soon as I could. I think she felt the same way because she turned her head to stare out the window.

'Or when they don't belong to him,' I told her. Then I turned to Black. 'So tell me about your werewolves.'

'Three years ago, my daughter survived an attack by a rogue werewolf,' he said, speaking quickly as if that would make it easier for him to handle. 'She was ten.'

'Ten?' whispered Honey. 'And she survived?'

Like Honey, I'd never heard of someone attacked so young surviving – especially not a girl. Females don't survive the change as well as males. That was why Adam's pack only had three females and nearly ten times that many males.

Lost in his tragic story, Black didn't seem to hear Honey's comment. 'There was another werewolf. He killed her attacker before it could finish her off. He brought her back to us and told us what to do for her. He told me to hide her. He said that a young girl might . . . might have it rough in a pack.'

'Yes,' said Honey fervently. At my questioning look she said, 'Unmated females belong to the Alpha. Your wolf instincts kick in, so it's not terrible' – her eyes said differently – 'even if you don't particularly like the Alpha. But a girl so young . . . I'm not certain that an Alpha would spare her.' She took a deep breath and whispered, almost to herself, 'I know some of them would even enjoy it.'

Black nodded, as if this wasn't news to him – though it was to me. I thought I knew all there was to know about werewolves.

'What about when she first changed?' I asked. Humans are not equipped to deal with a new-made werewolf.

'I built a cage in the basement,' he said. 'And every full moon I chain her and lock her in.'

Every full moon even after three years? I thought. She should have managed to gain control of her wolf by now.

'Two months ago she broke the chain to her collar.' Black looked ill. 'I got a thicker chain, but this time . . . My wife told me that she gouged a hole in the cement. I was in Portland covering a trade conference. I called the werewolf. The one who saved her. He told me she was getting stronger, that I had to find a pack for her. He told me our local Alpha would be a poor choice. When he found out I was in Portland, he gave me Hauptman's name – and yours.'

I felt sorry for his daughter – and for him. Sorrier still because finding an Alpha who wouldn't abuse her might be the least of his problems if she hadn't managed to control her wolf yet. Wolves who are out of control are killed by their Alpha so they don't hurt anyone else.

I didn't want to give Adam responsibility for a young girl's death.

'There may be someone closer to where you live,' I said. 'Let me make a phone call.'

'No,' said Black, taking two steps back. He might not

be a werewolf, but he was fast. I never noticed the gun until it was in his hands. 'It's loaded with silver,' he said, the spike of fear I felt from him made me want to pat him on the back and tell him it would be all right – or it would if he didn't shoot me and Honey didn't kill him.

I don't think he was used to combat situations, because he ignored Honey and kept the gun on me.

'He's not going to shoot anyone, Honey,' I told her as she started to move. 'It's all right, Mr Black, I won't mention your name. Has your contact told you anything about the Marrok?'

He shook his head.

Honey waited, her eyes locked on his gun.

'Okay. The Marrok is like, the Alpha of all the Alphas.' That there was a head werewolf was kind of an open secret. Everyone knew that there was someone pulling the were-wolves' strings, and there was a lot of speculation about who it might be. So I hadn't given away any great secret.

Bran wasn't out to the public – if things went badly, he wanted to make sure that the sanctuary he'd established in Montana remained a safe haven. Even if he had been out, no one would think that he was the Marrok. Being un-remarkable was one of Bran's favorite talents and he was good at it.

'He'll know which Alphas will take care of your daughter, and which ones to stay away from better than any lone wolf could. It's his job to take care of the werewolves, Mr Black, to make sure the ones like your daughter are safe.'

And to make sure the ones who were not able to control their wolfish side were killed quickly and painlessly before they started killing people, people like their parents and families.

'All right,' he said, at last. 'Call him. But if you say some-thing I don't like, I'll kill you.'

I believed him; he had the look of a man with his back to the wall. Honey eased closer, close enough that she'd probably be able to stop him before he pulled the trigger. Probably. If she wanted to badly enough.

I took out my cell phone and placed the call.

'Hello?' It was a woman's voice.

Damn. Bran's wife didn't like me. Not like Honey disliked me, but the I'll-kill-you-if-I-get-a-chance kind of not like. She'd tried it a couple of times. She was the reason I always called Bran's cell phone and not his home number.

'This is Mercedes,' I said. 'I'm calling on official business. I need to talk to your husband.' I heard Bran's voice, but he was speaking too low for me to hear anything except the command in his tone. There were a few clicks and unidentifiable noises and then Bran came on the line.

'How can I help you?' he asked sounding calm, though I could hear his mate's bitter voice in the background.

Briefly, I explained the situation to him. I didn't tell him that I was worried about a wolf who couldn't control herself after three years, but he must have heard it in my voice because he interrupted me.

'It's all right, Mercy. A child chained in the basement doesn't learn control because it is not expected of her. With a little help she might be fine. Any child who survives a werewolf attack before adolescence has willpower to spare. Where does he live?'

I relayed Bran's question.

Black shook his head. He still had his gun out, pointed at me.

I gave an exaggerated sigh. 'No one intends your daughter harm.'

'Fine,' said Bran's voice in my ear. 'Roughly three years ago? A rogue werewolf killed by a lone wolf. There were two incidents that might fit, but only one of the lone wolves would take it upon himself to help a girl. Tell your gentleman that he's from somewhere near Washington D.C., probably in Virginia, and his werewolf friend is Josef Riddlesback.'

'Not a good idea,' I told Bran as I looked Black in the eyes. It was hard to blame him for the gun when I could read the fear in his face. 'He's worried about his daughter. She's thirteen and he doesn't want her hurt.' I had to use the tone of my voice to convey just how worried Black was. Much too worried to amaze him with Bran's powers of deduction.

'I see. A little paranoid is he?'

'Absolutely,' I agreed.

There was a short pause, then Bran said, 'Do you have a sheet of paper handy?'

'Yes.'

'Right. Josef is right, neither of the pack leaders in that area are the sort I'd trust with a child. I'm going to give you the names of the pack leaders who would be safe with a child. Leaders who would not mind a reporter knowing who they are. It is very short, and none of them are anywhere near Virginia. There are others. Do you believe his story?'

'Yes,' I said.

'Then I'll also give you places where the Alphas have not come out to the public and don't want to do so, but who would take care of a young girl. If he wants to chance it, he could go there and see if the Alpha would meet with him.'

I wrote down the names he told me, four men, including Adam, complete with phone numbers. Then I wrote down fifteen towns. Nineteen Alphas out of maybe a hundred and fifty that Bran thought could be trusted to help a child without abusing her.

It made me acknowledge just how lucky I was that the werewolf relative my mother went to for help once she realized I could turn into a coyote belonged to the Marrok and not to some other pack.

'You can send them to me, too,' he said, when he was done.

'But—' I bit my tongue. I wasn't going to tell a reporter that the Marrok was one of the wolves who wasn't out yet.

'I trust your judgement, Mercy – and I've raised a few strays before.' Like me.

'I know.'

He must have heard the gratitude in my voice, because I heard the smile in his. 'One or two, anyway, Mercy. Tell your gentleman that he needs to find someone to help as soon as possible. Unless he uses silver, which will hurt her, I doubt he'll be able to keep her in his cage forever. Not to mention that she doesn't need the moon to change. Some day she's going to be hurt or startled into changing and then she'll kill someone.' Bran hung up.

I gave Tom Black the list and explained what it meant. Then I gave him Bran's warning. As the words sank in, he lowered his gun, but I don't think it was on purpose. It was more as though he was sunk in despair and nothing mattered anymore.

'Listen,' I told him. 'There's nothing you can do about her being a werewolf—'

'She tried to commit suicide,' he told me, tears welling in his eyes. 'The day after the full moon. She's worried she will hurt someone. She used a knife on her wrist, but the cuts kept healing too fast. I'd take her to a damned shrink, but I don't want to risk telling anyone what she is. She already thinks she's a monster, she doesn't need anyone else telling her so.'

I saw Honey's eyes widen, when he said that bit about being a monster. From the expression on her face, she thought she was a monster, too.

I frowned at her. I didn't want to have sympathy for Honey – it was so much easier to dislike her. She frowned back.

'Put the gun away,' I told Black in the firm voice that sometimes worked on werewolves. I guess it worked on grieving fathers, too, because he slipped the pistol back in his shoulder holster.

'She doesn't need a shrink,' I told him. 'Every thirteen year old girl wants to kill themselves at some point or other.'

I remembered being thirteen. When I was fourteen my foster father had killed himself, and that permanently removed the impulse. I'd never do that to people I cared about.

'I expect getting locked in the basement once a month doesn't help,' I continued. 'The Marrok told me that there's every reason to expect she'll be able to control her wolf if you find an Alpha to guide her.'

He turned away and raised his hands to his face. When he turned back his tears were gone, though his eyes were moist. He took the piece of paper I'd written on, and, only after I handed it to him, the roll of money. 'Thank you for your help.'

'Wait,' I said, glancing at Honey. 'Mr Black, that werewolf who talks to you, has he ever shown you his wolf?'

'No.'

'Has he shown your daughter?'

'We only saw him once, the night he brought her back to us. The night of the attack. He left a number where he could be reached.'

'So the only wolf you've seen is your daughter, chained and out of control in her cage – and the only wolf she's ever seen is the one who attacked her?'

'That's right.'

Honey was, if anything, more beautiful in her wolf form than she was in her human form. I looked at her. Wolves communicate very well without words; she understood what I asked her to do. She also very clearly didn't understand why, though she wasn't strictly opposed to it. Black had his own secrets; he wouldn't tell anyone that Honey was a werewolf.

After a few moments of silent arguing while Black grew puzzled, I finally said, 'Honey, as much as I hate to admit it, your wolf is glorious. No one would ever think you were a monster – any more than a Siberian tiger or a golden eagle is a monster.'

Her mouth opened and closed, then she glanced at Black. 'All right,' she said in a curiously shy voice. 'Can I borrow your bathroom?'

'It will take her a little time,' I told Black when she was gone. 'Fifteen minutes or so – and she might wait a few minutes beyond that. Changing is painful and newly changed werewolves tend to be a little grumpy about it.'

'You know an awful lot about werewolves,' he said.

'I was raised by them,' I told him. I waited a moment or two, but he didn't ask me why. I suppose he was more concerned with other matters right then.

'If I were you,' I told him. 'I'd bring your daughter here to Adam.' Bran thought the girl might make it with a little help – that she wasn't a hopeless case. Adam was very strong – and he had Samuel here, who was good with young wolves. Her chances in Adam's pack were better than they would be anywhere else. 'Adam has a big house because pack members and other wolves have the tendency to drop in on him without a moment's notice. Big enough that you and your wife could stay for a while.' Adam would honor my invitation. I knew him well enough to know that he wouldn't even resent it. 'With Adam around, your daughter wouldn't have to be caged – and I think that she, and the rest of your family, would benefit from being around a pack of wolves for a while. They are dangerous and terrifying, but they can be beautiful, too.' Adam would keep his pack from scaring the humans.

'Josef – the werewolf I know – told me that there are benefits to being a werewolf. He said—' Black's voice tightened and he had to stop for a moment. 'He said that hunting was the best thing he'd ever felt. The kill. The blood.'

Stupid werewolf, I thought. Heck of a thing to tell the parent of a thirteen-year-old girl, truthful or not.

'Werewolves heal incredibly fast,' I told him. 'They are strong, graceful. She'll never grow old. And the pack . . . I don't know how to explain it to you, I'm not sure that I understand it myself, but a wolf with a good pack is never alone.'

I looked him straight in the eye and said, 'She can be happy, Mr Black. Safe and happy, and not a danger to herself or anyone else. It's horrible that she was attacked and a miracle that she survived – I've never heard of a child that young surviving an attack. Being a werewolf is different, but it is not terrible.'

I smelled fur and turned to look at the doorway before Honey walked in. She was a small werewolf, about the height of a large German Shepherd though heavier in the body and leg. Her fur was a light fawn color with a darker undercoat and a silvery stripe down her back almost the same color as her crystal gray eyes.

A werewolf's shoulder is articulated more like a tiger or bear than a wolf, giving them lateral motion and the ability to use their impressive claws. With some of the bigger males, the effect can be almost grotesque, but Honey fit together well. When she moved she looked gracile and strong, just not entirely canid.

I smiled at her – she wagged her tail and ducked her head. It took me a moment to realize why she did that. Since Adam had claimed me as his mate, I was higher in the pecking order than she was.

I didn't remember any of the rest of Adam's pack acting

submissive to me, though. But then I didn't usually run into Adam's pack in wolf form – and in human form . . . well, theoretically their behavior should be the same. But some things were harder on a human mind than a wolf's. I imagine they all had a hard time being submissive to a coyote, especially because they all knew I was Adam's mate only as a courtesy.

I felt my smile widen though, as I thought about the havoc I could cause by insisting that they all treat me with proper pack etiquette. Wouldn't work; I was actually surprised that Adam's claim had worked well enough to keep some of them from bothering me, but it might be worth trying just to see Adam's face.

Honey's summer coat wasn't as splendid as her winter one, but it revealed the play of muscle in a way her thicker fur would not have. She knew it, too, and found a square of sunlight to pose in.

Black took a step back as she approached, but, after that first step, he held his ground. Honey gave him time to adjust before she continued forward, sitting down within touching distance.

'She's beautiful,' he said, his voice only a little tight. If I hadn't been able to hear the speed of his pulse, I wouldn't have known how scared he was. If he reacted this way to his daughter, it was no wonder she was having troubles.

Honey, though, had been a werewolf for a long time and her control was excellent. She gave no sign that he was able to detect how much the scent of his fear was exciting her, and after a few minutes his fear began to die down.

'My daughter could be like this?' he asked me, sounding more naked than a man should when surrounded by strangers.

I nodded my head.

'How soon?'

'On her own? That depends upon her. But in the presence of an Alpha, immediately.'

'No more cages,' he whispered.

I couldn't let him think that. 'Not metal ones,' I told him. 'But once she is a member of the pack, she'll fall out of your control and into the Alpha's. That can be a cage of sorts, though a more comfortable cage.'

He took a deep, shaky breath. 'Can she understand me?' he asked, nodding toward Honey.

'Yes, but she can't talk.'

'All right.' He looked straight in her eyes, not realizing he was challenging her. I almost said something to him, but Honey didn't seem to be bothered, so I let it go.

'If you had a daughter,' he asked her, 'would you bring her here? Would you trust her to Hauptman?'

She smiled at him, not so widely as to display her sharp white teeth, and wagged her tail.

He looked at me. 'If I bring her here, will he take her away from us?'

I wasn't sure how to answer him. Adam wouldn't see it that way, to him the wolves were all his family, but conveying that to someone who hadn't been around a pack was diffi-cult – and I'm not sure that a father would find it any better. How do you give up your child, even for their own good? That was a question I had never asked my mother.

'He'll take her under his wing,' I said at last. 'He'll take responsibility for her welfare – and he will not lightly give up that responsibility. He'd never refuse to let you see her. If she is unhappy in Adam's pack, there are other options, especially once she has control of herself.'

'She can become a lone wolf,' he said, relaxing.

I shook my head. I wouldn't lie to him. 'No. They'd never let a female out on her own. There are too few of them, for one thing, and the males . . . are too protective to allow a female to fend for themselves. But she could request to change packs.'

The lines on his face deepened and he swore. Three times. Honey whined. She might have been sympathetic, or just protesting the foul language. I didn't trust myself to predict Honey anymore.

'What are your alternatives?' I asked him. 'If she kills someone, the wolves will have to hunt her down. How would she feel if she hurts you or her mother?'

He took out his cell phone and stared at it.

'Would you like me to call him for you?' I asked.

'No,' he said and riffled around in his pocket for the paper with Adam's phone number on it. He stared at it for a moment, then almost whispered, 'I'll call him tonight.'

7

'Hey, Mercy, what'cha workin' on? Looks like a miniature Corvette.'

I looked up to see Tony, cop and old friend – usually in that order – leaning up against one of my work benches. Today he was dressed casually in a thin shirt and khaki shorts appropriate to the hot summer day. Tony looked a bit frayed around the edges. It had been a little over two weeks since the sorcerer had moved into town and, according to the local news, the crime rate had been skyrocketing.

'Good eye,' I told him. 'It's a '71 Opel GT, designed by the same guy who designed the Corvette. Friend of mine bought it from some guy who replaced its wussy original engine with a Honda engine.'

'He didn't do it right?'

'He did it fine. Excellent job of refitting it, as a matter of fact. I couldn't have done a better job myself.' I grinned at him. 'Only problem is that a Honda engine turns to the right and the Opel was designed for a lefty.'

'Which means?'

I patted the sleek fender and grinned at him. 'It only goes twenty miles per hour forward, but can break one hundred backward if you use all four gears.'

He laughed. 'Cute car.' He stared at it for a minute and the smile fell away from his face. 'Listen. Can I take you out to lunch? Business, so I'll foot the bill.'

'Kennewick PD needs a mechanic?' I asked.

'No. But I think you can help us.'

I washed up, changed out of my work clothes and met him back in the office. Honey looked up when I came in. Last week, her second week of guard duty, she'd turned up in jeans (pressed) with a folding chair, small desk, laptop and cell phone. Working out of my office was almost as good, she claimed, as working out of her own. Ever since the incident with Black, we'd been treating each other with cautious friendliness.

'I'm going to lunch with Tony,' I announced. 'I'll be back in an hour or so. Gabriel, would you call Charlie about his Opel, and tell him the price we got on that used Mazda RX7 engine? The cost won't make him happy, but the RX will fit.'

Honey looked up at me, but she didn't protest me leaving, as I half expected her to.

'I hope you don't mind if we walk,' Tony said as we stepped out into the sweltering heat. 'I think better when I'm moving.'

'Fine with me.'

We took the shortcut into downtown Kennewick, over the train tracks and through a couple of empty lots. Honey trailed behind us, but she was good enough that I don't think Tony spotted her.

Downtown is one of the older sections of town, small businesses in old buildings surrounded by Craftsman and Victorian houses, mostly built in the twenties and thirties. Efforts had been made to make the shopping area look inviting, but there were a few too many empty shops for it to look prosperous.

I expected him to talk to me while we were walking, but he didn't. I held my peace and let him think.

'It's pretty hot for walking,' he said finally.

'I like the heat,' I told him. 'And the cold. I like living somewhere that actually has all four seasons. Montana has two. Nine months of winter, three months where it almost warms up, then back to winter. Sometimes the leaves actually get to turn colors before the first snow hits. I remember it snowing on the Fourth of July once.'

He didn't say anything more, so I supposed he hadn't been trying to make small talk – but I didn't know what else he could have been trying for with his comment, either.

He took me to a small coffee shop where we ordered at the counter and then were escorted into a dark, cool room filled with small tables. The atmosphere the owners had been trying for was probably an English pub. Never having been to England, I couldn't tell how close they'd gotten, but it appealed to me.

'So what am I here for?' I asked him finally, after soup and a largish sandwich appeared before me, and the waitress left us alone. It was late for lunch and early for dinner so we had the room to ourselves.

'Look,' he said after a moment. 'That sour old guy who used to be your boss, the one who still comes in once in a while – he's fae, right?'

Zee had publicly acknowledged his heritage for a long time, so I nodded my head and took a bite of sandwich.

He took a gulp of water. 'I've seen Hauptman, the were-wolf, at your garage at least twice.'

'He's my neighbor,' I said. The sandwich was pretty good. I was betting they made their own bread. I'd had better soup, though, too much salt.

Tony frowned at me and said intensely, 'You're the only one who always knows who I am, no matter what disguise I wear.' Tony was an undercover cop with a talent for changing his appearance. We'd become acquainted after I'd recognized him and almost blown his cover.

'Mmm?' My mouth was full on purpose because I didn't want to say anything more until he got to his point.

'The fae are supposed to be able to change their appearance. Is that how you always know me?'

'I'm not fae, Tony,' I told him after I swallowed. 'Zee is. The fae change their appearance by magic – glamour, they call it. I'm not entirely sure that the fae can see through each other's glamour – I certainly can't.'

There was a short silence as Tony adjusted what he had been going to say.

'But you know something about the fae. And you know something about the werewolves?'

'Because Hauptman is my neighbor?'

'Because you were dating him. A friend of mine saw you at a restaurant with him.'

I looked at him and then pointedly around the restaurant.

He got it. 'He said it looked like you two were pretty hot and heavy.'

Defeated, I conceded. 'I went out with him a couple of times.'

'Are you still?'

'No.' I'd put too much emphasis on it.

I'd made a point to stay out of Adam's way since I'd almost made out with him in his garage. Remembering that made me feel like a coward. I didn't want to talk about Adam if I could help it. Truth was, I didn't know what to do about him.

'I'm not fae.' I decided not to eat the rest of the soup, but I opened the crackers and munched on them. 'I'm not a werewolf.'

He looked like he didn't want to believe me, but he chose not to confront my answer directly. 'But you know some of them. Some fae and some werewolves.'

'Yes.'

Tony set down his spoon and gripped the edge of the

table with both hands. 'Look, Mercy. Violent crime always goes up in the summer. The heat makes tempers shorter. We know that. But I've never seen anything like this. It started with that murder-suicide in the Pasco hotel a few weeks ago, but it didn't stop there. We're working double shifts trying to handle the load. Last night I took in a guy I've known for years. He has three kids and a wife who adores him. Yesterday he came home from work and tried to beat her to death. This just isn't normal, not even in the middle of a heat wave.'

I shrugged, feeling as helpless as I doubtless looked. I knew things were bad, but I hadn't realized how bad.

'I'll ask Zee, but I don't think it's anything the fae are doing.' I had to quash any hint of that – it might be dangerous for Tony if he started poking around. The fae don't like the police prying into their business. 'The last thing they want is to frighten the general population. If one of them were doing something like this, the whole community would search them out and take care of it.'

I hadn't talked to Zee for a few days. Maybe I ought to call him and suggest that the police were looking toward them for answers to the outbreak in violence – without using Tony's name. I didn't know what they could do against a vampire who was also a sorcerer. The fae weren't very organized, and tended to ignore other people's problems. They knew about Littleton – because Zee knew – but they seemed to be content to let the vampires and wolves search him out. But if the situation started to put a little pressure on them, maybe they'd help find him – Warren and Stefan hadn't been making much headway. The trick would be to make certain that the fae applied their efforts against the villain, and not against the police.

'What?' asked Tony sharply. 'What were you thinking?'

Whoops. 'I thought that it might be a good idea to let Zee

know what you just told me. Just in case there's something they can do about it.' I can lie, but living among werewolves, many of whom can smell a falsehood, had made me pretty adept at using the truth to my advantage.

'And the werewolves?'

I shook my head. 'Werewolves are pretty simple creatures – that's why they make good soldiers. If there were a rogue werewolf out here, there might be dead' – I found a hasty substitute for *bodies* – '*animals*, but not regular people going berserk for no good reason. The wolves aren't magical like the fae are.'

I slapped my hands lightly on my thighs and leaned forward. 'Listen, I am happy to help you with what little I know about fae and werewolves. I will make a point of talking to Zee – but, as you said, we're in the middle of a heat wave. We've been in the three digits for a long time with no sign of cooler weather. It's enough to make anyone crazy.'

He shook his head. 'Not Mike. He didn't lose his temper when his wife wrecked his '57 T-Bird. I tell you I know this guy. I played basketball in high school with him. He doesn't have a temper to lose. He wouldn't just lose it and beat up his wife because his AC frizzed out.'

I hate guilt. Hate it worse when I know that I have nothing to feel guilty about. I was *not* responsible for Littleton.

Still, how would it be to hurt someone you loved? I could see his friend's situation was eating at Tony – and I had a strong surge of sympathy, and guilt. I couldn't do anything either.

'Get your friend a good lawyer – and get him and his family to see a therapist. If you need names, I have a friend who is a divorce lawyer – I know he has a couple of counselors he recommends to his clients.'

Tony jerked his head in a motion I took to be a nod, and

we finished lunch in silence. I took a couple of dollars out of my pocket and tucked them under my plate for a tip. They were damp with sweat, but I expect the waitresses were used to dealing with that this summer.

As soon as we exited the restaurant, I could smell a were-wolf – and it wasn't Honey. I glanced at the people around us and recognized one of Adam's wolves looking in the window of a secondhand store. Since he didn't look the type to be really interested in the display of old baby buggies, he must be guarding me. I wondered what had happened to Honey.

'What's wrong?' Tony asked as we walked past my security detail.

'Stray thought,' I told him. 'I guess the heat's making me crabby, too.'

'Listen, Mercy,' he said, 'I appreciate you coming out with me like this. And I'd like to take you up on your offer to help us. Seattle and Spokane have specialists who deal with the fae for them – some of those cops *are* fae. We don't have anyone like that. We don't have any werewolves either' – they did, at least the Richland PD did, but if they didn't know that, I wasn't going to tell him – 'and it would be good not to be wandering around totally in the dark for a change.'

I hadn't meant to offer to help the police – that would be too dangerous. I opened my mouth to say so, and then stopped.

The trick to staying out of trouble, Bran had told me, is to keep your nose out of other people's business. If it became known that I was consulting with the police, I could find myself in big trouble.

Adam I could deal with, it was the fae I worried about, them and the vampires. I knew too much and I didn't expect that they would trust me to judge how much to tell the police.

Still, it didn't seem fair that the police were responsible for keeping the peace when they only knew the things that the fae and the werewolves wanted them to know. There were too many ways that could prove deadly. If something happened to Tony or one of the good guys and I could have prevented it, I'd never sleep a night through again. Not that I'd been doing particularly well at sleeping lately anyway.

'Fine,' I said. 'Here's some free advice. Make sure that none of your co-workers starts stirring up the fae over this.'

'Why not?' he asked.

I took my first step out into the abyss, and told him something that might get me in real trouble. I glanced around, but if the werewolf was still tailing us, he was doing a really good job. Since Adam's people were usually more than competent, I dropped my voice to a bare whisper. 'Because the fae aren't as gentle or powerless as they try to let on. It would not be a good thing if they decided someone was looking their way for this rise in violence.'

Tony missed a step and almost tripped over a railroad tie. 'What do you mean?'

'I mean never put yourself in a position where harm to you would make the fae community here safer.' I gave him a reassuring smile. 'It is not in their best interest to harm anyone – and they usually police themselves so that you don't have to. If one of them is breaking the law, he will be taken care of. You just need to be careful not to make yourself a threat to them.'

He absorbed that for half a block. 'What can you tell me about dealing with the werewolves?'

'Here?' I asked waving my hand vaguely at the city around us. 'Talk to Adam Hauptman before you try to question someone you think might be a werewolf. In another city, find out who's in charge and talk to them.'

'Get permission from their Alpha before speaking to

them?' he asked a little incredulously. 'You mean like we have to talk to parents before questioning a minor?' Bran had let the public know about Alphas, but not exactly how rigid the pack structure really is.

'Mmm,' I looked at the sky for inspiration. None came, so I tried to muddle through it on my own. 'A child can't rip your arm off, Tony. Adam can see to it that they answer your questions without hurting anyone. Werewolves can be . . . volatile. Adam can help with that.'

'You mean they'll tell us whatever he wants us to hear.'

I took a deep breath. 'This is important for you to believe: Adam is one of the good guys. He really is. That's not true of all pack leaders, but Adam's on your side. He can help you, *and* as long as you don't offend him, he will. He's been pack leader here for a long time because he's good at his job – let him do it.'

I don't know if Tony decided to believe me or not, but thinking about it kept him occupied until we stopped next to his car in my lot.

'Thanks, Mercy.'

'I didn't help.' I shrugged. 'I'll talk to Zee. Heck, maybe he knows someone who can give us a break in the weather.' Not likely. Weather was Great Magic, not something that most fae had the power to alter.

'If you were a real Indian, you could do a rain dance.'

Tony could tease me because his Venezuelan half was mostly Indian of one sort of other.

I shook my head solemnly. 'In Montana, the Indians don't have a rain dance, they have a Stop-this-Damned-Wind-and-Snow dance. If you've ever been to Browning, Montana, in the winter, you'll know it doesn't work.'

Tony laughed as he got in his car and started it. He left the door open to let the heat out, holding a hand in front of the vent to catch the first trickle of cold air.

'It'll probably cool down about the time I get to the station,' he said.

'Toughen up,' I advised him.

He grinned, shut his door and drove off. It was only then that I realized Honey's car wasn't in the lot.

Gabriel looked up when I came in. 'Mr Hauptman called for you,' he said. 'He said you should check your cell phone for messages.'

I found the cell phone where I'd left it, on top of a rolling tool chest in the shop.

'Just picked up Warren,' Adam's voice had that calm and brisk rhythm he only used when things were really bad. 'We're taking him to my house now. You should meet us there.'

I called Adam's house, but the answering machine picked up. So I called Samuel's cell.

'Samuel?'

'I'm on my way to Adam's house now,' he told me. 'I won't know anything until I get there.'

I didn't ask if Warren was hurt. Adam's voice had told me that much. 'I'll be there in ten minutes.' Not that it mattered, I thought, pressing the END button. There wasn't anything that I could do to help.

I told Gabriel to hold the fort, and to lock up at five.

'Werewolf troubles?' he asked.

I nodded. 'Warren's hurt.'

'You all right to drive?' he asked.

I nodded again and dashed out the door. I was halfway to my car when I realized that probably no one would have thought to call Kyle. I hesitated. Warren and Kyle weren't an item anymore – but I didn't think it was due to lack of caring on either of their parts. So I found Kyle's office number on my phone's memory and got in touch with his hyper-efficient office manager.

'I'm sorry,' she told me. 'He's unavailable right now, may I take your name and number?'

'This is Mercedes Thompson.' It wasn't easy to buckle in with one hand, but I managed. 'My phone number—'

'Ms Thompson? Hold on, I'll patch you through.'

Huh. Kyle must have put me on his important people list. I listened to classical music in my ear as I turned onto Chemical Drive and put my foot down. I was pretty sure the driver of the green Taurus behind me was the werewolf who had been tailing me.

'What's up, Mercy?' Kyle's soothing voice replaced Chopin before I made it to the WELCOME TO FINLEY sign.

'Warren's hurt. I don't know how badly, but Adam called in the troops.'

'I'm in my car near Twenty-seventh and 395,' he said. 'Where is Warren?'

Behind me, I saw flashing lights as the police car that usually hid just past the railroad overpass pulled over the Taurus. I put my foot down harder on the gas.

'At Adam's house.'

'I'll be there shortly.' As he hung up, I heard his Jag's big V-12 open up.

He didn't beat me there, but I was still arguing with the idiot at the front door when he skidded to a stop, splattering gravel all over.

I pulled out my cell phone and played Adam's message for the door guard. 'He's expecting me,' I grated.

The idiot shook his head. 'My orders are no one but pack.'

'She *is* pack, Elliot, you moron,' said Honey, coming to the door behind the big man. 'Adam's claimed her as his mate – which you very well know. Let her in.' Honey's hand clamped on Elliot's arm and dragged him back from the door.

I grabbed Kyle's arm and pulled him past the obstreperous

moron-guard. There were werewolves everywhere. I knew that there were only about thirty wolves in Adam's pack, but I'd have sworn there were twice that in the living room.

'This is Kyle,' I told Honey, leading Kyle to the stairs.

'Hello, Kyle,' Honey said softly. 'Warren's told me about you.' I hadn't realized she was a friend of Warren's, but her smeared mascara told me she'd been crying.

She didn't follow us up the stairs — doubtless she'd have a few unhappy moments with Elliot before she could do anything else. Idiot or not, Elliot was a dominant, and so higher in the pack than Honey, who took her rank from her submissive husband. Have I mentioned that werewolf etiquette is stuck in another century? Honey had really put her neck out for us.

Adam's house has five bedrooms, but I didn't have to guess where Warren was. I could smell the blood from the top of the stairs, and Darryl, Adam's second, stood watch at the door like a Nubian guarding the Pharaoh.

He frowned heavily at me. I was pretty sure it was for bringing a human into pack business. But I had no patience for it right now.

'Go rescue Honey from that idiot who was trying to keep me out.'

He hesitated.

'Go.' I couldn't see Adam, but it was his command that sent Darryl past us and down the stairs.

Kyle entered the room first, then stopped abruptly, blocking my sight of the room. I had to duck under his arm and scoot past before I got a good look.

It was bad.

They'd stripped the bed down to its bottom sheet and Samuel was working furiously over the battered, bloody thing that was Warren. I didn't blame Kyle for hesitating. If I hadn't smelled him, I would never have known who the man on the bed was, there was so little left that was recognizable.

Adam leaned against the wall, out of Samuel's way. Sometimes, if a pack member is badly hurt, flesh and blood of the Alpha can help heal him. Adam's left arm had a fresh bandage. He looked over at us, his gaze taking in Kyle. When he looked at me, he nodded once, in approval.

Samuel saw Kyle and directed him over to the bed next to Warren's head with a jerk of his chin.

'Talk to him,' Samuel said. 'He can make it if he wants to badly enough. You just need to give him a reason.' Then to me he said, 'Stay out of my way unless I ask you for something.'

Kyle, dressed in slacks that cost more than I made in a month, sat without hesitation on the bloodstained floor next to the bed and began talking quietly about baseball, of all things. I tuned him out and concentrated on Warren, as if I could hold him here by sheer force of will. His breath was shallow and unsteady.

'Samuel thinks the damage was done last night,' Adam murmured to me. 'I've got people out looking for Ben, who was with Warren, but there's no sign of him yet.'

'What about Stefan?' I asked.

Adam's eyes narrowed a bit, but I met his gaze anyway, too upset to worry about damned dominance or any other kind of games.

'No sign of any vampire,' he said finally. 'Whoever hurt Warren, dropped him at Uncle Mike's.' Uncle Mike's was a bar of sorts in Pasco, a local hangout for the fae. 'The man who opened today found him in the Dumpster when he was taking out the trash. He called Uncle Mike, who called me.'

'If it was done last night, why isn't he healing better than this?' I asked, hugging myself tightly. Anything that could do this to Warren could have done the same or worse to

Stefan. What if Warren died? What if Stefan were already dead — the never-to-rise-again dead — left somewhere else, in some other Dumpster. I thought of the joyous way Littleton had killed the maid. Why had I allowed myself to be convinced that the wolves and the vampires would be a match for him?

'Most of the damage was probably done with a silver blade,' Samuel told me in an absent voice — he was paying attention to his work. 'The other wounds, the broken bones, are healing more slowly because his body is overtaxed trying to heal everything at once.'

'Do you know where they went last night?' I asked. Samuel's hands were so quick with the needle. I couldn't tell how he knew where to set stitches because Warren looked like so much hamburger to me.

'I don't know,' Adam said. 'Warren called me with reports of what they did, not what they were planning to do.'

'Have you called Stefan's house?'

'Even if he were there, he wouldn't be awake yet.'

I pulled out my cell phone and called Stefan's number and waited for his answering machine to pick up. 'This is Mercedes Thompson,' I said clearly, hoping someone was listening. I knew that Stefan didn't live in the seethe, but he probably didn't live alone. Vampires need blood donors, and willing victims were much safer than taking someone off the street.

'Last night Stefan went out hunting. One of his comrades is in seriously bad shape and we don't know where the other one is. I need to know if Stefan came back last night.'

There was a click as someone, a woman, picked up the phone and whispered, 'No,' and then hung up.

Adam flexed his fingers, as if he'd been clenching them too much. 'Littleton took two werewolves and an old vampire—'

'Two vampires,' I said. 'At least Stefan had another vampire assigned to help him.'

'Warren said the second vampire wasn't much use.'

I shrugged.

'Two werewolves and two vampires, then.' Adam seemed to be working something out. 'Stefan had already fallen to him once; that makes Warren the strongest of the party. It wasn't chance that he was the one given back. 'See,' Littleton is telling us, 'send your best against me and see what I return to you.' Littleton didn't finish him off because he wanted us to know he didn't consider Warren a threat. He doesn't care if Warren survived to go after him again or not. This . . .' Adam's voice deepened into a rough growl '. . . *thing* has drawn a line in the sand and dared me to cross.'

Adam knew how to play mind games. I think it's a requirement for being an Alpha. Or maybe it was just from his time in the army, which, according to his stories, wasn't that different, politically speaking, from the pack.

'And the others?' I asked.

He didn't say anything, just shook his head. I hugged myself again, feeling cold.

'So what are you going to do?' I asked.

He smiled unhappily. 'I'm going to play Littleton's game. I have no choice. I can't leave him running around in my territory.'

Just then Warren's breathing, which part of me was listening to with rapt attention, stopped. Adam heard it too, crouching as if there were an enemy in the room. Maybe there was. Death is an enemy, right?

Samuel swore, but it was Kyle who came off the floor, tipped Warren's chin and began CPR with silent desperation.

I hadn't been able to hear Warren's heart, but it must have stopped, too, because Samuel started chest compressions.

Useless again, I watched them fight for Warren's life. I was really tired of being unable to do anything while people were dying.

After what seemed like a long time, Samuel pulled Kyle away saying, 'It's okay, he's breathing. You can stop now.' He had to repeat himself several times before Kyle understood.

'He'll be all right?' he asked, sounding quite different from his usual airy tones.

'He's breathing on his own, and his heart is beating,' Samuel said.

It wasn't exactly an agreement, but Kyle didn't seem to notice. He sank back onto the carpet and started telling a story as if he'd never been interrupted. His voice showed none of the strain in his face.

'Tell me what I need to know about demons,' I told Adam, though I couldn't take my eyes off of Warren. I had the strangest feeling that if I quit watching him, he would die.

There was a long pause. He knew why I wanted to know. If he didn't tell me what he could now – didn't help me with what I intended – then he wasn't the man for me.

'Demons are evil, nasty, and powerless unless they manage to attach themselves like a parasite to some damned fool. Either they are invited in as a guest – which is what makes a sorcerer, or they sneak in because someone weak of will does an evil thing. A simple demon possession doesn't last long because the possessed man cannot blend in: a demon in control wants one thing – destruction. A sorcerer, someone who controls the demon by means of a bargain, is far more deadly. A sorcerer may live undetected by the human population for years. Eventually, the sorcerer will lose control, and the demon takes over.'

Nothing I hadn't known.

'How do you kill a demon?' I asked. Samuel's hands were once more sliding needle and thread through bloody flesh.

'You can't,' Adam said. 'All you can do is remove the threat by killing its host. In this case, Littleton, who is a vampire, bolstered with the demon's magic.' He took a breath. 'Not any kind of prey for a coyote. You can leave it to us, Mercy. We'll see that he is dead.' He was right. I knew it. I was useless.

I noticed that Kyle was staring at us with wide eyes, though he didn't pause in his baseball story, something about when he was in Little League.

'Did you think that werewolves were the worst monster in the world?' I asked Kyle in a nasty tone. I didn't know until I spoke how angry I was. It wasn't right, taking it out on Kyle, but I couldn't seem to stop my mouth. He had rejected Warren for being a monster – maybe he ought to learn more about monsters. 'There are a lot worse things out there. Vampires, demons, and all sorts of nasties and the only thing that stands between the humans and them are people like Warren.' Even as I said it, I knew I wasn't being fair. I knew that being lied to had bothered Kyle as much as finding out that Warren was a werewolf.

'Mercy,' said Adam. 'Shh.'

It seemed as if his words carried a cool wind of peace that swept over me, washing away all the anger, the frustration and the fear, the Alpha werewolf calming his wolf – only I wasn't his wolf. He had done it again.

I jerked around to stare at him; he was watching Warren intently. If he'd done this to me on purpose, he wasn't concerned about it. But I was pretty sure he'd done it out of habit, because it shouldn't have worked on me.

Damn it.

Warren made a noise, the first one I'd heard out of him since we'd come into the room. I'd have been happier if he hadn't sounded scared.

'Easy, Warren,' Adam told him. 'You're safe here.'

'If you die on us, you won't be,' said Kyle with a growl that would have done credit to any of the werewolves in the room.

Battered, bruised, and bloody they might be, but Warren's lips could still smile. But only a very little bit.

Samuel, his work apparently finished, pulled the old bentwood rocker from its place in the hall and set it next to the foot of Warren's bed, leaving the space at the head of the bed to Kyle. Samuel leaned forward in the chair, elbows on the bentwood arms and rested his chin on his folded hands. He looked as though he was watching his shoes, but I knew better. His attention was on his patient, listening for a change in breathing or heartbeat that might signal trouble. He was capable of sitting there, motionless, for hours – Samuel had a reputation as a very patient hunter.

The rest of us mimicked his quiet stillness as Warren drifted to sleep – except for Kyle, who had dropped back into his trials as a ten-year-old third baseman.

While Warren dozed restlessly, there was a steady, but silent, stream of visitors over the next hour. Some of them were friends, but most of them were just checking out the damage. If Adam – or Samuel – had not been there, it would have been dangerous for Warren. Werewolves, outside of a well-run pack, will kill the wounded or weak.

Adam leaned on the wall, watching the visitors with brooding intensity. I could see the effect of his regard as his wolves (and even though they were in human form, they were still his wolves) entered the room. As soon as they saw him, their footfalls quieted further. They dropped their heads, tucked their hands under the opposite arms, took a quick, comprehensive look at Warren's wounds and left.

When Honey came in, she was sporting a bruise on the side of her face that was healing visibly fast. A half hour

later there would have been no sign of it at all. She gave
Adam a quick look from the hallway. He nodded his head
– it was the first reaction he'd given to any of the visitors.

She scooted around Samuel's chair, then sat down on the
floor beside Kyle. She gave Adam another look, but when
he didn't object she quietly introduced herself to Kyle,
touched him on the shoulder, then settled against the wall
with her head leaned back and her eyes closed.

A few visitors later a blond man with a short, reddish
beard came into the room. I didn't know him by sight,
though I recognized his scent as belonging to one of Adam's
pack. I'd quit paying attention to the visitors – and would
have ignored this one as well except for two things.

His posture didn't change as he walked through the
doorway – and Adam's did. Adam pushed against the wall
with his shoulders, propelling himself completely upright.
Then he took two steps forward until he stood between
Warren and the stranger.

The red bearded man was a head taller than Adam, and
for a second tried to use that extra height as an advantage
– but he was no match for the Alpha. Without a word or
an aggressive move, Adam backed him down.

Samuel appeared not to notice anything. I doubt that
anyone else would have seen readiness in the slowly tightening muscles of his shoulder.

'When he is well,' Adam said, 'if you give fair challenge,
Paul, I won't stop the fight.'

Under the Marrok's rule, there were very few sanctioned
fights – real fights, not just a couple of snaps and a bite or
two. That was one of the reasons there were more werewolves
in the New World than in Europe, where the werewolf, like
the fae, had originated.

I can usually sort out the pack from most dominant to
least (or the reverse), just from body language. Wolves are

better at it than I am. Humans, if they pay attention, do the same thing – though it's not nearly as important to them as it is to the wolves. For a human it might mean getting a promotion or not, or winning a hard-fought argument. For a werewolf, survival depends upon the pack – and a pack is a complex social and military hierarchy that depends upon each member knowing exactly what his place is.

Dominance among wolves is a combination of force of personality, strength of will, physical ability and a component of *other* that I can't explain to anyone without the eyes, ears, and nose to sense it – and those with the proper senses wouldn't need it explained. Willingness to fight is as close as I can come. It is because of that *other* that, outside of a pack, the natural dominance of a wolf changes within a fairly broad range. Like all of us, some days they are tired, depressed, or happy – all of these affect natural dominance.

In a pack, these natural swings are gradually sifted through. In wolves that are near-dominants, sometimes a fight between them will allow strength to determine pack rank. An Alpha's second and third were the next two most dominant males in the pack.

Warren, among enemies, was quiet and watchful, rather than adapting the more typical aggressiveness of a dominant male. His body language skills weren't even as good as mine because he'd spent so little time with a pack when he was first Changed. He ran beside the pack, rather than inside it. Because of that, he was vulnerable to challenge from wolves who thought they might be stronger, better, faster.

It was Adam, I knew, who told the others that Warren was his third. If Adam had been less dominant, less well-liked or respected, there would have been blood shed over his declaration. I knew Adam's determination was right – but I was one of the few people for whom Warren dropped his guard.

A significant minority of the wolves felt that Warren wasn't strong enough for the position he held. I knew – from Jesse rather than from any of the wolves involved – that some of the wolves wanted Warren out of the pack or, even better, dead.

Evidently this Paul was one of those, and one dominant enough to challenge Warren. Something Adam had just given him permission to do.

Paul gave a small, pleased nod and left the room with brisk steps, unaware that Warren would wipe the floor with him. If Warren survived – by Samuel's careful focus, I knew that was still in doubt.

Adam watched the man leave with a brooding gaze. He lifted it at last and saw me watching him. His eyes narrowed and he came up to me and took my arm, tugging me out of the room behind him.

He led me to Jesse's room, hesitated and dropped my arm. He knocked once, lightly, on her door and then opened it. She was sitting on the floor with her back against the bed, her nose red and tears running slowly down her face.

'He's holding his own,' Adam told her.

She scrambled to her feet. 'Can I go see him?'

'Be quiet,' he told her.

She nodded and headed for Warren's room. When she saw me, she hesitated, then gave me a smile like sunshine peeking out from the clouds of Warren's condition. Then she hurried past.

'Come,' Adam took my arm again – I really disliked that – and escorted me to another closed door. This one he opened without knocking.

I held hard to my irritation as I jerked free and walked all the way into the room. If I was irritated, I wouldn't be afraid. I really hated it that I was afraid of Adam now.

I folded my arms and kept my back to him, only then realizing that he'd brought me to his bedroom.

I'd have recognized it as Adam's room, even if it hadn't smelled of him. He loved textures and warm colors and the room reflected that from the dark brown Berber carpet to the Venetian plaster treatment on the buttercream walls. There was an oil painting as tall as I was and twice as wide on one wall, a mountain forest scene. The artist had resisted the impulse to add an eagle in the air or a deer in the stream.

A human might have found the painting boring.

I touched the canvas before I realized I had moved. I wasn't familiar with the name of the artist, which was scrawled almost illegibly on the lower right corner and on a small brass plaque on the center of the frame. The title of the piece was *Sanctuary*.

I turned away from the painting to find Adam staring at me. He had his arms crossed and there were the little white marks along his wide cheekbones that told me he was in a temper. That in itself wasn't unusual. He had a hot temper and I was pretty good at getting him worked up – though not lately. And not, I would have sworn, today.

'I had no choice,' he snapped at me.

I stared at him without the foggiest notion what he was talking about.

My doubtlessly stupid look seemed to enrage him further. 'This will keep Paul from ambushing him. It has to be a real challenge, in front of witnesses.'

'I know,' I told him. Did he think I was stupid?

Adam watched me for a few seconds then turned away and began to pace rapidly back and forth across the room. When he stopped, he faced me again and said, 'Warren has more control of his wolf than any of my others, and Ben, despite his attitude is nearly as good. They were the best of my wolves to send after the sorcerer.'

'Did I ever say differently?' I snapped. The painting had distracted me – but Adam reminded me that I was trying to be angry with him. Happily that wasn't difficult.

'You're angry with me,' he said.

'You're yelling at me,' I told him. 'Of course I'm mad.'

He waved his hands impatiently. 'I don't mean now. I mean earlier in Warren's room.'

'I was angry with the stupid wolf who came in to challenge Warren as soon as he was lying on his back,' which reminded me of how Adam had scared me when he'd used the Alpha thing to calm me down. But I wasn't up to talking about that yet. 'I wasn't mad at *you* until you grabbed me by the arm and dragged me out of the room to yell at me.'

'Damn it,' he said. 'Sorry.' He looked at me and then looked away. Robbed of his defensive anger, he looked tired and worried.

'Warren and Ben are not your fault,' I told him. 'They both volunteered.'

'They wouldn't have gone if I hadn't allowed it. I knew it was dangerous,' he snarled, the anger back as quickly as it had gone.

'Do you think that you are the only one entitled to feel guilty about Warren – and about Ben?'

'*You* didn't send them out,' he said. 'I did.'

'The only reason they knew about the sorcerer was because of me,' I said. Then because I could see that he really felt guilty I told him my own worse deed. 'I *prayed* that they would catch the sorcerer.'

He looked at me incredulously, then laughed, a harsh and bitter sound. 'You think that *praying* makes you responsible for Warren's condition?'

He didn't believe. I don't know why it shocked me so. I knew a lot of people who didn't believe in God, any God. But all the werewolves I'd grown up with were believers.

Adam looked at my face and laughed again at the expression.

'You are such an innocent,' he said in a low angry purr. 'I learned a long time ago that God is a myth. I prayed every hour for six months in a stinking foreign swamp before I opened my eyes – and a crazy werewolf finished teaching me that there is no God.' His eyes lightened from warm brown to cool yellow as he spoke. 'I don't know. Maybe there is. If so, He's a sadist who watches His children shoot at each other and blow themselves up without doing something.'

He was pretty wound up because he wasn't even making sense – and Adam usually made sense even when he was shouting at the top of his lungs. He knew it too, because he turned abruptly and strode over to the big picture window that looked out over the Columbia.

The river was nearly a mile wide just here. Sometimes, when it was stormy, the water could appear nearly black, but today the sun turned it a glittery, bright blue.

'You've been avoiding me,' he said, sounding calmer.

The other window looked out over my place. I was gratified to see that the partially dissected Rabbit was framed in the center of his view.

'Mercy.'

I just kept looking out the window. Lying would be pointless and telling the truth would lead to the next question, which I didn't want to answer.

'Why?' He asked it anyway.

I glanced over my shoulder, but he was still looking out the other window. I turned around and hitched a hip on the window sill. He knew why. I'd seen it in his eyes when I walked away from the garage. And if he didn't know . . . well, I wasn't going to explain it to him.

'I don't know,' I said finally.

He spun around and looked at me, as if spotting unexpected prey, his eyes still hunter's yellow. I'd been wrong. Lying was worse than pointless.

'Yes, you do,' he said. 'Why?'

I rubbed my face. 'Look, I'm just not up to your fighting weight tonight. Can it wait until Warren is out of danger?'

He watched me out of narrowed amber eyes, but at least he didn't prod any more.

Desperate to change the subject, I said, 'Did the reporter get in touch with you? The one with the daughter.'

He closed his eyes and took a deep, lingering breath. When he opened his eyes again they were the color of a good chocolate bar. 'Yes, and thank you for dropping that one on me without warning. He thought you had already called me: it took us both a while to realize I hadn't a clue what he was talking about.'

'So are they coming here?'

Adam waved his hand toward Warren's room, 'When there is something that can do that to one of my wolves here? They were supposed to come here. I'll have to call him and tell him it's not advisable. I don't know who to send them to, though. There's not an Alpha I know that I'd trust to watch over my daughter – and his is even younger than Jesse.'

'Send him to Bran,' I suggested. 'Bran said he's raised a few strays in his time.'

Adam gave me an assessing look. 'You'd trust the Marrok with a child?'

'He didn't hurt me,' I said. 'And a lot of Alphas would have.'

Adam grinned suddenly. 'And that's saying something. Did you really run his Lamborghini into a tree?'

'That's not what I meant,' I said hotly. 'A lot of Alphas would have killed a coyote pup thrust upon them.'

I strode across the room to the door. I stopped there.

'It was a Porsche,' I said with dignity. 'And the road was covered with ice. If it was Samuel who told you about it, I hope he told you he was the one who egged me into taking the car out in the first place. I'm going back to see how Warren is.'

Adam was laughing quietly as I shut the door behind me.

I drove home alone a few hours later. Samuel was staying all night to make sure nothing went wrong – at least nothing more wrong than it already had. Kyle was staying as well: I was pretty sure it would have taken more than a pack of werewolves to get him out of that room.

There was nothing I could do for Warren, or for Stefan. Or Ben. Why couldn't the people I cared about just need someone to fix their cars? I could do that. And when had I started worrying about Ben? He was a rat bastard.

But the sick feeling in my stomach was partly on his account, too. Damn it. Damn it all.

There were two phone messages waiting for me when I got home. One from my mother and the other from Gabriel. I returned Gabriel's call and told him that Warren had been badly hurt, but should be fine. My mother I couldn't face. Not without crying, and I didn't intend to cry until I found out for certain what had happened.

I ate ramen noodles for dinner and fed most of it to Medea who purred as she licked the broth. I cleaned up my meal, then vacuumed and dusted. You can tell the shape of my life by how clean my house is. When I'm upset I cook, or I clean. I couldn't eat anything more, so I cleaned.

I turned the vacuum off to move the couch and realized that the phone had been ringing. Had something else gone wrong?

I picked up the receiver and hit TALK. 'Thompson residence.'

'Mercedes Thompson, the Mistress would like to speak with you.' The voice was urbane and female, a secretary's voice. I looked out the window and saw that the sun was setting, bathing the Horse Heaven Hills in brilliant orange light.

All the frustrated anger I'd been working off returned with a vengeance. If Stefan's mistress had sent out all of her minions after the sorcerer, instead of playing petty power games, Warren wouldn't be fighting for his life.

'I'm sorry,' I said insincerely. 'Please inform your mistress that I am not interested in visiting with her.' I hung up the phone. When it rang again, I turned off the ringer and pulled the cushions off the couch so I could clean underneath them.

When my cell phone rang, I almost ignored it, too, because I didn't recognize the number. But it might have been one of Adam's pack calling, or Stefan.

'Hello?'

'Mercedes Thompson, I need you to help me find Stefan and kill this sorcerer,' said Marsilia.

I knew what I should do. If she'd said anything else I could have hung up on her, I would have done it, too, no matter how stupid hanging up on the Mistress of the vampire seethe would be. But she needed *me*, needed me to *do* something.

To kill the sorcerer.

But that was ridiculous – what could I do that two vampires and a pair of werewolves could not?

'Why me?'

'I'll explain it to you face-to-face.'

She was good, I had to give her that much – if I hadn't been listening for it, I don't think I'd have heard the satisfaction in her voice.

8

Though it was nearly midnight, the parking lot at Uncle Mike's was full and I had to park in the warehouse's lot next door. My little Rabbit wasn't alone, but it looked worried among all the SUVs and trucks. I don't know why the fae like big vehicles, but you never see one driving a Geo Metro.

There are several bars near the fae reservation in Walla Walla, about sixty miles up the highway, that claim to be fae hangouts to attract publicity. There was a new bar, not too far from my shop, that billed itself out as a werewolf den. But you won't find Uncle Mike advertising for customers, nor will you find many humans there. If some stupid human, attracted by the number of cars in the lot, stops by, a subtle spell has him hurrying along his way. Uncle Mike's is for the fae – though he tolerates most any kind of preternatural creature, as long as they don't cause any problems.

I'd refused to go to the seethe without Stefan. Stubborn, I might be, but not stupid. I wouldn't invite her to my house either – it's much easier to invite evil in than it is to keep it out afterwards. I wasn't even certain how you uninvited a vampire, beyond knowing that it was possible. So I'd suggested Uncle Mike's as a neutral meeting place.

I'd expected it to be less crowded since it was a work night. Apparently Uncle Mike's clientele wasn't worried about getting up in the morning like I had to.

I opened the door and noise poured out like water over a dam. Caught by the sheer volume of sound, I hesitated – then a firm hand caught my breastbone and pushed me, sending me stumbling back outside. The door swung shut, leaving me alone in the parking lot with my assailant.

I took a second step back, putting space between us, wishing I'd brought a gun. Then I took a good look and relaxed. He was dressed in a lincoln green tunic and hose, looking not unlike one of Robin Hood's Merry Men, the uniform of Uncle Mike's staff.

He looked about sixteen, tall and thin with just a faint shadow of hair about his mouth that might be a moustache in a few years. His features were ordinary, neither too big nor too small, but not neatly arranged enough to be overtly attractive.

He made a little gesture at me and I smelled the sharp astringent scent of fae magic. Then he turned on his heel and started back to the door. He was a bouncer. Damn it all, this was the second time today someone tried to throw me out of someplace.

'I'm not human.' I told him impatiently, following behind him. 'Uncle Mike doesn't mind me coming here.' Not that Uncle Mike had taken much notice of me.

The boy hissed and turned to face me, anger darkening his features. He held his hands up between us and cupped them. This time the smell of magic was as strong as ammonia, clearing my sinuses. I gave a choked cough at the unexpected strength of the scent.

I don't know what he intended to do to me because the door behind him opened again and Uncle Mike himself came out.

'Hsst now, Fergus, you'll not be wanting to do that, do ya hear me? Put that out. Of all the . . . You *know* better than that.' Ireland lay thick as honey on his tongue and his voice worked its own kind of magic on the bouncer, who dropped his hands at the first word.

Uncle Mike looked like a tavern owner ought to. As if he'd reached into my mind and pulled out all the tavern owners in all the books and movies and stories I'd ever experienced, and then distilled them to produce the perfect caricature. His face was pleasing, but more charismatic than handsome. He was average in height with wide shoulders, thick arms, and short-fingered, powerful hands. His hair was reddish brown, but there were no freckles on his tanned face. His eyes, I knew, though the night robbed them of their color, were bright hazel and he turned their power on his hapless employee.

'Now, then, Fergus, you make yourself useful and tell Biddy she's to guard the door for the rest of the night. Then you are to go to Cook and tell him I want you to stay busy until you remember that killing customers isn't good for business.'

'Yes, sir.' Thoroughly cowed, the bouncer scuttled through the door and disappeared inside. I might have felt sorry for him, if it hadn't been for the 'killing customers' part.

'Now then,' Uncle Mike said, turning to me. 'You'll have to excuse my help. That demon is raising all sorts of havoc for us here, keeping tempers at a killing edge as you have seen. I'm thinkin' that it might not be the best night for one of your kind to join us in revelry.'

It was more polite than a death curse perhaps, but even more effective at keeping me out. Damn it.

I swallowed my growl and tried to keep my voice as polite as his. 'If I am not welcome, would you have someone find Marsilia and tell her to meet me out here?'

His face went blank with surprise. 'And what are you doing meeting the Vampire queen? You play in waters much too deep to swim in for long, little girl.'

I think it was the 'little girl' that did it. Or maybe it was the shift in wind that brought the smell of garbage, wolf, and blood to my nose as well as the distinct scent that was Warren's alone – reminding me that he had been dumped here, bleeding and dying only hours ago.

'Maybe if the fae would stir their *asses* once in a while, I could stay in shallow water,' I said, all attempts at politeness gone. 'I know the old stories. I *know* you have power, damn it all. Why are you all just sitting around and watching the sorcerer kill people?' I was trying not to include Stefan among the dead, but part of me was already in mourning – it added a reckless edge to my tongue. 'I suppose if you are afraid it might put you "on a killing edge," it makes better sense to wait it out.' Warren could have done that, too. Then he'd be safe at home instead of bleeding in Adam's guest bedroom. 'Especially since it is a *vampire* matter. The people who die along the way are merely effluvia and nothing to be concerned about.'

He smiled, just a little, and it flamed my temper higher. 'Fine, *smile* away. I suppose you've killed your share. Well, this affects you, too. The humans aren't stupid, they know this is something out of the ordinary, something evil – and the only people they know who might do this are yours.'

He was grinning now, but he held up a staying hand. 'Sorry, love. It's just the image. One doesn't think of mechanics using words like *effluvia*, does one?'

I stared at him. Maybe there was something about being old, and I suspected Uncle Mike was very old, that gave him a different perspective, but . . .

'I'm sorry,' I said, and even I could hear that my voice was thick with rage. 'I'll try to keep to commonly used, very small words when discussing something that has a body count of what . . .' I tried to add it up in my head, though I was foiled somewhat because I didn't know how many people had died while Daniel had been under the sorcerer's control. 'Fifteen?'

The smile left his face altogether, and he stopped looking like a tavern owner. 'More like forty, I think, though I doubt not there are more we've yet to find. Not all of them here in the three cities, either. Demons deal in death and rot. Nothing to smile at, nor to let pass. My apologies,' he bowed, a jerky motion that was over so quickly I couldn't be absolutely certain I'd really seen it. 'I was amused as much at myself as at your use of the language. Even after all this time, I keep forgetting that heroes can be found in unlikely places and persons – like mechanics who can turn into coyotes.' He stared at me a minute and a sly smile slid into his eyes, nothing like the expressions he usually had on his face.

'So, as you have the right, being a hero about to throw yourself on a grenade for the rest of us, I'll tell you why we're not bestirring ourselves against it.' He nodded his head toward the tavern. 'We fae are holding to survival by our fingertips, Mercedes Thompson. We are dying faster than we are reproducing, even counting our half bloods. It started the first time a human forged a cold-iron blade, but bullet lead kills us just as quickly as steel ever did – gremlins like Siebold Adelbertsmiter being the exception among us.'

He paused, but I waited. I knew all of this, as did anyone who cared to turn on the TV or read a newspaper.

'There are beings of power here,' he said. 'Beings who would scare the human population into launching a geno-cidal wave that would wipe every fae off the face of the earth if they knew of them. If the sorcerer turns its attention to us, makes one of us kill humans in front of cameras – which it can do – there will be no more fae.'

'The werewolves are under the same constraints,' I said. 'It hasn't stopped Adam. He could have left it all to the vampires. I bet that there are four people in that bar right now that could destroy this monster before it even knew they were looking for him.'

He clenched his fists and turned away, but not before I saw something else on his face, something *hungry*. 'No. You underestimate its power, Mercedes. Most of us have no more resistance to vampiric powers than any human – nor are there many souls pure enough to resist the demon. You don't want it controlling one of us.' He swung back to me, and he looked just as he always had, that instant of something *more* was gone as if it had never been.

I took a step back anyway because my instincts were telling me that I wasn't the biggest predator here.

His voice was mellow and easy as he told me, 'But just in case someone was overly tempted to take this sorcerer on, the Gray Lords have declared this vampire business, and we are to stay out of it. The Gray Lords do consider humans to be *effluvia*, Mercy. Very dangerous effluvia. They are not inclined to worry overmuch about a few human deaths.'

Looking into his eyes, I knew three things. The first was that Uncle Mike was one of the few who would have gone after the sorcerer. The second was that he both hated and feared the Gray Lords. The third was that he didn't consider humans to be effluvia at all.

I wasn't certain which one surprised me the most.

'So,' I said, 'does this mean you'll let me come in and find Marsilia myself?'

He nodded his head slowly. 'I'll not stand in the way of it.' He held out his arm in an old-fashioned gesture. I put my fingers lightly on it and let him lead me back toward the bar.

Just before we reached the entrance, though, he paused. 'Don't take the wolves with you when you go after the sorcerer.'

'Why not?'

'That Fergus, he has served me for thrice times a score of years. In that time he ne'er once raised a violent hand to a customer of mine. That demon the sorcerer bears carries violence like a stream carries little fishies. His very presence takes away all self-control and encourages ragin' and fightin'. The effect of a demon on a werewolf is like vodka on a fire.'

It sounded like Tony's recitation of the growing unrest the police were fighting. Bran had mentioned something like that, too, but he hadn't made it sound as dire. Come to think of it, though Adam's outburst tonight might easily be explained by a combination of hot temper and worry, Samuel had been more volatile than usual lately.

'Why didn't you tell Adam that Warren and Ben were in danger?' I asked.

'I didn't know until that poor lad of his was laid on my doorstep today that Adam had sent his boyos out a-hunting – though I should have.'

Had Bran known the danger when Adam sent Warren and Ben with Stefan? I thought about it. Probably. But Bran had never been one to tell his people what their limits were. Likely he'd been right, too. Worry and fear from knowing that the demon could eat away their control would do half the demon's work for it.

I wouldn't tell them either, I decided. Which meant that I couldn't tell them that I was going hunting – and, whatever Marsilia had in mind, I was done with sitting around. Coyotes were good at skulking and could take down much bigger prey than most people would expect. If Marsilia could offer help, fine. If not I'd go after him on my own.

I entered the bar with Uncle Mike. There was a heavy metal band playing tonight and the thrum of the drums and the distorted guitar made my head throb in time with the beat and sent my ears into overdrive. I know some wolves who love places like this, where their sensitive senses turn off for a while. They find it restful. Not me. It makes me jumpy because I can't hear what's coming up behind me.

Uncle Mike escorted me past the woman at the cover charge desk, and she gave him a surprised look which he ignored. He bent down until his lips were near my ear and said, 'I have to go man the bar, but I'll keep an eye out for you while you're here.'

I opened my mouth to thank him, but he touched his fingers to my mouth before I said anything.

'None of that, girl. I know Zee has taught you better. Never thank a fae or you'll be washing his socks and paying his rent before you can say *effluvia* ten times.'

He was right. I knew better, and possibly I'd have remembered before I said anything. But I appreciated his courtesy just the same.

I raised my eyebrows and said with mock innocence, 'But *you* wouldn't do that.'

He grinned appreciatively and waved me away. 'Go find your vampires, girl. I've money to make.'

No one gave me any trouble, but I felt the weight of fae eyes on my back as I carefully moved through the crowd. It was hard not to bump people in a building as packed as this one was, but I kept Uncle Mike's warning in mind and kept my body parts to myself. The mood of the crowd was pretty ugly. My ears weren't doing me much good, but the emotions my nose picked up weren't happy ones.

I found the vampires on the far side of the dance floor. Marsilia was in a fifties-style white dress that brought up images of Marilyn Monroe, though the vampire had none of her soft curves. Even in the dim light, her skin was too pale against the white of her dress.

Someone should tell Marsilia that the style didn't flatter her. Maybe she'd tick me off enough to do it myself.

My temper seemed to be on edge, too.

Startled at that thought, I stopped where I was and turned in a slow circle, but I didn't see Littleton anywhere. Or smell him either. I started toward the vampires again.

Marsilia had brought only one escort, and I wasn't

surprised to see it was Andre, Stefan's friend and rival. Weaving through the crowd gave me a little time to think on how to play my part. Marsilia knew she had me on her hook already, all that was left was to decide who was in charge. Since it was almost certainly going to be my skin at risk, I had an interest in making sure I had control of the hunt. I pulled the necklace I always wore out from under my T-shirt so they could get a good look at the stylized silver sheep as I approached.

I don't wear a cross. As a child, I'd had a bad experience with one. Besides, a crucifix was the instrument of Our Lord's death – I don't know why people think a torture device should be a symbol of Christ. Christ was a willing sacrifice, a lamb, not a cross for us to hang ourselves on; or at least that's my interpretation. Maybe other people think of religion and God differently than I do.

Anyway, my little lamb works at least as well for me against vamp, as a cross is supposed to – and Marsilia knew it.

When I walked up to the table, I smiled at them, showing my teeth. Then I took the chair they'd left me and spun it so I could sit on it backward with my arms folded across the top. In a wolf pack, a little attitude can save you a whole lot of bruises.

I'd show no more weakness to these predators, I told myself. I wasn't in their territory now, and they had no power over me. Well, not unless I considered how much stronger they were, and how much more practice they'd had at killing. So I tried not to consider it. At least the noise would keep them from hearing my heart beat like a rabbit's.

'So,' I said, 'you want me to go hunt your vampire for you?'

Marsilia's face could hardly be any stiller, but Andre raised an eyebrow. 'Sorcerer hunting, surely,' he murmured. Like

Marsilia he wore white. His natural skin color – though pale as all the vampires were for lack of sun – was just dark enough that the white looked good on him. His shirt was rich silk, cut in a vaguely Oriental style with white on white embroidery. It looked better on him than his pirate shirts did.

'Hmm.' I flashed another smile at Marsilia. 'But you need me because I'm a walker, and we're supposed to be good at killing vampires. And this sorcerer is exactly that. A vampire.'

Marsilia smiled back, the expression looking more human than anything I'd seen on her face – she was probably making an effort.

She rolled the mostly empty glass in her hands, making the inky black liquid swirl. I didn't know if Uncle Mike's served blood in wine glasses, but since all I smelled was various flavors of alcohol, I expected not. Since she was making such a show though, I was pretty sure I was supposed to think it might be blood and be unnerved.

'Thank you for meeting me here,' she said at last.

I shrugged and exaggerated just a little bit. 'I was going after it anyway.' I realized only after I said it, that it was the truth. 'Since it's a vampire though, having your approval for this hunt makes it . . .' I pretended to search for a word. 'Safer – for both of us.'

I was playing a dangerous game. If she really thought I was a danger to her seethe she'd kill me. But if she didn't respect me, I was likely to end up just as dead.

She sighed and set her glass on the table. 'You were raised with the wolves, Mercedes, so I understand the need for playing dominance games. But two of mine are missing and I fear for them. Stefan was among the strongest of mine, but the return of the remains of one of his companions tells me that he has failed.'

All of her body language was just a little off. Perhaps she was really worried about her vampires, but her performance set my hackles up. To the wolves, body language is more important than words – and her body language was all wrong, sending messages that her voice did not. I couldn't tell which I should be listening to.

'"Remains" is a little strong,' I said. 'Warren's not dead.'

She didn't say anything more for a moment, tapping the table lightly in the same pattern that she'd used the last time I'd seen her. I thought that I hadn't reacted quite as she'd intended – was I supposed to have accepted her help eagerly?

Finally she said, 'I know you think it is my fault for sending Stefan off by himself. There were reasons to make it appear a punishment, but Stefan was a soldier. He knew an assignment when he heard one. He knew I believed him, just as he knew I had no choice but to send him after this creature.'

That I could believe.

'She meant for him to ask me for help,' Andre broke in. 'It is my fault that he didn't. Stefan and I had . . . have been friends for a long time. But I made a mistake and he was angry with me.' He looked at me and met my eyes for a moment, but looked away when I averted my gaze. I wondered what he would have done if I'd let him ensnare me.

He continued as if nothing had happened. Maybe it hadn't.

'Daniel was one of Stefan's when he was human. He was more fragile than he appeared and he died while he fed me. There is only an instant when the choice to bring one back can be made, Mercedes Thompson. Less than five human heartbeats. I thought to lessen the cost to everyone by bringing him back a vampire instead of putting him permanently to earth.'

Marsilia touched his hand, and I realized his speech hadn't been for me, but for her.

'You gave Daniel a gift,' she said. 'Ample recompense for your mistake.'

Andre bowed his head. 'Stefan didn't think so. Bringing him over made Daniel mine, and Stefan was convinced that I'd done it on purpose.'

The vampires were damned hard to read, but I thought Stefan probably had the right of it. Andre had been too pleased about something to do with Daniel and Stefan the night of Stefan's trial.

'Unkind of him,' Marsilia told him.

'I'd have given him back,' Andre said. 'But I was waiting for Stefan to ask.'

See. Vampires play stupid dominance games, too.

Marsilia shook her head. 'It was, perhaps, all to the good that Stefan did not take you. I might be here talking with this walker with both my best soldiers dead.' She turned her attention back to me. 'So here is how I propose to make your job easier, Mercedes. I will lend you my left hand to guard your back,' she said, nodding at Andre, 'my right being sundered. And I will give you what information I have.'

'In return for what?' I asked, though my question was automatic. She thought Stefan was dead.

She closed her eyes for a moment then stared at my forehead. The vampire version of courtesy, I think. It made me feel like I had a smudge on my forehead.

She said, 'In return for you finding this bedamned thing. Since it killed Stefan, I have to accept that any other vampires sent after it will likewise be destroyed. You are the best hope we have of eliminating it.'

'And besides,' I added dryly. 'If I don't succeed, what have you lost?' She didn't reply, but she didn't need to. 'So tell me, how do I kill this sorcerer?'

'Just like any other vampire,' she said.

'Most of what I know is from *Dracula*. Assume I'm totally ignorant, please.'

'Well enough,' she agreed. 'A wooden stake through the

heart works. Immersion in holy water or direct exposure to sunlight. It is said that the great saints could kill us with their faith, but I do not think, despite your lamb,' she waved her hand at my necklace, 'that your faith is great enough for that. But take your little sheep with you, Mercedes, because it should work as well on demons as it does on vampires.'

'What was it that walkers could do that made vampires fear them?' I asked.

She and Andre both went very still. I didn't think she would answer me. But she did. Sort of. 'The first you already know,' she said. 'Many of our powers do not work well on you. Most of our magic is useless.'

'Your truth spell worked,' I pointed out.

'That chair is not vampiric magic, Mercedes, not entirely. Though all magic, I believe, finds you difficult prey. But blood magic has a power all of its own, as do very old things. That chair is a very old thing.'

'I didn't mean to distract you from the subject,' I said politely inviting her to get back to the point.

She gave me a faint smile. 'No. I don't suppose you did. Walkers also speak to ghosts.'

I blinked at her. 'So what?' A lot of people, even otherwise perfectly normal humans, can speak to ghosts.

She pushed back her chair. 'I think that I have answered enough of your questions.' She gave Andre a look, so I knew that he wouldn't clarify anything for me. 'I believe that you ought to start by finding out where Stefan went last night.'

'Warren won't be talking, not for a while,' I told her. His throat had been crushed. Samuel thought it could take several days to heal.

'Stefan was in the habit of talking with his people,' she told me. 'They are afraid. They won't talk to me or mine. But I think they will talk to you. Andre will take you to Stefan's house where you can speak with the menagerie.'

Then she disappeared. I suppose she could have cloaked herself in shadows as some of the fae can, but I couldn't smell her, couldn't sense her anywhere.

'I hate it when she does that,' said Andre taking a sip out of his glass. 'Mostly envy, I expect. Stefan could do it, too – the only one of her get to receive that gift.'

I stayed silent a while, contemplating Marsilia. She'd been making an effort to be human tonight – though she'd only been moderately successful. Tentatively, I decided that she'd been mostly honest about what she wanted from me and why. I was pretty sure that she thought I held the key to finding this sorcerer – either through my resistance to vampire magic or through my 'ability' to speak to ghosts.

It wasn't like I saw ghosts all the time or anything.

I was already a freak, a shapeshifter not tied to the moon who turned into a coyote. Neither human nor werewolf nor fae. I didn't like thinking I might be even odder than I'd thought.

I looked up to see Andre watching me patiently. To my werewolf accustomed eyes, he didn't look like someone who was one of Marsilia's most capable warriors. There was no width in his shoulders, no substance to his muscles. She could have been flattering him, since he was in the room, but I didn't think so.

'Did she teleport?' I asked. I'd been told that will-o-wisps were the only creature who could really teleport.

He smiled and shrugged. 'I don't know how it is done. But it is one of the reasons we are certain Stefan is gone. If he were still with us, he could not be easily imprisoned.'

'You don't sound upset,' I said. I didn't want to think about Stefan being dead – permanently dead, I mean.

He gave me a shrug that might have meant anything. 'I think Stefan is gone, Mercedes Thompson – I wear the white to honor him, as does the Mistress. But there is nothing I can do about his death except hunt his killer.' He paused and set his glass down very gently. 'We do not know each other well enough for me to cry on your shoulder.'

The shadow of anger in his voice made me like him better.

'All right,' I said. 'Why don't you show me how to find Stefan's house.'

We'd made it halfway to the door when the crowd quit letting us through. Andre was quicker than I was. He stopped where he was while I tried sliding around a particularly sizable woman who was standing in front of me.

'Hold up, ducks,' she said in a voice that was low enough to vibrate my sinuses. 'I smell a human in a fae tavern.' On the tail of her words, the music stopped and the sounds of people talking and moving died down.

Once I realized she was talking about me, though she spoke to the room at large, I thought of several clever, but stupid remarks about her sense of smell – I wasn't human at all, not in the sense she meant. Stupid because only a very unwise person jumps up and down shouting on top of a beehive.

Sometimes, when one of them have committed a terrible crime, the whole wolf pack enjoins in the punishment, tearing the violating wolf to bits. But before it starts, there is a moment of oppressive stillness when the culprit is alone, surrounded by the pack. Then one wolf moves and starts the feeding frenzy. This crowd had that feel, as if they were waiting for someone to start something.

'I have Uncle Mike's permission to be here,' I said softly, giving no challenge. I didn't know what kind of fae she was, what to do to avoid a fight.

She opened her mouth, obviously unappeased when someone shouted, 'A forfeit.'

I thought the shout might have originated at the bar, but it was immediately taken up by a throng of voices. When they quieted, the woman in front of me looked around and asked the room at large, 'Wot kind of a forfeit then, ducks?'

Forfeit, I thought, some kind of gift, maybe. Or sacrifice.

Uncle Mike pushed forward, through the crowd until he stood in front of me, his face thoughtful. It was a sign of his power that they all waited for his judgement.

'Music,' he said at last. 'My guest will offer us a gift of music for our hospitality.'

The big woman sighed as Uncle Mike stepped back and swept the fae near him away until I could clearly see the small stage where three musicians still stood. There were two guitarists and a string bass. I don't know where the sounds of drums had come from because there were none in evidence.

One of the guitarists grinned, hopped off the stage and motioned to the others to do likewise. Leaving the platform to me.

I lifted my eyebrow at Uncle Mike and began walking to the stage. Andre, I'd noticed, had drawn back in the crowd. They wouldn't bother him, not a vampire. Neither would they have bothered one of the werewolves. I, who was neither werewolf nor vampire, was fair game.

I wondered if Uncle Mike would have let them tear me to bits if he hadn't been aware that, pack or not, the wolves would avenge me – fat lot of good vengeance would have done me. Uncle Mike's suspect help was of more use.

When I stepped onto the stage, one of the guitarists tried to hand me his instrument with a flourish.

'I appreciate the gesture,' I told him carefully, 'but I don't play.' I didn't play anything except piano – and that very poorly. I was just lucky that the piano lessons had included voice lessons, too.

I looked around for inspiration. The obvious answer was to pick a Celtic song, but I rejected it as fast as it came to

mind. Folk songs, for the most part, have dozens of variations and dozens of people claiming that their version was
true. In a group of mostly Celtic fae who were looking for
a reason to kill me, singing a Celtic song would be stupid.

There were a few German fae here, and the Germans were
not nearly as picky about their music, but the only German
song I knew was 'O Tannenbaum,' a children's Christmas
carol that wouldn't impress anyone — not that my voice was
going to impress anyone anyway. I had pitch and volume,
but no real talent.

Which made the choice of song very important. We played
a game and if I cowered too much, not even Uncle Mike
could save my skin. A subtle insult would be best. Not a
slap in the face, but a poke in the side.

I also needed a power song, because my voice isn't pretty
and soft. Something that sounded good a capella. Despite
the air-conditioning, the room was stifling hot and my
thoughts felt sluggish — of course that might have been the
fear.

I wished it was winter and the air was cool and crisp . . .
Maybe it was that, maybe it was the lingering thought about
'O Tannenbaum,' but I knew what I was going to sing. I
felt my lips curl up.

I took a deep breath, properly supported with my
diaphragm, and began singing. *'O holy night, the stars are
brightly shining . . .'*

So in the sweltering heat of a July night, I sang a Christmas
carol to a room full of fae, who had been driven out of their
homelands by Christians and their cold-iron swords.

I've heard that song sung softly, until the magic of that
first Christmas seems to hang in the air. I wish I could sing
it that way. Instead, I belted it out, because that's what my
voice does best.

I closed my eyes to my audience and let the simple belief

of the words run through me like a prayer until I got to, 'Fall on your knees.' Then I opened my eyes and glared at the woman who had started all of this and I sang the rest of the song at her.

When the last note died away, the big woman threw back her head and laughed. She turned to Uncle Mike and patted him on the shoulder, sending him half a step forward.

'Good forfeit,' she said. 'Huh.' Then she stomped off back through the crowd toward a corner of the room.

If I'd been expecting applause, I'd have been disappointed. The room settled down and the fae went back to doing whatever they'd been doing before I'd become so interesting. Still, it hadn't been any worse than singing at the Friday night performance in front of Bran at Aspen Springs.

One of the musicians, the one who'd offered his guitar, grinned at me as we switched places.

'A little thin on the highest notes,' he said. 'But not bad.'

I grinned back at him, a little ruefully. 'Tough crowd.'

'You're still alive, ducks, aren't you then?' he said imitating the cadences of the woman's voice.

I gave him a half wave and made a direct line for the exit. I didn't see Andre, but Uncle Mike met me at the door and held it open for me.

Standing on the porch I caught the door and looked back at him. 'How did you know I could even carry a note?'

He smiled. 'You were raised by a Welshman, Mercedes Thompson. And isn't that a Welsh name, Thompson? Then, too, one of the names for the coyote is the Prairie Songbird.' He shrugged. 'Of course, it wasn't *my* life on the line.'

I snorted in appreciation.

He touched a finger to his forehead and closed the door firmly between us.

9

Andre was waiting for me in the parking lot, standing beside one of the seethe's interchangeable black Mercedes, ready to drive me to Stefan's home — as if I were stupid enough to hop into a car driven by a vampire I didn't know.

Despite Andre's objections, I followed him in my car rather than letting him drive me. Aside from being safer, when we were done, I could drive straight home instead of waiting for him to drive me back out to Uncle Mike's.

He was right, it might have been useful to talk and come up with a game plan — if I had trusted him a little more or if I hadn't had to go to work in the morning. Bills don't wait just because my friend was cut to hamburger and the vampire's mistress wants me to find a sorcerer who has killed more than forty people.

I took a tighter grip on the wheel and tried not to look at the broken dash, where Stefan, calm, quiet Stefan, had put his fist. What had made him so angry? That the sorcerer had beaten him?

What had Stefan said? That he knew there was something wrong with his memories because he hadn't remembered me. That I was not unimportant to him.

Stefan was a vampire, I reminded myself. Vampires are evil.

I reached out and touched the dash. *He did it because I had been hurt*, I thought.

He wasn't unimportant to me either — I didn't want him to be gone forever.

Stefan's house was in the hills in Kennewick, in one of

the newer subdivisions on the west side of Highway 395. It was a big, sprawling brick house on a large lot with a circular drive, the kind of house that should have generations of children growing up in it. Surrounded by buildings with fake columns and two-story-high windows, it should have looked out of place. Instead it looked content with what it was. I could see Stefan in this house.

'You'd better knock on the door,' Andre said as I got out of my car. 'They've already refused to admit me once tonight – with every justification. Stefan might forgive me Daniel, but his flock will remember.' He sounded mildly regretful, about on the level of a child who'd thrown a baseball through a window.

Despite the late hour, there were lights on all over the house. When I thought about it, it made sense that a vampire's people kept late hours.

Coming here had sounded logical when Marsilia had directed us here. I hadn't really thought about what it would mean.

I hesitated before I knocked. I didn't want to meet Stefan's people, didn't want to know that he kept them the way a farmer keeps a herd of cattle. I liked Stefan, and I wanted to keep it that way.

The curtain in the window next to the door moved a little. They already knew we were here.

I rang the doorbell.

I heard a scramble behind the door as if a lot of people were moving around, but when it opened, there was only one person in the entryway.

She looked to be a few years older than me, in her mid- to late thirties. She wore her dark, curly hair cut to shoulder length. She was dressed conservatively in a tailored shirt and slacks; she looked like a business woman.

I think she might have been attractive, but her eyes and

nose were swollen and red, her face too pale. She stood back in silent invitation. I walked in, but Andre came to an abrupt halt just outside the threshold.

'You'll have to invite me in again, Naomi,' he said.

She drew in a shaky breath. 'No. Not until he returns.' She looked at me. 'Who are you and what do you want?'

'My name is Mercedes Thompson,' I told her. 'I'm trying to find out what happened to Stefan.'

She nodded her head and, without another word to Andre, shut the door in his face.

'Mercedes Thompson,' she said. 'Stefan liked you, I know. You stood up for him before the other vampires, and when you believed he was in trouble, you called us.' She glanced back at the door. 'Stefan revoked Andre's entry into the house, but I wasn't certain that it still worked with Stefan . . . missing.' She looked at the door a moment, then turned to me with a visible effort at composure. Control sat more comfortably on her face than fear.

'What can I do to help you, Ms Thompson?'

'You don't sound like the kind of person who would . . .' There was doubtlessly a polite term for someone who willingly feeds a vampire, but I didn't know it.

'What did you expect?' she asked tartly. 'Pale children covered with tattoos and bite marks?'

'Mmm,' I said. 'I met Daniel.'

Her expressive eyes clouded. 'Ah, Daniel. Yes. And we have a couple more like him. So, the stereotype is present here, but not all encompassing. If you went to another vampire's flock you might find it more like you expected. Stefan is seldom typical of anything.' She took a deep breath. 'Why don't you come into the kitchen and I'll pour you some tea while you ask your questions?'

There were at least ten people besides Stefan living in the house: I could smell them. They kept out of sight while

Naomi led me to the kitchen, but I could hear someone whispering nearby. Politely, I didn't stick my head into the room the whispers were coming from.

A butcher-block table that wouldn't have fit in most of the rooms in my trailer held sway in the center of the kitchen. Naomi pulled out a tall stool and sat down, motioning for me to take a seat as well. As she did, her hair fell away from the unblemished skin of her neck.

She saw my glance and pulled her hair back, so I could see that there were no red marks. 'Satisfied?' she asked.

I took a deep breath. She wanted me uncomfortable, but the adrenaline rush from Uncle Mike's was gone and I was just tired.

I pushed back my own hair and turned so she could see the bite marks on my neck. They were mostly healed, so I'd quit wearing a bandage, but the skin was still red and shiny. I'd probably have a scar.

She sucked in her breath and leaned forward to touch my neck. 'Stefan never did that,' she said, but with rather less conviction in her tone of voice than in her words.

'Why do you say that?' I asked.

'Someone just gnawed on you,' she said. 'Stefan has more care.'

I nodded. 'This was done by the thing that Stefan went hunting.'

She relaxed. 'That's right. He'd said it attacked you.'

Stefan talked to her, a hopeful sign.

'Yes.' I pulled out a second stool and climbed aboard. 'Do you know where Stefan went last night?'

She shook her head. 'I asked. He wouldn't tell me. He said he didn't want us chasing after him if he didn't come home.'

'He was worried about you?'

'Yes, but not the way you think,' said a new voice behind me.

I looked over and saw a young woman in baggy clothes and long, straight hair. She didn't look at us, just opened the fridge and studied the contents.

'How so?' I asked.

She looked up and grimaced at Naomi. 'He was worried that she would get the rest of us killed trying to rescue him. See, if he dies, so does she . . . not immediately, but soon.'

'That's not why I'm worried,' Naomi lied. I could hear it in her voice.

'See, the professor here has leukemia.' The younger girl took out a quart of milk and drank out of the carton. 'As long as she's playing blood bank, Stefan's return donations keep her cancer in check. If he quits' – she made a choking, gasping sound, then gave Naomi a faint pleased look. 'In return she acts as Stefan's business manager – paying bills, doing the taxes . . . shopping. Hey, Naomi, we're out of cheese.' She replaced the carton and shut the fridge.

Naomi slid off her chair and faced the younger girl. 'If he is dead, that means no more free ride for you. Maybe you should go back to your mother and her new husband. At least until the Mistress finds you and gives you to another vampire. Maybe Andre would want you.'

The teenager just stared at her, her gaze coolly mocking. Naomi turned to me and said, 'She doesn't know any more than I do.'

She glared at the girl one more time, then stalked off. The girl had come out the clear winner in their engagement. I found myself thinking she'd make a good wolf.

'I'm Mercedes Thompson,' I said, turning on the stool so I could put my elbows on the butcher-block table and lean back in a nonthreatening manner. 'I'm looking for Stefan.'

She glanced around as if looking for him, too. 'Yeah, well he ain't here.'

I nodded my head and pursed my lips. 'I know. One of

the wolves he was with last night was returned to us in very bad shape.'

She raised her chin. 'You aren't a werewolf. Stefan said.'

'No,' I agreed.

'Anything that could take out Stefan could wipe the floor with old Andre out there.' She jerked her chin toward the front door. 'What makes you think you can help Stefan?'

'Marsilia believes I can.' I watched the impact of the name hit her. For a moment, even with the veil of dark hair that covered her face, I caught a glimpse of the fear that rose from the depths of the house. Everyone here was very afraid. The house reeked of it.

'If Stefan doesn't come back,' she told me very quietly, suddenly sounding much older, 'I think we're all dead, not just Doctor Tightbritches. Sooner or later, we're all gone. The Mistress won't want us free to blabber about *them*. So she'll farm us out to the rest of her vampires, put us in their menageries. Most of them aren't as careful with their food as Stefan. No control when they're hungry.'

I didn't know what to say that didn't sound like a platitude, so I picked a thread out of her speech and plucked it. 'Stefan keeps you alive longer than the others are able to?'

'He doesn't kill those of us in his menagerie,' she said. I remembered that the London Zoo had once been known as a menagerie. She shrugged with studied casualness. 'Mostly, anyway. When he gets us, we have to stay a couple of years, but after that, 'cept for Naomi — and that's hardly Stefan's fault either — we're free to go.'

'Why a couple of years?' I asked.

She gave me a 'how stupid are you?' look. 'It takes that long for him to establish enough of a connection to make sure we won't go telling anyone we meet about vampires.'

'How long have you been with Stefan?'

'Five years this August,' she said, though she couldn't be over twenty. I hid my shock, but not well enough because she smirked at me. 'Twelve. I was twelve. Stefan's a big step up from my folks, let me tell you.'

Vampires are evil. Funny how I kept trying to forget that about Stefan.

'You probably know more about vampires than I do,' I told her, changing my tack so I could get a little more information. 'I grew up with the werewolves, and even though I've known Stefan a long time, most of our conversations are about cars. Would you mind if I asked you a few questions?'

'What do you want to know?'

'How much do you know about the thing that he was hunting?'

'He doesn't talk to us much,' she told me. 'Not like he used to talk to Daniel. He said it was a vampire demon thingy.'

I nodded. 'Close enough. Apparently if I can kill the vampire, the demon will just go away. No more vampire demon thingy. Marsilia told me how to kill vampires.' I stopped speaking and let her think about that a minute. She was pretty bright, it didn't take her long to come to the same conclusion I had.

'Man, that's pretty scary, going into a battle with the Mistress as your intel. Sure, I'll tell you what you need to know.' She ran her eyes over me and was unimpressed. 'She really thinks you can kill this thing?'

I started to nod, then stopped. 'I have no idea what Marsilia thinks.' Uncle Mike hadn't thought me hunting the sorcerer was stupid. I wasn't sure if I should trust the fae any further than I trusted the vampire. I shrugged finally and told her the truth. 'I don't really care. I'll kill the sorcerer or die trying.'

'What did she tell you?'

'She said I could kill a vampire with a wooden stake through the heart, holy water or sunlight.'

She leaned a hip against the fridge and shook her head. 'Look. The wooden stake thing works, but it's better if it's oak, ash, or yew. And if you kill them that way, you have to cut off their heads or burn the body to make sure they stay dead. Remember, a dead vampire is ashes. If there's a body, it'll come back – and it'll come back angry with you. Cutting off their heads is pretty good, but difficult. They're not likely to stand around and wait for the chainsaw. Sunlight's good, too. But the stake and sunlight, they're like kicking a guy in the balls, you know?'

I shook my head, fascinated.

'They all know about it. They're not going to put themselves at risk if they can help it. And if you screw it up all it does is piss 'em off more. Holy water's mostly out. You'd need a whole swimming pool full of holy water to kill one.'

'So how would you kill a vampire permanently?'

She pursed her lips. 'Fire's best. Stefan says they burn pretty well once they get started.'

'Stefan told you all of this?' I tried to imagine the conversation.

She nodded. 'Sure.' She gave me a considering look. 'Look, I don't know where he went, but I know he was keeping a sharp eye out on the local news and the papers. He had a map of the 'Cities and he marked where there was violence. Yesterday he was pretty excited about something he'd noticed about the pattern.'

'Do you have the map?' I asked.

'No. He took it with him. And he didn't show it to any of us.'

I slid off the chair. 'Thank you . . .'

'Rachel.'

'Thank you, Rachel.'

She nodded her head and then opened the fridge again, dismissing me. I walked to the front door slowly, but no one else appeared, so I let myself out.

Andre was waiting for me, sitting on the hood of his car. He jumped off and asked, 'Did they know anything?'

I shrugged. 'They didn't know where he was, but I found out how he decided where to look. Maybe it'll help.'

I looked at Andre and wondered if Marsilia had left out the part about decapitating the staked vampire on purpose. It didn't take much thought for me to decide she had.

'How would you kill Littleton?' I asked him.

'Fire,' he said promptly. 'That's the easiest way. Staking works, but you have to decapitate them afterwards.'

It didn't mean anything. From my question he'd have known I'd asked Stefan's people.

'That's not what Marsilia told me.'

He gave me a faint smile. 'If you just staked him, she could capture him, make him hers. There aren't a lot of vampires, Mercy, and it takes a long time to make them. If Daniel hadn't belonged to Stefan for so long, he'd have died permanently. Marsilia doesn't want to waste a vampire – especially not one who has all the powers of a demon at his touch. If he is hurt badly enough, there are ways of bringing him back under the control of a more powerful vampire, like Marsilia. He would make her position un-assailable.'

'So you intend to capture him?'

Andre shook his head. 'I want the bastard dead. Permanently dead.'

'Why is that?'

'I told you, Stefan and I, we have been friends for a very long time.' He turned his face into the light that illumin-ated the driveway. 'We have our differences, but it is . . . like family squabbling. I know this time Stefan was really angry, but he'd have gotten over it. Because of this sorcerer, I will never get the chance to make peace with him.'

'You are so certain Stefan is gone?'

Stefan's VW Bus was parked off to the side of the garage, covered by a tarp to protect its unusual paint job. What kind of vampire drove an old bus painted like the Mystery Machine? Last Christmas I'd gotten him a life-sized Scooby Doo to ride in the passenger seat.

He must have heard the answer I wanted in my voice because he shook his head slowly at me. 'Mercedes, it is difficult to keep a human captive. It is almost impossible to imprison a vampire. Stefan has ways . . . I don't think that he could be imprisoned – yet he has not come home. Yes, I think he is gone. I will do everything I can to see that this Littleton follows him.'

They made too much sense, he and Adam. I had to believe that Stefan was gone – and Ben and the young vampire I'd only met the once were dead as well. If I wasn't going to cry in front of him, I had to leave really soon.

I glanced at my watch. 'I have to be up in three hours.' If I knew how long it was going to take us to find the sorcerer, I'd have had Zee take over the shop, but I couldn't afford to do that for more than a few days a month, not and keep up on the mortgage and food.

'Go home and go to bed.' He took out a slim leather case and withdrew a card, handing it to me. 'My cell number is on this. Call me tomorrow at dusk and we can discuss where to go from here.'

I tucked the card in my back pocket. We'd stopped at the door to my car so I opened it and started to sit down when I thought of another question.

'Stefan said that Littleton was new. Does that mean there's another vampire controlling him?'

Andre inclined his head. 'A new vampire is under the

control of his maker.' He gave me a smile that was faintly bitter. 'It's not willing service. We all have to obey our maker.'

'Even you?'

He gave a short, unhappy bow. 'Even I. As we get older and accumulate power, though, the control diminishes. Or when our makers die.'

'So Littleton is obeying another vampire?'

'If the vampire who made him isn't dead, he should have to obey him.'

'Who was Stefan's maker?'

'Marsilia. But Stefan never had to play slave as the rest of us did.' There was sheer envy in his voice as he said, 'He was never a thrall. It happens sometimes, but such vampires are always killed upon their first rising. Any other vampire would have killed Stefan as soon as it was apparent that he wasn't under their control, but Marsilia was in love. He gave her an oath of obedience, though, and to my certain knowledge, he never broke it.' He looked out at the night sky.

Abruptly, he shut my door. 'Go home and go to sleep while you still can.'

'Did Marsilia make you too?' I asked, turning the key in the ignition.

'Yes.'

Damn it, I thought, this was so stupid. I didn't know *anything* about vampires and *I* was going to bring down one who had taken out two vampires and a pair of werewolves? I might as well shoot myself in the head right now. It would save time and effort.

'Good night, Andre,' I told him and drove out of Stefan's driveway.

I was tired enough to sleep as soon as my head hit the pillow. I dreamed of Stefan's poor menagerie, doomed, if Rachel was to be believed, by Stefan's death. I dreamed of Stefan driving his bus with that silly stuffed Scooby Doo perched in the passenger seat. I dreamed he tried to tell me something but I couldn't hear it over the noise.

I rolled over and buried my head under the pillow but the noise continued. It wasn't my alarm. I could go back to sleep. I was tired enough that even dreaming of dead people was preferable to being awake. After all, Stefan was as dead and gone when I was awake as when I was sleeping.

It wasn't a really loud sound. If it had been less irregular, I think I could have ignored it.

Scritch. Scritch – scritch.

It was coming from my window near the bed. It sounded like the rosebush that had grown outside of the window of my mother's home in Portland. Sometimes it would brush against the house at night and scare me. I wasn't sixteen anymore. There was no one but me who could get up, go outside, and move whatever it was so I could go to sleep.

I pulled the pillow tighter over my ears. But there was no blocking the noise. Then I thought – *Stefan?*

In an instant I was fully awake. I threw the pillow on the floor, sat up in a rush, and turned to press my face up against the window and look out.

But there was someone's face already pressed up against the window. Someone who wasn't Stefan.

Gleaming iridescent eyes stared at me through the glass, not six inches from my own. I shrieked Samuel's name and jumped out of bed, away from the window. It wasn't until I was crouched and shaking in the center of my bedroom floor before I remembered that Samuel was still over at Adam's.

The face didn't move. He'd pressed so hard against the glass his nose and lips were distorted, though I had no trouble recognizing Littleton. He licked the glass, then tilted his head and made the sound that had drawn me from my sleep. His fang left a white mark as he scored the glass with it.

There were a lot of little white marks, I noticed. He'd been there for a long time, watching me as I slept. It gave me the creeps, as did the realization that unless he was very, very tall, he was hanging in the air.

All my guns were locked in the stupid safe. There was no way I could get to them before he could burst through the window. Not that I was sure a gun would have any effect on a vampire anyway.

It took me a long time to remember that he couldn't get into my home without an invitation. Somehow that belief wasn't as reassuring as it ought to have been with him staring at me through a thin pane of glass.

Abruptly, he pulled away from the window and dropped out of sight. I listened, but I couldn't hear anything. After a long while, I accepted that he was gone.

I wasn't going to be able to sleep on that bed though, not unless I pulled it away from the window. My head was throbbing from lack of sleep and I staggered into the bathroom and got out some aspirin and gulped them down.

I stared at myself in the mirror, looking pale and color-less in the darkness.

'Well,' I said. 'Now you know where he is, why aren't you out tracking him?'

I sneered at my cowardly face, but some of the effect was lost in the darkness so I reached over and flipped the light switch.

Nothing happened.

I flipped it twice more. 'Stupid trailer.' The breakers often switched off on their own – someday I was going to have to rewire the trailer.

The breaker box was on the other side of the trailer, past

the big windows in the living room and the smaller one in the kitchen. The one in the kitchen didn't have a curtain.

'Fearless vampire hunter my aching butt,' I muttered, knowing I was too thoroughly spooked to go and reset the breaker unarmed. Stalking out of the bathroom, I opened the gun safe. I left the pistols in favor of the Marlin 444 rifle which I loaded with silver – though I didn't know if the silver would do any more harm to a vampire than regular lead. They certainly wouldn't do less.

At any rate, the Marlin would give me enough confidence to go back to sleep.

I shoved the finger-long bullets into the gun impatiently. If those things could stop an elephant, I had to believe they'd make a vampire sit up and take notice too.

I knew I shouldn't turn on the bedroom light. In the unlikely event that Littleton was still here, it would ruin my night vision and it would silhouette me in the light, making me a good target if Littleton the vampire and sorcerer decided to use a gun – unlikely considering how much he'd enjoyed killing that poor maid slowly. I wasn't enough of a threat to deprive him of that much fun.

I hit the bedroom switch next to the bathroom door, anyway. Nothing happened. The bedroom and the bathroom were on different circuits, they couldn't both be thrown at the same time. Had Littleton cut the power to the trailer?

I was still staring at the switch when someone screamed Samuel's name. No, it wasn't just anyone screaming – it was me. Except that I hadn't screamed again.

I jacked a shell into the Marlin and tried to take comfort from its familiar weight and the knowledge that Littleton couldn't come in.

'Little wolf, little wolf, let me come in.' The whisper filled my room, I couldn't tell where it was coming from.

Breathing hard through my nose to control my panic, I

knelt on the bed and looked cautiously out the window, but I couldn't see anything.

'Yes, Mercy?' Samuel's voice this time, light and playful. 'Sweet Mercy. Come out and play, Mercedes Thompson.' He had Samuel's voice down cold, too. Where had he heard Samuel speak?

Something scratched down the side of my trailer, next to the window, grating with the unmistakable sound of bending metal. I scrambled away and aimed the Marlin, waiting for his shadow to pass in front of the window.

'Little wolf, little wolf, come out, come out wherever you are.' Warren's voice this time. Then he screamed, a roaring sound of pain beyond bearing.

I had no doubt that Warren had made those noises, but I hoped he wasn't making them right outside my trailer. I hoped he was safe at Adam's house.

It was a good thing that he'd started with my voice – if I'd believed Warren was screaming outside my trailer I'd never have been able to stay inside. Where it was safe. Maybe.

The last of Warren's cries subsided, but Littleton wasn't finished with me yet. He tapped his way along the wall that was the end of the trailer. There was a window in that wall too, but I didn't see any sign of him, though it sounded as though he was tapping on the glass again.

He can't come in, I reminded myself silently, but I still flinched as the metal siding of my home shrieked and the trailer rocked a little. Then there was a brief silence.

He resumed his tapping, though it sounded more like banging now. Each time he hit the walls, both my home and I jerked. He continued around to the back, the sounds he made changing as he hit the bathroom wall. One of the tiles fell off the shower stall and shattered.

I kept the Marlin aimed toward him, but I kept my finger off the trigger. I couldn't see where I was shooting, and my neighbors' houses were well in range of the Marlin. Even if I managed not to kill any of them, shooting a gun would be bound to draw their attention. My nice neighbors wouldn't stand a chance against a vampire, especially not this vampire.

As far as my other, tougher neighbors were concerned . . . I was a little surprised the noise Littleton was making hadn't attracted them already. Still, Adam's house was well insulated. They might not hear Littleton's voice well enough to worry about it, but a gun shot would bring them running.

Werewolves and sorcerers were a bad combination, though, according to Uncle Mike. I believed him – which is why I hadn't tried calling for help. I was beginning to think that Littleton really couldn't come in. He could scare me, but he couldn't come in and hurt me unless I invited him in.

'Not by the hair of my chinny chin chin,' I muttered.

He banged the wall again and I jumped. Seconds passed, a minute, then two and nothing happened. No screams, no bangs, no ripping siding – how was I going to explain that to my insurance company?

'Yes, Ma'am,' I tried out. 'This vampire queen asked me to hunt a vampire and demon combo. He found out somehow and it ticked him off so he ripped the siding off my house.'

I sat down in the middle of my floor with the gun under my arm. 'I guess I'll have to fix it myself. I wonder how much siding costs. And whatever else he damaged out there.'

I couldn't remember if I'd gotten Medea inside before I went to bed. I usually did, but I'd been so tired . . . As soon as I got my courage up again, I'd go out and make sure Medea was sleeping in Samuel's room where she preferred to spend the night. I could call Andre – but . . .

My shoulders were stiff from the tension and I leaned my head to the side, stretching. Suddenly the floor underneath the carpet bent upwards with a tremendous noise. I sprang to my feet and shot my floor while it was still vibrating. I might not be super strong, but I am fast. I shot twice more in rapid succession. Then I waited, staring at the holes in my floor and the powder marks on my cream-colored Berber carpet.

Something moved in one of the holes and I jumped back, shooting again as several small objects were forced through holes that they were too large for. A moment later I heard a car door slam in my driveway and a German engine purred to life, a BMW like Littleton had been driving at the hotel. He drove off, not in a hurry, just another driver out on the road, and I stared at the four, misshapen, blood-covered, silver slugs he'd given back to me.

When my alarm went off, I was sitting in the middle of my bedroom floor with Medea curled up purring in my lap for comfort. Why is it that in all the adventure movies the heroine doesn't have to get up and go to work?

It had taken me an hour to send my neighbors back home. I'd told them the damage must have been done by some irate customer – or maybe one of the local gangs. Yes, I'd fired the shots to scare them off – I didn't think I'd hurt any of them. Maybe they hadn't known anyone was home. Of course I'd call the police, but there was no sense getting them out this late. I'd call them in the morning. Really.

I'd been planning on talking to Tony anyway, though I doubted I'd say anything about Littleton's attack. There wasn't anything the police could do about him.

I could call in Zee, just for the day, but I wasn't going to sleep today anyway. I might as well save Zee's help for another day. I turned off the alarm and pushed a protesting Medea off my lap and threw on clothes so I could take a look at the damage Littleton had done to my trailer in the morning light.

The damage was worse than it had seemed last night. He

hadn't torn off the siding, he'd cut it to ribbons from the roof to the bottom in segments a finger-length apart. I also had the answer to how he'd gotten underneath it. The cinder block foundation in the back had a person sized hole broken through it.

My trailer was a 1978, fourteen-by-seventy-foot model, long past its prime. It wasn't a showpiece, but it had, at least, been in *one* piece when I went to bed last night. Fixing it was going to cost an arm and two legs — if it could be fixed at all.

To that end, I'd better get ready to go to work or there would be no money to fix anything, including breakfast.

While I showered I thought about what I'd learned and what I hadn't. I didn't know where Littleton was now. I didn't know if a gun was useful against a vampire. I had three bullets that said perhaps not, but then they had been covered with blood so at least they'd done some damage. I didn't know why seeing ghosts made me dangerous to vampires, or how being immune to their magic was going to help me against a vampire who could do what he'd done to my trailer. And, after the demonstration Littleton had given me last night, I knew I was going to need Andre to destroy him.

I called Adam's house before I left for work to check on Warren. I was also wondering why no one had come over to check out the shooting. The phone rang ten times before someone picked it up.

'Hey, Darryl,' I said. 'How's Warren doing?'

'He's alive,' Adam's second told me. 'Unconscious but alive. We heard the shooting last night, but the wolf we sent over said you had it under control. Is Samuel around?'

'Samuel stayed over there last night,' I told him.

He made a noncommittal grunt. 'Samuel's not here, and Adam apparently left the house about two in the morning. I didn't think to ask the guard about Samuel.'

Darryl must be worried if he was telling me all of this. I rubbed my forehead. Two was a few hours before I'd had my visitor.

'Did anyone ask Kyle what they were talking about before they left?'

'Warren's . . . friend was asleep. Warren is drifting in and out, but he is pretty agitated when he is awake. He knows something, but his vocal cords are damaged and we can't understand a thing he tries to say.'

He was answering me as if I had some authority, I realized, as if he really were talking to Adam's mate.

'What do you think happened?' I asked.

'I think Adam – and Samuel if he is gone, too – figured out where the damned sorcerer is. I don't see Adam leaving Warren alone in this bad a shape otherwise.'

Neither did I. I pinched the bridge of my nose. 'That could be bad.'

'How so?'

'Last night, Uncle Mike told me that having a demon and a werewolf together could be very dangerous. Demons have a deleterious effect on self control, which is very, very bad for werewolves. Uncle Mike was *very* concerned.'

He absorbed that for a moment. 'That *could* be bad. It might have been nice to know that sooner.'

'Mmm.' I sucked in a breath. There was more that he should know, but I wasn't happy telling him. Still, with Samuel and Adam both missing, it wasn't smart to withhold information from one of the few allies I had left.

This was Darryl, and, since he was treating me as though I really was higher in the pack than he was – and since he was unlikely to care much about me one way or the other – he wasn't going to forbid me anything. 'I was in Uncle Mike's meeting Marsilia. She wants me to find Littleton and kill the sorcerer for her.'

There was a very long, telling pause. 'She thinks you can do this?' His disbelief might not be flattering, but I kinda felt that way myself so it was all right.

'Apparently. She's got one of her higher ranking vampires helping me out.'

'Mmm,' he said.

'I think he's actually okay. He's a friend of Stefan's.'

'Adam wouldn't let you do this.'

'I know. But he's not there. If Warren regains consciousness, I want you to call me.' I gave him my cell number, home number, and the number of the shop.

After he'd written it all down, I said, 'You need to call Bran and tell him everything.'

'Even about you?' he asked. He knew what Bran would think about me going after a sorcerer with a vampire.

'Yes,' I said. I wasn't going to put him in a position that would get Bran angry with him. Bran could get angry with me – I'd had a lot of practice at dealing with that once upon a time. I supposed I could get used to it again. It helped that he was hundreds of miles away and I had caller ID on my cell phone.

Even so . . . 'But only if he asks,' I added hastily.

Darryl laughed. 'Yeah, I remember using that trick on my mother. Hope it works better for you than it did for me.'

I hung up.

Adam and Samuel had disappeared before Littleton had started his little performance at my trailer.

Littleton had Samuel's voice down pat. After four hours, Adam hadn't called to check in on Warren, who was not yet out of danger – nor had Samuel.

Littleton had them both. If Littleton was like other vampires, he would not be active in the day. There was a chance they were still alive. Littleton liked to savor his prey.

I had to find him before nightfall.

I called Elizaveta and got her answering machine.

'This is Elizaveta Arkadyevna. I am unavailable. Please leave a message with your name and phone number and I will return your call.'

'This is Mercy,' I told it after it beeped at me. 'Adam and Samuel are missing. Where are you? Call me or Darryl as soon as you can.'

I didn't know enough about witchcraft to know if she could help or not. At the very least I could pick her brain about vampires and sorcerers – if I could convince her that Adam's orders not to talk to me were out of date.

I called all three of Tony's numbers and told him to call me on my cell. I called Zee, but only got his answering machine. I left a detailed message on his phone also. That way Darryl and Zee both knew what I was up to.

Then I took my cell phone and headed to work. I'd send Gabriel home for the day and close the shop.

My watch said I was fifteen minutes early, so I was surprised to see Mrs Hanna. She was hours ahead of her customary schedule.

When I parked in my usual spot, she was next to my car. Frantic as I was, Mrs Hanna's very presence demanded that I be polite. 'Hello, Mrs Hanna. You're early today.'

There was a pause before she looked up at me, and for a moment she didn't know me at all. A month or two more, I thought, and there would only be a little personality left.

But for today, her face eventually lit up, 'Mercedes, child. I was hoping to see you today. I have a special drawing just for you.'

She fumbled around in her cart without success, becoming visibly more agitated.

'It's all right, Mrs Hanna,' I told her. 'I'm sure you'll find it later. Why don't you leave it for me tomorrow?'

'But it was just right here,' she fretted. 'A picture of that nice boy who likes you. The dark one.'

Adam.

'Tomorrow will be fine, Mrs Hanna. What brings you out so early?'

She looked around as if bewildered by the question. Then relaxed and smiled. 'Oh that was Joe. He told me I'd better change my route if I wanted to keep visiting him.'

I smiled at her. When she'd been alive, she'd talked about John this and Peter that. I never had been sure if she really had boyfriends, or just liked to pretend that she had.

She leaned forward confidentially. 'We women always have to change for our men, don't we.'

Startled I stared at her. That was it exactly. I felt as though Adam was changing who I was.

She saw that her words had hit home and nodded happily. 'But they're worth it, God love them. They're worth it.'

She puttered off in her usual shuffle-shuffle step that covered a surprising amount of ground.

10

'No, sir, she's not—' Gabriel looked up as I walked into the shop. 'Wait. She's here.'

I took the phone, thinking it might be Tony or Elizaveta. 'This is Mercy.'

'This is John Beckworth, I'm calling from Virginia. I'm sorry, I forgot how much earlier you are than we.'

The voice was familiar, but the name was wrong. 'Mr Black?' I asked.

'Yes,' he sounded a little sheepish. 'It's Beckworth, actually. I just got off the phone with a Bran Cornick. He suggested that there is some trouble in the Tri-Cities.'

'Yes, we have something of a . . . situation here.' Either Adam had called Bran yesterday, or Darryl had remembered the Blacks/Beckworths and talked to him this morning.

'So Mr Cornick said. He suggested that we fly to Montana early next week.' He paused. 'He seemed less intense than Adam Hauptman.'

That was Bran, quiet and calm until he ripped out your throat.

'Are you calling to make sure he's safe?' I asked.

'Yes. He wasn't on the list of men you gave me.'

'If I had a daughter, I'd have no qualms leaving her with Bran,' I said sincerely, ignoring the question of why Bran's name wasn't on the list. 'He'll take good care of you and your family.'

'He talked to Kara, my daughter,' he said, and there was a world of relief in his voice. 'I don't know what he said, but I haven't seen her this happy in years.'

'Good.'

'Ms Thompson, if there is ever anything I can do for you, please don't hesitate to call.'

I started to automatically refuse, but then I stopped. 'Are you really a reporter?'

He laughed. 'Yes, but I don't cover celebrity sex lives. I'm an investigative journalist.'

'You have ways of finding out about people?'

'Yes.' He sounded intrigued.

'I need as much information as you can get on a man named Cory Littleton. He has a website. Fancies himself a magician. It would be particularly helpful if you could find out if he owns property in the Tri-Cities.' That was a long shot, but I knew that Warren had checked out all the hotels and rentals. If Littleton was here, he had some place to stay.

He read the name back to me again. 'I'll get what I can. It may take a few days.'

'Be careful,' I said. 'He's dangerous. You don't want him to know you're looking.'

'Is this connected to the trouble Mr Cornick was telling me about?'

'That's right.'

'Tell me how to contact you – probably an e-mail address would be best.'

I gave him what he needed, and thanked him. Hanging up the phone, I noticed Gabriel's eyes on me.

'Trouble?' he asked.

Maybe I should have worked harder to keep Gabriel out of my world. But he had a good head on his shoulders, and he wasn't stupid. I'd decided it was easier to tell him what I could – and safer than if he went looking.

'Yes. Bad trouble.'

'That phone call last night?'

'That's part of it. Warren's hurt badly. Samuel and Adam are missing.'

'What is it?'

I shrugged. 'That I can't tell you.' The vampires didn't like people talking about them.

'Is he a werewolf?'

'No, not a werewolf.'

'A vampire like Stefan?'

I stared at him.

'What? I'm not supposed to figure it out?' He shook his head reprovingly. 'Your mysterious customer who drives the funky bus painted up like the Mystery Machine and only shows up after dark? Dracula he isn't, but where there's werewolves, there certainly ought to be vampires.'

I laughed, I couldn't help it. 'Fine. Yes.' Then I told him seriously, 'Don't let anyone else know you know anything about vampires, especially not Stefan.' Then I remembered that wouldn't be a problem. I swallowed around the lump in my throat and continued seriously. 'It's not safe for you or your family. They'll leave you alone as long as they don't know you believe in them.'

He pulled his collar aside to show me a cross. 'My mother makes me wear this. It was my father's.'

'That'll help,' I told him. 'But pretending ignorance will help more. I'm expecting a couple of phone calls. One from Tony and the other from Elizaveta Arkadyevna, you'll know her by her Russian accent.' I'd intended to close the shop for the day, but I didn't have anything to do until Tony or Elizaveta called me back. If it had taken two weeks for Stefan and Warren to find the sorcerer, I was unlikely to find him by driving up and down streets at random. There are over 200,000 people living in the Tri-Cities. It isn't Seattle, but it's not Two Dot, Montana, either.

*   *   *

I couldn't concentrate on my work. It took me twice as long to replace a power steering pump as it should have, because I kept stopping to check my phone.

Finally, I broke down and called Zee again – but there was no answer on his phone. Elizaveta still wasn't answering her phone either, nor was Tony.

I started on the next car. I'd only been working on it for a few minutes when Zee walked in. From the scowl on his face, he was upset about something. I finished tightening the alternator belt on the '70 Beetle and scrubbed up. When I had most of the grease off my hands I leaned a hip on a bench and said, 'What's up?'

'Only a fool deals with vampires,' he said, his face closed up into a forbidding visage of disapproval.

'Littleton ripped Warren to bits, Zee,' I told him. 'It probably killed Stefan – and Samuel and Adam are missing.'

'I did not know about the Alpha and Samuel.' His face softened a little. 'That is bad, *Liebchen*. But to take direction from the vampire's mistress is not smart.'

'I'm being careful.'

He snorted. 'Careful? I saw your trailer.'

'So did I,' I said ruefully. 'I was there when it happened. Littleton must have found out that Marsilia asked me to find him.'

'You obviously found him last night – not that it did you any good.'

I shrugged. He was right, but I couldn't just sit around and wait for Darryl to call and tell me they'd found Samuel and Adam dead. 'Marsilia seems to think I can deal with him.'

'You believe her?'

'Uncle Mike did.'

That took him aback; he pursed his lips. 'What else did Uncle Mike say to you?'

The stuff about heroes was too embarrassing, so I told him what Uncle Mike had told me about the effect of demons on werewolves.

'Uncle Mike visited me this morning,' Zee told me. 'Then we both went out and visited some other friends.' He hefted a backpack at me.

I caught it and unzipped the bag. Inside was a sharpened stake as long as my forearm and the knife Zee had loaned me the first time I'd visited the seethe. It was very good at slicing through things – things a knife had no business cutting at all, like chains for example.

'I got the stake from a fae who has an affinity for trees and growing things,' he said. 'It's made from the wood of a rowan tree, a wood of the light. She said that this would find its way to the heart of a vampire.'

'I appreciate your trouble,' I said, skirting around an outright 'thank you.'

He smiled, just a little smile. 'You *are* a lot of trouble, Mercy. Usually you're worth it. I don't think that knife will do anything to the vampire when his magic is still working. But once he's staked he will be more vulnerable to it. Then you can use it to cut off his head. Zzip.'

I reached down to the bottom of the bag, where something else was hidden. I brought it out into the light and saw it was a flat disk of gold. On the front was a lizard, and on the back were marks of some sort that might have been letters. Both the lizard and the lettering were battered.

'A vampire is not dead until its body is ashes,' Zee said. 'Put this on its body, after you've cut off the head, then say the medallion's name.' He took it, brushed his fingers over the lettering, and, though I don't think the lettering actually changed, I could read it. *Drachen*.

It had been ten years ago, but I *had* taken two years of German in college. '*Kite?*' I said incredulously.

He laughed, the smile flashing wide on his narrow face. 'Dragon, Mercy. It also means dragon.'

'Do I say it in German or English?' I asked.

He pulled my hand forward and put it in my reluctant palm, closing my hand upon it. '*Macht nichts, Liebling.*' It doesn't matter.

'So if someone says either word it burns whatever it's touching to ashes?' I hadn't meant to sound quite so appalled. How often did I really hear the word in everyday life anyway?

'Would I give you such a thing?' He shook his head. 'No. Uncle Mike has given it your name, no one else may invoke it, and even then it takes both word and desire.'

'So I have to say it and mean it,' I said. I imagined if I was holding it against a vampire, desire to burn the creature to ashes wouldn't be hard to come by.

'Right.'

I leaned forward and kissed him on the cheek. 'This will help a lot.'

He frowned at me for the kiss. 'I would like to do more, but it is *verboten*. Even in so much as we have managed there is risk.'

'I understand. Uncle Mike told me.'

'If it were just risk to me, I would go with you to fight this thing. It is the whole of the Walla Walla Reservation who will suffer.'

Because of the violence shortly after the fae had revealed themselves, most of the fae who were not still hidden, had voluntarily relocated to one of several fae reservations, where they could live in safety. Zee lived there; I'm not sure about Uncle Mike. But I did know that the Gray Lords weren't above killing one fae to ensure the good behavior of others.

'I do understand,' I told him. 'Besides, didn't you tell me once that your talents are not much use against vampires?'

His eyebrows lowered even further. 'My magic would not

help. But strength I have – I am a blacksmith. I worry for you who are so human-fragile.'

'That's why I'm taking one of Marsilia's vampires with me,' I told him.

My cell phone rang before he could say what he thought about that. I picked it up and looked at the caller ID, hoping for Tony or Elizaveta. It was Bran. I considered not answering it, but he was all the way in Montana – all he could do is yell at me.

'Hey, Bran,' I said.

'Don't do it. I will be there tomorrow morning.'

Bran said he wasn't psychic, but most of the werewolves were convinced otherwise. Moments like this made me agree with them.

I was tempted to feign innocence, but it was too much work. I was tired, and I doubted I was going to be able to sleep until Adam and Samuel were safe at home – or until Littleton was dead.

'Good,' I said. 'I'm glad you're coming, but both you and Uncle Mike told me demons are very bad news for werewolves. What happens if *you* lose control?' It didn't even occur to me that Bran wouldn't know who Uncle Mike was. Bran just knew everything and everyone.

He said nothing.

'We don't have enough time to wait for you,' I said. 'If Samuel and Adam are still alive, I have to find them before nightfall.'

He still didn't say anything.

'It doesn't matter if you object,' I told him gently. 'You can't stop me, anyway. With Adam missing, I'm the highest ranking werewolf in town – since he declared me his mate.' Fancy that. And I wasn't even a werewolf – not that I expected my mythological rank to stand up without Adam around. Still, Bran of all people would have to follow his own laws.

'I'm not helpless,' I told him. 'I have my very own super-hero vampire/sorcerer-slaying kit, and the vampires have given me one of their own to guard my back.' Going after Littleton was probably suicidal, even with a vampire to back me up – it hadn't helped Warren any – but I wasn't going to sit around and wait for Adam's body to show up in Uncle Mike's garbage.

'You trust this vampire?'

No. But I couldn't tell him that – and I knew better than to try to lie to Bran. 'He wants Littleton permanently dead.' I was sure of that much, I'd heard the anger in Andre's voice, the hunger for vengeance. 'He was a friend of one of the sorcerer's victims.' I could almost say 'sorcerer's victim' fast enough that I didn't think, 'Stefan,' or 'Adam,' or 'Samuel.' A victim was someone nameless and faceless.

'Be careful,' he told me, finally. 'Remember, the walkers may have taught vampires to fear them, but there are still lots of vampires, and only one walker.'

He hung up.

'He's right,' Zee told me. 'Don't get too cocky.'

I laughed. It came out sounding tired and sad. 'You saw my trailer, Zee. I'm not going to get cocky. None of your people know where he is?'

Zee shook his head. 'Uncle Mike is looking into it, but he has to be careful. If we find anything, we'll tell you.'

The phone rang again, and I answered without looking at the number. 'Mercy.'

'You need to get over here.' Kyle spoke very softly, as if he didn't want anyone to overhear him – but he was in a werewolf's house.

'They can hear you,' I told him. I could hear Darryl saying something in Chinese. It was a very bad sign that Darryl was speaking Chinese because he only did that when he was really ticked off. 'I'll be right over.'

I turned toward Zee.

'I'll work the shop today – and tomorrow, maybe longer,' Zee said. 'And you won't pay me.'

When I started to object, he raised one hand. 'No. I cannot hunt Littleton, but I can help this much.'

Fixing the trailer was already turning next month into a macaroni-and-cheese month. If Zee donated his time, at least it wouldn't be a ramen noodle month. I kissed his cheek again and ran for my car.

Remembering the fate of the wolf who'd tailed me yesterday, I drove exactly five miles an hour over the speed limit down the highway. Getting a ticket would eat up a lot of time.

My cell phone rang again as I drove past the traffic cop who was parked on the other side of the bridge over the train tracks. This time the phone call was from Tony.

'Hey, Mercy,' he said. 'I got all six messages. What did you need?'

'Is there any way you could get me a list of all the violent incidents the police were called to over the past month? I need it for all the Tri-Cities, not just Kennewick.'

'Why?' The friendliness had left his voice.

'Because there *might* be something causing them, and it *might* help stop it if I can find out where the incidences are taking place.' I watch TV. I've seen the way the police track serial killers – at least in detective shows. It made sense that demon-caused problems might center around the demon. Stefan had apparently run into success using that method.

If I ever become a serial murderer, I'll be very careful to kill people in a pattern that centers around a police station – and not my home or work.

'We have a map,' he told me as I turned down Adam's road and put my foot down. Sure the speed limit on the road was thirty-five but I'd never seen a police officer out here. 'Why don't you come over to the station and I'll show it to you – if you answer a few questions.'

'All right,' I said. 'I have a few errands to run first. Can I meet you in an hour or so?'

'I'll be here,' he said, and hung up.

Honey opened the door of Adam's house before I got to the porch.

'They're upstairs,' she said unnecessarily. Darryl was still saying something rude in Chinese.

No, I don't speak Chinese, but some things don't require translation.

I ran up the stairs with Honey on my heels.

'I talked Darryl into coming downstairs after Kyle called you,' Honey said. 'But just a few minutes ago Warren tried to get out of bed and Kyle yelled at him. So Darryl went back up.'

I'd have asked for more details – like why Warren and Darryl were arguing in the first place, assuming it wasn't Kyle and Darryl – but there wasn't time.

The guest room door was open. I stopped just outside and took a deep breath. When you walk into a room with two angry werewolves (and I could hear two growls), it is a good idea to be calm. Anger just exacerbates the situation – and fear can make both of them attack you.

I shoved the last thought to the back of my mind, tried to think serene thoughts, and walked in.

Warren had shifted into his wolf form – and he looked no better than he had last night. Splatters of his blood crusted the sheets, the walls and the floor.

Darryl was still in human form and was struggling with Warren. It looked like he was trying to hold him in the bed.

'Lie down,' he roared.

In the pack, Darryl outranked Warren, he was Adam's second and Warren, Adam's third. That meant Warren had to do what Darryl told him to.

But Warren, hurt and confused, his human half submerged under the wolf, had forgotten that he was supposed to submit to Darryl's authority. It should have been an instinctive thing. That Warren wasn't listening to Darryl meant one thing – Darryl wasn't really more dominant, Warren had been faking it all along.

Under these circumstances it was a very, very bad thing. A wounded werewolf is dangerous, the wolf nature superceding the human control – and a werewolf is a very nasty creature. Much, much nastier than his natural counterpart.

The only reason Warren hadn't killed everyone in the house was because he was half dead and Darryl was very, very strong.

Kyle was standing against a wall, as far as he could get from the bed. His purple silk dress shirt was ripped and the skin under it torn and dripping blood. The expression on his face was worried, but he didn't smell of fear or anger.

'You're the highest ranking wolf,' Honey whispered. 'I told Kyle to call you when Darryl just seemed to irritate Warren. He was all right with Kyle until a few minutes ago.'

Hadn't I just told Bran that I outranked Darryl? But Honey, like the rest of Adam's wolves, knew I wasn't really Adam's mate – and even if I was, my authority would be law – not real. Not as real as it would take to help Warren control his wolf. But Honey watched me with faith in her eyes, so I had to try.

'Warren,' I said firmly. 'Lie down.'

If I was the most surprised person in the room when Warren subsided immediately, Darryl was a close second. I've always thought it was stupid, the way female pack members take their rank from their mate. I thought it was one of those dumb things that the wolves' human halves tacked onto nature to make life difficult, something the human part of the werewolves paid attention to, not the wolf.

Darryl slowly let go of Warren and sat on the end of the bed. Warren lay limply where he'd been, his splendid brown coat ragged and coated with blood, some old, some fresh.

'Well,' I said, to cover up my confusion. 'It's a good sign that he can shift – and he'll heal faster in this form.' I looked at Kyle. 'Did he say anything about why Samuel and Adam left?'

'No,' Kyle frowned at me. 'What did you do?'

I shrugged. 'Werewolf politics,' I told him.

'How did you do this when I could not?' Darryl asked.

I looked over and saw that his dark eyes had lightened to yellow – and he was staring at me.

'Not my fault,' I told him. 'Adam didn't even ask me before he claimed me as mate before the pack – I certainly didn't think it was anything more than a way to keep me from getting eaten. As far as dominance goes, you and Warren will have to sort things out when Adam gets back.' I looked back at Kyle and asked him again, 'How badly are you hurt?'

Kyle shook his head. 'Just a scratch.' He raised his face to me. 'Am I going to howl at the moon, too?'

I shook my head. 'It's not that easy to become a were-wolf. He'd have had to nearly kill you. A scratch wouldn't do it.'

Kyle was a lawyer – nothing showed on his face. I couldn't tell if he was relieved or disappointed. Maybe he didn't know either.

'We're going to have to move him down to the safe room,' I told Darryl.

The safe room was a room in the basement that was re-inforced to withstand a full grown werewolf. If Darryl wasn't dominant enough to make sure Warren stayed quiet, the cell was the only alternative.

'We can leave him on the mattress,' suggested Honey. 'Darryl and I can carry him down the stairs.'

Which is what we did. Kyle and I followed, and I explained what we were doing as quickly as I could.

Warren didn't object to being imprisoned, but we had trouble keeping Kyle from following him.

'He didn't hurt me on purpose,' he said, standing just inside the cell door. 'I was trying to help Darryl keep him down.'

'It'll get worse before it gets better,' I told him.

'He didn't hurt me before.'

Which let everyone in the room, except Kyle, know just how much Warren cared about him. Even a crazed werewolf won't harm his mate.

'I don't want to have to explain to Warren why we let him eat you,' I said. 'Look, you can sit in this couch right here and stay all day.'

There was a little sitting room outside the cell, with a couch, matching easy chair, and big-screen TV.

'It'll only be for the day,' Darryl said, his voice still a little growly, making me glad we weren't closer to a full moon. 'He'll be well enough to be on his own tonight.'

Warren and his wolf might have accepted me as Adam's mate, but I doubted Darryl did – and finding out that Warren was dominant to him was going to make him touchy for a while. A long while.

We left Warren in the cell, with Kyle leaning against the silver-coated bars. It wasn't the smartest place for him to wait, but at least he wasn't inside.

'I have to go,' I told Darryl, once we were upstairs. 'I'm still trying to locate Adam and Samuel. Can you handle it from here?'

He didn't answer me, just stared down toward the cell.

'We'll be all right,' said Honey, softly. She stroked Darryl's arm to comfort him.

'They won't accept him as second,' Darryl said.

He was probably right. That Warren had survived being a homosexual werewolf as long as he had was a tribute to his strength and intelligence.

'You can sort it out with Adam when he gets back,' I said. I glanced at my watch. I had just enough time to call Elizaveta before I left for the police station.

I didn't leave a third message on her answering machine. It might have annoyed her.

When I got off the phone, Darryl said, 'Elizaveta left town after Adam found Warren. She said it was too dangerous for her to be here. If the demon got too close to her, it might be able to jump from Littleton to her, which, she told us, would be a disaster. She gathered her family and took a trip to California.'

I knew that Elizaveta wasn't a Wiccan witch. Her powers were inherited and had nothing to do with religion. That she was so afraid of a demon told me that she had already had some dealings with the powers of darkness – otherwise the demon wouldn't have been able to take her over without an invitation.

'Damn it,' I said. 'I don't suppose you have any ideas on how to kill Littleton.'

He smiled at me, his teeth very white in the darkness of his face. 'Eat him,' he said.

'Very funny.' I turned to leave.

'Kill the vampire and the demon goes away,' he told me. 'That's what the witch told Adam. And you kill a vampire by staking him, cutting off his head and then burning him.'

'Thank you,' I told him, though it was nothing I didn't know. I'd been hoping Elizaveta would have some knowledge of the demon that would make it easier to kill Littleton.

After I shut the door behind me, I heard Darryl say, 'Of course, eating him would work, too.'

*   *   *

The Kennewick police station was not too far from my shop, right next to Kennewick High. There were a bunch of high schoolers crowded into the small entryway, mobbing the pop machine. I waded through them to the glass fronted booth where a young man, who looked like he'd have been more at home with the kids on the other side, sat doing paperwork.

He took my name and Tony's, then buzzed me through the first door into an empty waiting room. I'd never been inside a police station before, and I was more intimidated than I'd expected. Nervousness always made me claustrophobic, so I paced back and forth in the air-conditioned room. It smelled strongly of whatever cleaner they'd used, though I expect that wouldn't have bothered anyone with a less sensitive nose. Beneath the antiseptic smell, it smelled of anxiety, fear, and anger.

I must have looked a little wild-eyed by the time Tony came to get me, because he took one look and asked, 'Mercy, what's wrong?'

I started to say something, but he held up one hand. 'Wait, this isn't private. Come with me.' Which was just as well, because I wasn't sure what I was going to tell him.

As I followed him down the corridor, I decided that the problem with deciding to bend the rules was trying to figure out just how far I could bend them.

The fae weren't going to step in against Littleton, at least not yet. The werewolves, according to Uncle Mike and Bran, didn't stand a chance. If the vampires were asking my help, it was a good sign they didn't know what to do about him either.

Bran had said that eventually sorcerers fall victim to their demon and all hell breaks loose. It just might be that the KPD would be the people on the front lines when that happened.

On the other hand, if it ever got back to the seethe that I told the police about their existence, I might as well kill myself right now.

Tony led me to a smallish office room, and shut the door behind us, closing out the sounds of the department. It wasn't his office. Even if it hadn't smelled like someone else, I could have told from the wedding picture on the desk. It was about thirty years old, and both of the smiling young people in it were blond.

Tony sat on the edge of the desk, set a manila file folder he'd been carrying beside him, and waved me vaguely to one of the chairs against the wall. 'You look like something the cat dragged in,' he said.

I shrugged. 'Rough morning.'

He sighed and tapped his finger on the folder. 'Would it help if I told you I have here a report from a concerned citizen who called in at 7:23 this morning. It seems that her nice young neighbor, one Mercedes Thompson, had to fire her rifle in order to drive off a bunch of hooligans last night or early this morning. One of our patrolmen stopped by to see the damage.' He gave me a somber look. 'He took pictures.'

I gave him a wry smile. 'I was surprised at how bad it was when I saw it this morning, too.'

'Is this because someone saw you talking to me yesterday?'

It would have solved a lot of problems if I let him think that – but I prefer not to lie. Especially when that lie might start a fae-hunt.

'No. I told my neighbors it was probably just kids – or someone angry with my work.'

'So they came after your trailer with can openers? How long were they there before you came after them with the rifle?'

'Am I under arrest?' I asked brightly. Shooting a rifle where I lived might be illegal, I'd never checked it out.

'Not at this time,' he said carefully.

'Ah,' I settled back in the uncomfortable chair. 'Blackmail. How fun.' I tried to see the best way through this. Honesty was always the best policy.

'Okay,' I said finally, having decided how much I could tell him. 'You were right. There is something that's causing people to become violent. If I tell you what it is, however, I won't live to see tomorrow. Also, even if you know what it is, you won't be able to do anything to stop it. It is not a werewolf, and not a fae. Nor is it human, though it might appear that way.'

He looked . . . surprised. 'We were right?'

I nodded my head. 'Now, let me tell you this. It came last night and ripped my trailer to pieces, but it couldn't come in because I didn't invite it. You have to invite evil into your home – that's one of the rules. I shot it four times with my Marlin 444, loaded with silver. I hit it at least three times without even slowing it down. You need to stay away from it. Right now it's in hiding. The rise in violence is just a – a side effect. If you bring it out into the open, there will be a lot more bodies. We're trying to contain it without getting anyone killed. Hopefully very soon.'

'Who is "we"?' he asked.

'Some *acquaintances* of mine.' I looked him square in the eye and prayed that he'd leave it there. The heavy emphasis I used was straight out of a gangster movie. He didn't have to know how underpowered we were; the police would be even more helpless than Andre and I.

'I promise I won't lie to you about the preternatural community,' I told him. 'I may leave things out, because I have to, but I won't lie to you.'

He didn't like it, didn't like it at all. He tapped his fingers unhappily on the top of the desk, but in the end, he didn't ask more questions.

He got off the desk and walked over to a cabinet mounted in the wall behind my chair. I moved when he opened it and pushed back the doors to reveal a white board in the center and corkboards on the inside of each door. On one of the corkboards someone had pinned up a map of the Tri-Cities and covered it with roundheaded colored pins. Most of the pins were green, some were blue, and a double handful were red.

'This isn't all of them,' he said. 'A couple of weeks ago a few of us wondered if there was a pattern to the violence, so we pulled all reports of violence since April. The green pins are usual stuff. Property damage, arguments that get a little hot and someone calls them in, someone bangs his girlfriend around. That kind of stuff. Blue is where someone ended up in the hospital. Red is where someone ended up dead. A few of them are suicides.' He put a finger on a cluster of red near the highway in Pasco. 'This is the murder-suicide at the motel in Pasco last month.' He moved his hand to a green pin all by itself near the east edge of the map. 'This is your trailer.'

I looked at the map. I'd expected to get a list of addresses, but this was exactly what I needed – and not. Because there was no pattern I could see. The pins were scattered evenly around the Tri-Cities. Denser where the population was heavier, light in Finley, Burbank, and West Richland where there weren't so many people. There was no neat ring of pins like you see in the movies.

'We can't find a pattern either,' he said. 'Not an overall pattern. But the incidences do tend to come in clusters. Yesterday it was East Kennewick. Two fistfights and a family disturbance that roused the neighborhood. The night before it was West Pasco.'

'He's moving around,' I said. That wasn't good. Where was he keeping Adam and Samuel if he was moving around? 'Is there a time of day that the violence is the worst?' I asked.

'After nightfall.'

I looked at the pins again, silently counting the red ones. They were short of Uncle Mike's count – and I don't think either of them knew about the family who died during Daniel's experience with Littleton.

'Did you learn anything?' he asked.

'Hunting serial killers is easier on TV,' I said sourly.

'Is that what we're dealing with?'

I shrugged, then remembered Littleton's face when he killed the woman at the motel. 'I think so. Of a sort. The incidental violence is really bad, Tony, but this monster likes to kill. If he decides he doesn't need to hide anymore, it would be very bad. What can you tell me about serial killers?'

'I haven't seen one here,' he said. 'Doesn't mean we don't have one we don't know about — but there are things we watch for.'

'Like what?'

'Most of them start with easy victims for practice.'

Easy like Daniel? I thought.

'I have a friend in the Seattle PD who tells me his whole department is waiting for someone to get killed. For three years they've had neighborhood pets turn up dead. They're patrolling extra heavily near their at risk populations: the homeless, runaways, and prostitutes.'

I shivered. Had Littleton been a killer before he became a sorcerer and a vampire? Had he been a vampire first or a sorcerer? Had he been evil, or had he been made evil? Not that it mattered.

Someone knocked on the door. Tony reached past me to open it.

'Come on in, Sergeant,' he said. 'We're finished here. Sergeant, this is Mercedes Thompson. Mercy, this is Sergeant Owens, our watch commander. This is his office.'

Sergeant Owens was lean and fit, an older, more cynical version of the smiling young man in the wedding photo. He held out his hand and I shook it. He kept mine a moment, examining the traces of grease I could never quite get out from under my nails.

'Mercedes Thompson,' he said. 'I hear that you had trouble last night. I hope there is no recurrence.'

I nodded. 'I expect they got it out of their systems,' I told him with a faint smile.

He didn't smile back. 'Tony tells me that you have ties to the werewolf and fae communities and you've agreed to help us out.'

'If I can,' I agreed. 'Though I'm probably more qualified to tune up your cars than to give you advice.'

'You'd better be a very good mechanic,' he said. 'My people put their lives on the lines. I don't need bad advice.'

'She fixed Sylvia's car,' Tony said. In addition to being Gabriel's mother, Sylvia was a police dispatcher. 'She's a very good mechanic, her advice will stand up.'

In point of fact, Zee had fixed Sylvia's car, but that was beside the point.

The Sergeant relaxed. 'All right. All right. We'll see how it goes.'

We were back in the hall, when I stopped.

'What?' Tony asked.

'Take off the pins for the incidents at night. We need the daytime violence,' I told him. His very presence would cause violence. 'This thing moves around at night, but I don't think he can move during the day.'

'All right,' he said. 'It'll take a while. I'll get a rookie on it. Do you want to wait?'

I shook my head. 'I can't afford to. Would you call me?'

'Yes.'

I thought he'd drop me back at the waiting room, but he escorted me all the way out. This time the little entryway was empty of students.

'Thank you,' I said as I got in my car.

He held my door opened and saw what Stefan had done to my dash.

'Somebody hit that,' he said.

'Yep. I have that effect on people.'

'Mercy,' he said somberly. 'Make sure he doesn't hit you like that.'

I touched the broken vinyl where Stefan had put his fist. 'He won't,' I told him.

'You're sure I can't help you?'

I nodded. 'I promise that if that changes, I'll call you right away.'

I stopped at a fast food restaurant and ordered lunch. I ate a couple of cheeseburgers and a double order of fries, though I wasn't particularly hungry. I hadn't had any sleep, so staying alert meant fueling up – the large, caffeinated soda would help, too.

When I was through eating, I got in my car and drove around, thinking myself in circles. I just didn't have enough information to find the sorcerer, and I needed to find him before dark. Before he killed Samuel and Adam – I refused to believe they might already be dead. He hadn't had time to play with them yet.

Why had Marsilia sent me after Littleton knowing I was too stupid to find him?

I jerked my car over to the side of the road and parked it abruptly, too busy thinking to be safe driving.

Never trust a vampire. It was the first thing I'd ever learned about vampires.

Despite her performance at Stefan's trial, Marsilia claimed she had believed Stefan when he told her there was a vampire who was a sorcerer loose in the Tri-Cities. She could have sent the whole seethe after him – instead she'd sent Stefan and Daniel. No, Stefan had chosen Daniel. She'd expected Stefan to pick Andre. As had Andre, for that matter.

Even after she believed Stefan dead, she still didn't send

the seethe after Littleton. Instead she sent me with Andre. Me. I was supposed to find Littleton, or so she said. Andre was to keep me alive while I did so – or follow me around so Marsilia knew what I was doing.

Andre thought that Marsilia meant to see if she could take control of Littleton rather than kill him. Was that what Marsilia wanted him to do? Was that what he'd been supposed to do if he'd gone hunting with Stefan?

If Marsilia told him not to kill Littleton, he wouldn't. She was his maker and he couldn't disobey her – though apparently Stefan could.

I rubbed my face and tried to clear my thoughts. Knowing what Marsilia was up to might be important in the long run, but it wasn't going to help me find Littleton.

Littleton wasn't leaving my traces for me to follow.

'So what do you do when you're out hunting and you can't find any tracks or scent?' I asked aloud. It was a basic question, one that Samuel used on new werewolves who were ready to go for their first hunt.

'You go to places that will attract your prey,' I answered. 'Come on Samuel, that's not going to help. I don't know what attracted the sorcerer here in the first place.'

To know how to find them, you have to understand your prey.

Some little thought nudged at me. Littleton was not from the Tri-Cities. He'd been traveling though when he ran into Daniel. He'd come back, and Stefan and I had found him. He'd been waiting for Stefan. Why?

Then it hit me.

I'd read the Faust story in several versions, from Benét's 'The Devil and Daniel Webster' to Marlowe and Goethe. Sorcerers sell themselves to demons for knowledge and power. There was nothing in Littleton's actions that I could see as a search for knowledge or power.

Demons crave chaos, violence, and death. Littleton brought

that in abundance, but if the demon were directing his actions wholly, there would be more bodies. Demons are not patient creatures. The demon would not have let Warren go, would not have let Stefan and me go that first night.

But Littleton was a new vampire, and new vampires do what their makers tell them to do.

So what would a vampire get from Littleton's actions?

Littleton had almost certainly killed Stefan and Ben, and nearly killed Warren – but I was pretty sure that the wolves were collateral damage. No one would have predicted that the werewolves would get involved at all.

So, what could Daniel's disgrace and Stefan's death gain a vampire? Stefan had been Marsilia's favorite. Was the sorcerer an indirect attack on Marsilia?

I drummed on the steering wheel. If the seethe had been a wolf pack, I'd have been able to interpret her actions better. Still . . . she sent Stefan out and pretended it was punishment. Pretended for whose benefit? If all of the seethe were her get, obedient to her will as Andre told me vampires had to be, she wouldn't have had to pretend at all. So maybe she was having trouble controlling her people.

Maybe someone sent Littleton here to destroy her, to take over the seethe. How did a vampire become the leader of a seethe? Could Littleton's maker be in the Tri-Cities? If he was, could he hide from the other vampires?

I needed more information. More information about Marsilia and her seethe. More information about how vampires worked. And I knew only one place I might get it.

I started the car again and headed for Stefan's menagerie.

11

There was a gleaming red Harley-Davidson motorcycle in the driveway that hadn't been there last night. I pulled in behind it and stopped my car. The poor old Rabbit looked out of place in such an upscale neighborhood.

I rang the doorbell and waited a long time. My mother had taught me to be polite and part of me felt guilty for disturbing them during a time when they were probably used to sleeping. Guilt didn't keep me from ringing the doorbell again.

It was Rachel who opened the door – and like me, she looked like she'd had a hard night. She wore a thin, bright yellow T-shirt that left a four inch gap between its hem and the top of her low-rise jeans. Her navel was pierced and the sapphire-colored stone in the ring twinkled when she moved. It drew my eye and I had to force myself to look at her face – which was sporting several blue bruises along her jaw that hadn't been there last night. Her upper arm bore a purple handprint where someone had grabbed her.

She didn't say anything, just let me look my fill as she did the same to me. Doubtless she saw the puffy skin and dark circles that showed my lack of sleep.

'I need more information,' I told her.

She nodded and backed away from the door so I could come inside. As soon as I was in the house I could hear someone crying: a man. He sounded young and hopeless.

'What happened here?' I asked following her into the kitchen, the source of the sobs.

Naomi was sitting at the butcher-block counter, looking

ten years older than she had last night. She was wearing the same conservative clothes — and they looked the worse for wear. She looked up briefly as we walked in, but then turned her attention back to the mug of coffee she was sipping with deliberate calm.

Neither she, nor Rachel, paid any attention to the young man curled up in the corner of the room, next to the sink. I couldn't see his face because he had his back to all of us. He was rocking, the rhythm of the motion interrupted by the infrequent sobs that made his shoulders jerk forward. He was muttering something just under his breath, and even my ears couldn't catch exactly what he said.

'Coffee?' asked Rachel, ignoring my question.

'No.' The food I'd eaten was sitting like a lump in my stomach as it was. If I added coffee to it, I wasn't sure it would stay down.

She got down a mug for herself and poured some coffee out of an industrial-sized coffeemaker on the counter. It smelled good, French vanilla, I thought. The scent was soothing, better than the taste would have been. I pulled up a chair next to Naomi, the same one I'd used last night, and, glancing again at the man curled up in the corner I asked again, 'What happened to you?'

Naomi looked at me and sneered. 'Vampires. What happened to you?'

'Vampires,' I replied. Naomi's sneer sat oddly on her face, and seemed out of character — but I didn't know her enough to be sure.

Rachel tugged a chair around so she was opposite Naomi and me. 'Don't take it out on her. She's Stefan's friend, remember. Not one of them.'

Naomi looked back at her cup and I realized that she wasn't calm at all, she was in that place beyond fear where nothing you do matters because the worst has already happened and there's nothing you can do about it. I recognized that look. It's an expression I see a lot around the werewolves.

It was Rachel who told me what had happened.

'When Stefan didn't come back yesterday morning, Joey – that's short for Josephine – decided to leave while she could.' Rachel didn't drink her coffee, just turned her cup this way and that. 'After you left, though, I heard her motorcycle in the driveway. Can't mistake the sound of Joey's hog.' She moved her hands away from the mug and wiped them on her thighs. 'I was stupid. I know better – especially after Daniel. But it was Joey . . .'

'Joey has been here the longest,' Naomi said, when it became obvious Rachel was finished speaking. 'She was bound to Stefan already.'

She saw my puzzlement because she explained, 'That means she's almost one of them already. Everything except the actual changeover. The longer they stay bound before they die, the better the chance they'll rise again. Stefan is patient, his people almost always rise because he waits for years longer than most vampires.'

She was telling me all this so she wouldn't have to go on with the story.

'Daniel?'

She nodded. 'He was bound, just barely. It doesn't happen to all of us – but Daniel was still too new for the changeover to be certain. It was a miracle he survived. Stefan was so angry.' She took a sip of coffee and grimaced. 'I hate cold coffee.' She took another sip anyway. 'Andre did it on purpose, you know. One of those stupid one-upmanship games. He was terribly jealous of Stefan because Marsilia favored him – and at the same time he loved Stefan like a brother. So when he was angry he attacked one of us instead. Vampires don't usually care too much about the sheep in their menageries. I don't think Andre realized just how angry Stefan would get.'

'What happened to Joey?' I asked.

'She's dead,' Naomi told her coffee cup.

'Permanently dead,' Rachel said. 'I thought it was her on the motorcycle. She was wearing a helmet, and she doesn't let anyone, not even Stefan, touch the hog. When I finally realized the rider wasn't tall enough to be her, I tried to run back to the house.'

'She grabbed your arm?' I suggested. It wasn't a difficult guess, with the armband of bruises she wore.

Rachel nodded. 'And covered my mouth so I couldn't scream. About then, a car drove up – one of the seethe cars.'

Like the one Andre had driven last night. I worked on them from time to time in lieu of making a cash payment to the seethe. All the businesses in the greater Tri-Cities who weren't affiliated with more powerful groups paid protection money to the vampires. That's how I first met Stefan. He had helped me negotiate my payment from cash (which I couldn't afford) to work – mostly on his van, as it turned out, though I did the upkeep on the seethe's cars as well. They were Mercedes and BMWs, big, black sedans with dark, dark windows – just what you'd expect a bunch of vampires to drive.

'They popped open the trunk – and I thought they were going to shove me in, but it was worse than that. They already had Joey in there.' She jumped up abruptly and ran from the room. I heard her throwing up.

'They killed Joey, cut off her head so she wouldn't ever become one of them.' Naomi spoke evenly, but had to set down her coffee so she wouldn't spill it. 'They told Rachel that we were to stay inside this house until they decided what to do with us. They didn't have to kill Joey to deliver that message. They could just have brought her back here – or one of them could have brought her over, the way Andre brought over Daniel.'

'Rachel said "she". Was it Marsilia?' I asked.

Naomi shook her head. 'It was the Teacher. Marsilia . . . Stefan was a favorite of hers. I don't think she'd have killed one of us.'

'The Teacher?' I asked.

'Her real name is Estelle – she reminds me of an evil Mary Poppins.'

I knew the one she meant.

'They all have names among themselves,' she explained. 'Stefan was the Soldier, Andre is the Courtier. Stefan said it had to do with an old suspicion that if you spoke evil's name, you drew its attention. Stefan didn't believe in it, but some of the older vampires won't use real names when they talk of others.'

'So Estelle,' I said her name deliberately, 'went against Marsilia's wishes?'

'No. Well, probably, but not against her orders.'

'I'm trying to understand how the seethe works,' I told her. 'That's why I came here.'

Rachel came back in the room looking even more pale than she had before. 'I thought you were looking for Stefan?'

I nodded. They wouldn't care about Samuel and Adam. 'I think . . . *I think* that there is more going on than just a vampire turned sorcerer. I wonder, for instance – *who* turned the sorcerer into a vampire.'

'You think there's another vampire involved?' Naomi asked.

'Stefan said that the sorcerer was a new-made vampire. It occurred to me that his maker might be pulling the monster's strings. But I don't really know enough about vampires to make an educated guess.'

'I do,' Naomi said slowly, straightening in her chair.

Something shifted in her face and I saw yesterday's competent woman take control. 'I can help you, but there's a price.'

'What price?' I asked.

I somehow doubted that she wanted me to sing for her;
she didn't have Uncle Mike's sense of humor. And as the
thought occurred to me, I finally figured out that once Uncle
Mike claimed me as his guest, the fae couldn't do anything
bad to me without challenging him – which was why the
big woman had sighed in disappointment when Uncle Mike
told them I was his guest, even as he condemned me to sing
in front of the whole lot.

I was so lost in thought, I almost missed Naomi's answer
to my question.

'You have connections to the werewolves. I want you to
ask the Alpha to intercede for us. If Stefan is dead, then so
are we. Marsilia will scatter us among the menageries of the
other vampires who will imprison us until we die.'

'All the other vampires kill their . . .' I almost said food
and I couldn't think of any more diplomatic way to put it
so I just stopped speaking.

She shook her head. 'Not on purpose, but most of them
don't have Stefan's control. But we are Stefan's. That means
that their mind tricks won't work as well on us – and those
of us who are bound like Joey . . . When a bound one is
made over by someone they're not bound to, odd things
happen. I've heard people say that's why Stefan was never
properly subservient to Marsilia, that he was bound by a
different vampire. They won't want to keep us around long.'

'So if Stefan is permanently dead . . .'

She smiled bleakly at me. 'We all are.'

'And you believe the werewolves could do something about
this?'

She nodded. 'Marsilia owes them blood price. This sorcerer
is a vampire – which makes him Marsilia's business. When

the two werewolves joined the hunt they became her responsibility. Since one was hurt and the other—' she shrugged expressively. 'If your Alpha asks us as his price, she'll give us to him.'

'What about worries over your silence?' I asked.

'If we belong to the werewolves, our silence becomes their problem.'

'I'll speak to the werewolves,' I promised. 'But I don't have much influence.' Especially if Adam and Samuel were dead, too. The thought made it hard to breathe, so I shoved it away. 'Tell me about the vampires and how the seethe operates.'

Naomi gathered herself together visibly, and when she spoke she sounded like the professor she had apparently once been.

'I'll start from the general and then go to the specific, shall I? You understand that generalities do not account for variations – just because most vampires follow this pattern, doesn't mean that they all do.'

'All right,' I told her, wishing I had a notebook so I could take notes.

'A vampire likes to keep a food supply at hand, so they live with a small group of humans, usually anywhere from three to seven. Three are enough to provide food for a month before they die, seven is enough for six months – because if the vampires feed lightly on each, their prey lasts longer.'

'There aren't forty people disappearing from the Tri-Cities every month,' I protested. 'And I know that Marsilia has more than ten vampires.'

Naomi smiled grimly. 'They don't hunt in their own territory. Stefan found me in Chicago teaching at Northwestern. Rachel's from Seattle. I think the only one of us Stefan found in the Tri-Cities was Daniel, and he was hitchhiking down from Canada.'

For some reason, her speaking of Daniel made me glance over by the sink, but sometime while we'd been talking, the young man must have left. When I thought about it, I realized that I hadn't heard him for a while. It bothered me that I hadn't heard him leave.

'So the vampires have to continually replenish their menageries?'

'Most of them.' Naomi nodded. 'Stefan, as you know, does things differently. There are fourteen of us who live here, and maybe a dozen more who visit occasionally. Stefan doesn't usually kill his prey.'

'Tommy,' said Rachel in a small voice.

Naomi waved her hand dismissively. 'Tommy was ill anyway.' She looked at me. 'When the fae came out, Stefan began to be concerned about the same things that caused the fae to reveal themselves. He told the seethe – and the ruling council of vampires – that they could no longer live as they were and expect to survive. He had already been maintaining a large menagerie because he didn't kill his people – he has a reputation for being softhearted. I'm told Marsilia thinks his concern for us is "cute".' She gave me an ironic look.

'He began to experiment. To look for ways the vampire could benefit the human race. He found me dying of leukemia and offered me a chance at life.'

I did some adding in my head and frowned at her. 'Rachel said you were a professor and he found you about the time the fae came out. How old were you?'

She smiled. 'Forty-one.' That would mean she was in her sixties now – she didn't look it. She didn't look much older than I did. 'Stefan already knew that longevity was something he could offer: one of his bound children had belonged to him for over a century before another vampire killed her.'

'How does feeding a vampire make you live longer?' I asked.

'It's the exchange of blood,' said Rachel. She put a finger against her lips and licked it suggestively. 'He takes and then gives a little back. Since I started feeding, I've been able to see in the dark — I can even bend a tire iron.' She glanced at me from under her lashes to see how I took her revelation.

Ick, I thought hard and she frowned at me as if my re-action disappointed her. Maybe she expected me to be more horrified — or intrigued.

'And my leukemia has been in remission since 1981,' Naomi added prosaically. 'Joey said she was always a little psychic, but after she became Stefan's she could move things without touching them.'

'Not much,' said Rachel. 'All she could do was wiggle a spoon across the table.'

'So vampires can heal diseases?' I asked.

Naomi shook her head. 'With blood-borne diseases the vampires help a lot, things like sickle-cell anemia and a host of lesser known stuff. Stefan had some success with some of the autoimmune diseases, like MS and HIV. Except for the leukemia, though, Stefan found that he couldn't help cancer patients — or full-blown AIDS patients like Tommy, either.'

'So Stefan was trying to create a politically correct vampire?' I asked. The idea was mind boggling. 'I can see the headlines, *Maligned Vampire Only Wants to Save People*. Or better yet, *Vampire Estates — Come to our modern community compound. We'll heal your ills, make you stronger, and give you eternal life*.'

'*Join us for lunch*,' contributed Rachel with a toothy smile.

Naomi gave me a dry look. 'He's not that ambitious, I don't think. And he's run into problems.'

'Marsilia?'

'Mmm.' Naomi looked thoughtful. 'For a long time Marsilia was more of a figurehead than a leader. Stefan said she was pouting because she was exiled. After last winter, she began noticing more. He was hoping for her support in his efforts. Hoping she could push some of the others into more humane treatment of their menageries.'

'But . . . ?' I started.

'*But* there are a lot of problems with what Stefan is trying to do. First of all, not many vampires can afford to support as many people as he is – and any less than twelve of us and we start dying. And too, most vamps cannot control as many people as Stefan. There aren't many vampires who can make their sheep love them.' She looked pointedly at Rachel as she said the last sentence.

'Stefan says that the biggest problem is self-control.' Rachel said, ignoring Naomi. 'Vampires are predators. They kill things.'

Naomi nodded. 'A lot of them choose not to control themselves, they say it ruins the enjoyment of their meal. But all of them lose control sometimes when they are feeding. Even Stefan.' For a moment I caught a glimpse of horror in her eyes, but she lowered her eyelids and banished it. 'The longer a person belongs to a vampire, the harder it is for the vampire to keep from killing him. Stefan says that with the bound ones the urge to kill is very, very strong – and it only gets worse with time. He used to send Joey off to her family in Reno for months on end. The urge affects all vampires, not just the one the person is bound to. That's why Stefan didn't kill Andre outright. Daniel was bound – it could have been accidental.'

'Andre's menageries don't last very long,' Rachel told me. 'He's never created a vampire except for Daniel because he kills them before their time.'

I don't know what she saw in my face, only heard her start to speak quickly – something to the effect that Andre wasn't evil. '. . . not like Estelle or some of the others who like to play with their food.'

But I wasn't listening to her, I was looking at Daniel's tear-streaked face. I'd only met him the once, and I recognized his scent more than his features. He was standing behind Rachel, looking at me and whispering. It took me a few seconds to realize that it had been him I'd seen curled up by the sink. I hadn't recognized his scent then, but the dead don't always appear to all my senses.

Then I realized what he was saying and stopped fretting about why I hadn't realized who he was the first time I'd seen him.

'He ate me,' he whispered in a quietly frantic voice. 'He ate me.' Over and over.

'Where?' I asked coming to my feet. 'Where is he, Daniel?'

But it was no use. Daniel was no Mrs Hanna, who had died quietly and gone on with her usual routine. Some ghosts have urgent business to conduct − stopping over for a few minutes to leave a final message of love, or anger, with someone important. Some of them, especially the ones who died in traumatic ways, are caught in the moment of their death. Those are the most common kind − like Henry VIII's fifth wife, Catherine Howard, who runs screaming in the halls of the Tower of London.

'Daniel?' I asked, though his lack of reaction had robbed me of some of my urgency.

Rachel had quit speaking, hopped off her stool, and looked at Daniel. Naomi was just staring at me.

He faded after a moment more, and even after I couldn't see him anymore his voice lingered.

'Did you see him?' whispered Rachel.

'That's a cruel trick to play,' Naomi snapped at me.

I looked at her. 'You live with vampires and don't believe in ghosts?' I asked.

'Daniel's dead,' Rachel whispered.

I nodded. I wondered how a vampire could be a ghost — weren't they already dead? I was starting to get punchy from lack of sleep.

Naomi turned to the girl, 'Rachel—'

'I saw him, too,' she said hollowly. 'Just for a moment, but it was him. If Daniel's dead . . . Stefan wouldn't let anything happen to him, not if he were alive.' She looked around a little wildly and then left the room. I heard her quick footsteps up the stairs.

'What did he tell you?' I couldn't tell by her words if Naomi believed me or not, but it didn't really matter.

'Nothing.' I decided not to share what he had said. It wouldn't help anyone here, and it didn't sound as if Rachel had heard him. I got up and opened cupboards at random until I found a glass. I filled it with water and drank, pretending my throat was dry because I was thirsty, not because I was scared. Had the sorcerer really eaten Daniel?

Unwelcome, the memory of Littleton killing the woman at the hotel hit me as a full-throttle flashback: sight, smell, and sound. Just for a moment, but for that moment I was back in the hotel room. I must not have acted strangely, because when I turned back to Naomi she wasn't looking at me like she'd have stared at someone who'd screamed. I set the glass carefully down on the counter.

'If vampires live in their menageries,' I said, proud of my steady tone, 'who lives in the seethe?'

'Only the strongest vampires can live on their own and survive purely on human blood. All the others live in the seethe. They are the Mistress's menagerie,' Naomi told me after a moment.

I worked it out. 'She feeds on the vampires?'

Naomi nodded. 'And gives them a little, very little, blood in return. Without that blood, the weaker vampires would die – and only the Mistress is allowed to feed other vampires and feed from them. She keeps humans there, to nourish them all, but without her, the lesser vampires would die.'

'Allowed to feed?' I asked. 'If there is a rule against it, that must mean that she gains something from feeding off vampires.'

'Yes. I'm not sure what – strength and power, I think. And the ability to limit the actions even of those vampires she didn't directly beget. She made Stefan, and, I think Andre. But Estelle and most of the others aren't hers. When she quit paying attention to the seethe, Stefan and Andre ran things for her. But some of the older vampires became unruly.'

'Estelle and Bernard,' I suggested remembering the man in the dapper suit.

Naomi nodded. 'The four of them, Stefan, Andre, Estelle, and Bernard are the only vampires strong enough to live outside the seethe. Stefan says that once they can live without feeding from the Mistress, vampires start to get territorial, so they're sent out to gain their own menageries.' She paused. 'Five, actually. The Wizard lives on his own.'

'The Wizard?' I asked.

She nodded her head. 'Wulfe. You've seen him because Stefan said he was present at the trial. He looks younger than Daniel and has white blond hair.'

The boy who'd worked the magic on the chair.

'While Marsilia wasn't paying attention, Estelle and Bernard managed to make a few new vampires and kept them to themselves.'

'They're feeding off the new vamps,' I said, following her story. 'That makes them more powerful than they otherwise would be.'

'Right. This part I'm not certain of.'

'Okay.'

'There's some reason that Marsilia can't take the new vampires from them. I think it's because once the new vampires have exchanged blood with their maker a few times, they'll sicken and maybe die without the blood of that particular vampire. Vampires reproduce very slowly so they are very careful with new ones – even if it means that Bernard and Estelle gain power that Marsilia cannot afford for them to have.'

'So,' Naomi continued, 'there's dissension in the ranks. Stefan believed that Marsilia is losing her grip on the seethe. No one is in outright rebellion, but the Mistress is not in absolute control either.'

'What does the addition of the sorcerer do to her position?' I asked, and she smiled at me like a student who'd come to the right conclusion.

'A vampire is in town causing trouble,' she said. 'It's a matter for Marsilia to handle – but this one has proven stronger than Stefan. Vampires . . . the older they get the more afraid they are of death. Stefan told me that he thought the reason she sent only him out after the sorcerer wasn't to punish him – but because she could send no one else because they wouldn't go. Of the five most powerful vampires, only Stefan and Andre are truly hers.'

So she really had been desperate when she came to me.

'Why doesn't Marsilia go after him herself? She's the Mistress and the most powerful of them all.'

Naomi pursed her lips. 'Would your Alpha go after such a dangerous creature when he had warriors to fight in his stead?'

'He already has,' I told her. 'An Alpha who counts on others to fight his battles doesn't stay Alpha long.'

'He's not dead.' I turned at the sound of a masculine voice behind me.

The man who filled the doorway looked to be somewhere in his fifties, with an underlying strength buried beneath his somewhat thickened midsection. I glanced at his hands and was unsurprised to see them roughened from a lifetime of hard work. Like me, this was a man who'd made his living with his hands.

'Who's not dead, Ford?' Naomi asked, but he ignored her entirely.

His bright eyes on mine, he took another step into the room. I couldn't look away from his gaze. 'He's not dead,' he said intensely. 'If he were dead, the threshold would be gone. I was here when Andre couldn't get through. Only Stefan made this a home. *I'd* know if he were dead.'

'Stop it, Ford,' Naomi said sharply and the scent of her fear distracted me from Ford's brilliant, liquid-crystal gaze.

I blinked and jerked my gaze away. It was still daylight, so Ford couldn't be a vampire – but I was guessing he was the next thing to it.

He grabbed my arm and hauled me off the stool with less effort that it should have taken. I was used to big men – Samuel was over six feet tall, but this man made me feel small. He didn't know how to fight though, because I didn't have any trouble breaking his grip.

I took two steps back and Naomi put herself between us. 'Daniel is gone,' I told him. 'I saw his ghost myself. Warren, one of the werewolves who was with Stefan, was badly injured and left for the pack to find. I don't know how our other wolf is or Stefan either. I intend to find out.'

Naomi stepped closer and patted him on the chest. 'Shhh. It's all right.' Her soothing tones were very close to what Adam used on his new wolves when they became overset. 'You might want to go now, Mercedes,' she said in the same soothing tones. 'Ford is one of the bound.'

And that meant more than his being able to become a vampire when he died, I saw. The brightness of his eyes wasn't some genetic fluke, but the precursor to the glowing gems I'd seen vampires display in anger or lust.

He grabbed Naomi impatiently, I think to thrust her aside so he could get to me. But she tilted her head and presented the side of her neck to him, and he hesitated, clearly caught by the sight of her pulse.

If she'd been merely afraid, I'd have stayed there and tried to help her – but her eagerness for him was uncomfortably strong. I turned and left as he bent for her neck.

I was a half mile from Stefan's house before I took my first full breath. I'd learned a lot there, more than I'd expected – and nothing that would help me find Littleton. I'd no idea where the other vampire menageries were, and even if I did, I doubted that the sorcerer would be living with his master – assuming Littleton's maker was one of Marsilia's vampires.

There were any number of vampires who might have made the sorcerer to cause trouble for Marsilia. Or a vampire from another seethe might have noticed the trouble she was in, and sent the sorcerer to soften the seethe up in preparation for a hostile takeover.

All of that was Marsilia's problem and not mine. I needed to find out where the sorcerer was.

I was fully engaged in fruitless speculation and it wasn't until I was guiding the Rabbit down the twisty drop from the hills back down into the alluvial plain of east Kennewick that I realized I'd driven halfway home.

Maybe Warren knew what had sent Adam and Samuel after Littleton. I headed for Adam's house. It had only been a few hours but werewolves heal very fast once they're able to change.

The werewolf I'd had to argue with last night was back on door duty, but he dropped his eyes and opened the front door without arguing. There were a few of the pack draped over the couches in the living room, but no one I was particularly friendly with.

'Mercy?'

Jesse was in the kitchen, a cup of hot chocolate clutched in her hands.

'Has your father or Samuel called?' I asked, though the answer was obvious from her face.

She shook her head. 'Darryl said you were looking for them.' Her tone asked me a whole slew of questions. What kind of danger was her father in? Why was it me looking for him and not the whole pack?

'How is Warren?' I asked because I didn't have any answers I wanted to tell Adam's daughter.

'Still bad,' she told me. 'Darryl is worried he's not going to make it because he's not healing like he should be, and he won't eat.'

'I need to see if I can talk with him.'

I left Jesse to her cocoa and her worries.

The door to the basement was shut, but I opened it without knocking. Anyone likely to be in the room, with the possible exception of Kyle, would have heard me talking to Jesse. Darryl's dark eyes met mine from the rocking chair he sat in. I stood in the doorway and stared into his eyes.

'Mercy?' Kyle's voice was strained and he sounded almost as tired as I felt.

'Just a moment,' I murmured without taking my eyes off of Darryl. I don't know why he felt he had to challenge me right now – but I didn't want to be taking orders from him today.

Finally Darryl looked down. It wasn't submissive as much as it was dismissive, but it was good enough for me. I turned away from him without a word and walked over to the barred wall that Kyle was still leaning against.

'What's wrong?' Kyle asked.

'Stupid werewolf games.' I crouched in front of the cage door. Warren had changed back into human form. He was curled up with his back to us. Someone had thrown a blanket over him. 'Darryl's just a little confused right now.'

Darryl snorted.

I didn't look at him but I felt my lips curl in sympathy. 'Following a coyote would stick in any wolf's craw,' I said. 'Sitting around when there's things that need doing is worse. If Darryl were a lesser wolf, he'd have killed me when I walked into the room.'

Darryl's snort evolved into an honest laugh. 'You're not in any danger from me, Mercy. *Confused* though I might be.'

I risked a glance and relaxed because Darryl'd lost the look of lazy readiness and appeared merely exhausted.

I smiled at him. 'Can Warren talk?'

Darryl shook his head. 'Samuel said he thought it would be a few days. Apparently there was some damage to his throat. I don't know what effect changing had on his prognosis. He won't eat.'

'He talked in his sleep,' Kyle told me.

He was watching Darryl without bothering to conceal his dislike. Darryl had always had a problem with Warren, even before he'd found out Warren wasn't subservient to him. Dominant wolves were always prickly around each other, unless one of them was the Alpha. It meant that Darryl tended to be nastily autocratic when Warren was around.

'What did he say?' Darryl snapped, his chair rolling abruptly forward.

'Nothing that matters to you,' Kyle replied, uncaring of the danger of irritating a werewolf.

I was more interested in the way Warren's shoulders were tightening.

'You're going to disturb him if you start fighting,' I said. 'Darryl, have you heard from Bran?'

He nodded, his attention still focused on Kyle. 'He's

coming up. He's got some business to finish so he won't be able to get here until late tonight.'

'Good,' I said. 'I want you to go up and eat something.'

He looked at me, surprised.

I smiled. 'A hungry werewolf is a cranky werewolf. Go eat something before you eat somebody.'

He stood up and stretched, the stiffness in his movement told me that he'd been in that chair for a very long time.

I waited until he was gone then opened the door of the cell.

'I've spent most of the last few hours with Darryl telling me that wasn't a good idea,' commented Kyle.

'Probably isn't,' I agreed. 'But Warren listened to me this morning.'

I sat on the end of the mattress and pulled the blanket down so it covered Warren's feet better. Then I crawled onto it between the wall and Warren.

His face was just a few inches from mine and I saw his battered nostrils flutter a little and breathed into them so he'd know it was me. The hours since I'd last seen him hadn't improved his appearance any, his bruises had darkened and his nose and lips were more swollen. Darryl was right: he should be healing faster than this.

But Kyle said he had spoken.

'It's all right,' I told Warren. 'It's just Kyle and me here.'

His lashes moved and one eye opened just a slit then closed.

'Adam and Samuel are missing,' I told him. 'Daniel is dead.'

His eye opened a little and he made a soft noise.

'Was he alive when you last saw him?' A shift that might have been a nod. I reached up and touched a place on his cheek that looked unbruised and he relaxed infinitesimally. Among the wolves, body language can tell me almost as much as words.

'Did you tell Adam and Samuel where to find Littleton?'
I asked.

Warren's heart rate picked up and he shifted on the bed,
his eye opened again and a tear of pure frustration spilled over.

I touched his lips. 'Shh. Shh. Not you. I see. But someone
told them.'

He stared at me, tormented.

'Do you know where they went?'

'Samuel got a phone call last night before they left,' said
Kyle.

Dumbfounded I lifted my head to stare at Kyle who was
kneeling on the floor on the other side of Warren's bed. 'Why
didn't you tell anyone?'

'Darryl didn't ask,' he said. 'He assumed I was sleeping
the whole time – and wasn't in the mood to listen when I
tried to talk to him. I should have told you earlier today –
but to be quite honest, I was a little distracted.'

I relaxed back on the bed. Damned werewolves. I suppose
it never even occurred to Darryl to pay attention to a human.
Darryl had a PhD, damn it. You'd think he'd be smart enough
to pay attention to a man with the brains to be one of the
top attorneys in the state, an attorney moreover with an Ivy
League education.

'If you think being a human around them is frustrating,
you should try being a coyote,' I told him. 'So what did
Samuel say?' I didn't have much hope of anything useful. If
he'd said where they were going, for instance, Kyle wouldn't
have let pride keep him from giving Darryl the information.

'Samuel didn't have a chance to say anything to whoever
called. They called, said a few sentences, and hung up. Samuel
grabbed Adam and said, "Let's go."'

I gave him a rueful look. 'They ignored you, too.'

He smiled at me this time, a tired smile. 'I'm not used
to being ignored.'

'Irks me when they do it to me, too.' I shifted my gaze back to Warren. 'Did you hear what the caller said?'

I didn't expect he had, so his stillness took me by surprise.

His battered mouth tried to shape a word. I listened carefully but it was Kyle, leaning over the bed, who caught it.

'Trap?'

'Warren, I know the werewolves have to stay away from Littleton,' I told him. 'Did he call them and get them to come to him?'

He moved his head just enough for an affirmative.

'Did you hear where?' He lay unmoving. 'Warren, I won't let any of the wolves go near him. Neither Kyle nor I will tell the pack where they are, not until Bran gets here. I'll just tell the vampires – it's their problem in the first place.'

He tried but neither Kyle nor I could tell what he said. Finally Kyle said, 'Look, it's obviously not a yes or a no. Warren, my dear, did you hear part of it?'

Clearly exhausted by his efforts, Warren nodded. He relaxed and said one thing more.

'Church?' I said and saw by Warren's face I'd gotten it right. 'That's all?' I touched his face as he relaxed. 'Go back to sleep, Warren. We'll make sure Bran knows everything.'

He gave a shuddering sigh and relaxed fully into unconsciousness.

'Kyle, would you make sure to tell Bran this much when he gets here? He should be here late tonight or early tomorrow morning.' I got out of Warren's bed as carefully as I could.

'All right. What are you going to be doing?'

I rubbed my face. It had taken a lot of willpower to crawl out of that bed when my whole body wanted to curl up with Warren and sleep. 'If I can find out where Littleton is before nightfall, I might be able to kill him.' With the handy-dandy vampire-killing kit in the trunk of my car.

'Can I help?'

'Only by staying here with Warren. See if you can get him to eat when he stirs again.'

Kyle looked at Warren and his face held none of its usual sardonic humor when he said, 'When you find the bastard who did this, kill him and make it hurt.'

I made him get up and come out of the cell with me. I didn't think Warren would hurt him, but I wasn't willing to take the chance.

My cell phone rang. It was Tony.

'You won't believe this,' he said. 'And I don't know if it helps.'

'What?' I asked.

'The daytime incidents – with a few outliers – are in Kennewick. There's a broad pattern that seems to be centered around the KPD.'

'The police station?' I asked.

'That's right. Although I suppose it could just as easily be centered around Kennewick High or your place, for that matter. But the police station's right in the middle.'

'How broad's the pattern?' I asked.

'About three, three and a half miles. Some of the incidents are across the river in Pasco. There are outliers – our specialist tells me that there are enough to be significant. A few in Richland, Benton City and Burbank. Does this help?'

'I don't know,' I told him. 'Maybe. Thanks, Tony. I owe you a few favors for this.'

'Just stop this thing.'

'I'll do my best.'

I met Darryl at the top of the stairs.

'You were right,' he told me. 'Food helped.'

'Mmm,' I said. 'Samuel got a call last night. Warren doesn't know where they went, though.'

'Warren's awake and talking?'

I shook my head. 'I wouldn't call it talking, and he's asleep again. It was Kyle who heard the phone call. As he apparently tried to tell you.' I watched it sink in. 'You might think about listening to Kyle,' I told him gently, then to let him off the hook, I asked, 'Do you know why my being able to talk to ghosts would scare the vampires?'

He grunted a negative. 'I don't see how that would help. Last I heard, ghosts avoid evil.' He walked past me without touching me.

I don't think he even realized what he'd given me.

Ghosts are not people. No matter how well Mrs Hanna conversed, she was still just a memory of the person she had been.

I was so stupid.

She'd told me that she changed her routine and all I'd thought was how sad it was, because without her usual habits she'd probably fade quickly. I hadn't wondered *why* she'd changed her routine. Ghosts, pattern ghosts, just don't do that. Someone had told her to, she'd said – I couldn't remember who, just that it was a man's name. Her route wandered all over Kennewick. If the sorcerer was in Kennewick, she might have run into him.

Jesse looked up from the kitchen table as I ran down the stairs. 'Mercy? Did you find out something?'

'Maybe,' I told her as I kept going to the door. 'I have to find someone though.' I looked at my watch. Eight twenty-seven. I had an hour and a half before dark – if the sorcerer had to wait for full dark to awaken.

12

For most of the time that I'd lived in the Tri-Cities, Mrs Hanna had pushed her grocery cart along the same path from dawn to dusk. I'd never actually followed her, but I'd seen her any number of places so I had a pretty good idea about most of her route. I didn't have any idea about how she'd changed it, so I had to look everywhere.

When I passed the first church, I pulled over to the side of the road and pulled out a notebook I kept in the car and wrote down the name of the church and its address. After an hour I had a list of eleven churches, reasonably near the KPD, none of which had flaming signs that said SORCERER SLEEPING HERE. The sun was noticeably low in the sky and my stomach was tight with dread.

If I was wrong that the reason Mrs Hanna had to change her route was to avoid Littleton, then I'd wasted the last hour. If I was right, I was still running out of time.

I was also running out of places to look. I pulled over by Kennewick High and tried to think. If Mrs Hanna hadn't changed her route it would be easier to find her. If she hadn't been dead it would have been easier yet. I was counting on being able to see her, but ghosts quite often manifest only to some senses: disembodied voices, cold spots, or just a whiff of perfume.

If I didn't find her soon it would be dark and I'd have to face Littleton during the height of his power – both as a demon and a vampire.

I stopped at the light on Garfield and Tenth. It was one of those lights that stayed red for a long time even when there was no oncoming traffic. 'At least I wouldn't have to face Littleton alone after dark because I can call Andre.' I pounded my hands on the steering wheel, impatient with the red light. 'But if I don't find Mrs Hanna before night, I won't find her at all.' Mrs Hanna went home at night.

I said it out loud because I couldn't believe how stupid I'd been. 'Mrs Hanna goes home at night.'

There was still no traffic coming so I put my foot down, and for the first time in my adult life I ran a red light. Mrs Hanna had lived in a little trailer park along the river, just east of the Blue Bridge and it took me five minutes and three red lights to get down to that area. I ran those lights, too.

I found her pushing her cart on the sidewalk next to the VW dealership. Parking my car on the wrong side of the street, I jumped out, biting back the urge to shout her name. Startled ghosts tend to disappear.

With that in mind I didn't say anything at all when I caught up to her. Instead I walked along beside her for a quarter of a block.

'What a nice evening,' she said at last. 'I do think we're due for a break in the weather.'

'I hope so.' I took two deep breaths. 'Mrs Hanna, pardon my rudeness, but I was wondering about that change in your usual walk.'

'Of course, dear,' she said absently. 'How is that young man of yours?'

'That's the problem,' I told her. 'I think that he's run into some trouble. Could you tell me again why you came by my shop at a different time?'

'Oh, yes. Very sad. Joe told me the way I usually walk wasn't safe. Our poor Kennewick is getting to be such a big city, isn't it? Terrible when it's not safe for a woman to walk in the daytime anymore.'

'Terrible,' I agreed. 'Who is Joe and where is it he doesn't want you walking?'

She stopped her cart and smiled at me gently. 'Oh, you know Joe, dear. He's been the janitor at the old Congregational church forever. He's very upset at what's happened to his building, but then who consults the janitor?'

'Where is it?' I asked.

She looked over at me with a puzzled look on her face. 'Do I know you, dear? You look familiar.' Before I could form a suitable reply she glanced up at the setting sun, 'I'm afraid I must be going. It's not safe after dark you know.'

She left me standing alone in front of the trailer court.

'Congregational church,' I said sprinting for my car. I knew that none of the churches I'd written down had the word Congregational in it, but I also had a phone book I kept in the car.

There were no listings for a Congregational church in the yellow pages so I turned to the white pages and found a single listing in Pasco, which was not helpful. Mrs Hanna's route didn't take her across the river.

I pulled out my cell phone and called Gabriel's phone number. One of his little sisters had a thing about ghosts. If her mother wasn't there, and you let her get started, she'd tell ghost stories the whole time she worked cleaning the office.

'Hi, Mercy,' he answered. 'What's up?'

'I need to talk to Rosalinda about some local ghost stories.' I told him. 'Is she there?'

There was a little pause.

'Are you having trouble with ghosts?'

'No, I need to find one.'

He pulled his mouth away from the phone. 'Rosalinda, come over here.'

'*I'm watching TV, can't Tia do it? She hasn't done anything today.*'

'It's not work. Mercy wants to pick your brains.'

There were a few small noises as Gabriel handed over the phone.

'Hello?' Her voice was much more hesitant when she was talking to me than it had been when she was talking to her brother.

'Didn't you tell me you did a report on local ghosts for school last year?'

'Yes,' she said with a little more enthusiasm. 'I got an A.'

'I need to know if you've heard anything about the ghost of a janitor named Joe who used to work at a church.' He didn't have to be a ghost, I thought. After all, I talked to Mrs Hanna, and I wasn't a ghost. And even if he was a ghost, that didn't mean there were stories about him.

'Oh, yes. Yes.' Gabriel didn't have an accent at all, but his sister's clear Spanish vowels added color to her voice as it brightened with enthusiasm. 'Joe is very famous. He worked his whole life cleaning his church, until he was sixty-four, I think. One Sunday, when the priest . . . no they called him something else. Pastor, I think, or minister. Anyway when he came to open the church he found Joe dead in the kitchen. But he stayed there anyway. I talked to people who used to go to church there. They said that sometimes there were lights on at night when there was no one there. And doors would lock themselves. One person said they saw him on the stairway, but I'm not sure I believe that. That person just liked to tell stories.'

'Where is it?' I asked her.

'Oh. Not too far from our apartment,' she said. 'Down on Second or Third, just a couple of blocks from Washington.' Not far from the police department either. 'I went over to take pictures of it. It isn't a church anymore. The church people built a new building and sold the old one to another church about twenty years ago. Then it sold to some other people who tried to run a private school. They went bankrupt, there was a divorce, and one of them, I can't remember if it was the husband or the wife, killed themselves. The church was empty the last time I went by there.'

'Thank you, Rosalinda,' I said. 'That's exactly what I needed to know.'

'Do you believe in ghosts?' she asked. 'My mother says they are nonsense.'

'Perhaps they are,' I said, not wanting to contradict her mother. 'But there are a lot of people who believe all sorts of nonsense. Take care.'

She laughed. 'You too. Goodbye, Mercy.'

I hit the END button and looked at the darkening sky. There was one way to tell if the vampires were up. I pulled Andre's card out of my back pocket and called him.

'Hello, Mercy,' he answered. 'What are we doing tonight?'

As soon as Andre answered the phone, I knew that my chance at finding the sorcerer in a daytime stupor was gone. I could wait until the next morning. Then we could go after him with Bran. Bran was, in my mind, exempt from the effects of the demon. I just couldn't imagine the thing that could break his icy calmness.

But if we waited for help, waited for the morning, I was almost certain that both Adam and Samuel would be dead.

'I know where he is,' I told Andre. 'Meet me at my shop.'

'Marvelous. I will be there as soon as I can,' he said. 'I have some preparations to do first, but I won't be long.'

I drove there to wait for him. I called Bran's cell phone and got a voice mail request. I took it as a sign that he would be too late to help. I told him to look in the safe in my shop and gave him the combination. Then I sat down at the computer and typed out everything pertinent about what I was doing and where I was going. I wasn't going to leave everyone wondering what happened to me the way everyone else who had gone after Littleton had.

When I finished, Andre still wasn't there, so I checked my home e-mail. My mother had sent me two e-mails, but the third was from an unfamiliar address with attached files. I was about to delete it when I saw that the subject line read CORY LITTLETON.

Beckworth, true to his word, had gotten information about Littleton for me. His e-mail was short and to the point.

Ms Thompson,
    Here is all the information I could find. It comes from a friend of mine who is with the Chicago police and owes me some favors. Littleton disappeared from Chicago about a year ago where he was being investigated as a murder suspect. My friend told me that if I knew where this guy was, he'd appreciate hearing about it – and the FBI are looking for him as well.
    Thanks again,
    Beckworth

There were four pdf files and a couple of jpgs. I opened the jpgs. The first picture was a full color shot of Littleton standing on the corner of a city street. On the bottom right-hand corner the photo was date-stamped April of last year.

He was a good forty pounds heavier than when I'd last seen him. There was no way to be certain, but something about the way he was standing made me believe that he'd been human then.

I opened up the second picture. Littleton in a nightclub talking to another man. Littleton's face was animated, as I'd never seen it in real life. The man he was talking to was turned so all I could see was his profile. But that was enough: it was Andre.

Andre pulled up just as I finished printing out a second letter to Bran. I tossed it into the safe, grabbed Zee's vampire-slaying backpack and went out to meet my fate.

Andre drove us out of my parking lot in his black BMW Z8. It suited him in the same way that Stefan's version of the Mystery Machine had suited him. It surprised me a little because Andre had never impressed me as elegant and powerful. I gave him a quick look under my lashes and realized that tonight he was both, reminding me that he was one of the six most powerful vampires in the seethe.

He'd turned a sorcerer into a vampire so that he could be the most powerful. And I was betting my life that he had lost control of the sorcerer the night Stefan and I met Littleton.

Andre was something of an enigma to me, so I was trusting Stefan's judgement, and the judgement of Stefan's menagerie that he was loyal to Marsilia and jealous of Stefan.

Daniel had been a trial, to see what Littleton could do against a new-made vampire. If matters had not worked out well, Andre could have dealt with it – Daniel was his, after all. But Littleton had proven himself, so Andre had set him up against Stefan. But if Andre were still Marsilia's man, then he would not have condoned the bloodbath at the hotel. It was too likely to have drawn attention to the vampire. But the one thing that made me believe that Littleton was not following orders that night was that Stefan survived. Andre, I thought, would have killed Stefan. Not because of Marsilia's affection – but because Stefan was always, so clearly, the better man.

So I got in a car with the vampire who'd created Littleton

because I believed he wanted the sorcerer as much as I did – he couldn't afford for Littleton to continue to run free, making more and more trouble for him. And I got in that car because I knew that Andre was my only chance to keep Adam and Samuel alive.

'A church is holy ground,' Andre informed me when I told him where we were going. 'He can't be in a church: he's a vampire.'

I rubbed my face, ignored the little voice that kept repeating 'we have to find them,' and tried to think. I was so tired. I'd been up, I realized, for over forty hours without sleep.

'Okay,' I said. 'I remember hearing vampires can't stand on holy ground.' Slipped in among a dozen things that weren't true – say, for instance, the one about vampires crossing water. 'But if Littleton was staying in a church, how could you explain it?'

He turned onto Third and slowed way down so we could look for likely buildings. Gabriel's sister hadn't told me which side of Washington the church was on. Since my shop was east of there, that's where we started. I pressed several buttons and finally got my window to roll down so I could sniff the air.

'All right,' he said. 'Maybe the demon changes the rules, but they're not supposed to be able to abide holy ground either. Or, the church could have been desecrated.'

'It was a school for a while,' I said hopefully.

He shook his head. 'Not unless it was a whorehouse. It takes one of the great sins to desecrate a church – adultery, murder – something of that nature.'

'How about a suicide?' I asked. Gabriel's sister hadn't said the suicide had taken place in the church – but she hadn't said it hadn't happened there either.

He glanced at me. 'Then I think a demon would take great delight in living in a desecrated church.'

The traffic on Washington was light tonight and he goosed the little sports car across all four lanes without stopping for the stop sign.

'When this is over,' I muttered darkly, 'I am never getting in a car with a vampire driving again.'

Rosalinda was right. The church was two blocks off of Washington. There were no signs around it, but it was unmistakably a church.

It was bigger than I expected, almost three times the size of the church I attended on Sundays. The old church had once had a fair sized yard, but there was little left of it but sunburnt weeds chopped almost level with the ground. The parking lot had fared little better, the blacktop had worn down until it was more rock than tar and bleached weeds poked out through branching cracks in the surface. I looked, but I couldn't see any sign of the BMW Littleton had been driving.

Andre pulled over as soon as we saw the church, parking his car across the street, in front of a two-story Victorian home that looked as though it might once have been a farm house.

'I don't see his car,' I said.

'Maybe he's already out hunting,' said Andre. 'But I think you're right, he was here. This is someplace he would stay.' He closed his eyes and inhaled. It made me realize that he hadn't been breathing tonight except a couple of shallow breaths before he talked. I must be getting used to being around vampires. Ugh.

I took a deep breath myself, but there were too many scents around. Dogs, cats, cars, blacktop that had baked all day in the hot sun, and plants. I knew without looking that there was a rose garden behind the house we were standing in front of – and that someone nearby was composting. I couldn't smell werewolf, demon, or vampire – except for Andre. I hadn't realized how much I'd been counting on some sign that Adam or Samuel had been here.

'I don't smell anything.'

Andre lifted an eyebrow and I realized that under the right circumstances he was very good looking – and that I'd been right, there was something different about him, something *more* tonight.

'He's not stupid,' he said. 'Only a stupid vampire leaves a trail to his doorstep.' There was a little bit of pride in his voice.

He looked at the church a moment, then started walking across the street, leaving me to trot after him.

'Shouldn't we be practicing a little stealth?' I asked.

'If he's at home, he'll know we're here anyway,' he told me helpfully. 'If he's not, then it doesn't matter.'

I stretched my senses as far as I could, and wished that the roses didn't have quite so strong a scent. I couldn't *smell* anything. I wished I was certain that Andre would fight on my side tonight.

'So if we're not trying to take him by surprise,' I asked, 'why did you park across the street?'

'I paid over a hundred grand for that car,' Andre told me mildly. 'And I'm moderately fond of it. I'd hate to see it destroyed in a fit of temper.'

'Why aren't you more afraid of Littleton?' I asked. I was afraid. I could smell my own fear over and above the roses, which had, oddly enough, grown stronger after we crossed the street.

Andre stepped off the road and onto the sidewalk, then came to full stop and looked at me. 'I fed deeply this evening,' he said with an odd smile. 'The Mistress herself did me that honor. With the ties that already bind us, and her blood fresh within me, I can call upon her gifts and her power at my need. It will take more than a new-made vampire, even one aided by a demon, to defeat us.'

I remembered how easily Littleton had subdued Stefan

and had my doubts. 'Then why didn't Marsilia just come herself?' I asked.

His jaw dropped in genuine shock. 'Marsilia is a lady. Women do not belong in combat.'

'So you brought me instead?'

He opened his mouth then closed it again, looking a little embarrassed by what he'd been about to say to me.

'What?' I asked, beginning to be a little amused – which was better than terrified. 'Isn't it polite to tell someone she's expendable because she's not a vampire?'

At a loss, he started up the cement steps that led to the worn double doors that hadn't been painted in too many years. I followed, but stayed a step behind.

'No,' he said finally, his hand on the doorknob. 'And I prefer to be polite.' He turned to look down at me. 'My mistress was certain that you were the only person who would be able to find this vampire. She gets glimpses of the future sometimes. Not often, but what she does see is seldom wrong.'

'So do we all survive?' I asked.

He shook his head. 'I do not know. I do understand, though, that you have taken great risk for the honor of the seethe. You are so fragile—' He reached out and rested his fingertips against my cheek. 'Almost human. On my honor, I promise to do everything in my power to see that you are safe.'

His eyes caught me for a moment before I took two quick steps back, all but falling over the steps. Stefan's honor I trusted – Andre's was questionable.

Both of the front doors were locked, but neither had been designed to keep out a vampire. He put a shoulder against one of the doors and broke the frame so the door swung open freely. Apparently we weren't being subtle tonight.

I slid Zee's backpack down my arms and retrieved the stake and knife. Zee'd included the belt and sheath for the knife so at least I didn't have to run around with the knife in one hand and the stake in the other. I waited for Andre to ask me what I was doing with a knife, but he ignored me. All of his attention was on the church.

Andre stood poised outside the threshold.

'What happens if it is still holy ground?' I asked, hurriedly tying the belt.

'Then I burst into flames,' he said. 'But if it was holy ground I should have felt it before this.' As he spoke, he stepped through the doorway and stood fully inside the church. 'This isn't hallowed ground,' he told me, rather redundantly.

I followed him into a large foyer and then looked around. The foyer was large enough for ten or twenty people to have milled around comfortably. The flooring was linoleum tile, cracked and pitted with age. There was a wide stairway leading upward that had a rather nicely carved handrail. Beside the stairway was a pair of double doors, propped open so I could see the large, empty room beyond them that must have been the sanctuary.

The whole church was dark, but there were windows high up that let in a little illumination from the streetlights outside. A real human might have had trouble navigating, but it was light enough for Andre and me.

He stalked over to the sanctuary doors and sniffed. 'Come here, walker,' he said, his voice dark and rough. 'Tell me what you smell.'

I could have told him from where I stood, but I stuck my head into the sanctuary.

The ceiling soared two stories above our heads with frosted windows on both walls that glimmered silver with the dim light of the city night. The floor was hardwood, scarred where pews had once been bolted in.

The walls and some of the windows of the sanctuary had been covered with graffiti – probably done by the neighborhood kids. I just didn't see either a vampire or demon writing things like *For a Good Time Call* – or *Juan loves Penny*. There were a few gang tags, too.

At the far end from us was a raised platform. Like the rest of the room, it was stripped as well, the podium and organ or piano long gone. But someone had cobbled together a table out of cinder blocks. I didn't have to go closer to know what that table had been used for.

'Blood and death,' I said. I closed my eyes. It helped me catch the fainter scents and kept me from crying. 'Ben,' I said. 'Warren. Daniel. And Littleton.'

We'd found the sorcerer's lair.

'But not Stefan.' Andre stood behind me, and his voice echoed in the rafters of the room.

I couldn't read anything from his voice, but I was not comfortable with him at my back. I remembered Naomi telling me that all of the vampires lost control sometimes – and the room smelled of blood and death.

I walked past him back out to the foyer. 'Not Stefan,' I agreed. 'At least not in there.'

There was a hallway on the other side of the foyer with doors opening off either side. I opened the doors and found three rooms and a closet with a hot water heater and a large fuse box.

'He won't be up here,' Andre said. 'There are too many windows.' He hadn't followed me, just waited in the foyer until I finished my search.

His eyes weren't glowing, which I took to be a good sign.

'There's a basement,' I told him. 'I saw the windows outside.'

We found the stairs to the basement tucked neatly behind the stairway to the choir loft. He didn't seem to mind me being behind him, even with my stake, so I followed him down.

Our footsteps, quiet as they were, sounded hollow in the

stairwell. The air was dry and dusty. Andre opened the door at the bottom and the scents in the air changed abruptly.

Now I smelled Stefan, Adam, and Samuel as well as Littleton – but the strongest scent of all of them was the demon. As it had at the hotel, after only a few breaths, the reek of demon drowned out everything else. The door at the bottom of the stairway had kept the scents contained.

We walked even more quietly now, though, as Andre had said, if Littleton was here, he'd have heard us come in.

The basement was darker than upstairs, and someone without preternatural sight might have had trouble seeing at all. We were in an entryway, similar to the foyer upstairs.

There were a pair of bathrooms next to the stairway; and the MEN sign fell off when I pushed open the first door. Streetlights filtered through glass block windows allowing me to see that the room was empty except for a broken urinal leaning crookedly against one wall.

I let the door close. Andre had checked the other restroom and was already walking past a cloakroom and into a short hallway, the duplicate of the one upstairs complete with doors.

I left him to it and started on the other side of the stairs. The first room I walked into was a generous-sized kitchen, though there were only empty spaces where a refrigerator and stove had been. The cabinets were hanging open and bare. Along the inside wall there was a folding half-door covering the top of the counter. With it open, the church members could have served food from the kitchen to the room on the other side without walking back out to the foyer.

Something scuttled behind me and I spun around, but it was only a mouse. We stared at each other for a moment before it went on its way. My heart was beating like a drum in my ears – stupid mouse.

I came out to find Andre standing in front of the double

doors next to the kitchen. The door was chained shut and locked with a shiny new padlock.

He put his hand on the door and something beyond the door growled softly – a werewolf.

'He won't have left them free,' Andre said, though he made no effort to break the chain. 'That door would never hold a werewolf who wanted out.'

'*Andre?*' Stefan called out. 'Is that you? Who's with you?'

'Stefan?' Andre whispered, frozen in place.

'Open the door.' I pushed on his shoulder urgently. Stefan was alive. If I could have ripped the doors off the hinges myself, I would have. Stefan and at least one of the wolves were still alive.

Andre took hold of the chain gingerly and pulled until one of the links broke.

I reached past him and jerked on the chain, letting it fall to the floor as I pushed one of the heavy doors open. I slipped past Andre and found myself in a gymnasium the size of the sanctuary upstairs. The small windows on one side had been covered with black paper and taped with duct tape, but there was a torchiere lamp with a dim bulb hooked up to a car battery that provided enough light to see by.

In the very center of the room, Stefan sat cross-legged inside a large dog crate, the kind you can buy at a pet store. About ten feet away there were more crates lined up next to each other. Something tight and angry eased as my eyes found a leggy red wolf, a muscular silver and black wolf, and a huge white wolf with crystalline eyes: Ben, Adam and Samuel.

Andre rushed past me and knelt in front of Stefan's cage. He touched the latch and the dim bulb flickered. Magic sometimes has an odd effect on electricity – I heard a humming noise and Andre jerked his hand back, shaking it briskly.

'The cages are spelled,' said Stefan dryly. 'Otherwise don't you think my companions over there would have torn them to pieces?'

I noticed then that he was being very careful not to touch the bars on the side of the cage. He looked drawn and as pale as I'd ever seen him. His usual T-shirt was splattered with old blood, but other than that he looked like himself.

'A lot of people think you're dead,' said Andre.

'Ah,' said Stefan, turning his brooding gaze toward me. 'They are mistaken.'

Stefan was alive and well, but I wasn't so certain about the rest.

I took a step toward the wolves, and the red wolf in the nearest cage threw himself at me. The light blinked out entirely for a few moments and when it came back on Ben was crouched in the very middle of his cage making hoarse grunting noises and staring at me with hunger in his eyes. Despite the ferocity of his lunge and the laws of physics, his cage hadn't moved. Magic.

Ben hadn't wanted out. He'd wanted to eat me. Uncle Mike had been right. Demons had a bad effect on werewolves.

'The demon's magic makes it quite impossible to escape these cages,' said Stefan behind me. His voice was mild, but somehow I knew he was angrier than I'd ever seen him.

'Sam?' I said approaching the white wolf. He was too big for the cage and had to bend oddly in order to avoid touching it. As I came closer, he began to shake. He whined at me, then snarled.

In the farthest cage, Adam growled but he was looking at Samuel, not at me.

'Adam?' I asked and he looked back at me. He was angry all right, the scent of the werewolves' frustrated rage rose over the scent of demon. But his brown eyes were clear and cold. It was Adam in control. Samuel, I wasn't sure of.

I reached out and touched Adam's cage. Nothing happened. No flash of power, no blinking lights. The magic didn't bother me though the bars felt warm under my fingers. I set the stake down on the floor and tried Zee's knife, but I couldn't get it to touch the bars – all it did was make the light go out again.

The door was locked with a stout padlock, but there were lynch pins in all the corners, holding the cage together. I tried to pull one out, but I couldn't budge it.

Adam whined. I reached my fingers through the bars and touched his soft fur.

'When Littleton is here, Adam loses it, too,' warned Stefan. 'If I'd known the effect the demon would have on the werewolves, I'd have left them out of this. Warren and Daniel are dead.'

'Warren's not dead. He's badly hurt, but he's recovering at Adam's house,' I said. 'And I knew about Daniel.'

Andre gave me a strange look, and I realized I hadn't told him that Daniel was dead.

'I am glad to be wrong about Warren. I was expecting Andre sooner or later' – Stefan leaned toward me and his voice took on a chiding note – 'but Mercedes Thompson, what in the *name of Hell* are you doing here?'

Suddenly, as if they were all puppets on the same strings, the werewolves jerked their heads toward a door I hadn't noticed on the outside wall. Adam growled and Samuel hit the side of his cage. Slowly, carefully I pulled my fingers out of Adam's cage, but he paid me no attention. I picked up the stake again, but it seemed a flimsy weapon to use against a vampire.

The door opened to the night outside, and a dark figure hesitated a moment, then strolled in. The door slammed shut behind him.

'Andre, how lovely to see you,' crooned Littleton. As his

face came into the light I saw that Zee had been right – sooner or later, all sorcerers stop being demon riders and become demon ridden. Littleton was still in control, because his prisoners were still alive, but he wouldn't be for much longer.

'I'm sorry that you came while I was out getting a snack.' The T-shirt he wore had a dark stain on it. He stopped before he was halfway across the floor and smiled at Andre. 'But I am here now so all is well. Come here.'

I'd let Andre convince me that he was right, that Marsilia had managed to give him enough power to handle Littleton. I was so certain of it, that I thought he had some plan in mind when he walked around Stefan's cage.

I took a better grip on the stake, hiding it from Littleton with my body as I dropped the backpack quietly to the floor, ready for Andre to do something.

Andre was shorter than Littleton so I could see Littleton's face even though Andre stood between us. I was still waiting for Andre to make his move, when Littleton tipped Andre's head to the side and struck while Andre just stood there.

He didn't feed, just bit into the side of Andre's neck and then licked the blood. He laughed. 'Thank you. How unexpected. Who'd have thought the selfish bitch would have shared her power with you? Did she think that would allow you to overcome us when we have the lovely and powerful Stefan to feed upon?' He kissed Andre's cheek and whispered, 'He tastes better than you do.'

He held Andre against him for a moment. 'You know, if it were only me, I'd let you serve us. But my friend, the one who shares my head, the nameless one, he's been getting very bored. Yesterday we had the wolf and Daniel to entertain us. Today I thought to use the Master of the wolves, but then you came to play.'

Andre didn't fight, didn't pull away. He just stood there like Stefan had done while Littleton killed the maid.

My fear caught Littleton's attention.

He left Andre standing where he was and walked over to where I was crouched in front of Adam's cage.

'The little girl Marsilia sent hunting me,' he said. 'Yes, I knew about you. A master vampire can listen in on his children, did you know? I am master now, and he the child. I know all of his plans.' He could only be speaking of Andre.

Littleton bent down too close to me. My hands were trembling and I could smell the stink of my fear even above the smell of demon. I should have used the stake, but my own fear paralyzed me where I was.

'Why did Marsilia think that you could hunt me down? What is a walker?' he asked.

Quoting scripture doesn't work well on vampires, Zee had once told me, *though it is sometimes effective on demons and the like.*

'*For God so loved the world, that He gave His only begotten son*,' I said, so frightened that I could only whisper. He cried out, covering his ears. I grabbed my sheep necklace and pulled it out of the neck of my shirt. I held it out, a blazing shield. When I said the next bit, my voice was stronger. '*That whosoever believeth in—*' Covering his ears must not have worked because he dropped them and grabbed me by my shoulder with one hand and hit me with the other.

I opened my eyes and it felt as if no time had passed at all – except that I was lying on the floor about fifteen feet behind Stefan's cage, my face pressed against the cool, dark linoleum tile. I tasted my own blood when I licked my lips and my face was wet.

Someone was fighting.

I moved my head until I could see better.

It was Andre and Ben. Ben's fur looked black as he danced in the shadows, looking for an opening against the vampire. He lunged forward, but Andre was faster, clipping him in the muzzle with his open hand. Ben slid away, mostly unhurt.

I think if they'd been fighting on dirt or something that gave Ben's claws a proper grip, Ben would have had the upper hand. But in the dark, on the slick linoleum, it was almost even.

Littleton stood with his back to the light, watching.

'Wait,' he said, sounding like nothing so much as a disappointed film director. 'Stop.'

Ben snarled angrily and whirled to face his tormentor. Andre just stopped where he was, like a windup toy that had been suddenly turned off.

'I can't get a good view from here,' Littleton said. 'Come upstairs. You can play in the chapel while I watch from the loft.'

He turned and strode off toward the doors that we'd left hanging open. He didn't turn to make sure that the others followed him – though they did. Andre walked a few feet behind the sorcerer, Ben's blood dripping from his fingertips. Ben was less obedient.

He stopped to snarl at Adam and Samuel who growled and snarled in return. Samuel hit his cage with a full force blow that turned out the light for a count of three.

When the light turned back on, Ben was standing in front of me.

'Wolf,' said Littleton impatiently from outside the room.

Ben took one step closer to me and licked his lips.

'Come, Wolf.' There was power in that voice, I could feel it myself.

Ben's lips lifted off his fangs, then he turned and ran out of the room. I heard the sound of his claws on the steps.

'Mercy, can you come to me?' asked Stefan in an urgent whisper.

Good question. I tried to move, but there was something

wrong with my shoulder joint. My left arm didn't move at all. I tried moving my legs and saw stars. Hastily I dropped my head back to the floor and concentrated on breathing in and out. Cold sweat dampened my back.

After a count of twenty I tried again. This time I think I actually did pass out, but not for more than an instant.

'Nope,' I said. 'Not moving anytime soon. Something's wrong with my shoulder and neither of my legs is very excited about moving either.'

'I see,' said Stefan after a moment. 'Can you look at me then?'

I tilted my chin and left my head on the floor where it wanted to stay. He was facing me, his eyes shimmering like a river of fire.

'Yes,' I said – and that was all the invitation he needed.

'Mercy,' he said, and his voice filtered through the cells of my body, filling me with purpose. 'Come to me.'

It didn't matter that my arm didn't work or that I couldn't get to my feet. Stefan wanted me and I needed to go to him.

Someone was snarling and the light was flickering crazily. Vaguely I noticed that Adam was throwing himself against his cage over and over again.

My breath came out in pained grunts as I pulled my uncooperative body over the cool floor using the elbow of my good arm, because I still had the stake in my hand.

'Shut up, wolf,' Stefan's voice was soft. 'Do you want him down here? I have a plan, but if he comes down here too soon, we'll all be dead – including Mercy.'

When his voice stopped calling me, I rested, keeping my gaze on Stefan's. When he asked me to, I started moving again.

It took a long time, and it hurt a lot, but at last my cheek pressed against Stefan's cage.

'Good girl,' he said. 'Now put your fingers through the

bars. No. You'll have to set the stake down for now. Good. Good. That's it. Rest now.'

While Adam growled quietly, something sharp cut into my index finger. The pain was over too fast to worry about – just one small pain among many. But when Stefan's mouth closed around it I felt a sudden euphoria and all the pain went away.

13

Cold and bitter, something dripped into my mouth. I would have spit it out but it was too much effort. Gentle fingers, chill as ice, touched my cheek and someone whispered words of love against my ears.

A snarl wove its way into my world as the freezing liquid turned to fire and slipped down my throat into my stomach, forcing me back into awareness. The wild anger in that wolf's tone called an adrenaline rush of fear that brought me fully awake.

I lay curled around Stefan's cage. The stake had rolled under me and lodged uncomfortably between my ribs and the floor. The light was off again and I could smell burning flesh, even over the scent of demon.

Part of me knew I shouldn't be able to see anything this clearly, but for some reason my night vision was even better than usual. I could see Adam staring over my head, his muzzle wrinkled and his eyes brilliant yellow lit with rage that promised death.

I rolled my head a little so I could see what Adam was looking at. All I saw was Stefan.

The vampire had threaded his fingers through the bars a few inches above my hand. He had a cut on his hand, a wide open slash that was pouring blood. Some of it caught on the bars, but most of it slid down his fingers to drip on the floor. My neck and cheek were wet with it.

I licked my lips and tasted something that might have been blood – or it might have been the finest elixir of some medieval alchemist. One moment it tasted like blood, iron and sweet, and the next it burned my tongue.

Sparks glittered in the dark blood on the bars and sizzled on his skin where it touched the cage.

His face was hidden against his upright knee. 'It's done now,' he murmured.

I pulled back from the cage and then pushed awkwardly with my single good hand at his smoking limb, which was very cool to the touch, shoving Stefan back inside, away from the bars.

Slowly, he pulled his hand in toward his body and then raised his head, shutting his eyes when the dim light-bulb, freed from the odd effect of the cage's sorcery, came back on.

'It'll only last for a little while,' he told me. 'You're still hurt, so be careful not to damage yourself more than you can help.'

I started to ask him a question, but Samuel howled and Adam, turning his attention away from Stefan and I, joined in the chorus. As their cries died away, I heard someone coming down the stairs. It sounded like Littleton was dragging something.

I dropped back to the ground, my hair over my face to hide it – only then realizing that I felt better. A lot better. Amazingly better.

One of the hallway doors was pushed open with a crash. Through the curtain of my hair I watched Andre fly through the doorway and land in an ungraceful heap on the floor.

Littleton liked to throw things.

'You didn't do it right,' the sorcerer complained as he dragged a limp red werewolf through the doorway by one hind leg. 'You have to do what I tell you. I didn't tell you to kill the wolf, it's not even midnight yet. You are not going to ruin my fun with an early kill.'

He looked over at us, or rather at Stefan. I closed my eyes most of the way, and hoped my hair hid them well enough that he didn't realize I was awake.

'I *am* sorry,' he said contritely as he approached Stefan, still dragging Ben. 'I haven't been much of a host. I didn't realize you were thirsty or I'd have provided a meal. But then I suppose I just did.'

He dropped Ben in front of me, then nudged me with a toe. 'I might have played a little with this one,' he said with a sigh. 'But humans don't last as long anyway. Maybe I'll bring in a few more for food for you though. It might be fun to turn them loose in here and make you call them to you.'

Ben wasn't dead, I could see his ribs rising and falling. He wasn't healthy either. There was a flap of torn skin on his hip that oozed blood, and one front leg bent oddly about two inches below the joint. I couldn't see his head because the rest of his body was in the way.

Littleton went back to get Andre. He picked him up and carried him like a lover as he brought him to the light in the center of the cages.

With Andre still in his arms, he sat down next to the light. He arranged the other vampire on the ground like a doll, pulling Andre's head on his knee. Andre's face was covered with blood.

I licked my lower lip and tried not to enjoy the buzz of vampire blood on my tongue.

Littleton bit himself on the wrist, giving me a glimpse of his fangs and then he put the open wound over Andre's mouth.

'You understand,' he murmured to Andre. 'Only you. You understand that death is more powerful than life. More powerful than sex. If you can control death, you control the universe.'

It should have sounded melodramatic. But the fevered whisper lifted the hair on the back of my neck.

'Blood,' he told the unconscious Andre. 'Blood is the symbol of life and death.'

Andre moved at last, grabbing Littleton's wrist and holding it to him, curling around it. Much as a starving Daniel had curled around Andre's wrist during Stefan's trial. I wished the lingering touch of Stefan's blood didn't taste so good.

Andre opened his eyes and looked up.

I expected his eyes to be glowing, as Daniel's had been. Instead they were intent. Like Adam's had been, his eyes were focused on Stefan.

Littleton was muttering in Andre's hair, his eyes closed. So I took a chance and shifted my body just a little, drawing Andre's gaze. When he looked at me, I moved an inch more so he could see the stake.

He closed his eyes again, then abruptly let Littleton's arm fall away and he rolled to his hands and knees, somehow managing to shift so that Littleton was between us, his back toward me.

'Blood is life,' said Andre in a voice I'd never heard him use. It drifted through the room like a mist and settled on my skin. 'Blood is death.'

'Yes.' Littleton sounded dazed and I remembered how it had felt when Stefan fed from me. Until that moment I'd almost forgotten he had fed from me.

Littleton, unconcerned by my fears, said, 'Blood is the life and the death.'

'Who commands death?' Andre asked, his voice calling for a response that my mouth wanted to form.

Littleton came up to his knees and I could see the imprint of his spine on the back of his shirt. 'I do!' he shrieked. He reached over and grabbed Andre under the jaw and pulled the vampire where he wanted him. He bit down right over the top of the wounds he'd made in Andre's neck earlier.

It was the best chance I was going to get. I tried to surge to my feet and almost fell. One of my ankles wouldn't hold any weight, though it didn't hurt.

I didn't have far to go.

Bent over Andre, Littleton's ribs were clearly outlined on his shirt. Someone should tell him that thin people shouldn't wear fabrics that cling. I picked a spot between the delicate, arching bones, just to the left of his spine, and struck with my whole body, just as Sensei had taught me to hit.

If my ankle had been working, I might have managed it. Training worked against me and I instinctively tried to use my weight to help push the sharpened wood through. My leg collapsed under me and the stake only went in an inch before it stuck between his ribs instead of breaking through them.

Littleton jerked to his feet with an outraged cry. He struck out blindly, just missing me because I was already rolling away as fast as I could. Luckily I was faster than the vampire. I rolled until I bumped against the car battery powering the light.

'Bitch,' Littleton hissed.

I felt my neck, but my sheep necklace was gone, lost when he'd thrown me across the room. While I was fumbling, the sorcerer leapt at me.

Andre grabbed him around the middle and they both crashed to the ground just short of me. Littleton managed to put Andre on the bottom and I saw that the stake was still embedded in his back.

I grabbed the car battery by its plastic handle and hefted it in my right hand. Grunting with the effort, I raised it above the struggling vampires and brought it down on the end of the stake.

The light, still attached to the battery, crashed to the

floor, leaving the room in darkness once more. This time I had trouble seeing clearly — the benefits of Stefan's blood were fading.

I twisted until I could free Zee's knife from its sheath. It took more effort than it should have.

Littleton had gone limp, his body flopped over faceup when Andre pushed him off. The stake had gone all the way through Littleton and protruded several inches through his chest. It had sliced into Andre, just above his collarbone, but he didn't seem to mind. He lay flat on his back and laughed, though he didn't sound happy.

The pain was back with interest, making me nauseous and light-headed. I swallowed bile and sat up using my good arm to push down and lever myself into a useful position. The knife in my hand clicked on the floor.

I'd killed mice, rabbits, and, once, a deer while running as a coyote. I'd killed two men — three, now. It didn't help me face the next task. Bryan, my foster father, used to hunt, both as a wolf and with a gun. He and Evelyn, his wife, had butchered the meat while I wrapped it in freezer paper. I'd never had to cut up the carcass myself.

Zee's knife cut into Littleton's neck with a wet slurping sound. I'd thought Littleton to be dead . . . deader than he'd been before, I mean. But as the knife slid in, his body began to spasm.

The motion attracted Andre's attention and he sat up, 'What? No, wait!'

His hand closed on mine hard enough to leave bruises, and he jerked my hand back. Littleton's head flopped to the side. The effect was somehow more grisly than if the head had been completely severed.

'Let go,' I said, almost not recognizing the hoarse croak as my own voice. I jerked my hand, but he wouldn't release his grip.

'Marsilia needs him. *She* can control him.'

Metal fell with a loud crash: the sorcerer's power was failing, allowing his prisoners to escape. Adam crouched beside me just a hair sooner than Samuel appeared on my other side. Both werewolves were snarling almost soundlessly and I knew, almost without looking at them that the human parts of them were gone, leaving only the predator behind.

That the knowledge didn't frighten me to death is a measure of how traumatized I was.

'Let go of me,' I said again, this time softly so as not to alarm the werewolves who were quivering with eagerness and the smell of fresh blood. I wasn't really sure why they hadn't just attacked.

Andre stared first at Adam, then at Samuel. I don't know that he was trying to control them, but if he was, it didn't work. Adam growled and Samuel whined eagerly and took a half step closer.

Andre released my wrist. I didn't wait any longer, pressing the knife through meat, gristle, and bone until Littleton's head rolled free and the knife cut into the linoleum.

I'd been wrong: it *was* worse when the head was all the way severed.

Throw up later, I thought. *Destroy the body now*.

The backpack wasn't more than a body length from me, but I couldn't find the energy to get to it.

'What do you need?' asked Stefan who was crouched on the other side of the body, next to Andre. I hadn't noticed that he'd left his cage, too – or that he'd moved at all. He was just suddenly in front of me.

'The backpack,' I said.

He got up like it hurt, and moved with none of his usual energy, returning with the backpack in hand. Both of the wolves stiffened when he held the pack out toward me, over

Littleton's body. Stefan was moving slowly because he was in bad shape – but it was probably a good thing. Making sudden moves around the werewolves would have been a bad idea, even if they had relaxed, just a bit, when I'd removed the sorcerer's head.

As I reached out to take the pack, Andrew spoke again. 'Marsilia needs him, Stefan. If she has a sorcerer at her beck and call, the others will have to cower in her presence.'

'Marsilia can cow them on her own,' Stefan responded tiredly. 'A sorcerer is not a comfortable pet. Marsilia has allowed greed to overcome her common sense.'

The medallion wasn't a very big item and it hid from my fingers. It was heavy though, so I finally managed to locate it in the bottom. I took it out and put it on Littleton's chest.

'What is that?' asked Stefan.

Rather than answering him, I leaned over Littleton's chest and whispered, '*Drachen.*' *Burn you bastard, burn.*

The metal disk started to glow cherry red. For a moment I thought that was all it would do. But after a moment the body burst into flame, the almost-invisible blue flame of a Bunsen burner with the gas adjusted perfectly. I had a moment to wonder at the suddenness of it, then Stefan leapt over the body, grabbed me under the arms and pulled me back before I was caught up in the hungry flames.

His grip reminded me I had an injured shoulder in the worst way. The sudden pain was so intense I screamed.

'Shh,' said Stefan ignoring the werewolves who were eyeing him with hungry eyes. 'It'll settle down in a minute.'

He sat me down and put my head between my knees. His hands were still cold, like those of a corpse. Which he was.

'Breathe,' he said.

I couldn't help a hiccoughing laugh at having a dead man tell me to breathe.

'Mercy?' he asked.

I was saved from trying to explain why I was laughing because the outside doors were pulled open with a screech of bending metal.

Stefan turned to face this new threat, a werewolf on either side. Andre stood up as well. All of them kept me from seeing the doorway, but I could smell them.

Darryl and two others. The frightened child inside my heart, unappeased by Littleton's immolation, relaxed at last.

'You're late, Bran,' I told him as the light from the burning vampire flickered and died.

It wasn't the Marrok who answered me, but his second son, Charles. 'I told Darryl he shouldn't speed. If the police hadn't pulled us over, we'd have been here ten minutes ago.'

Bran walked by the vampires as if they didn't exist. He touched Samuel and then Adam. 'Charles has clothing for you,' he told them and they melted away into the darkness, presumably to change and get dressed. Bran's presence did as much to allow them to regain enough control to change back to human as Littleton's death had. His permanent death, I mean.

The dim light from outside backlit Bran, so it was difficult to see his face.

'You've been busy,' he said, his tone neutral.

'No choice,' I told him. 'Did you read the papers I left for you?' *Do you know that all the villains aren't ashes?*

'Yes,' Bran said, and something inside of me relaxed. He couldn't know which of the vampires was Andre – but he'd manage, I knew.

Uncaring of vampire dust – or whatever else of Littleton might be scattered about on the floor – Bran knelt in front of me so he could bend down and kiss my forehead.

'It was a damned stupid thing to do,' he said in a voice so soft as to be almost inaudible.

'I thought you couldn't make it here until morning,' I said.

'I hurried.' He put his hand on my shoulder.

'Ouch,' I said, sinking farther down on the floor.

'Samuel,' he called. 'If you could manage to hurry a bit, I think you have a patient.'

My shoulder was only out of joint and Samuel put it back as gently as he could. It still hurt like the blazes. I shuddered and shook, and managed not to throw up on anyone, while Adam, his voice harsh with barely controlled rage, told everyone what had happened after Andre and I showed up.

Andre seemed stunned by Littleton's death. Stefan knelt beside him with a hand on his shoulder and a wary eye on all the wolves stalking around.

I waited until I was sure I could talk without sounding too shaky – and until Adam was finished speaking. Then I looked at Stefan and said, 'Andre is the one who made Littleton.'

Andre looked at me in shock, then threw his weight forward – I don't know if he'd have attacked me, or just tried to run, but Stefan caught him. Before it turned into a real struggle, Charles and Darryl helped to hold him.

'I was going to ask if you were certain,' Stefan said, releasing Andre to the werewolves who were obviously in better shape to hold the other vampire. 'But Andre has answered that question himself.'

'I have proof,' I told him.

'I would like to see it,' Stefan said. 'If only to present to the Mistress. Right now, though, is there a cell phone I might use to call my seethe? As much as I appreciate your help, Adam, I think that it would be a bad thing to bring your wolves into the seethe right now while tempers are still uncertain.'

*   *   *

The vampires came and spirited Andre away. I had expected that Stefan would go with them, but he didn't. Samuel insisted on bringing me to the hospital, though Charles and Darryl took Ben, who was in worse shape than I was, to Adam's house in Darryl's car.

'How come I can't just go home?' I whined. My shoulder ached and I just wanted to go to my bedroom and pull my blankets over my head.

'Because you aren't a werewolf,' Stefan said. 'If your ankle is broken, you need a cast.'

The werewolves who weren't driving (Adam and Samuel) gave him cold looks. Bran had brought Adam's SUV and being stuffed inside it with the three werewolves and the vampire was a new experience in testosterone. When Samuel and Adam had gotten into the back seat with me, Stefan had slipped into the front. Bran was continuing to ignore the vampire, so Stefan stayed.

The five of us staggered into the emergency room. The only one remotely respectable was Bran, and he was carrying me. It wasn't until we were under the intense lights of the hospital that I realized just how bad we looked. I was covered with blood, Stefan was covered in blood. His face was drawn and tired, though the expression on it was peaceful. I didn't want to know what I looked like.

Samuel, even in clean, fresh clothing, looked as though he'd spent a week on a wild binge and Adam . . . The nurse at the triage station took one look at Adam and hit the innocent-looking black button underneath her desk.

It wasn't the wear and tear that panicked her, but the look in his eyes. I know I was really glad that Bran was with us.

'It's all right, Elena.' Samuel managed a rough growl that only barely sounded human. 'I'll take them in.'

She looked at him again and shock spread over her face. 'Dr Cornick?' She hadn't recognized him when we'd come in.

'Call the Kennewick police,' I told her. 'Ask for Tony Montenegro. Tell him Mercy has some news for him if he can get his butt down here.'

Samuel would be questioned by the hospital administrators, I thought. I didn't know if he'd missed a shift or not, but they wouldn't overlook him coming in with this crew. Police business would cover his rump – and I thought that Tony might benefit from seeing that the werewolves had taken his concerns seriously. It would also let the wolves know they had allies among the police here. People who could be trusted. That was important if they were ever to integrate into the citizenry.

There were a few people in the waiting room and all of them stopped whatever they were doing to look at Adam. The smell of fear overpowered the scent of illness and blood. Even Bran stiffened a little under the flood of triggered scents.

Samuel strolled right through the room, ignoring the woman who bravely came up to us to get insurance information.

Bran paused before he followed Samuel through a pair of swinging doors. 'Not to worry, my dear,' he told the woman gently. 'Dr Cornick will see to it that all the proper forms are filled out.'

Tony walked into the emergency room as if he'd been there a time or two before. He was wearing civilian clothes, jeans and T-shirt, but the cheery-faced young man with him was in uniform.

He strolled into my curtained cubicle and looked around. Samuel was off doing doctor stuff, but the others were all there. Stefan and I had scrubbed up. I was in one of those stupid hospital gowns, but Stefan's clothes were still covered with blood. Bran sat on the doctor's chair, slowly spinning it around, looking like a bored teenager. Like the people in the waiting room, Tony and his companion ignored Bran and watched Adam, who was leaning against a wall. Stefan was slumped in a corner and got a swift, assessing glance before the police both looked back at Adam.

'Tony, this is Adam Hauptman, we were talking about him just the other day. Adam, this is my friend Tony.' I didn't bother to introduce the others.

Tony's face froze and he stopped where he was. I guess he hadn't recognized Adam from his newspaper pictures until I'd used his name. Adam's publicity shot showed a conservative businessman. There was nothing conservative or businesslike about him tonight. Anger radiated off of him in waves even humans should be able to sense.

'Hey, John,' Tony said casually, after quickly looking away from the Alpha. I guess the information sheet that had gone out on werewolves had explained that it was not a good idea to have a staring contest with one. 'Why don't you get both of us a cup of coffee.'

The other cop gave Tony a narrow-eyed look, but he only asked, 'How long should I take?'

Tony glanced at me. I shrugged and instantly regretted it. 'This won't take more than ten minutes.'

When the other cop had gone, Tony pulled the curtains closed. It didn't give us much privacy, but the cacophonous chatter of dozens of mysterious machines would mask whatever we had to say from human ears.

'You look like death warmed over,' he told me.

'It wasn't at the police station,' I told him, too tired for our usual teasing. 'But it wasn't more than a half mile away.'

'You found it.'

'I killed it,' I said. 'I think that you'll find the nightlife will calm down a little from here on out.'

Tony frowned. 'It?'

'Yes.' Stefan's voice was weary. 'Something that should never have been allowed to roam the streets. It was not murder, sir. It was self-defense.'

'Don't worry,' offered Bran meekly. 'There isn't a body.' Only because he'd noticed Littleton's head lying around and we'd used Zee's medallion to get rid of it, too. I'd forgotten all about it. Presumably it wouldn't have done anything except scare the begeebers out of whoever found it – since the body was gone – but I was just as glad to have that last bit taken care of as well.

Tony looked at Bran more closely. 'Do I want to ask who you all are?'

'No,' I told him.

'So why did you call me in?' Tony asked.

I opened my mouth to answer and Samuel pulled the curtains aside and stepped in, an X-ray in his hands.

'Dr Cornick,' Tony greeted him like an old friend – I supposed that cops might see a lot of emergency room doctors. Then something about the wariness of everyone in the room clued him in.

'Samuel needs to have the shield of police business to hide behind,' I said before he could ask if Samuel was a were-wolf, too.

Tony frowned, taking a careful look at the people in the room – avoiding eye contact. 'All right,' he said slowly. 'You're sure everything will get back to normal?'

I started to shrug, but nodded my head instead. 'As normal as it gets.'

'Fine.' He looked at Samuel. 'Tell me that you're not a danger to your patients.'

I waited anxiously for a smart-ass comment, but Samuel was tired, too. He only said, 'I'm not a danger to my patients.'

'All right,' Tony said. 'All right. Dr Cornick, if anyone asks about this, just tell them it was a police matter you were helping in.' He took out his wallet and pulled out a card. 'Give them my number if you need to.'

Samuel took the card. 'Thank you.'

Then Tony turned back to Adam. 'Mr Hauptman,' he said. 'Mercy tells me that I ought to speak with you first on matters concerning werewolves.'

Adam rubbed his face tiredly. It took him so long to speak that I worried. Finally he said, in an almost civil tone, 'Yes. Did Mercy give you my number?'

'We didn't get that far.'

Adam collected himself and managed a small smile that made him look like a hungry tiger. Tony took a discreet step back. 'I'm not carrying my cards tonight, but if you call my office, I'll instruct them to give you my cell phone number – or Mercy usually knows how to get in touch with me.'

My ankle was just sprained. Stefan left while Tony was talking with Adam. No one but me seemed to notice. I don't know if he did some vampire thing, or that no one else cared.

Adam wanted me to stay at his house. But he had half the local pack, part of the Montana pack, and Kyle staying at his house. I had no intention of joining the crowd.

After the others left for Adam's house, Samuel carried me into my battered trailer and started toward my bedroom, but I didn't want to sleep. Not ever.

'Can you take me to the office, instead?' I asked.

He still wasn't speaking much, but he obediently switched directions and took me into the tiny third bedroom that hummed with various bits of electronics.

He set me in the chair, then dropped to his knees in front of me. His hands were shaking when he closed them on my knees and pulled them apart so he could fill up the space between. His body was hot as he pressed himself against me and buried his face in my neck.

'I knew you'd come,' he whispered and the power of his wolf ruffled my hair as it rushed over me. 'I was so worried. And then . . . and then the wolf came. Adam kept control – he tried to help me, but I was in a worse state than Ben, who had been there far longer. I am losing control of my wolf, I'm a danger to you. I told my father that as soon as you are well, I will return to Montana.'

I held him with my good arm. 'Demons aren't good for a werewolf's control.'

'Of the three of us there,' he told my neck, 'I had the least control.'

That wasn't true. I'd been there and seen him still fighting when Ben had given up entirely to the wolf. But before I took up that argument, I realized something.

'That church is less than half a mile from the hospital,' I told him. 'Uncle Mike told me the demon's presence causes violence anywhere near him – and the police records confirm that. When Tony worked it up for me, we found that the area of effect was over three miles in diameter. You've been fighting the demon since the night I first ran into Littleton. It had Ben for a few days – you, it's been working on for weeks.'

He stilled, thinking about it.

'The night you lost control after that accident with the baby,' I said. 'It wasn't you, it was the demon.'

The arms of my chair creaked a protest under his hands. He took a deep breath of my scent and then pulled back a little so he could look me in the face. Very slowly, giving me plenty of time to pull away, he kissed me.

I thought I might love Adam. Samuel had hurt me once before – very badly. I knew that he might only want me now for the same reason he had wanted me then. Even so, I couldn't pull away.

I had come so close to losing him.

I returned his kiss with interest, leaning into his body and threading my fingers through his fine hair. It was Samuel who ended the kiss.

'I'll get you some cocoa,' he said, leaving me in my chair.

'Sam?' I said.

He stopped at the door, his back to me and his head lowered. 'I'll be all right, Mercy. For tonight, just let me get us both some cocoa.'

'Don't forget the marshmallows,' I told him.

14

'He's not come to trial yet?'

'No,' Stefan sipped at his tea, which he had requested. I hadn't known vampires could drink tea. 'How's the ankle?'

I made a rude noise. 'My ankle is fine.' Which wasn't strictly true, but I wasn't going to let him change the subject. 'It took them only a day to bring you to trial and it's been two weeks for Andre.'

'Weeks that Andre spends in the cells beneath the seethe,' Stefan said mildly. 'He's not out vacationing. As for how long it is taking, I'm afraid that is my fault. I've been in Chicago to see what I can ferret out about Andre's activities there. To make sure that Littleton was the only person he managed to turn.'

'I thought Andre didn't have enough control to turn his people into vampires.'

Stefan set his tea on the table and gave me an interested look. 'Rachel said you'd been over to visit. I hadn't realized how much you learned.'

I rolled my eyes at him. 'I grew up with werewolves, Stefan, intimidation isn't going to work. Tell me how Andre managed to turn a sorcerer when he can't turn one of his minions.'

His face lit up in one of his generous smiles. 'I don't know. I'll tell you what I do know. Cory Littleton has been flirting with evil since he was a very young boy. His apartment in Chicago – which Andre has paid for up until next December – had a secret room I sniffed out. It was full of interesting things like black wax candles and books on ancient ceremonies that would have been best left uncatalogued. I burned them, and the notebooks he kept his journals in – written in mirror writing of all things. At least it wasn't in Greek.'

'Does Andre know how Littleton became a sorcerer? Could he make more of them?' asked Samuel, his sleep-roughened voice emerging from the hallway.

'Hello, Samuel,' Stefan said. Medea came out of the hallway shadows first, meowing sharp little complaints as she trotted across the kitchen floor and hopped onto Stefan's lap.

Samuel followed, half dressed and sporting a day's growth of beard. Samuel hadn't been himself since Littleton captured him – or maybe since that night he told me about the baby his girlfriend had aborted. His temper was shorter and he was too serious – when I tried to bring up the subject of that kiss we'd shared, he wouldn't discuss it. I worried about him.

'Does Andre know how to create a sorcerer?'

Stefan nodded his head slowly. 'According to Littleton's journals he does. Littleton told him.'

Samuel pulled out a chair and spun it around so he sat on it backwards. 'Was it something about Littleton being a sorcerer that allowed him to survive being turned?'

Medea batted Stefan's hand and instead of picking up his cup, he rubbed her behind her ears. She purred and settled more firmly on his lap.

'I don't know,' Stefan answered finally. 'I'm not certain even Andre knows. He fed off Littleton for several years before turning him. I don't think that he has any more Littletons waiting in the wings, though. It's not all that easy to find someone willing to sell his soul to the devil.'

Samuel relaxed.

'He was a sorcerer before he was a vampire?' I asked.

'Yes.' Stefan wiggled his fingers in front of Medea's nose

and she batted at them. 'He was a sorcerer before he met Andre. He thought that being a vampire would make him more powerful – Andre told him so. Neither he nor the demon was pleased to find out that being a vampire meant that they had to follow Andre's orders.'

'He wasn't following Andre's orders that night in the church.' Samuel reached over and grabbed a cup and filled it from the teapot on the table.

'No. It *is* possible to break the bond of control the maker has over his children, just difficult.' Stefan sipped his tea and I wondered what his careful expression was hiding.

'Speaking of bonds,' I said, finally asking the question that had haunted me since the night I'd killed Littleton, 'will there be any permanent effects from your sharing blood with me that night?'

I wanted him to say 'no.' Instead he shrugged. 'Probably not. One blood exchange isn't much of a connection. Any effects from it will fade. Have you noticed anything odd?'

I shook my head – no telekinesis tricks for me.

'Why were you able to call her to you?' asked Samuel. 'I thought she was immune to vampire tricks.'

'Mostly immune,' murmured Stefan. 'But you don't have to worry about that. Calling is one of my talents. If Mercy hadn't been mostly unconscious – and willing to come – I couldn't have called her. She's not going to suddenly find herself unable to resist coming to my call or the call of any other vampire.'

I didn't ask him about the memory I had of him murmuring loving words into my ears. I hoped it was just something to do with how he'd called me.

'Why did you come here tonight?' I asked instead.

Stefan smiled at me with such power I wasn't sure he was truthful when he said, 'I had to strengthen my stomach. Visits with you are always bracing, Mercedes, if not completely comfortable.' He glanced down at his watch. 'But it's time for me to go while you still are able to get a full night's sleep. The Mistress will expect a full report.'

He put the cat down with a final pat and got up to leave. In the open doorway he hesitated, and without looking at me he said, 'Don't fret, Mercy. I've learned all I can, and she won't hold back the trial again. Andre will face justice.'

I waited until Stefan had left before I asked Samuel, 'They have that chair, the one that makes you tell the truth. Why did he go out to investigate?'

Samuel gave me a dark look. 'Sometimes I forget how young you are,' he said.

I glowered right back at him. 'Don't think that ticking me off will get you out of answering. Why did he delay the trial?'

Samuel took a sip of tea, grimaced and set it down. He wasn't a tea drinker. 'I think he's worried about what questions will get asked and what questions will not. If he knows enough, he can testify himself.'

It sounded fine, but I couldn't see why he'd tried not to tell me that. There must be something more.

He looked at my face and laughed wearily. '*Sufficient unto the day is the evil thereof*. Go to bed, Mercy. I need to get ready to go to work.'

'Dad told me to ask you when you're going to fix that eyesore the sorcerer made of your house,' Jesse said levering herself onto a shelf in my shop.

'When I win the lottery,' I told her dryly and went back to tightening the belt on the old BMW I was working on.

Jesse laughed. 'He told me you'd say that.'

My shoulder was still pretty sore and I limped, but at least I could work now. Zee had taken over the shop for two weeks – he didn't want me to pay him. But he'd saved my life with his vampire kit, I owed him enough. If I was lucky, after paying him I'd still be able to cover the bills, but not much else. It would be a few months before I could afford to even look at replacing the siding on the trailer.

'What are you doing here, anyway?' I asked.

'I'm waiting for Gabriel to get off work.'

I looked up at that.

She laughed harder. 'If you could see your face. Who are you worried about, him or me?'

'When you break his heart, it'll be me who'll have to live with the moaning.' If there was real fear in my voice, it was only because Zee's son Tad, Gabriel's predecessor, had had a very rocky love life.

'When *she* breaks *my* heart? If anyone's heart breaks, it'll be hers,' Gabriel informed me grandly, from the office doorway. 'Unable to resist my charms, she'll be devastated at my callousness when I tell her I must go to college. The loss will cause her to resign herself to a long and lonely life without me.'

Jesse giggled. 'If my dad stops in, tell him I'll be home around ten.'

I gave Gabriel a stern look. 'You know who her father is.'

He laughed. 'A man who will risk nothing for love is not a man.' Then he winked. 'I'll have her home before ten, though, just in case.'

Alone, I buttoned up the BMW and closed down the shop. Stefan hadn't called me this morning before I came to work, so I didn't know if anything had happened with Andre.

There was nothing to worry about. Andre was clearly guilty of creating a monster. Still, there had been a weariness in Stefan's manner last night that made me fret a little. If it was an open and shut case, why had he spent weeks in Chicago investigating?

I had company waiting for me in the parking lot. Warren had lost some weight and still limped, even worse than I did. It hadn't stopped him from wiping the floor with Paul who now cringed whenever Warren walked by. And if there were occasional nightmares, he still looked much happier than he had been.

Much of that was due to the handsome man leaning on the fender of Warren's battered truck wearing, of all things, a lavender cowboy outfit complete with purple hat. The only good thing that had come out of the Littleton business was that Warren and Kyle were an item again.

'Who ticked you off?' I asked Kyle, who had exquisite taste.

'I was meeting a client's husband and his high-powered Seattle lawyer. The longer they think I'm a lightweight poof, the higher I'll hang them in court.'

I laughed and kissed him on the cheek. 'It's good to see you.'

'We're going to catch a show at my place,' Kyle said. 'We thought you might like to join in.'

'Only if you change clothes,' I told him seriously.

The truck rocked a little and Ben stuck his head over the side of the bed where he'd been resting. His red coat was rough and his eyes were dull. He let me touch his face before curling back up in the truck bed.

When I got in the cab, Warren said, 'Adam thought it would do Ben some good to get out. We thought it would do you some good, too.'

'He's still not shifting,' I asked.

'No. And he wouldn't hunt with us at full moon.'

I glanced out the back window, but, although he doubtless could hear us talk about him, Ben didn't raise his head off his front paws.

'Is he eating?'

'Enough.'

Which meant that he wasn't likely to lose control and

eat me like he'd eaten Daniel — that's what Daniel had been telling me. Vampires, not even vampires possessed by demons, don't eat other vampires.

It surprised me a little that Ben was taking it so hard. He had always seemed to me like the kind of person who could strangle his granny for her pearls then eat a peanut butter sandwich in her kitchen afterwards. Maybe I was wrong — or else eating someone was tougher. Warren had told me that Ben and Daniel had struck up an odd friendship while they were out hunting Littleton. It hadn't been strong enough to save Daniel, but it might be enough to destroy Ben.

We watched Japanese anime, ate take-out Mexican food, and made rude jokes while Ben watched us with empty eyes. Warren drove us both home in the early evening, dropping me at my house first.

There was a note on the fridge from Samuel. He'd been called into work because one of the other physicians was sick. The phone rang while I was still reading Samuel's note.

'Mercedes,' said Stefan's voice in my ears. 'Sit down.'

'What's wrong?' I don't take orders well: I stayed where I was.

'Andre was tried last night,' he said. 'He confessed to turning Littleton, confessed to everything: the creation of Littleton, the incident with Daniel, setting me up to meet Littleton at that hotel.'

'It was about you,' I said. 'He was jealous of you.'

'Yes. It was during a conversation with him that I decided there was something odd about Daniel's experience. He made sure someone told me Littleton had registered at that hotel.'

'Littleton was supposed to kill you,' I said.

'Yes. He was supposed to kill me — but that was the night he broke Andre's control. Andre thinks that all the killing strengthened the demon so Littleton didn't have to listen to him anymore. Andre couldn't find him after that night. But he wasn't too worried until Littleton started leaving presents on his doorstep.'

'Presents?'

'Body parts.' When I didn't say anything Stefan continued. 'Andre was getting pretty desperate, and when Littleton captured Daniel, Warren, Ben and me, he convinced Marsilia that you were the only hope of finding Littleton. He was around when the walkers nearly drove the vampires out of the Western territories. It should please you that he was really shocked when you found Littleton so soon.'

'He confessed,' I said. 'So what is bothering you?'

'There was no permanent harm done to the seethe,' he said, biting off the words.

I sat down on the floor of the kitchen. I'd heard those words before.

'She released him.' I couldn't believe it. 'Did she just let him go?'

Samuel had known it might happen, I thought. Both he and Stefan had known there was a good chance he'd be freed: that's why Stefan had worked so hard to get evidence.

'I told them that by calling you into the hunt, the seethe was responsible for the damage to your trailer and for you missing work for almost two weeks. The seethe has retained the services of a contractor to replace the siding, though that may take a while – this is their busy season. In the next few days, though, our accountants will issue you a check to compensate you for your loss of work.'

'They just let him go.'

'He sent Littleton here, hoping to destroy those he perceived as Marsilia's enemies. The chair witnessed his truthfulness.'

'You aren't Marsilia's enemy.'

'No. I just stood between him and what he wanted. Such things are understood in the seethe.'

'What about all the people who died?' I asked. 'The family of harvest workers, the people in the hotel?' The poor woman whose only crime was working a crummy job at the wrong place and time. What about Warren, screaming in agony, and Ben who refused to be human again?

'The seethe does not consider human life to be of much worth,' Stefan said softly. 'Marsilia is intrigued by the idea of a sorcerer who is also a vampire. She thinks that such a one might bring the end to her exile here. The Tri-Cities is not the deserted wasteland it was two hundred years ago when she was sent here for trespasses against the Old One who rules in Italy, but neither is it Milan. The Old Master would be intrigued by the power of a creature who can make a vampire as old as I bow to his will. Maybe even intrigued enough to call us home.'

'She wants him to make another one,' I whispered.

'Yes.'

Samuel called me from his work the next morning. Ben had been confined to the cell in Adam's house. He'd attacked another male werewolf without provocation – attempted suicide, werewolf style. He was badly hurt, but expected to recover.

I thought of Ben's dull eyes, of Warren's limp and the dead woman who haunted my dreams. I thought of the 'nearly forty' deaths Uncle Mike laid at Littleton's feet; many of them were killed while Andre was still in control. I remembered Stefan's admission that the vampires didn't consider human lives to be of much worth.

With the vampire's judgement given, if the wolves did anything to Andre it would be seen as an attack on the seethe and precipitate a war that would cost many more lives on all sides. So, even though Bran and Adam were livid, their hands were tied. If Samuel hadn't been the Marrok's son, he could have done something.

Stefan couldn't do anything, even if he wanted to. He had to obey Marsilia. His hands were tied, too.

But mine weren't.

It was a good thing I hadn't given Zee the vampire-hunting kit back. I was going to need it. The first thing I had to do was find Andre's home, and I had everything I needed to do that — a keen nose and time.

I ran after the ball and caught it, running slowly so the boys who were chasing me would think they might have a chance. They laughed as they ran, which wasn't very efficient of them if they intended to catch me. I sprinted between them, and across the yard, dropping the ball at their father's feet, wagging my tail. Something wild coyotes don't usually do.

'Good girl,' he said and pretended to throw it.

I gave him a reproving look, which made him laugh. 'Look out you hooligans,' he called out to the boys. 'I'm sending her your way.'

I darted through the trees after the ball, then realized the children's excited cries had died completely. I spun around to see what had happened, but they were both all right. Just staring at the man who'd gotten out of the black SUV.

Adam had that effect on people.

I turned back and looked for the ball, finding it hiding under a rosebush. With it in my mouth I danced back across the yard and dropped it at Adam's feet.

'Thank you,' he told me dryly. Then he turned to the man who had called him.

'I really appreciate you letting me know where she was. My daughter took her out to her boyfriend's house and forgot to keep watch.'

'No problem.'

They shook hands, one of those strong-but-not-painful manly handshakes.

'You need to keep an eye on her, though,' the man told Adam. 'She looks a lot like a coyote. If she'd gone out a few miles more she might have been shot before anyone noticed the collar.'

'I know,' Adam gave a rueful laugh. 'She's half coyote, we think, though her mother was a German Shepherd.'

I jumped in the SUV when Adam opened the door. He got in, gave the little family who'd 'found' me a friendly wave. Then he started the car and drove off.

'That's the third time this month I've come to pick you up,' he told me. Twice in Richland and today in Benton City. I was costing him a small fortune in gas and rewards. I'd seen him slip money to both boys.

I wagged my tail at him.

'I brought clothes this time,' he said. 'Hop in the back and change so we can talk.'

I wagged my tail at him again.

He raised an eyebrow. 'Mercy, you've been avoiding talking to me for long enough. Time to quit running and talk. Please.'

Reluctantly, I hopped to the backseat. He was right. If I hadn't been ready to talk, I wouldn't have been running around the Tri-Cities in a collar with his phone number on it. Of course escaping from the Animal Control Shelter might have had something to do with it as well.

He'd brought sweats that smelled like him. They were big, but I could tighten the cord on the pants so they didn't slide off. I rolled up the sleeves and then crawled back over the seat.

He waited until I was buckled in before he spoke. I expected to be grilled about my recent habit of wandering around the city in coyote guise.

'I scare you,' he told me, instead.

'Do not.' I huffed indignantly.

He glanced at me and then at the road. I noticed he was taking the long way home, the narrow highway that followed the Yakima River and would eventually drop us off in the north side of Richland.

There was a smile on his face.

'Okay. What if I said that your reactions to me scare you?'

My heartbeat picked up. That just wasn't fair, women were supposed to be a mystery to men.

'You're a control freak,' I said hotly. 'You'll have to excuse me if I don't like being controlled.'

'I don't control you,' he said in that rich-as-night voice he could use when he wanted to. The rat bastard. Upset as I was it still had an effect on me. 'You chose to submit.'

'I don't submit to anyone,' I snapped, looking out the side window to show him I wanted this conversation over.

'But you want to.'

I had no answer for that.

'It's taken me this long to figure out an answer to our problem,' he said. 'What if I let you take charge?'

I gave him a suspicious look. 'What do you mean by that?'

'I mean just what I said. When we go out, you pick where we're going. If we kiss — or anything else — it'll be because you started it. That way, even if you want to submit to me, you can't because I'm not asking anything.'

I crossed my arms over my chest and stared hard at the river. 'Let me think about it.'

'Fair enough. So, do you want to tell me what you were doing in Benton City?'

'Hunting.'

He sucked in a deep breath. 'You won't find him that way.'

'Find whom?' I asked innocently.

'The vampire. Andre. You won't find him that way. They

have ways of confusing their scent and magic to hide their daytime resting places even from other vampires. That's why Warren and Ben couldn't track Littleton down when they went looking.'

'Their magics don't work so well on me,' I told him.

'And you can talk to ghosts that the rest of us can't see,' he snapped impatiently. 'Which is why Marsilia sent you after Littleton.' He was still mad at me for doing that, even if, maybe *especially because*, it had worked. 'How long have you been looking for Andre? Since Marsilia let him go?'

I didn't give him an answer. Didn't *want* to give him an answer. It occurred to me that this was the first time I'd felt myself in his presence since we'd gone on our first date. Maybe it was the vampire blood.

'What did I do to deserve that look?' he asked.

'Why don't I feel like obeying you now?' I asked.

He smiled at me and turned onto the bypass highway that ran along the outskirts of Richland. It was four thirty and the road was clogged with traffic.

'Being the Alpha is different from just being dominant,' he said.

I snorted. 'I know that. Remember where I grew up.'

'If I'm away from the pack, I can make the Alpha go dormant. Bran can do it whenever he feels like it, but for the rest of us, it takes real effort.'

I don't know how he expected me to react to that, but it didn't make me happy. 'So it was deliberate, the way you made me feel?'

He shook his head, and I let out the breath I hadn't realized I'd been holding. I don't like being manipulated at all, and being manipulated by paranormal means is worse.

'No. I told you it takes an effort – and the . . . effect you have on me makes it difficult.' He wasn't looking at me now. He was a product of his times. He might look like he was in his late twenties, but he'd been born just after WWII, and a man raised in the 1950's didn't talk about his feelings. It was interesting watching him squirm. I was suddenly feeling much more cheerful.

'I can't help how I'm wired,' he said after a moment. 'I don't even know how much is being an Alpha werewolf and how much is just me – but being around you brings out the predator in me.'

'And so you had to make me want to please you?' I made sure he heard how I felt about that.

'No!' He sucked in a big breath and then said, 'Please don't antagonize me right now. You want an explanation. You want me to stop influencing you. I'm trying to do both – but it isn't easy. Please.'

It was the 'please' that got to me. I leaned my back against the door so I was as far from him as I could get. 'Tell me, then.'

'Bran can control his Alpha effect until he can fool werewolves who don't know who and what he is. I'm not so talented, but I can stuff it down so it doesn't interfere with my everyday life. When I negotiate contracts, I don't like to exert undue influence on the people I'm dealing with. Even in the pack, I don't use it much. Cooperation is always better than coercion – especially when that coercion only lasts until they're out of my presence. I only bring out the big guns when there's trouble in the pack that can't be solved by talking.' He glanced at me and almost hit the car in front of him when traffic stopped unexpectedly.

If my hearing hadn't been so good I wouldn't have heard him when he said, 'When I am with you, my control is shot. I think that's what you've been feeling.'

So he could command my obedience whenever he wanted to. Only because he chose not to do so was I left with my free will.

'Before you act on that fear I can smell,' he said more confidently, 'I'd like to point out that you had no trouble turning Samuel down when you were sixteen – and he's more dominant than I am.'

'He's not an Alpha and I didn't turn him down to his face. I left without talking to him.'

'I've seen you go toe-to-toe with Bran and not back down.'

'No, you haven't.' I wasn't stupid. No one faced off with Bran.

He laughed. 'I've heard you. Remember when Bran told you to be a good little girl and let the wolves deal with the scary stuff and so ensured that you would go out and find the bastard who'd taken Jesse?'

'I didn't argue with him,' I pointed out.

'Because you didn't care if you had his permission or not. The only reason you submit to me is because some part of you wants to. I'm willing to admit that my being an Alpha brings that part of you to the forefront, but it is you who relaxes your guard around me.'

I didn't talk to him all the rest of the way home. I was fair enough to admit to myself that I was angry because I was pretty sure he was right, but not fair enough to tell him so.

Being a master strategist, he let me stew. He didn't even get out of the car to open my door – which he usually did. I hopped out and stood with the door open for a minute.

'There's supposed to be a good movie coming out,' I muttered. 'Would you like to come with me Saturday afternoon?' I hadn't intended to ask. The invitation just popped out.

He smiled, that slow smile that started in his eyes and never quite made it to his mouth. I shifted my weight uneasily because that smile had an unsettling effect on me.

'Which theater?'

I swallowed. This was not a good idea. Not at all. 'The one behind the mall, I think. I'll check.'

'Fine. Call me later with the time.'

'I'll drive.'

'Okay.' His lips were curling up now.

Dumb, I thought, *dumb sheep waltzing right into the slaughterhouse*. I shut the door without saying anything more and went into the house.

Out of the frying pan and into the fire, I thought, meeting Samuel's gaze.

'Going to the movies?' he asked, having obviously overheard what I'd said to Adam.

'Yes.' I jerked my chin up and refused to give in to the tight feeling in my stomach. Samuel wouldn't hurt me. The problem was, I didn't want to hurt him either.

His eyes were half-shut and he breathed in. 'You smell like him again.'

'He picked me up when I was running in coyote form, so he brought me clothes.'

Samuel moved with the speed of a born predator and put his hand behind my neck. I stood very still when he put his nose under my ear. I couldn't help but smell him also. How could his scent have as powerful an effect on me as Adam's smile? It was wrong.

'When you go with him,' he growled, his body trembling with readiness or pain – I couldn't tell which because I could smell both, 'I want you to remember this.'

He kissed me. It was utterly serious, beautiful – and, given the rage in his eyes when he started, surprisingly gentle.

He backed away and gave me a small, pleased smile. 'Don't look so worried, Mercy love.'

'I'm not a broodmare,' I told him, trying not to hyperventilate.

'No,' he agreed. 'I won't lie to you about how I feel. The

thought of having children who won't die before they are born is powerful. But you should know that the wolf in me doesn't care about such things. He only wants you.'

He left while I was still trying to come up with a reply. Not to his room, but all the way out of the house. I heard his car start up and purr away.

I sat down on the couch and hugged one of the pillows. I was trying so hard not to think about Samuel or Adam, that I had to think about something else. Something like hunting down Andre.

Marsilia told me that the reason vampires feared walkers was that we were resistant to vampire magics and could talk to ghosts.

But as Darryl had reminded me, ghosts avoid evil – like vampires. I might not be susceptible to some vampire magics, but evidently the magic that kept me from sniffing their lairs out worked just fine. Maybe the other walkers had been more powerful than me.

Medea jumped on the couch beside me.

Marsilia couldn't have meant something like the way I'd used Mrs Hanna to find Littleton. That was a special case. Most ghosts aren't capable of communication.

There aren't many ghosts in the Tri-Cities, it is too newly settled for that. There weren't very many people here until WWII, when the efforts to develop a nuclear bomb spawned the Hanford Project. Despite, or maybe because of, the military cause of the cities' growth, the Tri-Cities didn't have a lot of violence in its past – and violent, senseless death was the main cause of ghosts.

Violent, senseless deaths happened at a vampire's menagerie.

I set the pillow down and Medea climbed into my lap.

I wasn't the only person who could see ghosts. There are lots of haunted places in Portland where I'd gone to high school – and normal, everyday people see them. Of course, most humans don't see them as well as I do, and then usually only at night. I never understood that. Ghosts are around in daytime as often as at night, though there are a lot of things that cannot bear the light of day.

Like vampires.

It couldn't be that easy.

The next day, after work, I went out looking for Andre on two feet instead of four. I wasn't sure that looking for ghosts would work. In the first place, ghosts aren't all that common. A thousand people could die in a battle and there might be no ghosts at all. And even if there were ghosts, there was no guarantee I'd see them – or figure out they were ghosts if I did. Some of the dead, like Mrs Hanna, appeared as they had in life.

I was looking for a needle in a haystack, so I could kill Andre.

I understood it wouldn't be like killing Littleton – and that had been bad enough. Andre would be asleep and defenseless. Even if I managed to find him, I didn't know that I could actually execute him.

And if I did kill him, Marsilia's seethe would come after me.

At least then I wouldn't have to make a choice between Adam and Samuel. Every cloud has its silver lining.

I hunted every afternoon and returned just before dark. Samuel was making himself scarce, but he'd started leaving meals in the fridge for me. Sometimes take-out, but usually something he'd cooked. When he was home, he acted as if he'd never kissed me, never told me that he was still interested. I didn't know if that was reassuring or frightening. Samuel was a very patient hunter.

I took Adam to the movies on Saturday. He was very well behaved. Afterwards we drove out to the Hanford Reservation and ran as wolf and coyote through the open terrain. He didn't have Samuel's ability to throw off all his humanity and revel in the joy of being a wild thing. Instead, he played with the same intensity he used for everything else. Which meant that when I chased him, I wasn't really sure I wanted to catch him – and when he chased me, I felt like a rabbit.

We were both tired out when I dropped him off at his home before dinner. He didn't kiss me, but he gave me a look that was almost as good.

I didn't want to go home to Samuel after that look. So I drove back into Kennewick and just cruised around. Watching Adam play tamed beast had been . . . heart wrenching. Adam wasn't like Bran, who enjoyed role-playing. I didn't like myself very much for making Adam do it. Playing in the Reservation had been better, he hadn't subdued the wolf as well there.

I stopped at a stop sign in one of the plethora of new housing developments that had sprung up over the past few years, and there it was. Hollow eyed and sad, the middle-aged man stood on the porch of a respectable-looking house and stared at me.

I pulled the Rabbit over and parked it, and returned his stare. As I sat there, another one appeared beside him, this one an old woman. When the third ghost appeared, I got out of the car. The house was only a couple of years old: three people were a bit much for a normal household to lose in a couple of years – especially three people who had become ghosts rather than going on to the other side as most dead people do.

I took the backpack that held Zee's vampire-hunting kit and walked across the street. It was only as I started up the porch that I realized he'd have some people here, too. For some reason, I'd forgotten that I'd have to deal with the vampire's menagerie before I killed the vampire.

I rang the doorbell and did my best not to look at the ghosts, of which there were now significantly more than three: I could smell them even if I couldn't see them.

No one answered the door, though I could hear them inside. There was no smell of fear or anger, just unwashed bodies. When I turned the door knob, the door opened.

Inside the smell was bad. If vampires have almost as good a sense of smell as I do, I don't know how any vampire could have stayed here. But then vampires don't have to breathe.

I tried to use my nose to tell me whose house I was in. His scent was partially masked by the sour smell of sweat and death, so I couldn't be certain I had the right vampire, just that he was male.

The ghosts followed me. I could feel them brush up against me, pushing me onward as if they knew what I was here for and were determined to help. They pushed and pulled until I came to a doorway next to the bathroom on the main floor. It was narrower than the other doors, obviously built to be a linen closet. But, at the urging of my guides, I opened the door and was unsurprised to see a set of winding stairs that led down into a dark hole.

I have never been afraid of the dark. Even when I can't see, my nose and ears work pretty well to guide me. I'm not claustrophobic. Still, climbing down that hole was one of the hardest things I've ever done, because, even knowing he would be inactive during the day, the thought of trying to kill a vampire scared me silly.

I hadn't brought a flashlight. Hadn't expected to need one: it was daylight after all. There was a little light from the stairway. I could see that the room wasn't very big, just a little bigger than the average bathroom. And there was something, a bed or couch, stretched across the far side of the room.

I closed my eyes and counted a full minute, when I opened my eyes again, I could see a little better. It was a bed and the vampire on it wasn't Andre. His hair was lighter. The only blond male in the seethe who had his own menagerie was Wulfe, the Wizard. I had no quarrel with him.

I had to fight the ghosts as I climbed back up the stairwell. They knew what I was there for, and they wanted the vampire dead.

'I'm sorry,' I told them after I made it back up to the hallway. 'I can't just kill for no reason.'

'Then why did you come?'

I swallowed my heart and turned around, expecting to see the vampire behind me, but there was only the dark stairway. But I couldn't dismiss the voice as my imagination because all of the ghosts were gone. I touched the sheep on the necklace I'd bought to replace the one Littleton had broken.

He laughed. 'Are you after Andre? He doesn't live around here. But you could kill me, instead.'

'Should I?' I asked, angry because he'd scared me.

'I know how a sorcerer is made,' he said. 'But no one has asked me.'

'Why haven't you made a sorcerer and turned him then?' I asked, growing more confident. The hallway was dim, but I could see that there was light coming in the house from the windows still. If Wulfe was awake, he'd be confined to the dark room where he was safe.

'Because I'm not a fool. Marsilia knows better, too, but she is obsessed with returning to Milan.'

'Then I have no reason to kill you,' I told him.

'Then again, maybe you couldn't have killed me,' he said, crawling out of the stairway. He moved very slowly, like a lizard who had gotten too cold.

I heard a whimper from behind one of the closed doors next to the bathroom, and sympathized. I wanted to whimper, too.

'I'm not hunting you,' I told him firmly, though I stepped backward until I stood in a circle of light at the end of the hallway.

He stopped halfway out of the stairway, his eyes were filmed over like a dead man's.

'Good,' he said. 'If you kill Andre, I won't tell – and no one will ask.'

And he was gone, withdrawing from the hallway and down the stairs so fast that I barely caught the motion, though I was staring right at him.

I walked out of his home because if I'd moved any faster, I'd have run screaming.

15

I found another vampire's lair in Pasco, but this time I played it smarter. I drove back at noon the next day when the sun was high in the sky and changed into my coyote self because my nose was sharper when I ran on four paws.

I hopped over the fence and cast about, but whatever vampires did to hide their lairs almost worked. I could find no clear scent around the house, but the car smelled of a female vampire, Estelle.

The third menagerie I found a few days later was Andre's.

He lived in a pretty little house mostly hidden behind a huge pole building. It sat on a couple of acres of land next to the wildlife preserve near Hood Park, just outside of Pasco.

I wouldn't have thought to look out that far since vampires, unlike werewolves, are city creatures. It was only luck that had me test-driving a VW Bus out that way. I pulled over to make a few adjustments and as soon as I got out of the car, I knew that people had died inside that house, a lot of people.

I got into the back of the van to change to coyote.

Either Andre was careless, or he wasn't as good as Estelle or Wulfe because I found his scent all over the property. He liked to sit at a picnic table and look out over the preserve. It was a beautiful view. I didn't see any ghosts, but I could feel them, dozens of them, waiting for me to do something.

Instead, I drove back to the shop and went to work.

If I could have killed him the day Marsilia released him, or even the night I killed Littleton it would have been easier. I'd killed animals to eat them, and because it was the coyote nature to prey upon mice and rabbits. Three times I'd killed in self-defense or defense of others. Cold-blooded murder was more difficult.

An hour before closing I left Gabriel in charge of the shop and drove home. Samuel wasn't there again, which was probably just as well. I sat down in my room and wrote a list of the people I knew Littleton and Andre, between them, had killed. I didn't know all the names, but I included Daniel twice, since Andre had killed him once – and Littleton was responsible for his second death. At the end of the list I put down Warren's name. Then below it, Samuel, Adam, Ben and Stefan. All of them had been damaged by the sorcerer.

Andre intended to create another monster like Littleton. Could I kill him while he was held helpless by the day?

Stefan couldn't touch him because he was oath bound to Marsilia. The wolves couldn't touch him or a lot of people would die.

If *I* killed Andre, the only person who would suffer was me. Sooner or later, Marsilia would figure out who had killed him even if Wulfe didn't tell her – and I trusted Wulfe about as far as I could throw him. When she knew, she would have me killed. I could only trust she wouldn't be stupid enough to do it in such a way that Samuel or Adam would get involved: she wouldn't want a war either, not with the seethe poised for rebellion.

Was it worth my life to kill Andre?

Deliberately I recalled the maid's face and the sound of her hoarse cries as Littleton killed her slowly in front of me. I remembered the shattered expression that Adam had tried to hide behind anger in the bright lights of the hospital, and the long days following that night before Samuel had strung two words together. Then there was Daniel, broken and starving, at Stefan's trial. Andre had sacrificed him twice, once for revenge and a second time to see how powerful his monster was.

I went to my gun safe and pulled out both of my hand-guns, the 9mm SIG Sauer and the .44 Smith & Wesson. I had to put a linen jacket on over my T-shirt so I could wear the SIG in its shoulder harness. The .44 would have to ride in the backpack with the rest of the vampire-hunting treasures. I was pretty sure the guns wouldn't do me any good against Andre, but they'd take out any of his human sheep – though if Wulfe's menagerie was anything to judge by, I might not have to worry about Andre's blood donors.

I hoped they'd stay out of the way. The thought of killing more people made me sick, especially as Andre's menagerie wasn't guilty of anything except being victims.

Even with the guns, when I got in the Rabbit, I wasn't entirely certain I was going to go after Andre. Impulsively I turned down Adam's street and drove to his house.

Jesse opened the door. 'Mercy? Dad's not back from work yet.'

'Good,' I told her. 'I need to see Ben.'

She stepped away from the door, inviting me in. 'He's still confined,' she told me. 'Whenever Dad isn't around to stop him, he goes after the nearest wolf.'

I followed her down the stairs. Ben was curled up as far from the doorway as he could get with his back to us.

'Ben?' I asked.

His ear twitched and he flattened a little against the floor. I sat down on the floor in front of the bars and put my forehead against the door.

'Are you all right?' Jesse asked.

Ben's misery smelled sour, almost like an illness.

'I'm fine,' I told her. 'Would you leave us for just a few minutes?'

'Sure thing. I was in the middle of a show anyway.' She gave me a quick grin. 'I'm watching *An American Werewolf in London*.'

I waited until she was gone and then whispered, so none of the other werewolves I could smell in the house would overhear. 'I found Andre,' I told him. I wasn't certain how far he'd sunk into the wolf, but at the mention of the vampire's name, he came to his feet, growling.

'No, you can't come with me,' I told him. 'If Marsilia thinks one of the werewolves is involved in Andre's death, there will be retaliation. I came here . . . I guess because I'm afraid. I don't know how I can kill Andre while he sleeps and still be me afterwards.'

Ben took two slow steps toward me. I reached up and touched the cage with the tips of my fingers. 'It doesn't matter. It has to be done and I'm the best one to do it.'

Abruptly impatient with myself, I stood up. 'Don't let them win, Ben. Don't let them destroy you, too.'

He whined, but I didn't stay to talk anymore. I had a vampire to kill.

The weatherman had been predicting a break in the weather for three days, and when I left Adam's house the dark clouds that had been moving in all day had thickened impressively. Hot wind snatched my hair and whipped it across my face.

When I got in my car, I was careful to hold onto the door so the wind couldn't fling it into the shiny new Toyota I'd parked next to.

It still hadn't started to rain when I drove the Rabbit onto the gravel drive that stopped at Andre's house, parking in front of the motor home-sized, garage door side of the pole barn. There were neighboring houses, but they were closer to the highway than Andre's house and the pole barn, along with strategically planted foliage, protected his privacy.

Anyone passing by would be able to see my car, but I wasn't really worried about the neighbors. I'd destroy Andre's body, and the vampires would never allow the human police to find anyone else's remains – including mine.

The grass was knee high and crunched as I walked across it. No one had watered the lawn for a month or more. There were flowers planted around the edge of the house, long dead. I suppose Andre didn't care about how nice his place looked by daylight.

I shouldered my backpack and walked around the pole barn to knock on the door. No one answered and the door was locked tight. I walked around the house and found a patio door on the other side. It was locked, too, but suitable application of a paving stone solved that nicely.

No one came to investigate the sound of breaking glass.

The dining room I walked into was spotlessly clean and reeked of Pine-Sol, the smell making me sneeze as well as disguising any other scent that might be present.

Like the house, the room was small but pretty. The floor was oak, antiqued with a white wash that made the room feel bigger than it was. On one side of the room was a brick fireplace. Family photographs covered most of the surface of the mantelpiece. Curious, I looked at them. Children and grandchildren, I thought, and none of them related to Andre. How long would it be before one of them realized they hadn't heard from their grandparents for too long? How long had he been here to leave so many ghosts?

Maybe the owners of the house were off touring the countryside in the motor home that the pole barn had been built to house. I hoped so.

I started to turn away and something knocked one of the photos off the mantel. Glass shattered on the floor and a chill breeze touched my face.

I left the dining room and walked into the kitchen, which was surprisingly big for the size of the house. Someone had painted the wooden cabinets white, then toll-painted flowers and vines all over. The window over the sink was covered with dark green garbage sacks sealed with duct tape so no light would get through.

There were no vampires in the living room either, though it wasn't as clean as the dining room and kitchen had been. Someone had left a dirty glass on an end table – and there were dark stains on the beige carpet. Blood, I thought, but the Pine-Sol was still crippling my nose.

The bathroom door was open, but the two doors next to it were not. I didn't think Andre was behind either of them, because someone had put shiny new bolts on the outside to keep whoever was inside prisoner.

I opened the first door gingerly and had to take a quick step back, even with my deadened nose, because of the strong smell of human waste.

The man was curled up on a pile of filthy sleeping bags. He curled up tighter when I opened the door and whimpered, muttering, 'They're coming for me, Lord. Don't let them. Don't let them.'

'Shh,' I said. 'I'm not going to hurt you.'

The smell was appalling, but it would have had to be a lot stronger to keep me out. He cried when I touched his shoulder.

'Come on,' I told him. 'Let's get you out of here.'

He rolled onto his back and grabbed my head in both hands.

'Vampire.' Eyes wild, he shook me slowly. 'Vampire.'

'I know. But it's daylight now. Come outside with me where he can't get you.'

He seemed to understand that part and helped me get him to his feet. I pulled his arm over my shoulder and we did a drunken dance out to the living room. I unlocked the door and took him out.

The skies were darker, making it look hours later in the

day than it really was. I sat him down on the picnic table with orders to stay there, but I wasn't certain he'd heard me because he was muttering about the dark man. It didn't matter. He wasn't in any shape to get very far.

I left the living room door open and hurried back to the second room. This time the occupant was an older woman. Bite marks trailed up both arms. If the puncture wounds hadn't been in pairs she would have looked like a junkie. She was more alert than the man had been. She didn't smell as bad, and, though she didn't make any more sense than he had, she helped me get her out of the room. I had a harder time getting her to let go of me once I had her at the picnic table.

'Run,' she said. 'Run.'

'I'm going to take care of him,' I told her. 'It's all right.'

'No,' she said, though she let me go. 'No.'

The house protected them from the worst of the wind, and it still hadn't started raining, though I heard the crack of thunder. If it didn't rain soon we'd have some grass fires out of this storm.

The mundane worry steadied me as I went back into the house to hunt for Andre. I left the bedrooms for last. Partially because I was in no hurry to go back into either, but also because I was pretty sure that Andre had to be on the outside of the rooms in order to lock them.

There were no secret passages I could see in the bathroom, and the closet next to it was full of furnace and water heater: there was no room for vampire. I walked back out to the living room and heard another crash from the dining room.

I got there just as the last framed photo fell onto the floor, just in front of a small throw rug. Something shoved me between my shoulder blades and I took another step forward.

'Under the rug?' I said. 'How unoriginal.' Sarcasm, I've found, makes terror more bearable. I hoped that Andre would be helpless in the daytime even if Wulfe had not been. Andre was the same age as Stefan, and Stefan told me he died during the day.

I moved the rug and there was a trapdoor, complete with an inset iron ring pull. I took out my flashlight before opening the trapdoor.

Here there was nothing so sophisticated as Wulfe's circular stairway. A free standing wooden ladder stood directly beneath the opening. I ducked my head into the hole, hoping the ghost who shoved me once wouldn't do it while I was hanging my head down.

It wasn't a basement so much as a very deep hole dug into the dirt to allow access to the plumbing under the house. There were a few old shelves leaned up against a foundation wall, and some fencing materials. On the other side of the room was a canopy bed straight out of a bodice-ripper romance.

My flashlight picked out an embroidered pattern on dark velvet fabric that enveloped the bed, hiding its occupant, if there was one.

I lowered myself down onto the top of the ladder, and very carefully stepped down two rungs. From there on it was an easy scramble to the ground. I opened my backpack and took out the stake and a mallet I'd taken from the shop: I'd learned it was harder than I'd thought to punch the stake through a vampire's heart.

I left the backpack and its remaining goodies near the foot of the ladder. They wouldn't do me any good until I'd staked Andre, and I had as much as I could carry with the mallet, stake and flashlight.

Above me, lightning struck somewhere nearby, making me jump. If I didn't calm down, I was going to have a heart attack before I killed Andre – and wouldn't that be a waste?

I stood as far from the bed as I could and used the stake to pull open the bed curtains.

Andre was there. When the beam of the flashlight caught

him in the face he opened his eyes. Like Wulfe's had been, his eyes were filmed over and blind. I took a step back, ready to run, but he just lay there with his eyes open. He was fully dressed in a pink knit shirt and beige slacks.

Heart in my throat, I forced myself to walk forward and lay the flashlight on the bed where it still gave me some light, but wasn't likely to roll around and blind me. I set the point of the stake down on his chest. It probably would have been smarter to open his shirt, but I couldn't force myself to touch him. The stake had gone through Littleton's clothing, it ought to go through Andre's as well.

Though I'd been suffocated with qualms all day, finding his prisoners had freed me from my conscience at last. Andre needed to die.

His hands started to move, startling me so that my first hit was off and the stake slid across his ribs instead of going in. He opened his jaws, showing fangs and his hands moved toward his chest.

Quickly I set the stake again and this time I hit the end squarely with the mallet. I felt the wood hit bone and push forward through the softer tissues beneath. I hit it again and the stake buried itself in his chest.

Like Littleton, Andre's body began to spasm. I ran toward my backpack chanting, 'knife, knife, knife,' and tripped over some unevenness of the dirt floor. I was still on my hands and knees when Andre knocked the flashlight off and it rolled under the bed, enclosing us in shadows.

I scrambled forward, finding the pack with my nose and fingers. Zee's knife in one hand, I walked slowly back into the now silent black corner. The flashlight's muffled light showed me where the bed was, but it made it more difficult to see inside the bed where the curtains shielded the vampire with shadow.

Did you really think it would be so easy?

The toneless voice burned in my head. I tried instinctively to block it out with my hands over my ears, but it was useless.

Did you think I'd be easy prey like my poor Cory, who was just a baby.

I wanted to turn around and run. I wanted to hide as far from the vampire as I could. I was no match for a vampire, especially not this vampire. The old bite on my neck started throbbing, the ache spreading into the shoulder Littleton had damaged.

That was his mistake, because the pain cut through the fear and allowed me to realize that the fear was imposed from outside myself. Once I knew that, it was easier to ignore.

I continued forward, stopping when my knees hit the edge of the bed. My fingers found his chest, then the stake and I moved my hand forward into the blackness until I touched his throat.

He turned his head, quick as a snake and bit into my wrist. Pain blossomed like a mushroom in my head. I moved my hand and his head followed, stretching upward as if the only muscle control he had was in his jaw.

Zee's knife had no trouble cutting his head off. I used it more carefully to pry my wrist free of his bite – I didn't want to slice myself up any more than Andre already had. I had to cut through his jawbone to free my wrist.

When I was through, I took a moment to be sick and then used Zee's knife once more to cut strips off my linen jacket sleeve so I could wrap my wrist. It wasn't as if anything would ever get the jacket clean again anyway.

I was disoriented and shocky, so it took me a while to find the backpack again. The dragon medallion was warmer than my fingers.

It was easier to find the bed this time. My eyes were

accustomed to the dark and the flashlight beam, as dim as it was, was the only light in the room.

I set the medallion on his chest.

'*Drachen*,' I said and suddenly there was more light than my eyes could handle.

Blinded, I had to stay where I was for a moment. By the time I could see, the fire had spread from the vampire to the bedding and smoke filled the room. I couldn't wait and reclaim the medallion or the stake without suffocating from smoke inhalation. So I left them behind and scrambled up the ladder. Zee's knife was still in my hand.

The skies were dark, boiling with energy, and as I stumbled out of the broken patio door, the wind pulled a tree limb off a nearby tree. The wind, or something else tugged and pulled me away from the house. I had to cover my eyes because dirt and plant matter filled the air.

I staggered to the picnic table and touched the man's shoulder. 'Come on,' I said. 'We need to get to the car.'

But he fell over, off the bench, and onto the ground. Only then did my brain catch up to what my nose and ears had been trying to tell me. He was dead. The woman was lying forward on the table, as if she'd set her head down and fallen asleep. My heart was the only one beating. She was dead, too.

As I stood dumbfounded, I became aware that there was something missing. The whole time I had been here I could feel the weight of the dead teasing the outer edges of my senses. There were no ghosts here, now.

Which meant that there were vampires nearby.

I spun around, looking, but I would never have seen him if he hadn't wanted me to.

Wulfe was leaning against the wall of the house, looking up at the sky, his head banging rhythmically against the wall of the house in time with my furiously beating heart.

Then he stopped and looked at me. His eyes were fogged, but I had no doubt he could see me.

'It's daytime,' I said.

'Some of us aren't as limited as others,' he answered me. 'Andre's death cries have roused the seethe by now. Marsilia will know he is dead – they have been bound for a long time, she and Andre. It won't have to be much darker before the rest of us are here. You need to get her away.'

I stared at him, then realized he wasn't talking to me – because a cold hand wrapped around my upper arm.

'Come on,' Stefan said, his voice strained. 'You need to get out of here before the rest come.'

'You killed them,' I said, digging in my heels. I didn't look at him because I didn't want to see him looking the way Wulfe and Andre looked in the daylight. 'They were safe and you killed them.'

'Not him,' Wulfe said. 'He told me you would never forgive him if he did. It was a clean death, they weren't frightened – but they had to die. They couldn't be allowed to run free crying, "vampire." And we need culprits to give to the Mistress.' He smiled at me and I took a step closer to Stefan. 'I came to find the house on fire,' he said, 'and two humans, Andre's current menagerie, outside of his house. I always told Andre that the way he kept his sheep would be the death of him someday.' He laughed.

'Come on,' Stefan said. 'If we get you out of here in the next ten minutes or so, no one will know you were ever here.'

I let him urge me away from Wulfe, still not looking at him.

'You knew I was hunting Andre.'

'I knew. There was nothing else you would have done, being you.'

'She'll question you with the chair,' I said. 'She'll know I did this.'

'She won't question me because I've been locked up in the cells under the seethe for the past week because of my "unfortunate attitude" about the Mistress's plans to create another monster. No one can escape from the cells because Wulfe's magic ensures what is locked there stays locked there.'

'What if she questions Wulfe?'

'The chair is Wulfe's creation,' said Stefan, opening my door. 'He'll tell her that no vampire, werewolf, or walker is responsible for Andre's death and the chair will verify it — because Andre caused his own death.'

I looked up at him then, because I couldn't help it. He looked just as he always did, except for a pair of impenetrable black sunglasses that hid his eyes.

He leaned over and kissed me full on the mouth, a quick gentle kiss that told me I hadn't imagined the passionate words he'd murmured as I'd drunk his blood the night I'd killed Littleton. I'd really hoped they had been my imagination.

'I gave you my word of honor you would not take harm,' he said. 'I was not able to redeem my word completely, but at least you will not suffer to lose your life because I chose to involve you in this.' He smiled at me. 'Don't fret, Little Wolf,' he said, and shut the door.

I started the car and zipped out of Andre's driveway, running from Stefan more than Marsilia's wrath.

Andre's house burned to the ground before the fire department could get to it. The reporter interviewed the fire marshall as rain pounded down. The rain, the fire marshall said, kept the fire from spreading to the dry grass. They'd found two bodies inside the house. The owners of the house had been contacted, they were spending the summer at their cabin in Coeur d'Alene. The bodies probably belonged to vagrants who had discovered the house was empty.

I was watching the special report on the ten o'clock news when someone pounded on my door.

'If you put dents in it,' I said, knowing Adam could hear me, despite the closed door, 'I'll make you replace it.'

I turned off the TV and opened the door.

'I have chocolate chip cookies,' I told him. 'Or brownies, but they're still pretty hot to eat.'

He was shaking with rage, his eyes brilliant yellow wolf's eyes. His cheeks had white marks from the force he was using to clench his jaws.

I took another bite out of my cookie.

'Where have you been?' he asked in a softly menacing voice. The weight of his power enveloped me and compelled me to answer.

So much for his promise not to exert undue influence.

Fortunately, having been terrified and traumatized well beyond my limits, there was nothing left to answer the Alpha's demand. I finished my cookie, licked the warm chocolate off my fingers and waved him inside.

He caught my hand and pulled back my sleeve. I'd doctored myself out of Samuel's first aid kit, which was much better stocked than mine. I'd cleaned the wound Andre had left in my wrist with hydrogen peroxide – I owed Samuel a new bottle. In a fresh, clean bandage the wound didn't look as bad. It felt as though he'd all but chewed my arm off.

'Ben said you found Andre,' Adam told me while he looked at my wrist. A muscle vibrated in his cheek. 'He was waiting for me in human form. But you didn't tell him where you found him so we went out hunting, Ben and I – until Jesse called to tell me your car was back.'

'Andre is gone,' I told him. 'He won't be coming back.'

He held my wrist in one hand and cupped my face in the

other, his thumb resting just over the pulse in my throat. 'If *I* killed you, it would at least be quick and clean. The Mistress will take a lot more time if she gets her hands on you.'

'Why would she?' I said softly. 'Two of Andre's flock burned down the house while he was asleep.'

'She'll never believe it,' he told me.

'Stefan thinks she will.'

He stared at me until I dropped my eyes. Then he pulled me against him and just held me.

I didn't tell him I was still scared — because he knew. I didn't tell him that I'd thrown up four times since I'd gotten home. I didn't tell him that I'd had to turn on every light in the house, that I couldn't get the faces of the two poor souls the Wizard had killed because Stefan wanted to protect me out of my head. I didn't tell him that I kept thinking about how the stake felt as it slid through flesh, or that I was never going to sleep again. I didn't tell him that Stefan had kissed me — Stefan who had killed two people to save me. He'd been right that I wouldn't have forgiven him for doing it — he just hadn't realized that I still held him respon-sible no matter who had done it. Wulfe didn't care whether I lived or died. If he was at Andre's house, it was some kind of favor exchange with Stefan.

Adam smelled so good. He would never kill an innocent bystander — not even to save me. I buried my nose between his shoulder and his jaw and let the warmth of his body sink into my soul.

Then I fed him cookies and milk until Samuel came home.

I awoke the next morning because someone was pounding on the side of my house. I was pulling on my jeans when I heard the front door open and the pounding stop.

They'd woken up Samuel, too.

Two big red trucks were parked outside my door, HICKMAN CONSTRUCTION written in wide white letters on their sides. There were three men in overalls with big grins on their faces chatting with Samuel.

'Damned if I know how they did it,' Samuel said. 'I wasn't here. My girlfriend scared 'em off with a rifle, but they sure did a number on the house while they were here, didn't they.'

We all obediently looked at the trailer.

'Might be cheaper just to buy a new trailer and cart this one off,' the oldest of the men said. He wore a hat that said *The Boss* and his hands had calluses on their calluses.

'The kid's parents are paying for the repairs,' I said. 'And repairing this trailer is a lot less hassle for us than moving into a new one would be.'

The Boss spit a hunk of chewing tobacco on the ground. 'That's for darn sure. Okay. We'll have this done in a day or two, depending on the damage to the underlying structure. The work order also says something about holes in the floor? I'm to repair them and replace the carpet.'

'In my bedroom,' I said. 'I didn't want to hurt my neighbors so I shot into the floor.'

He grunted. I couldn't tell if he approved or not. 'We'll do that tomorrow. Can we get in the house?'

'I can be here,' said Samuel. 'I work nights this week.'

'Where?'

'At the hospital.'

'Better than a convenience store, anyway,' said the Boss.

'I've done that, too,' agreed Samuel. 'The pay is better at the hospital, but the Stop and Rob was less stressful.'

'My Joni's an RN at Kadlec Hospital,' said one of the other men. 'She says those doctors are miserable to work with.'

'Terrible,' agreed Dr Samuel Cornick.

*   *   *

I looked up from the bus I was working on, and saw Mrs Hanna pushing her cart. I hadn't seen her since the night she'd helped me find Littleton though I'd caught her scent a time or two. I wiped my hands and went out to meet her.

'Hello,' I said. 'Beautiful day, isn't it?'

'Hello, Mercedes,' she said with her usual warm smile. 'I love the smell of the air just after a rain, don't you?'

'Absolutely. I see you're back on schedule today.'

Her face went a little blank. 'What was that, dear?' Then she smiled again. 'I found that picture I was looking for.'

'Which one?'

But she was finished talking to me. 'I have to go now, dear. Be good now.'

'Goodbye, Mrs Hanna,' I said.

She disappeared, but I could hear the clatter of her cart and the click of her heels on the pavement for a while after she left.

I finished working on the bus around lunchtime, so I headed back into the office. Gabriel looked up from the computer screen.

'Mail for you on your desk,' he said.

'Thanks.'

I picked up the box. There was no return address, but I'd seen enough of Stefan's handwriting to recognize it. So I waited until Gabriel left to get us some lunch before I opened it.

There were three packages wrapped in Scooby Doo paper: a scorched stake, a small gold medallion with a dragon on it, and a solid, dark chocolate VW Bus.

I gathered the paper and the box and put it in the trash, only then noticing that there was something else on the desk, a pencil sketch of a man's face. I turned it right side up and saw that it was Adam, his eyes watchful but a hint of a smile on his mouth. On the bottom of the page the artist had signed her name, *Marjorie Hanna*.

EXTRAS

www.orbitbooks.net

About the Author

Patricia Briggs lived a fairly normal life until she learned to read. After that she spent lazy afternoons flying dragonback and looking for magic swords when she wasn't horseback riding in the Rocky Mountains. Once she graduated from Montana State University with degrees in history and German, she spent her time substitute teaching and writing. She and her family live in the Pacific Northwest and you can visit her website at www.patriciabriggs.com

Find out more about Patricia Briggs and other Orbit authors by registering for the free monthly newsletter at www.orbitbooks.net

An interview with
PATRICIA BRIGGS

I really like the fact that Mercy is a mechanic. It sets the scene for Mercy to meet a variety of different people, providing helpful plot opportunities, but is a twist on the usual PI / investigator set-up, plus reinforces Mercy's status as a rather unusual and independent female. What was the inspiration behind Mercy's career choice?

Write what you know, right? Well I thought about the kinds of careers that put people in harms way: lawyer, police officer, private investigator. They're all fun, but I know virtually nothing about them. While I was fretting, I looked out to my back yard where my husband had a pair of Opel GTs he was trying to use to build a single running car.

I'm not a mechanic, but I've played hunt and fetch the tools for my husband and son while they tried to keep our miscellaneous old VWs on the road. We also had a good friend who was a VW mechanic who was something of a local hero to all of the people in the Tri Cities who owned Volkswagens.

Being a mechanic wasn't going to put her in harms way the same way being a police officer would, but by that point I needed a way to keep her grounded in human affairs anyway. And making her a small business owner who had to keep her business going while hell broke loose just gave me ammunition to keep the tension up in her stories.

Your books belong to a genre that has been called urban fantasy, paranormal romance, mystery and horror amongst other things. Do you have a preferred description of what you write and if so why?

It is, of course, a fusion of horror, noir mystery, detective mystery, and fantasy with bits of romance thrown in. Here in the states, a paranormal romance is a romance with paranormal elements: the romance is the most important part of the story. I usually call it an urban fantasy so that way romance readers won't expect it to be something it's not. There is romance, because I like it, but the stories are ultimately about the human worlds interactions with the monsters and not about the romance. Also, as evidenced with the "urban" part of the genre title, where the stories takes place is important. Not so much as a travelogue, but as a way to ground the story in reality.

Do you find it frustrating that so much excellent work is currently being produced in SF & Fantasy but that by and large it is still ignored by the literati?

No. I write the books I want to write – and I read the books that appeal to me. I got over having to read/write Great Literature when I was a teenager. Anyway, ultimately it is the common people who determine what classics are, not the literati. Tolkien and Rowling will be read a hundred years from now. I don't aspire to such heights, though. I'm happy to write stories that I enjoy – and a few other people seem to like them, too.

I am please that the literati have books written and published that they like to read, too. That way we can all be happy.

Why do you think people seek out Fantasy fiction?

This question usually comes up in some variant as a panel topic at science fiction conventions, and I've even been a participating panelist on it a time or ten – and I think that the answer varies with the author, the book and the reader. The most obvious function of fantasy literature is escapism. Allowing people to put aside the trials of their lives to live in a different world is valuable to our society. Escapist art reminds us that there is beauty in the world when our lives look pretty bleak. The best art, whether books, paintings, or music can console us, lift our expectations. When I was in high school, I used to take Christopher Stasheff's wonderful novel, *The Warlock In Spite of Himself* with me to dentist visits – or any other high stress times. I wore out five or six copies – that was in the days before he made a big splash so those copies were hard to find. No matter how upset I was, I could always laugh when I read that book.

Another traditional role of fantasy (and science fiction) is to disguise some current issue and examine it in abstract. George Orwell's *Animal Farm* was a grim fantasy designed to make us examine our lives. Voltaire's lively fable *Candide* made fun of complacency and the general self-congratulatory spirit of his era. Ellen Kushners' brilliant *At Swords Point* gently asks us to evaluate our place in society. Sometimes taking away the familiar norms of our world allows us to see things in a different light.

Which brings me to another important thing fiction, of any kind, does: Fiction, good fiction, allows the reader to see the world through someone else's eyes. When I read I can be a black man or a young child. I can be an old woman or a deer named Bambi. Understanding how someone else thinks is the first step to accepting their differences. In a world that, between faster communication and growing population, decreases in size every day, and in the light of the events of 9/11, it is important for us to be able to 'walk a mile in another's moccasins'. Books are, in my opinion, the single best medium to develop the understanding necessary to live together on our earth.

Do you still find time to read for pleasure? And if you do, do you like to stay within the genre or do you advocate a complete change?

If I didn't read, I don't think I could write. The faster I have to write, the more I have to read. I don't know why that is.

However after my first book, *Masques*, was published, it was almost a full year befire I could read fantasies (except for old favourites, or favourite authors). Either I picked them apart or I was jealous because they were so much better than my book <grin>.

Currently, I read a lot of fantasy, but I also read a lot of romance, mystery, and Science Fiction. I enjoy reading a wide variety of genres and I read a lot, usually at least one book a day (before I had children it was more like three books a day). I joined a reading group last year to broaden my horizons into, what I like to call, "The Reading Group Books" like *The Kite Runner* and *Reading Lolita in Tehran*. These are great books that I'd never otherwise read.

Some authors talk of their characters 'surprising' them by their actions; is this something that has happened to you?

Absolutely. Though I really think it is mostly that the longer I write about a character the better I know them. So when I present them with a problem, sometimes they attack it a different way than I expected. That's when I know that I have the character down and the rest of the story will be good.

This is a favourite question, so I expect you have been asked it many times – but it's always interesting to hear if you have any particular favourite authors who have influenced your work?

Andre Norton wrote both the first fantasy I ever read (*The Year of the Unicorn*) and the first science fiction novel (*Beastmaster*). From her I learned that the best stories are the ones about the underdog, about people who have it rough and survive.

When I was learning to write, I quite often turned to favourite authors when I was struggling with something. I learned to write conversation from Dick Francis and Jayne Anne Krenz for example.

I know from your previous interviews that your first love when a child was books about horses, being weaned onto SF/F by your big sister. Are you eternally grateful to her, or do you think the conversion was inevitable?!

I am eternally grateful to her. I suspect I'd have gone on to read SF/F without her, but she saved me a lot of time by pointing out the best books to start with.

If you have even more questions after reading this interview, almost(!) everything you might want to know about Patricia and her books can be found at www.hurog.com

If you enjoyed
BLOOD BOUND,
look out for

IRON KISSED

Book 3 of the

Mercy Thompson sequence

by

Patricia Briggs

Chapter 1

'A cowboy, a lawyer, and a mechanic watched *Queen of the Damned*,' I murmured.

Warren – who had once, a long time ago, been a cowboy – snickered and wiggled his bare feet. 'It could be the beginning of either a bad joke or a horror story.'

'No,' said Kyle, the lawyer, whose head was propped up on my thigh. 'If you want a horror story, you have to start out with a werewolf, his gorgeous lover, and a walker . . .'

Warren, the werewolf, laughed and shook his head. 'Too confusing. Not many people still remember what a walker is.'

Mostly they just confused us with skinwalkers. Since walkers and skinwalkers are both Native American shapeshifters, I can sort of understand it. Especially since I'm pretty sure the walker label came from some dumb white person who couldn't tell the difference.

But I'm not a skinwalker. First of all, I'm from the wrong tribe. My father had been Blackfoot, from a northern Montana tribe, and skinwalkers come from the Southwestern tribes, mostly Hopi or Navajo.

Second, skinwalkers have to wear the skin of the animal they change into, usually a coyote or wolf, but they cannot change their eyes. They are evil mages who bring disease and death wherever they go.

When I change into a coyote, I don't need a skin or – I glanced down at Warren, once a cowboy and now a werewolf – the moon. When I am a coyote, I look just like every other coyote. Pretty much harmless, really, as far down the power scale of the magical critters that lived in the state of Washington as it was possible to get. Which is one of the things that used to help keep me safe. I just wasn't worth bothering about. That had been changing over the past year. Not that I'd grown any more powerful, but I'd started doing things that drew attention. When the vampires figured out that I'd killed not one, but two of their own . . .

As if called by my thoughts, a vampire walked across the screen of the TV, a TV so big it wouldn't have fit in my trailer's living room. He was shirtless and his pants clung inches below his sexy hipbones.

I resented the shiver of fear that surged through my body instead of lust. Funny how killing them had only made the vampires more frightening. I dreamed of vampires crawling out of holes in the floor and whispering to me from shadows. I dreamed of the feel of a stake sliding through flesh and fangs digging into my arm.

If it had been Warren with his head on my lap instead of Kyle, he would have noticed my reaction. But Warren was stretched out on the floor and firmly focused on the screen.

'You know,' I snuggled deeper into the obscenely comfortable leather couch in the upstairs TV room of Kyle's huge house and tried to sound casual, 'I wondered why Kyle picked this movie. Somehow I didn't think there would be quite so many bare manly chests in a movie called *Queen of the Damned*.'

Warren snickered, ate a handful of popcorn from the bowl on his flat stomach, then said with more than a hint of a Texas drawl in his rough voice, 'You expected more naked women and fewer half-clothed men, did you, Mercy? You oughtta know Kyle better than that.' He laughed quietly again and pointed at the screen. 'Hey, I didn't think vampires were immune to gravity. Have you ever seen one dangle from the ceiling?'

I shook my head and watched as the vampire dropped on top of his two groupie victims. 'I wouldn't put it past them, though. I haven't seen them eat people yet either. Ick.'

'Shut up. I like this movie.' Kyle, the lawyer, defended his choice. 'Lots of pretty boys writhing in sheets and running around with low-cut pants and no shirts. I thought you might enjoy it, too, Mercy.'

I looked down at him – every lovely, solar-flexed inch of him – and thought that he was more interesting than any of the pretty men on the screen, more real.

In appearance he was almost a stereotype of a gay man, from the hair gel in his weekly cut dark brown hair to the tastefully expensive clothes he wore. If people weren't careful, they missed the sharp intelligence that hid beneath the pretty exterior. Which was, because it was Kyle, the point of the facade.

'This really isn't bad enough for bad movie night,' Kyle continued, not worried about interrupting the movie: none of us were watching it for its scintillating dialogue. 'I'd have gotten *Blade III*, but oddly enough, it was already checked out.'

'Any movie with Wesley Snipes is worth watching, even if you have to turn off the sound.' I twisted and bent so I could snitch a handful of popcorn from Warren's bowl. He was too thin still; that and a limp were reminders that only a month ago he'd been so badly hurt I'd thought he would die. Werewolves are tough, bless 'em, or we'd have lost him to a demon-bearing vampire. That one had been the first vampire I'd killed – with the full knowledge and permission of the local vampire mistress. That she hadn't actually intended me to kill him didn't negate that I'd done it with her blessing. She couldn't do anything to me for his death – and she didn't know I was responsible for the other.

'As long as he's not dressed in drag,' drawled Warren.

Kyle snorted agreement. 'Wesley Snipes may be a beautiful man, but he makes a butt-ugly woman.'

'Hey,' I objected, pulling my mind back to the conversation. '*To Wong Foo* was a good movie.' We'd watched it last week at my house.

A faint buzzing noise drifted up the stairs and Kyle rolled off the couch and onto his feet in a graceful, dancelike move that was wasted on Warren. He was still focused on the movie, though his grin probably wasn't the reaction the moviemakers had intended for their bloodfest scene. My feelings were much more in line with the desired result. It was all too easy to imagine myself as the victim.

'Brownies are done, my sweets,' said Kyle. 'Anyone want something more to drink?'

'No, thank you.' It was just make-believe, I thought, watching the vampire feed.

'Warren?'

His name finally drew Warren's gaze off the TV screen. 'Water would be nice.'

Warren wasn't as pretty as Kyle, but he had the ruggedman look down pat. He watched Kyle walk down the stairs with hungry eyes.

I smiled to myself. It was good to see Warren happy at last. But the eyes he turned to me as soon as Kyle was out of sight were serious. He used the remote to raise the volume, then sat up and faced me, knowing Kyle wouldn't hear us over the movie.

'You need to choose,' he told me intently. 'Adam or Samuel or neither. But you can't keep them dangling.'

Adam was the Alpha of the local werewolf pack, my neighbor, and sometimes my date. Samuel was my first love, my first heartbreak, and currently my roommate. Just my roommate – though he'd like to be more.

I didn't trust either of them. Samuel's easygoing exterior

masked a patient and ruthless predator. And Adam . . . well, Adam just flat scared me. And I was very much afraid that I loved them both.

'I know.'

Warren dropped his eyes from mine, a sure sign he was uncomfortable. 'I didn't brush my teeth with gunpowder this morning so I could go shooting my mouth off, Mercy, but this is serious. I know it's been difficult, but you can't have two dominant werewolves after the same woman without bloodshed. I don't know any other wolves who could have allowed you as much leeway as they have, but one of them is going to break soon.'

My cell phone began playing 'The Baby Elephant Walk.' I dug it out of my hip pocket and looked at the caller ID.

'I believe you,' I told Warren. 'I just don't know what to do about any of it.' There was more wrong with Samuel than undying love of me, but that was between him and me and none of Warren's business. And Adam . . . for the first time I wondered if it wouldn't just be easier if I pulled up stakes and moved.

The phone continued to sing.

'It's Zee,' I said. 'I have to take this.'

Zee was my former boss and mentor. He'd taught me how to rebuild an engine from the ground up – and he'd given me the means to kill the vampires responsible for Warren's limp and the nightmares that were leaving fine lines around his eyes. I figured that gave Zee the right to interrupt *Friday Night at the Movies*.

'Just think about it.'

I gave him a faint smile and flipped open my phone. 'Hey, Zee.'

There was a pause on the other end. 'Mercedes,' he said, and not even his thick German accent could disguise the hesitant tone of his voice. Something was wrong.

'What do you need?' I asked, sitting up straighter and putting my feet on the floor. 'Warren's here,' I added so Zee would know we had an audience. Werewolves make having a private conversation difficult.

'Would you drive out to the reservation with me?'

He could have been speaking of the Umatilla Reservation, which was a short drive from the Tri-Cities. But it was Zee, so he was talking about the Ronald Wilson Reagan Fae Reservation just this side of Walla Walla, better known around here as Fairyland.

'Now?' I asked.

Besides . . . I glanced at the vampire on the big-screen TV. They hadn't gotten it quite right, hadn't captured the real *evil* – but it was too close for comfort anyway. Somehow I couldn't work up too much sorrow at missing the rest of the movie – or more conversation about my love life either.

'No,' Zee groused irritably. 'Next week. *Jetzt*. Of course, *now*. Where are you? I will pick you up.'

'Do you know where Kyle's house is?' I asked.

'Kyle?'

'Warren's boyfriend.' Zee knew Warren; I hadn't realized he hadn't met Kyle. 'We're out in West Richland.'

'Give me the address. I will find it.'